LORI FOSTER

Worth
the Wait

HQN™

ISBN-13: 978-1-335-01698-0

Worth the Wait

Recycling programs for this product may not exist in your area.

This edition published by arrangement with Harlequin Books S.A.

For questions and comments about the quality of this book, please contact us at CustomerService@Harlequin.com.

® and TM are trademarks of Harlequin Enterprises Limited or its corporate affiliates. Trademarks indicated with ® are registered in the United States Patent and Trademark Office, the Canadian Intellectual Property Office and in other countries.

www.HQNBooks.com

Printed in U.S.A.

Worth
the Wait

CHAPTER ONE

FIVE O'CLOCK ON a Friday and Hogan Guthrie found himself smiling in anticipation as he closed the books on his work and powered down his computer. He could work from home, and sometimes did, but the scope of the new client meant some coordinating with other employees. For a week now he'd spent hours at the desk for his usual nine-to-five shift, poring over past records and updating them to a better, more cohesive platform. Popping his head to the side, he released tension gathered in his neck. A glance at the clock showed he'd have time to run home, shower and change into more casual and comfortable clothes before heading to the diner.

Friday nights at the diner usually ran late, but he didn't mind. Hell, he was actually looking forward to it.

Of course he knew why.

Violet Shaw.

Violet with that sexy Southern drawl, her rich red hair and vivid blue eyes. And that pale, creamy skin—

He jumped when a small, warm hand settled on his shoulder and he looked up to see his boss, Joni Jeffers, smiling down at him.

"You look tense," she said, and her fingers dug into his muscles in an impromptu and very inappropriate massage. "It was a grueling week, wasn't it?"

Wondering, with facetious cynicism, if he should file a sexual harassment suit, Hogan said only, "Too much time reformatting numbers. I should have remembered to stretch more."

"I can tell you stay in shape." Her other hand settled on him, too, and she leaned close as she kneaded his shoulders. "How's that feel?"

Like a blatant come-on. Not that long ago, he'd have jumped on Joni's unspoken offers. After having his life turned upside down, he'd spent damn near a year belatedly sowing his wild oats with a single-minded vengeance. He'd been a miserable bastard, too, and had probably made others around him miserable.

He hadn't known Joni then. Probably a good thing since he now worked for her. He'd done a lot of stupid things lately, but he wasn't an idiot.

Joni was cute with her bubbly personality, curly brown hair and top-heavy figure. At the moment, he felt not only her warm breath on his ear, but her lush boobs on his back.

Yet he wasn't even tempted. Again, he knew why.

These days, along with feeling more content in general, he had a preoccupation with his two jobs, his seventeen-year-old son—and unrequited lust for Violet.

Standing—and dislodging Joni's hands—he asked, "Ready to head out?"

"I was thinking about grabbing a drink." Her tongue slicked over her bottom lip in blatant suggestion. "Interested?"

Hell no. "Sorry, I can't. I have to get home in time to see my son before he leaves on a date." He assumed Colt would have a date, so that wasn't a lie.

Her eyes, sultry a moment before, flared. "Your son?"

"Yeah." The mention of a kid had often proved to be effective discouragement with a certain type of woman. Apparently, Joni was that type. "Colt's seventeen, almost eighteen now," he added, hopefully putting the nail in the coffin of her interest.

Straightening, Joni looked him over with suspicion. "You're not old enough for that."

"I'm thirty-five and I had Colt young." One of the few things he didn't regret from his youth.

"Your wife?" she asked bluntly.

Just as blunt, he answered, "Dead." And he wasn't explaining beyond that. "I have to run, but it looks like Derrick is hanging around. Given the way he smiles at you, I'm betting he'd love to get a drink."

She wrinkled her nose, but sighed as if resigned. Proving she wasn't yet entirely dissuaded, she gave him a long look and said, "I'll catch you next time." Turning, she headed for Derrick, who perked up at her approach.

Colt wasn't there when Hogan got home. Neither was Diesel, their dog, but then, the dog often hung next door when he and Colt were away.

He checked his phone but didn't see a message from his son. At almost eighteen, he understood that Colt wanted his independence, but one of his few rules was that he needed to give his father a call when he'd be late.

It wasn't until Hogan stepped out of the shower that he heard Colt coming in, Diesel with him. Drying off, Hogan opened the bathroom door and asked, "Where've you been?"

"I was at Uncle Jason's. You didn't see my truck?"

Relaxing, Hogan shook his head. It wasn't only the dog that liked to visit next door. He'd bought the small house next to his brother, Jason, when Jason married the woman who'd previously owned it.

Diesel hurried in to get some pats and show some love, then went back to sit next to Colt. Hogan should have realized where Colt would be but he'd been in such a rush, he hadn't been aware of anything except his anticipation.

Insane—yet he seemed to have found his calling, and it wasn't accounting.

While Hogan pulled on jeans, Colt leaned in the doorway, Diesel sitting beside him. At six-three, Colt was taller than both his father and his uncle. Broad-shouldered. Lean and muscular. Both Colt and Jason had dark brown eyes, whereas Hogan's were a much lighter blue.

Colt hadn't inherited much from him. Diesel, a shepherd mix they'd rescued that had first belonged to Honor but now adored Colt. He was fond of many people, but he was clearly Colt's dog.

"I'm coming to the diner tonight, okay?"

"Sure." Hogan glanced up after pulling on a polo. "A date?"

"Maybe." Colt smiled crookedly. "It's a group of us, but..."

"But?"

While he stroked the dog's head, he said, "A new girl joined my chemistry class today."

"Ah." Hogan guessed, "Pretty?" Maybe his son had inherited something after all. Not entirely a good thing.

"Very." Colt grinned. "I'm hoping to win her over before anyone else does."

Probably wouldn't take much effort. Once Colt had settled in after the move from Columbus to the much-smaller, quaint town of Clearbrook in Ohio, the girls had been flocking after him.

"So," Hogan said, "is this a request that your old dad stays away, or can I meet her?"

Looking far too serious, Colt said, "You don't need to hide away, ever."

Hogan sat to pull on his boots. "If it becomes an issue—"

"It won't be."

Unsure when he'd become philosophical on the issue, Hogan said, "You know, if the girl is new around here, she might need a friend more than a hot date."

"I'll be both." Colt straightened off the wall. "Gotta go. I've got grass-cutting jobs this weekend, so I want to finish my homework now. C'mon, Diesel." The dog was already on his heels.

"Be sure to cut our grass, too, before you take off."

With a wave, Colt headed to his incredibly messy room, so messy, in fact, that it kept him from being too perfect. Not that Diesel minded. He tended to sprawl on the piles of discarded clothes.

Smiling, Hogan wondered how he'd gotten so damn lucky. Lucky, at least when it came to his son.

He grabbed his keys and helmet, yelled a goodbye to Colt and headed out the door to his bike. The late-August evening hit his face like an open oven.

As he rode, the sweltering air tore across his face and he loved it. Sure, he'd first gotten the bike to indulge some idea of being a rebel with a "fuck you" attitude, as if that could make up for the past year of hell. He was over that now, mostly anyway, but he still loved the bike.

A few minutes later he pulled into the already-crowded lot of Screwy Louie's, the town's most popular diner. *Accountant by day,* Hogan thought as he strode in, *barbecue master by night.*

He stored his helmet and keys in a locker, found a stiff white apron and greeted the others who worked the evening weekend shift with him.

When he didn't see Violet bustling about as was

her usual preference, he stopped one of the waitresses. "Where is she?"

Knowing exactly whom he meant, the girl said, sotto voce, "Back office," and added, "I think she's sick."

Frowning, Hogan started his massive grills so they could heat, took the racks of previously prepared ribs from the industrial refrigerators and then headed for the tiny office at the back of the building.

He and Violet had an understanding of sorts. He wanted her; she resisted. He didn't make it easy on her, and she didn't give him any leeway. So far, the cat and mouse game had been fun. He was still patient.

And still very determined.

It didn't matter that he also worked for Violet; since this was a part-time job, not his career, the usual issue of mixing work with pleasure didn't apply.

Grinning, he rapped his knuckles against the door and opened it.

With her rich red hair fanned out around her on the surface of the cluttered desk, Violet rested her head on her folded arms. Without looking up, she asked, "What do you want, Hogan?"

"How'd you know it was me?"

She tipped her face and one vivid blue eye peeked up at him through that fall of incredible hair. "Honey," she drawled, "I know the sound of your walk, the way that you knock, and I know your scent."

His brows lifted. "My scent?"

Sitting back with a grumpy sigh, she asked again, "What'd you want?"

Ignoring her mean mood, he said, "Besides you?" He heard her growl and his grin widened. "Why are you in here moping? Late night yesterday?"

"Yes."

Before he could get jealous over that, she gestured at the scattered papers. "I fired my accountant, the miserable bastard."

"Why?"

"None of your business. But now the accounts have piled up. I despise paperwork—you know that. I worked on it off and on all day yesterday and a big chunk of today, but I'm still not done."

God, he loved her twangy voice, the way she drawled her words.

She gathered the papers together into a file and closed it, then stood to tuck it into an old metal file cabinet.

Her office was ancient and Hogan suspected her accountant's ideas might have been, as well. Hesitating to overstep, or to take on more work, he asked, "Anything I can help with?"

"You already are, darlin'. Your ribs are a huge hit." Using both hands, she finger-combed her hair into a high ponytail, then secured it with a cloth-covered rubber band that she pulled from her wrist. "I'm even looking into buying a special oven so you can keep it going through the winter months."

Standing in the doorway, blocking her exit, he asked, "Who said I want to be here in the winter months?"

"You're not stupid. You know you were born to do this."

Since he'd recently thought the same thing, he said, "I don't mind grilling in the snow."

With a seductive smile teasing her lips, she sidled closer and patted his face. "If you ever decide to give up that stuffy shirt and tie during the week, I'd hire you full-time in a hot minute." Her warm fingertips trailed down his neck, his chest and away. "Customers would love it, and I bet you'd make more in tips than you do sitting in an office."

Paying no attention to the job offer, Hogan caught her wrist. "You just love playing with fire, don't you?"

With her gaze on his mouth, she whispered, "You got those ribs ready yet?"

"I just got here."

"Best get a move on, then." She ducked past him.

Sometimes, Hogan thought as he watched her sashay away, Violet deliberately distracted him. Why? If she truly didn't want to get physical, why taunt him?

He glanced back at that file cabinet and wondered again about her accounting.

An hour later he didn't have time to think about anything except cooking. The orders were pouring in. Since they weren't served during the week, it seemed that come Friday night and through the weekend, everyone wanted barbecued ribs. Standing just outside the restaurant, near the side of the building where Violet had added more outdoor seating, Hogan whistled and slathered on more of his special sauce. The heat of the day waned as the sun fell lower in the sky, bleeding over the horizon in shades of crimson, purple and sunflower yellow.

Until coming to Clearbrook, he couldn't remember ever paying much attention to the sunset. He breathed deep of cooking meat, freshly mowed grass and humid air.

All around him, customers chatted and laughed, some sitting on picnic tables under shade trees, others using the metal tables and chairs under the overhang. After lifting three more racks onto a platter, Hogan rang a bell.

It was Violet, this time, who came to collect them.

Damp tendrils of her fiery hair escaped her ponytail and clung to her temples. Her flushed cheeks made the blue of her eyes even brighter. He'd already noticed the T-shirt she wore with Screwy Louie's scrawled across her breasts and a pair of khaki shorts with tennis shoes. Now the shirt stuck to her in select places. Eyeing her toned and shapely legs, he couldn't help thinking—

"We've got a real crowd tonight," she crowed, sounding a little breathless but pleased with the action. "Keep cooking, sugar!"

What did she think he would do? Abandon his station? Giving a theatrical sigh, he said, "Chained to my grill. A man's work is never done."

She crossed her arms and cocked a shapely hip against the wall. "There are ladies out front, gossiping about you."

Hogan quirked a brow while basting sauce over a slab of meat. "All compliments, I hope?"

"Suggestions, actually."

He waited.

"These ladies want to see you grilling…shirtless."

The smile came easily. Had her voice sounded a bit hoarse? No doubt from speaking over the rambunctious crowd. "Not sure that's allowed, is it? There has to be a code or something?"

Her eyes flared. "You would consider it otherwise?"

Shrugging, he said, "I'm not selfish. I'll do what I can to help your business thrive."

Violet snorted. "Not selfish, not modest…" Her nose wrinkled. "You have a hairy chest."

"True enough." Slanting her a look, he added, "Hairy thighs, too. And on my stomach, there's this line of—"

"It's enough that you don't wear a net on your head.

I don't want to have to worry about chest hair in the sauce."

She definitely sounded hoarse. "I don't exactly shed, you know." He frowned at her and saw she appeared distracted, leaning a hand against a table and drawing a slow breath.

"You okay?" he asked, wondering if the waitress was right about her being ill.

"Exhilarated." Quickly she straightened, patted his shoulder and took off again, her hands loaded with platters of meat.

For a little while, Hogan wondered about her. But they were too busy for him to dwell on anything but his job. The night droned on, and during small respites, Hogan prepared more ribs for the following day. His process required hours of precooking before the meat ever touched the grill. He worked alone, guarding his secret recipe—what a joke—which required him to hustle back and forth between the rear kitchen area and where the grills were set up.

Colt and his friends sat at a picnic table nearby, drinking tea and devouring burgers. The new girl was indeed cute, and if Hogan was a judge, his son had already won her over.

When Colt introduced him, Hogan felt a familiar, unmistakable pride. Despite the not-too-distant-past turmoil of their lives, Colt was a remarkable young man, and not just physically. He did well in school and he enjoyed helping others. Hogan knew he couldn't take all the credit for that, but he didn't want to think about his wife.

Before long, he saw that Colt had his arm around the girl and she rested her head on his shoulder. Hiding his smile, Hogan repeatedly glanced their way.

The move had been tough on Colt, but things were looking up for both of them.

The lingering crowds grew mellow as they neared the midnight hour. It was a few minutes to closing time when Kristy, a waitress, found him cleaning the grills.

"Hey, Hogan, got a minute?"

He glanced at her. She was young, cute and exceptionally friendly. Tonight, though, she looked worried. Aware of Colt watching him, Hogan said, "What's up?"

"I wasn't sure who to talk to."

He closed the grill and cleaned his hands on a dish towel. "Something's wrong?"

"It's Violet. I think she's really sick."

An unfamiliar emotion tightened in his chest. Worry, he decided. Only worry for the boss. He wouldn't allow it to be anything else. Not since his wife…

He shook his head. "Where is she?"

"In her office. But she's been in there awhile and it's time to shut down. You know Violet always oversees things."

Colt appeared at his side. "Anything you want me to do?"

Now see? How could he not beam with pride?

"Maybe." Often when Hogan worked at the restaurant, Colt was around. He probably knew the routine better than the actual employees. "Where's Beth?" She was Violet's assistant manager, and one of them was always around.

"She had her baby, so she's on maternity leave. Violet's in charge tonight."

Well, hell. He turned to his son. "You mind giving Kristy a hand?"

The way Kristy smiled at Colt made Hogan want to

growl. He said, "You're not eighteen yet, so don't touch any alcohol, all right?"

Kristy laughed. "That's his way of telling me you're off-limits." She patted Hogan's shoulder. "I'm already aware, Dad." Then she added to Colt, "You do look a lot older, though."

Colt grinned, not in the least embarrassed. "Let me say 'bye to my friends, and then I'm all yours."

Kristy watched him walk away, a hand to her heart.

Hogan rolled his eyes, hooked his arm through Kristy's and hauled her back into the restaurant, giving directions along the way.

It never occurred to him that he might be overstepping.

Since he could still be considered relatively new with only a month under his belt, there were others at the restaurant probably more qualified, but they all seemed relieved to have him take charge.

After setting things in motion, he peeked in on Violet. She was asleep at her desk. For only a moment he looked down at her. Those damned strange feelings stirred again; this time he ignored them.

He wanted to immediately wake her and suggest she go home, but instead he slipped back out of the office without making a sound. Far as he could tell, the restaurant was Violet's number one priority. If he woke her before everything was done, she'd probably start pitching in when clearly she needed some rest.

The employees knew their jobs, but still welcomed his reminders of how Violet preferred things done. He, himself, did her usual duties, running the end-of-day reports, balancing the books and closing out the cash drawer. He locked the remaining money in the safe and left the register open.

After Colt and Kristy left, Hogan did a final sweep of the building, set the security alarms on all but the back door and finally went to Violet's office. Before he could open the door, he heard a rasping cough. Again, he opened it and stepped in.

Violet, looking messier than he'd ever seen her, leaned over the papers again scattered across her desk.

"Violet?"

Slowly she turned her face toward him.

Her bloodshot eyes surprised him. *Sick.* He stepped in farther. "Hey, you okay?"

She looked from him to the paperwork. "I don't know." More coughs racked her.

Hogan strode forward and put a hand to her forehead. "Shit. You're burning up."

"What time is it?"

"A few minutes after midnight."

"Oh." She pushed back from the desk but didn't make it far. "The restaurant," she gasped in between strained breaths.

"I took care of it." Holding her elbow, he helped to support her as she stood. His most pressing thought was getting her home and in bed. No, not the way he'd like, but definitely the way she needed. "Where are your car keys?"

Unsteady on her feet, she frowned. "What do you mean, you took care of it?"

"You have good employees—you know that. They're aware of the routine. Colt pitched in, too. Everything is done."

"But..."

"I double-checked. I'm not incompetent, so trust me."

Her frown darkened.

"You can thank me, Violet."

She tried to look stern, coughed again and gave up. "Thank you." Still she kept one hand on the desk. "I'm just so blasted tired."

"I know." He eased her into his side, his arm around her. "Come on. Let me drive you home."

Giving him a lost look, she said, "I can't be sick. I don't have time to be sick. Beth's gone for at least four weeks. I have to—"

"You don't have to do anything, not right now." Hogan remembered once when Meg, his wife, had gotten pneumonia. Her cough had sounded the same and she, too, had been tired and run a fever. "It'll be okay. I'll be here for the weekend. I can handle things."

"It's not your restaurant!" Soon as she rasped the words, she began to cough.

Worried, Hogan set her against the desk. "Stay put." Then he found her purse and, without a qualm, dug through it for her keys.

He found them. He also found two condoms. His gaze flashed to hers, but her eyes were closed and she looked asleep on her feet, her body utterly boneless as she drew in shallow, strained breaths.

"Come on." With an arm around her, her purse and keys held in his free hand, he led her out the back way to the employee lot, securing the door behind her. Her yellow Mustang shone bright beneath security lights.

His bike would be okay. Or at least, it better be.

VIOLET TRIED TO get herself together but it wasn't easy. She honestly felt like she could close her eyes and nod right off. "The trash—"

"Was taken out." He opened the passenger door and helped her in.

"If you left on even one fan—"

"It would set off the security sensors. I know. They're all off." He fastened her seat belt around her and closed her door.

As soon as he slid behind the wheel, she said, "But the end-of-day reports—"

"Are done." He started her car. "Try not to worry, okay?"

Easier said than done.

Because the town was so small, Hogan seemed to know where she lived even though she'd never had him over. She hadn't dared.

Hogan in her home? Nope. Not a good idea.

Even feeling miserable, her head pounding and her chest aching, she was acutely aware of him beside her in the enclosed car, and the way he kept glancing at her. He tempted her, always had, from the first day she'd met him.

He was also a major runaround. Supposedly a *reformed* runaround, but she didn't trust in that. Things had happened with his late wife, things that had made him bitter and unpredictable.

Yet no less appealing.

She wasn't one to pry; otherwise she might have gotten all the details from Honor, his sister-in-law, already. She figured if he ever wanted to, Hogan himself would tell her. Not that there was any reason, since she would not get involved with him.

Hogan was fun to tease, like watching the flames in a bonfire. You watched, you enjoyed, but you did not jump in the fire.

More coughs racked her and she wheezed for breath.

"You know what?" he said, veering away from the direction of her house. "I'm taking you to the ER instead. You need some meds. Tonight."

She wanted to argue, to tell him that it wasn't his decision, but she wasn't stupid. Tomorrow was Saturday, so finding a doctor would be no easier then. She couldn't even imagine how much worse she might feel in the morning, given that she felt more wretched by the minute.

"Yes," she said, her head back and her eyes closed—not that he'd waited for her agreement. "I think you're right."

Three hours later, after a long visit in a crowded waiting room where he'd held her against him, a few tests that had shown she had pneumonia and a script for antibiotics that he'd filled for her at an all-night pharmacy, Violet finally slogged through her house for the bedroom.

Her throat was so dry; she desperately needed a bottle of water. And she'd dearly love to lose her bra.

She managed only to drop facedown into her bed, on top of the comforter. She missed the pillow.

It didn't matter. For someone who never got sick, she'd gone all out. Pneumonia. They should call it "debilitating weakness" instead.

Hogan stood over her. She pulled together enough energy to say, "Thank you. Lock the door on your way out."

Instead she felt him tugging off her sneakers.

Her eyes popped open; she was sick, not dead. "What are you doing?"

"I won't steal your shorts, so relax." After removing her shoes, he lifted her as if she weighed nothing. Holding her with one arm—something she couldn't help but notice—he turned down her bed and tucked her in.

When he walked away, she felt like crying.

She, who cried about as often as she got sick, which was never.

But instead of leaving, he came right back with the coveted bottle of water. "Here, let me help you." Sitting on the side of the bed, he slipped an arm beneath her and levered her up, put the bottle in her hand and supported her while she drank. "Better?"

"You know," she whispered, "since we're doing this, I may as well go all in."

"All in?"

She was in a bed—her bed—with Hogan Guthrie right next to her. Not ideal circumstances, but still… "Help me out of my shorts."

Across her back, his arm tightened until she thought she could make out every lean, hard muscle.

Maybe it was lack of oxygen caused by the pneumonia, but she heard herself say, "Unhook my bra, too—I'll take care of the rest. And thanks in advance."

"Um…"

"It's uncomfortable. I usually sleep naked, so—"

Letting her recline again, he quickly stood, then stared down at her with a gaze so intent she would have blushed if she'd had the energy.

After struggling over onto her stomach, she waited. Silence ticked by, and then the bed shifted and Hogan's hands, so incredibly large and warm, slipped up her back. She felt a brief tug and the bra cups loosened.

Heaven. She muttered, "You're pretty good at that. Guess you've had lots of practice."

"Don't try baiting me right now. You're not up to it." One by one he slid his hand up her arms, beneath each short sleeve of her T-shirt, and pulled the straps down and over her elbows, freeing her arms.

He turned her to her back, gave her a long look with

his incendiary blue eyes and said softly, "I believe in finishing the job."

She could barely keep her eyes open, but awareness burned through the lethargy as he reached under her shirt, hooked a finger in the front of her bra and tugged it out and away.

All the while, those hot blue eyes of his stared at her body.

Through a hazy gaze, Violet watched him look at her now-freed bra. It was beige with black lace and tiny polka dots, making him smile slightly before he tossed it onto her rocking chair. He wasn't above copping a feel—this was Hogan, after all—so his palm coasted across her ribs, her waist and over her stomach.

He drew in a breath, held it and opened the top snap of her shorts.

As he slowly tugged down the zipper, she said, "If I wasn't sick—"

He growled. "I know."

"—we wouldn't be doing this."

That made him laugh. "I think you enjoy torturing me."

"Sometimes," she admitted. And why not? His presence tortured her plenty.

He finished stripping off her shorts, then took his time looking at her in great detail. "Your panties match your bra."

"I'm aware."

He pulled the sheet up and over her, and when she shivered, he layered on the comforter. Now more detached, he said, "They're sexy."

Yup, she knew that, too. Since, by necessity, she was forced to be more celibate than not, wearing sexy underthings was her balm, her way of reminding herself that she was still an attractive, healthy woman.

Bracing one hand on the nightstand, the other on the back of the headboard, Hogan loomed over her. "*You're sexy.*" He kissed her forehead in a most sexless way. "Do you need more ibuprofen? A cough drop? Anything else?"

She needed to get well. She needed a man.

She needed Hogan Guthrie, but she wasn't a stupid woman, so she tried to never court trouble. "No, and thank you again."

"Try to get some rest." He turned out the light and left the room, pulling the door behind him until it almost closed.

Violet turned onto her side, snuggled tight and faded into sleep.

CHAPTER TWO

HOGAN STEPPED OUTSIDE the front door, but didn't secure the door behind him.

He had no intention of leaving.

God, the sight of her in nothing more than a snug T-shirt and boner-inspiring panties will be forever burned on my brain.

Her nipples had been visible through the thin cotton of the top, making his damned mouth water. And her skin, especially over the gentle curve of her belly, had felt like silk. Warm silk.

The urge to brush his mouth over her, to inhale her scent, had been nearly impossible to ignore. But despite his more recent lacks, he wasn't completely lost to civility, so he'd tucked her up and escaped.

No, he definitely wouldn't leave her.

Sitting on the front step of her porch, he called Colt first.

Without a single sign of sleepiness, Colt answered, "What's up? She okay?"

It was the middle of the damned night, practically morning, so Hogan asked, "Why aren't you in bed?"

"I was, but I was also waiting to hear from you."

"You're there alone?"

"No, I sneaked in three girls. Make it four. Uncle Jason and Honor never noticed. I mean, there's what? Thirty feet separating the houses? And Honor called twice to check on me, but I completely fooled her. I hid all the girls under my bed."

"Smart-ass." Hogan grinned. Colt was, by far, the best part of him.

Colt laughed as he said, "It's just Diesel and me."

The dog was good company, and good protection—not that Colt needed it. "I won't be home tonight at all, but I'll check back in the morning." Briefly, he explained about Violet and that he didn't want to leave her alone in case she needed anything.

Colt said, "At least she doesn't make you hide under the bed."

Frowning, Hogan wondered at his joke. "Don't make more out of this than there is."

"I won't." With definite amusement in his tone, Colt added, "I know you do goodwill sleepovers with all kinds of women. Doesn't mean anything at all."

"Colt," he warned.

"Good night, Nurse Guthrie. Tell Violet I hope she feels better soon."

As he disconnected the call, Hogan blew out a breath. Great, all he needed now was for rumors to get started. Who wouldn't believe them, especially if they were spread by his son?

He glanced back at the door. Would Violet mind? He didn't think so. She didn't strike him as a woman who cared much what others thought. Then again, no one would have any reason to think anything less than positive.

Violet was a strong woman—intelligent, warm, hardworking, beautiful, sweet… Jesus. Hogan ran a hand over his face.

What struck him most was the fact that Colt had teased him about it. Because it was Violet? Since the death of his mother, Colt hadn't said much about Hogan dating, but his silence on the matter had been more damning than words anyway.

He'd hurt Colt, and he hated that. Didn't matter that he'd been hurting, too.

Colt hadn't been silent about Violet. No, instead he'd joked. Maybe he knew Violet was too discriminating to get involved with him.

Rather than brood, he dialed his brother next.

Jason, at least, had been sleeping. He answered with a very groggy "What's wrong?"

"Sorry to wake you. I'm going to stay over at Violet's and Colt is already in bed. He's got Diesel there with him, but if you wouldn't mind—"

"Honor's been mothering him," Jason said around a yawn. "No worries."

Of course she had. Honor was a true sweetheart; she and Colt had a very special relationship. Diesel did sometimes stay the night with Jason, sort of picking and choosing between the two houses at his own whim, but likely he'd either known Colt was alone and felt protective, or Honor had insisted he keep the dog with him. Either way, he was relieved.

Hogan felt like a schoolboy explaining, but he did so anyway. "Violet has pneumonia. She was pretty hammered by the time we got back from the ER. She's crashed right now, but I figured I'd—"

"Got it. Take good care of her, okay?"

In the background, Hogan heard Honor ask, "What's going on? Take care of who? Is Colt okay?"

Jason said only, "Hogan's sleeping over at Violet's."

Alarmed by how he put it, Hogan protested, "Don't make it sound like—"

Honor seemed far more alert when she sang, "Oh, he is, is he?"

"Damn it, Jason, tell her—"

To Honor, Jason said with far too much gravity, "You know how noble my brother is."

They both laughed. At *him*.

Hogan heard some shuffling, a few whispers, and Jason said, "Later, brother."

Standing, Hogan put away his phone and leaned on the rail, looking out over the quiet street, most of the porch lights glowing in boxy homes set close together. Single-car driveways, mature trees everywhere.

Before long the sun would be up. On Saturdays, kids played in their yards and on every cul-de-sac, crowding the sidewalks with their bikes. Older folk walked their older dogs and groused about the bikes. Hogan smiled. The area was as different as night and day to where he used to live in Columbus.

He didn't use to think so, but now he knew it was better. Cleaner. Calmer.

A whole new life greeted him here—now if only the old life didn't still plague him.

Pushing that aside as he often did, he wondered if Violet was sleeping okay. He'd like to go in and check on her, but she thought he'd left. She was in her bed, not fully dressed, and he didn't want to intrude further. It was enough to stay over on her couch.

He saw again her slim body nestled in that big bed. From the day he'd met her, he'd appreciated her fair skin and red hair. She was so petite that with one splayed hand he could span the width of her from hip bone to hip bone. But her breasts weren't small. Not really large, either. Just full and soft and perfect.

Closing his tired eyes, Hogan breathed deeply.

Heavy humidity thickened the night air and filled his lungs. Insects carried on a cacophony of sounds, and when he listened closely he could even hear frogs in the large creek that served as a social gathering spot for the small town.

Clearbrook was a good place. Peaceful, close-knit, filled with friendly people. He discounted the remaining crime element since incidents were fewer and far between. The refurbishing of the town had been, by all accounts, a huge success. What used to be a slum area was now occupied by middle-class families.

Since he'd gone from a prestigious accounting firm to a small local business, supplemented by weekend restaurant work—that now included him and Colt.

Heading back inside, he quietly closed and locked the door. He flattened his mouth at the sight of the short, squat couch, but he wouldn't roam her house looking for a guest room.

After turning down the volume on his phone and setting it on the coffee table, he sat on the couch and removed his boots and socks, peeled off his shirt, then unsnapped and unzipped his jeans. He'd like to lose the jeans, but yeah—probably not a good idea.

There was no way to stretch out, so he sprawled as best he could, his head and one calf on the sofa arms, one leg dropping over the side. He snagged the knit throw over the back of the couch, half-heartedly tossed it over his body and closed his eyes.

He thought of Violet.

He thought of her panties.

Soon he was sound asleep and dreaming.

VIOLET FOUND HIM on her couch. At 8:00 a.m., it was too early to be up, especially after the late night, but when she'd gotten up to use the bathroom and find more ibuprofen, she'd heard a snore.

It didn't scare her only because she immediately guessed the source.

Her first thought when she found him there was that he was too big for her couch, his shoulders too wide, his legs too long.

Keeping the comforter swaddled around herself, she tipped her head and studied him—specifically she studied his body. Still wearing jeans, now open, he rested on his back, one arm above his head, the other folded over his stomach. Only a corner of the throw blanket covered him; the rest was on the floor with his right leg. He looked in danger of sliding over the side with it any moment.

Of course she'd seen him without a shirt many times at neighborhood picnics, but she hadn't been able to stare then, not with him so aware of her and neighbors all around them.

Now her eyes felt gritty, and she stared anyway. A sparse covering of crisp, dark hair went from his collarbone to just below his pecs, faded in a narrow line to his navel, then widened a little before disappearing into his jeans. Beneath his raised arm she saw softer hair.

She'd teased him about being hairy, but in truth, she thought he was the sexiest man she'd ever known. She loved his masculinity, which included that enticing dark hair.

Sleep masked his usual edgy persona so that he looked more peaceful now. His hair stuck up in tufts and beard shadow darkened his face. He, his brother and his son all had the most amazing, enviable lashes. They were long and thick, and looking at him, Violet liked the way they rested on his high cheekbones.

He wasn't overly muscle-bound, but there was no denying the strength of his lean, toned body. Even in sleep his biceps were pronounced. Her gaze traveled over his shoulders, down his body again to his flat stomach. Out of self-preservation she skimmed her gaze over the bulge inside his jeans to glance along the length of his long, strong legs and down to his feet. She admired them, as well.

She would have gone on admiring him except that she drew in a breath—and coughed.

Hogan stirred, shifting his big body, stretching a little before opening one eye.

Violet froze. Damn him, he looked gorgeous sleep-rumpled, while she knew she looked completely wrecked. Only half her hair remained in the ponytail, and she was so weak, she started to shake.

"Morning," Hogan rumbled.

"Good morning." Trying for sarcasm, she asked, "Comfortable?"

"Not really. Your couch is too short." He stretched again and sat up with a wide yawn.

Unmoving, Violet watched him scratch his belly, and she said with accusation, "You stayed over."

"Yeah." After running both hands through his mussed hair, he checked the time on his phone. Giving her another long look, he patted the seat beside him, no doubt still warm from his body. "Sit before you fall."

She didn't want to, but her body wasn't giving her much choice. She stepped around the table and dropped at the far end of the couch, which wasn't all that far.

Scooting closer to her, he touched his palm to her forehead. "Still feverish. You need more medicine?"

"I just took it. That's how I found you."

"Gotcha." He frowned at her hair, deftly removed

the band to free it and smoothed it down, massaging her scalp in the process.

Heaven.

He stole his magic fingers away. "Are you a coffee person or a juice person?"

"I'm not a baby."

With a short laugh, he agreed, "Definitely not."

She started to say she could get her own coffee, but she truly didn't feel like it. Putting her head back and closing her eyes, she said, "Maybe both?"

"Juice now, coffee when it's ready?"

She nodded, her eyes still closed.

"You can thank me, Violet."

"Thank you."

His fingers skimmed her cheek and she heard the smile in his voice when he said, "Be right back."

Somehow in the time it took him to pour orange juice into a glass, she'd fallen asleep. She opened her eyes to see the juice on the end table beside her. In the kitchen, the coffeemaker spit and hissed.

Down the hall, a toilet flushed, water ran and Hogan emerged, his jeans now fastened, his shirt still off, his feet still bare.

Damn, he looked good like that.

He also looked good in her house.

"Sleep if you want," he said as he passed her. "It's the best thing for you."

She drank half the juice and nodded off again.

Hogan's voice, talking quietly on the phone, awoke her the second time. She saw that sunshine now flooded her front windows. More sluggish than she ever could have imagined, she sat up and tried to gather her wits.

She focused on Hogan in the kitchen, fully dressed, his hair less messy but with whiskers still on his face.

"I can probably take Violet's car this morning, but I don't want to leave my bike in the parking lot." After waiting for a reply, Hogan said, "Yeah, that'd work. Appreciate it."

Who said he could take her car? Take it where?

"No, she won't make it in today. Damned pneumonia has really leveled her." As he softly spoke, Hogan turned to face her, then smiled at seeing her awake. Holding her gaze, he nodded, saying, "Yeah, I'll figure it out. Thanks again." He pocketed the phone and moved out of sight.

"I'm going into work," she told him, but raising her voice put her into a coughing fit.

He appeared with the coffee. "I reheated it."

Grudgingly, she accepted. Because he'd worked with her for a few weeks now, he knew she liked cream and sugar and the coffee was perfect, even better than the juice. "Thank you."

He surveyed her. "Are you hungry?"

"No." More than anything, she wanted to sleep. More and more sleep. She tried for a slow breath and managed to do it without coughing too much. "I'm sorry I keep conking out."

"I'm glad you did." He frowned, then sat beside her. "You can't go into work. You're an intelligent woman and you know it, but you're also stubborn. Put the stubbornness aside for now, okay?"

"I have to go in. It's mine and—"

"I can handle it. I have the weekend free and I know what I'm doing."

"What, no hot date?" Hogan always had hot dates on the weekends, and sometimes during the week—at least until recently. "What about what's-her-name? That kid."

The corner of his mouth curled. "Emma? She was twenty-five, not a kid—"

"Ten years your junior!"

"—and I only saw her once."

"I guess with you, once is enough?"

He cocked a brow. "Are you always this nasty in the mornings?"

"Yes," she lied. God, she felt so awful, she wanted to curl up and sleep until she felt normal again. "Go away, okay?"

"I haven't had a date since I started working for you."

No, she didn't want to hear that! That would mean he'd been dateless for weeks. "Poor baby, am I using up all your free time?"

Shrugging a shoulder, he grinned. "I could go out during the week, I guess. In fact, Friday, before I left the office, my boss hit on me."

Violet stared at him, scowled and guzzled the rest of her coffee. *I don't want to picture you with another woman.* Of course, it was already too late.

Glaring, she asked, "When are the two of you getting together?"

His gaze went to her mouth. "Never." Gently, he took the coffee cup from her and set it aside.

"I take it she's homely? Not built to your specifications?"

"She's attractive enough. Big boobs."

Trying for mock surprise, Violet said, "And you turned her down?"

"Let's say I redirected her attention."

"Redirected it how?"

"To a coworker who looked interested."

"Oh my God, you're bragging about passing her off to someone else?"

"*Redirecting* her," he emphasized. "It's not like she was looking to get married."

"Because that would have really sent you running!"
Good God, just shut up, Violet.

After a long look, he picked up the cup and stood.
He was halfway to the kitchen when he stopped. Keeping his back to her, he said, "Obviously you know I was
married once."

Violet's heart started to pound. "Yes." And she was
sorry she'd brought it up.

He looked back over his shoulder at her. "Marriage
doesn't scare me. But cheating, lying women do."

WHY THE HELL had he opened his mouth? So she'd been
needling him. So what. Nothing new in that, not with
Violet. The woman lived to give him a hard time.

Hours had passed since he'd left her sleeping on her
sofa, and still he wanted to chew nails. Colt rapped at
the back door of the diner and Hogan let him in.

"Uncle Jason said you were here. I was going to work
with him today but he said you might need me instead."

"Yeah." Hogan rubbed the back of his neck. "I rearranged the schedule for Violet since she's down for
the count. In between taking medicine, she sleeps. The
doctor at the ER said she'd be feeling better by Monday,
but I think that only means less miserable, not ready
to work."

"She's home alone now?"

Hogan didn't like it, either, but he'd set her up on her
couch as best he could, arranging her medicine nearby
with a glass of juice, a bottle of water and the TV remote. "She'll be okay. My guess is she'll sleep most of
the day away."

Colt looked around. "So what can I do?"

Since Violet didn't have a breakfast menu, the diner
opened at noon. Kristy would be in soon, along with an-

other employee. He'd already come up with a plan, so he got Colt going, then did some prep work on his ribs.

With that done, curiosity got the better of him and he moved to Violet's office to take a look at her paperwork.

Just as he suspected, it was horribly dated, and as far as he could tell, she didn't have a menu profitability analysis. Critical stuff in restaurant bookkeeping. He'd work on that, he decided, as well as catching her up, but he'd maintain all her regular records, too.

Violet could be prickly. No reason to fire her up more.

Around three, Nathan Hawley, the sheriff, stopped in. Hogan wasn't surprised when he came around back to sit in the shade.

"I went by to check on Violet."

Hogan stiffened a little. Nathan was single, and he wasn't blind. If he hadn't been tempted by Violet, he had to be dead. "Yeah? How's she feeling?"

"She told me to go away, and that if I saw you, to tell you to go away, too."

"How can I go away when I'm not even there?"

"I didn't ask her," Nathan said. "She was too limp for me to tease her. But I did notice she was propped on the couch watching a movie. Or pretending to watch it. Overall she looked like a zombie. I told her…"

Just then a single woman, carrying a drink and salad, dark glasses on her eyes, walked out. Ignoring them both, she went to the farthest section of the seating area, to a worn picnic table under a large maple tree.

She sat alone, with her back to them.

Hogan watched her, wondering about her since he'd never seen her before, then realized Nathan was watching her, too.

Amused by the sheriff's distraction, he grinned. "You were saying?"

Without taking his gaze from the woman, Nathan asked, "What?"

Hogan shook his head. "Never mind. Who is she? Do you know?"

"New neighbor," he murmured. "Real private." Finally, Nathan got his gaze off her. "I saw her step outside this morning to jog. I waved, but she didn't acknowledge me."

"Does she know you're the sheriff?"

"My car is parked in the driveway and it's emblazoned on the side, so yeah, I assume so."

"If being sheriff doesn't impress her, maybe she needs to hear you sing." Nathan cut a mean guitar and sang for the local garage band, the Drunken Monkeys. Where they'd gotten that name, Hogan had no idea. It all happened before he'd moved into the area.

"I wasn't trying to impress her," Nathan growled. "Just being neighborly."

"She's pretty." Thick, straight, light brown hair, secured in a low ponytail, hung to the middle of her back. Snug yoga pants and a tank top showed a very nice figure. She still wore running shoes, looked a little sweaty, and gigantic sunglasses hid half her face. "She lives on the other side of you?"

"Moved in a few days ago."

"Alone?"

"Far as I can tell."

Just then the woman peered over her shoulder. Those ridiculous sunglasses kept them from knowing if she looked right at them or not, but it seemed likely.

Nathan said nothing, so Hogan did the honors and waved.

She turned back around.

"See what I mean?" Nathan frowned. "What are we supposed to think about that?"

"No idea." Hogan swiped up a dish towel, wiped his hands, then headed toward her.

Startled, then quickly on board, Nathan followed.

Stopping at her table, Hogan smiled down at her. "Hi. Welcome to Screwy Louie's."

Very slowly she put her fork on her salad dish and looked up at him. "Thank you."

"I'm Hogan Guthrie, the barbecue guru, and this is Nathan Hawley, your neighbor, the sheriff, and part of Drunken Monkeys, the local band."

After all that, which he considered plenty to be a conversation starter, she only glanced up at Nathan and nodded.

Talk about a tough act… "New to the neighborhood, huh?"

Her mouth tightened—a very nice, very full mouth, Hogan noticed—and then she said, "Yes." She hesitated, pulled off her sunglasses and tried a smile. "Thank you for the welcome. The salad was delicious. I need to get going now." She stood, her "delicious" salad only half-eaten.

Nathan and Hogan stared.

She had beautiful eyes. Calling them light brown wouldn't have done the unique color justice. They were brown, definitely, but golden flecks lightened the color. Fox eyes, maybe. Really startling.

Hogan got it together first. "Sorry we intruded. It's a small neighborhood. No strangers, if you know what I mean." He offered his hand. "Hope we'll see you around again soon. Violet—she's the owner here—would love to meet a new face, I'm sure."

After replacing the sunglasses, she accepted a quick

handshake, her hand small in his, her grip firm. Then she gathered up stuff.

To escape.

Before she left, she paused. "You're here often?"

"Weekends only, usually."

Nathan said, "I usually stop in for my lunch, then sometimes on weekends, too."

Ho, so Nathan finally found his voice? Not that Hogan could blame him. He couldn't wait to tell Violet about this little meet and greet. She loved to observe her customers.

As the woman left, Nathan fell into step beside her. "I'll walk you out."

She didn't appear all that receptive, but still Hogan smiled at Nathan's determination.

It occurred to him that she hadn't given her name.

THROUGHOUT THE DAY, Hogan got reports on Violet. The first time he called, she'd been napping and he'd disturbed her. After that, he asked her to call him and he kept his phone on him. She called twice, both times asking only about the restaurant.

She tried to dodge his questions, but he played tit for tat and wouldn't answer her questions until she answered his.

No, she hadn't eaten.

Yes, she had slept.

Yes, she'd taken her meds.

No, she didn't need anything.

He sent Colt over to her house with some soup the cook made and a big glass of raspberry iced tea.

To Colt, she was apparently all sweetness, at least according to Colt. He'd stayed long enough to watch her eat and to pick up afterward.

By the time Hogan finished things that night it was nearly one in the morning. He packed up Violet's accounting records and headed out.

She was still on the couch when he let himself in. A comb hadn't touched her hair, and she was still in the same clothes.

The second he stepped in, she stirred awake, then forced herself to sit up. "Everything went okay?"

"Of course." Keeping the files at his side, he strode into the kitchen and set them on top of the refrigerator. He'd rather give her his suggestions and his improvements when he finished. "How do you feel?"

"I managed to brush my teeth and wash my face. That's as far as I got."

He couldn't help but smile. "Would you like a bath? I'll get it ready for you."

She pulled the comforter to her chin. "Yeah, I just bet you would."

"I'm not into molesting near-comatose women, I promise."

"Huh, so you do have some standards?"

Hogan drew a breath. She was sick, making her usual wit more sarcastic and mean-spirited. "Yes," he said evenly, "I have standards."

Their gazes held for a moment, and then she slumped farther on the couch. "I'm sorry. I'm being a bitch and I know it. I don't like being sick and I detest relying on—"

"Me?"

"Anyone." She rubbed her temples. "So far Colt is the only person I've managed not to offend. He's just too damned sweet to be mean to." She glanced over at him. "You're sure he's yours?"

Hogan laughed. "Yeah, I'm sure. Colt looks enough

like Jason, who looks like our dad, to ensure the parentage."

Hogan knew the moment she harked back on his earlier comment about cheating women.

Despite the fever, her face paled. "Oh God, I wasn't suggesting—"

Gently, he said, "I know." Coming to sit by her, he brushed back her hair. "You meant it as an insult to me. Comparisons, right?" He winked to let her know he hadn't taken offense or thought she was serious.

"Yes, a joking insult, I swear."

Luckily, Violet knew nothing about Colt's mother. Otherwise she might have had some real questions.

But even if Colt hadn't been his—after all, his wife had proved herself more than deceitful—it wouldn't have mattered. Not to his heart. Colt was his, now and forever.

"About that bath?" He tugged at the sleeve of her very rumpled T-shirt. "I can run the bath, set out towels, then even help tie up your hair, if you want. You'll probably feel better afterward."

"You're right about that. I wanted a bath, but it seemed like so much work…"

"It won't be, not for me. Give me just a few minutes to set it up. And afterward, I'll tell you about the new lady in town who almost made Nathan trip over his own feet."

CHAPTER THREE

VIOLET RESTED BACK in the steamy tub, her body so lax she knew she could nod off. But she wouldn't. No, she wanted to talk to Hogan.

He'd insisted she get the bath taken care of first.

Smart thinking, given her present limited supply of energy.

She'd already scrubbed head to toe, getting that out of the way before she tired. Now she just enjoyed breathing in the dampness in the air and feeling the warmth of the water sink into her bones.

"You okay in there?"

"Go away." She smiled, then glanced over to the closed toilet lid. Hogan had put a fresh T-shirt and another pair of panties there.

The man was making himself at home all right.

But the bath felt so good she didn't care.

He'd also put a thick towel on the side of the tub and her fluffy housecoat on the door hook.

Why did getting clean make her feel more human?

"If you stay in there much longer," came his deep, seductive voice, "am I going to have to carry you out?"

"You wish," she muttered low enough that he couldn't hear.

But he replied, his tone laced with amusement, "As a matter of fact, it's a current fantasy. You all warm, naked and—" he paused for effect "—wet."

Violet caught her breath, promptly coughed and grouchily wheezed, "I'll be out in five more minutes."

"Okay, calm down." She could almost picture his negligent pose against the door. "Hungry?"

Violet bit her lip. She was hungry. It was hours earlier that she'd eaten the soup Colt had brought her. But Hogan had already done so much—

"I'll take that heavy pause as a yes."

"Hogan, no, wait."

No answer. She heard him walking away.

Blasted perfectly flawed man. She closed her eyes, felt herself fading and decided she had to get out. His fantasy, nice as it would be, could not become her reality.

She liked him. She *loved* his barbecued ribs. And she enjoyed him as an employee and a friend.

Intimacy would only screw up the dynamics.

She dragged out of the bathroom, mostly dry and bundled in her clothes and housecoat, to the scent of pancakes.

How does he know all my weaknesses?

She followed her nose into the kitchen just as he dropped a pat of butter onto a stack of three fluffy pancakes.

He glanced at her, looked back to his skillet, then returned for a longer look. "It would help," he said low, "if you looked worse."

She almost laughed. "Ratty hair, bloodshot eyes and chapped lips appeal to you?"

"On you, yeah." He gave his attention back to the prep of the food. "I started to ask you what you'd like, but figured you'd just give me another smart-ass answer, so I decided on pancakes."

She pulled out a chair and slumped into it. "My comfort food. Thank you."

Smiling now, he set the first plate of pancakes and the bottle of syrup in front of her. "Juice, milk?"

"Juice, thank you."

Hogan gave her a piercing look. "Keep thanking me and I'll assume you're delirious. You might find yourself back at the hospital."

She grinned, filled her mouth with a big bite of syrup-drenched, fluffy pancake and moaned. "So good."

Hogan said nothing.

She looked up and found him staring at her intently. When she raised a brow, he shook his head and joined her at the table with his own plate of pancakes.

In short order, without her having to ask, he told her about the day and how busy they'd been and how smoothly everything had run.

Without her.

Feeling glum, she asked, "What about your bike?"

"Jason got it home for me." He eyed her. "I'm taking your car again tomorrow."

The independent woman in her rebelled. "You just assume I'll miss work again?"

Reaching out, he fingered one long, damp curl at her temple. "Ratty-haired women with bloodshot eyes and chapped lips should give themselves time to recoup."

Instead of debating that, Violet asked, hopefully with enough indifference, "Are you staying over again?"

Sounding supremely confident, he said, "Yes."

It was crazy. Beyond crazy. Bordering on dangerous. But Violet was thrilled. "Okay." Hoping to coast past that, in case she'd given herself away and shown how much she wanted him to stay, she poked his shoulder. "Now tell me about Nathan and this other woman."

He did, in exaggerated detail.

Once he'd finished, she said, "That doesn't sound

like Nathan." Love struck? Nathan was so alpha, so very take-charge. Sure, he performed with Drunken Monkeys, but even then he remained, in every way, the sheriff—just a more lighthearted version. "He got that macho scar while part of a SWAT team, you know."

Hogan's brow quirked at her "macho" comment, but it was true. Explaining to him, she said, "Nathan is as much a man as a man could be."

Now he frowned.

"It's a little overbearing," she added and watched his frown fade.

As if pledging the truth, Hogan lifted a hand. "Macho or not, his tongue was on the ground, I swear. And his eyes were glazed. He's after her all right. But she didn't even crack a smile for him."

"Or for you?"

Hogan grinned. "I finagled a very perfunctory hand-shake from her, and a clear dismissal."

"Huh. I like her."

"I thought you might." He waited while she yawned, then stood to get the dishes. "You ready to turn in?"

Her heart started thumping hard enough to lay her low again. She slid from her chair, didn't look at him and said, "After I brush my teeth. Be right back."

She wasn't occupied for more than five minutes, and during that time she thought mostly about Hogan, him being so darned nice, so blasted domestic and caring.

Sure enough, when she returned to the kitchen it was cleaned, everything put away. She didn't see Hogan— then the front door opened and he stepped in with an overnight bag.

While she watched, he stepped out of his shoes and put them by the door.

"Not boots?" she asked, noticing that he wore athletic shoes tonight.

"Only when I ride my bike." Carrying the small bag, he headed down the hall. "I'm going to grab a shower and brush my teeth, too." He disappeared into her bathroom.

So he'd assumed she'd want him to stay again? She should just go to bed, go into her own bedroom and close the door. Maybe even lock it.

She didn't.

She was on the couch, her feet curled up under her, when Hogan emerged. His hair was damp and he wore only shorts, nothing else, and he looked so damned good she breathed deeper and ended up coughing.

"Have you taken your meds?"

Shooting for defensive snippiness, she said, "Yes, Dad."

Pausing, Hogan grinned. "You know, if I didn't have a seventeen-year-old son, I might find that game kinky, especially with you being such a brat who could probably use some discipline." He shook his head. "But with Colt around, it'd just be too weird."

Heat rushed into her face. "I didn't mean—"

"I take it you want to visit for a while?" He checked that the front door was locked, then joined her on the couch. "I can manage to stay awake another hour if you can."

Violet stared at him, at his tanned chest with the inviting warmth, the crisp curling hair, and she fought herself.

Either he read her expression, or he was just that good at knowing women, because he asked softly, "Would you rather just cuddle a bit?"

She took a slow, shallow breath and admitted,

"Maybe." She felt like hell. Cuddling sounded even better than the bath and the pancakes.

He didn't tease her. In a voice pitched low and soft, he asked, "You want to stay here on the couch, or would you rather get in the bed? I promise to behave either way."

But could *she* behave? Even sitting a few feet away, a sizzle of awareness played over her skin. She looked at the couch cushions. The blasted couch was so short...

Without waiting for an answer, Hogan stood. "Tell you what—why don't I decide?" He scooped an arm under her legs and easily lifted her. "That way, you don't have to debate yourself so long."

Giving in, she rested her head against his shoulder. "I might blame you for this later."

"I'm a big boy," he said on his way down the hall. "I can take it."

Oh, she imagined he could take all kinds of things. More and more, she was the weak link, the one unable to stay strong.

In the bedroom, he shoved the door shut with his heel and carried her toward the bed. At first, he just held her. Violet knew he was looking down at her, but she was too cowardly to meet his gaze.

Not this close. Not with his mouth right there and a bed behind her.

It was tempting enough, this easy display of his strength, the warmth of his body and how good he smelled, like soap and sunshine and man.

Letting her ease down the length of his body, he put her on her feet. Casually, as if he'd done so a dozen times already, Hogan untied the belt to her housecoat and, without haste, pulled it off her shoulders.

Keeping her gaze on his bare chest, Violet stood there

in another T-shirt, this one oversize so it covered her better, but she knew he could still see her black panties.

Panties that *he'd* picked out for her.

Putting a finger under her chin, he lifted her face. "You're okay?"

Breathing became more difficult, and not just because of her illness. "You must think I'm a terrible tease."

A slow rascal's smile only made him more appealing. "Definitely a tease. But I understand not wanting to be alone when you feel bad." He kissed her forehead. "And I'm glad I'm here."

It didn't feel like a come-on, like an effort to soften her up so she'd finally give in.

She knew that Hogan had been hurting for a long time. He'd lost his wife, his job, and uprooted his life. For a while there, he'd been about as miserable as any human could be while still functioning and pretending nothing was wrong.

She admired his strength, the way he'd pushed forward instead of giving in to grief. Had he loved his wife a lot? It seemed likely, given they'd been together so long.

Yet she remembered his comment about cheating, lying women. Had he meant one of the random one-nighters he'd indulged? She didn't think so. None of those ladies had warranted even a second date, as far as she knew.

Testing the waters, she said, "It's easy to see why you're successful with women." His wife, that murky lady who might have hardened him, had to have been a complete fool.

Hogan shook his head. "Come on. Into bed." He straightened the messed covers and got her settled, then scooted in next to her, covering them only with the sheet.

Until now, she'd been so cold.

But lying next to Hogan warmed her up from the inside out—and he wasn't even touching her yet.

He stretched out a long arm to turn off the bedside lamp.

She was wondering how this would work, what she should do, when the bed dipped as he adjusted, and he very naturally drew her into his side.

"Comfortable?"

Oh yes. She cleared her throat, but managed only, "Mmm-hmm." God, he was hot. The entire front of her was snuggled close to the side of him, one strong arm under and around her, keeping her close. She wanted to lift her leg over him, but held herself still instead.

"You don't sound comfortable."

"I've never slept with a guy before unless... Well, I never have, not without sex first."

"It's a unique experience, that's for sure."

But he'd been married. Surely he and his wife hadn't had sex every night. Then again, if she was married to Hogan... Whoa. *No.* She put the brakes on those thoughts real quick.

"I don't know when you even have time to date," he said, and he sounded tentative, like maybe he was asking for more than the obvious.

"I don't."

His arm tightened around her. "So why the condoms in your purse?"

Violet reared up over him. She couldn't see him in the dark, but she stared toward his voice. "How do you know—"

"I got your keys from your purse."

"And you snooped!"

"Nope." His hands closed around her waist. "They were right there, front and center."

She felt like an idiot. Of course they were—she'd carelessly tossed them there a few days ago, worried that she might give in to him and wanting to be prepared just in case.

She wouldn't tell him that, so instead she told a half-truth. "They're just a precaution."

"Yeah?" He pulled her down to rest against his chest. She felt his hand sift through her hair until he'd freed it from the band. He smoothed it down her back, saying, "In case Nathan got interested? Or a customer?" Bitterness sounded when he added, "You know Jason is married now, so he wouldn't—"

Slowly balling up her fist, Violet drew back and punched him in the ribs. She was too close to him and feeling too weak to make it very forceful.

In fact, he laughed, caught her wrist and held it against his chest. "Legit question, Violet."

"No, I'm not interested in Nathan that way. I told you he's too macho. And I don't do random—unlike *some* people I know."

He laughed again, a sarcastic sound. "And my brother?"

If she could go back in time, she'd erase the very brief relationship she and Jason had indulged. But she couldn't, and obviously Hogan knew about it.

It was before Hogan had ever moved to the area, and it hadn't lasted long enough for anyone to remember. But in a small town, everyone was in everyone else's business.

Knowing this was a serious subject, a touchy subject, knowing that even though she and Hogan hadn't hooked up it mattered a lot to him, she searched for the right words to explain.

"I shouldn't have asked."

Hogan did that often, letting her off the hook. But not this time. "Jason and I are friends, nothing more."

"Friends with a history."

"Not that it matters—not to him and not to me. Honor is good for him, and vice versa. I'm happy for them both."

With one hand he continued to hold her one wrist while with the other he stroked her back. "You slept with him."

Violet winced. "Just that once." Her heart thundered so hard, she didn't know if that's what hurt her chest, or if it was the pneumonia. "It was stupid, for both of us, and it never meant anything. For a while there I was afraid it would ruin our friendship, maybe make things awkward. But Jason was no more interested in a repeat performance than I was."

The seconds ticked by, then Hogan teased, "Should I be insulted on my brother's behalf?"

Knowing he believed her, Violet relaxed. "No. The chemistry just wasn't there." *Not like the chemistry I have with you.* Because it was uppermost in her mind, and here, now, in the dark discussing such intimate things, seemed like a good time to bring it up, she asked, "What about you? Am I likely to run into one of your…" She didn't want to insult other women, so she settled on, "Flings?"

"No idea. Would you mind?"

If he'd let her go, she'd punch him again. He seemed to know it and held her snug even as she felt the laughter rumbling in his chest beneath her cheek. "Jerk."

"I've never claimed otherwise."

He didn't have to. Anyone who knew him saw right away that he was, overall, a really terrific guy. Definitely a great dad. A good brother, a friendly neighbor.

Gorgeous, and sexy and—

"If you need anything during the night, let me know, okay?"

What if she needed him? *No, bad thought. Bad, bad thought.*

The quiet settled around them.

When she squirmed, getting more comfortable against him, he whispered, "For the record, I'm not proud of my temporary stint as a hound dog."

Heat, scented by his body, wafted around her, making her warm and sleepy. "No?"

His fingertips trailed up and down her bare arm. "It was stupid and immature."

"I didn't realize."

He squeezed her. "Are you laughing at me?"

"No." She surprised herself when she kissed his chest. Just a quick kiss, but still… "Do you know why you became a hound dog?"

"Yeah, I do. Now go to sleep."

"Okay." She was too lethargic to argue with him.

Even as she drifted off, she stayed very aware of Hogan against her—and she knew he was still awake.

THE KNOCK ON the door woke Hogan and he opened his eyes before realizing that Violet sprawled half over him. He lifted his head, awareness hitting him hard.

Her slender thigh draped his lap, a warm, soft weight against his morning erection. Her hair spilled over his chest and shoulder, her hand in a loose fist over his right nipple.

The knock came again.

Well, hell.

He didn't want to move, definitely didn't want to disturb her, but he glanced at the clock and saw it was after nine. He came up to an elbow, and she awakened.

He watched her dark brown lashes flicker before her eyes slowly opened. She looked at his chest, down his body—then shot her gaze to his face.

"Good morning." Jesus, she was beautiful in the morning. He opened his hands on her back and resisted the urge to fondle her bottom.

Her eyes flared.

She hadn't yet caught on, obviously. "Someone's at your door."

As if she expected to see someone standing outside the bedroom, she scrambled up and pulled the sheet to her chin.

Hogan laughed. "The front door." Ready to be gallant, he stood.

Her interest went directly to his lap and stayed there.

"Keep that up," he warned her, while pulling on his shorts, "and it'll be an R-rated greeting I give to your visitor." Already he had more than usual morning wood, but then, given how he'd awakened, it made sense.

When she stayed silent, he sighed. "Clearly, you're not a morning person. Stay put and I'll do the honors."

Hoping it wasn't a boyfriend of some sort coming to call on her, Hogan opened the door.

Honor and Jason stood there.

"You didn't hear the door?" Jason asked, looking past him at the couch—where clearly no one had slept. His expression changed. "Damn, sorry. Maybe we can just—"

"Come in." Brain scrambling, Hogan stepped back

to allow them entrance. What might have happened if his brother and sister-in-law hadn't intruded?

Nothing, you ass. The woman is sick. Still, conversations from the night before flooded back on him. He wanted to dissect everything that had been said, the assurances she'd given him, the subtle ways she'd started to soften toward him.

Instead he had to entertain.

"I thought you'd be up." Jason barely kept his humor in check. "I know it was a late night, but you'll be opening the diner today, right?"

"Yes." He didn't bother explaining that he'd still been in bed, Violet half atop him, their legs entwined. He could still feel the softness of her, the cushion of her breasts against his chest, her silky hair tangled over him—

Honor looked around, then whispered, "Violet is still sleeping?"

Get it together. "Yes, she's—"

"Right here," Violet mumbled, coming down the hall in her thick housecoat, the comforter once again dragging in her wake. She glanced at Hogan, then away, in her sluggish beeline for the couch.

Honor immediately went after her. "You're still so sick. I'm sorry."

"She's a little better," Hogan said. "But she's lousy in the mornings."

Jason said, "Antibiotics are an amazing thing."

"I don't know," Honor mused. "Could be your brother's good nursing skills that are doing the trick."

"Maybe." Arching a brow, Jason grinned at Hogan. "Colt's on his way." He nodded at Hogan's lap. "You, ah, might want to get on some pants. Denim maybe. Something sturdy."

"Shut the hell up." But he went down the hall, taking deep breaths with each step, and found his pants. *Behave*, he told his dick. Now, with the house full, it should be easier to do.

On his way to the bathroom, he heard Violet say, "You guys, this isn't—"

"Any of our business," Honor happily finished for her.

Hogan could almost see Honor smiling. Such a caring person, and not a snide bone in her body.

He wondered if she woke up grouchy. Didn't seem likely; Honor was always a sweetheart.

In rapid order, Hogan dressed, brushed his teeth and finger-combed his hair. He would have liked to shave, but he'd just made it back to the small living room when Colt arrived.

For his son, nothing seemed amiss.

Jason had coffee going and Honor pulled a bag of homemade chocolate chip cookies from her tote.

They gathered in the kitchen. Hogan saw to it that Violet took her medicine, and to everyone else's amusement, she let him. It didn't occur to him that it might seem uncommon for him to feel her head for fever, or to suggest ibuprofen. At least, it didn't until he realized they were all gawking.

Honor quickly said, "The cookies aren't really homemade. All I do is bake them, but Colt likes them."

"I do," Colt agreed, putting three on his plate and then serving Violet.

She smiled at Colt, thanked him and said, "I'm not dying, people. I don't have to be coddled."

Except that she'd wanted to be coddled last night—by him.

"I can help again today," Colt offered. "I'm cutting grass this morning, but then I'm free."

"You don't mind? You don't have a date or something else you'd rather be doing?"

"The date was last night—sort of. She hung out at the diner with some of our friends. I got to visit on breaks, and I'll see her Monday at school. You'll be well soon, so it's not a problem." He grinned. "You've slipped me enough free refills and always give me double orders of fries. I'm glad to pay it back a little."

That was news to Hogan. So Violet had been pampering his son? Nice.

Violet turned to Hogan. "You can fill out a time card for him?"

Hogan and Colt protested at the same time.

She held up a hand. "For once, you two look alike." She frowned at Colt. "You are the nicest young man ever, but you can't work for free. I wouldn't want you to, and I won't let you. And you," she said to Hogan, "shouldn't let him."

Jason laughed. "Well, he is saving up for college, so…be gracious, Colt, and thank the lady."

"Thank you."

As the cookies and coffee were consumed, Hogan stewed. Yes, his son was saving for college—because his college fund had been robbed, wasted. And he, Hogan, had been blind to it, never once suspecting. It still made him ill. God, he'd been such a fool.

Violet's bare foot thumped his calf under the table.

He looked up and saw her glowering at him. "What?"

Rolling her eyes, coughing briefly, she said, "Your brother asked you a question."

"Oh." He gave his attention to Jason. "What was it?"

"I asked if you wanted us to stay with Violet so you could go home and do whatever for a while."

"And I," Violet said, "told him I didn't need a baby-sitter."

"No, she doesn't," Hogan agreed. He stood. "And yes, I'll be heading home now." He waited until the others caught his not-so-subtle hint and abandoned their chairs.

"I need to get started on a new gazebo today," Jason said.

Honor hooked her arm through her husband's. "And I have to be at the salon in an hour."

Glad to get them on their way, Hogan nodded. "I'll walk you guys out."

"You're leaving now, too?"

Violet looked small and vulnerable and as far from "sweet" as a woman could get. "We'll talk first," he promised her. "Then I'll go."

"Honor, thank you for the cookies. Jason, thank you for the coffee. And, Colt, thank you for helping out at the diner."

Colt slung his arm around her. "Thank *you* for the temporary job." He gave her a squeeze, said, "Let me know if you need anything, all right?" and followed his uncle out.

Hogan gave her a long look. "I'll be right back."

After a few minutes spent chatting with Jason and Honor, Hogan watched them drive away. He turned to his son. "So, how's everything going?"

"What do you mean?"

"New girl? Odd jobs? School?"

"Everything's great, Dad. No worries." He rattled the keys to his old pickup in his hand, anxious to be on his way.

Hogan settled against the fender. "You like the girl?"

The slow smile reminded him way too much of himself, and his uncle. "Yeah. She's shy, but really nice."

"Pretty, too, I noticed."

Colt gave one nod. "Definitely pretty."

"Working at the diner won't put a crimp in things?" Colt carried a lot of AP classes, worked nights and weekends cutting grass and doing yard work, plus odds and ends jobs for neighbors, and still fit in time for girls and his friends.

"No, it'll be fine."

He didn't often feel uncomfortable with his son, but over a touchy subject like college, he couldn't help but frown. "I'm setting up another college fund—"

"It's fine." Colt opened the truck door in a rush. "I should get going. I've got five lawns to finish up before the diner opens."

"Five?"

"They're the size of postage stamps, Dad. Won't take me long."

Clearly Colt didn't want to talk about it, either. Hogan let out a long breath. "I'll see you at noon?"

"Probably quarter till. I'll help you open." He put the key in the ignition, but didn't start it. "What'll happen tomorrow?"

Hogan shook his head. "She'll insist on coming in. She's still got five days of meds to take, and she's still running on empty, but there's no way I can stop her."

"I guess not." Colt gave it some thought. "Tell the others to step up as much as they can."

"Good idea. I'll do that." He clasped his son by the shoulder and gave him a squeeze. "Be safe."

Colt grinned. "You, too, Dad."

Hogan closed the door, then turned to go back up the walk. He saw Violet standing at the window.

CHAPTER FOUR

NATHAN SAT ON his front porch early Monday morning, drinking coffee, thinking about the day and, admittedly, waiting for his neighbor to show herself.

He'd learned her pattern by observation.

Lights out at ten each night. Her porch light stayed on.

No visitors, but she ventured out to her porch early evening to read.

And each morning, between seven and seven thirty, she exited her front door, went down the walk putting in earbuds, her iPod attached to the waistband of yoga pants, and she jogged.

It was now seven fifteen.

When he heard her door open, he didn't look her way. Just set aside his coffee cup and flexed his arms.

He was ready. More than ready.

Today she wore running shoes, black compression shorts, a yellow tank top, and if he was any judge of breasts—and he was—a sports bra. She had her thick dark blond hair in a fat braid down her back. Instead of sunglasses, she wore a visor that cast a shadow over her amazing eyes.

Without looking his way, she picked up her pace and fell into a light jog, her braid bouncing behind her.

Nathan watched her go, flexed again, then headed down the walk. His legs were longer, he was stronger and he'd catch up easily enough. But first he wanted to do more observing.

Why was she so aloof?

Trailing a good distance behind her, he watched the movement of her toned, shapely legs, the swing of her slim arms and the gentle sway of her round ass. She turned the corner.

Knowing she wouldn't hear him, not over the rhythmic *thwap-thwap-thwap* of her sneakers, he picked up his pace.

Did his scar bother her? Sure as hell bothered him, but he couldn't do anything about it. Well, he'd retired from his position in one of the largest SWAT teams in the country and taken a much less demanding position in southern Ohio. That was something, he supposed. Wouldn't rid him of the scar, but maybe it'd keep him from getting more.

Thinking about that day and the changes he made always left him hyperaware of the memory, the people who had died—and the people who had lived.

He touched his face where the scar cut across his cheek from his temple to the corner of his mouth.

Stopping suddenly, she turned and looked right at him.

Nathan dropped his hand and continued jogging.

So did she, but not for long.

She paused at the stop sign to a cross street and turned to face him.

Anticipation crackling, Nathan slowed as he reached her.

The second he was close enough, she demanded, "Are you following me?"

A direct attack. He hadn't expected that, not when

she'd been so cagey previously. Lying, he said, "Just out for a jog."

She eyed him like she didn't believe him.

Smart lady. "Do you jog every day?"

"Yes." She unbent enough to ask, "You?"

He lied again. "Sometimes." These days he did most of his cardio in the gym in his basement. But he'd always enjoyed jogging, so why not? "What did you say your name is?"

Giving him "the look," she shook her head. "I never said. And you don't strike me as the obtuse type, so I'm guessing you already knew that."

Of course he did, and the curiosity drove him nuts. Hell, he'd thought about her all night. "Is it a secret?"

"No, I just…" Hands on her hips, she looked across the street.

Was she thinking about running? Away from him? Nathan took a step back, ensuring he didn't crowd her.

She surprised him by holding out a hand. "Brooklin Sweet."

Warmth uncurled inside him. Trying not to rush her, he gently took her hand. "Nathan Hawley."

"I remember." She pulled away. "Your friend introduced you."

"Hogan."

"Yes."

Clipped answers. Trying to get rid of him quickly? Too bad, because he wasn't in a mood to accommodate her. Perversely, the more remote she acted, the more he dug in. "I'm pleased to meet you, Brooklin."

Her beautiful eyes stared into his. "Did I have a choice in the matter?"

"I don't know," he said, pretending to think about it. "I was pretty determined."

A smile cracked, but she controlled it. "Nathan." She spoke gently, as if to a half-wit. "You're a very handsome man. And clearly successful. Being sheriff, I imagine people fall into line pretty quickly for you."

Not really. Not in Clearbrook. He could debate the successful part, but he stayed quiet, anxious to hear what else she'd say. He thought it would be just as surprising as the rest of this meeting had so far been.

"Please don't take it personally. But I really value my privacy right now."

He lifted a brow.

"I'm not interested in dating."

He folded his arms over his chest. "I don't recall asking you."

She almost flinched. "No, you didn't, did you? That's good." She rallied together a look of optimism. "Saves us both the awkwardness—"

"But now that you've mentioned it," he said, cutting her off. He smiled over her groan. "How about a no-pressure, meet-your-neighbor visit? Screwy Louie's would do. Lunch, or maybe dinner?"

"Has a woman ever told you no?"

"Often. It's never as much fun as yes."

Her mouth twitched. "You're dangerous."

Hands up, he denied that. "Swear I'm not. I'm the sheriff, you know. I have to be on the up-and-up." When she looked ready to bolt again, he said, "Odd. Your eyes look much darker with the sun behind you." Almost like whiskey, instead of topaz. But that sounded absurdly poetic, so he kept the description to himself.

"How tall are you?" Staring up at him, she said, "I'm five-eight, not exactly petite, but you still tower over me. I'm thinking six-two?"

Wondering at that observation, he shrugged. "About

that." In case she wanted all his stats, he added, "I'm thirty-four, a hundred and eighty pounds."

"What? No credit report? Marital status? Financial statement?"

Nathan laughed. "Never been married, no kids, and I'm financially comfortable. Not rich, so don't get greedy. But I don't struggle."

Brooklin blew out a breath. "I never asked for any of that. My point, if I can remember it now, was that I don't like men towering over me."

"You're into shorter guys, huh?" Maybe he should stoop down a little.

"I'm not into guys at all."

That brought both his brows up. "Gay?"

Rolling her eyes, she said, "No. Just very uninterested in…" She waved a hand between them. "This."

"Me?"

"*Anyone.* For crying out loud, pay attention."

"Yes, teacher."

She backstepped, breathed a little faster and said, "I need to go."

Nathan gestured. "Lead the way."

"No…" Hand to her temple, she groaned. "Alone. I want you to go away now."

He would.

For now.

But first… "Just in case you think you can dodge me by jogging in the opposite direction tomorrow—"

The look on her face assured him he'd nailed it.

"—you should know that it's going to be a nice day, which means Mr. Westbrook will be cutting his grass early. In his Speedo." He watched her face. "He's sixty-eight and let's say he's on the stocky side." Very stocky.

Thick lashes lifted. "You're joking."

At least she wasn't so jumpy now. "He claims it keeps his *boys* healthy, like maybe they need the fresh air, too."

"His boys?"

"Balls."

"Oh." She snickered.

"A few neighbors have complained, but I figured at least he's wearing the Speedo, right? Even though he somewhat overflows them." Nathan touched a hand to his own trim middle. "He's a beer drinker you know, and has the gut to go with it."

"If I jog your way, will you follow me again?"

Once more direct and to the point. Nathan looked up at a bird on the lamppost near them. "Possibly." *Definitely.* He met her worried gaze. "Has this little chat been so painful?"

Brooklin shook her head. "I guess as long as it's only chatting, it's okay."

Headway. He crossed his heart. "Only chatting." Until she relaxed enough for him to push for more.

JONI JEFFERS WAS every bit as annoying on Monday as she'd been on Friday. Without an ounce of encouragement from Hogan, she'd set her mind to furthering their association beyond the professional.

She hovered around his desk until Hogan knew he wouldn't get anything done.

Her continued interruptions for intimate, too-close chitchat, along with his preoccupation worrying over Violet, added to a lack of sleep over the weekend, and he could barely see the numbers in the columns.

He turned his chair to face Joni, ignored the few co-workers around them and said, "I was thinking of working from home the rest of the week."

The way she smiled, you'd think he'd invited her over. "If that's what you need to do…"

"I'll get more done there." And it'd give him time to check on Violet. "I'm missing a few returns, but I've already emailed the client. I've got the basics down on the restructuring and modernizing of the system used. Everything is online now and I should be able to present it by the end of the week, or next Monday."

"Did you see any savings?"

"Plenty, actually."

"Perfect." She smiled down at him while trailing a finger up and down her cleavage.

Thank God her back was to everyone else.

"You know, Hogan, I might stop by middle of the week just so you can show me everything."

"I can come back in Friday," he said quickly. Then, to shore that up—because he seriously didn't want a surprise visitor—he said, "My son has friends over a lot." A lot, meaning occasionally. "You know how loud boys can be."

Her gaze became assessing. "How old did you say he is?"

"Almost eighteen."

"Closer to a man than a boy now."

"No." Hogan didn't trust Joni, not at all, and he wanted those thoughts out of her head real quick. "He's still in high school."

"You weren't much older than him when you became his father."

"True. Colt is a hell of a lot smarter than I was." As he spoke, Hogan gathered up his papers, saved his files and stood.

Joni didn't back up.

Jesus, half the office—all of five other employees—

were watching this farce play out. "I'll check my email first thing every morning. Let me know if there's anything else you need."

"I'll walk you out," she said.

Short of telling her to go to hell, what could he do? Is this how women felt when being sexually harassed? No, for a woman it'd probably be worse. After all, Joni didn't physically threaten him.

She just annoyed the hell out of him.

VIOLET WANTED TO CRUMBLE. She wanted to sink down to the floor and put her head on her knees and give in to the need to sleep. Thanks to the meds, her chest didn't feel quite so tight and the coughing was now at a minimum, but the awful exhaustion remained.

Where had her usual energy gone? After being a complete slug all weekend, having Hogan wait on her—even hold her while she slept—she should have had a little more pep.

To everyone she saw, she explained that she wasn't contagious, but still, she tried to avoid direct contact with the food and the customers, just so no one would worry.

In a diner, there was always something else to do, and she stayed busy doing it. Too busy.

Once the lunch-hour traffic died down, she decided she could finally head to her office and tackle some paperwork. She was just leaving the seating area when Hogan stepped in.

Doing a double take, she watched him talk with Colt for a bit.

Damn, he was a good dad. Very hands-on and available. So what if he'd had a temporary lapse while chasing tail? Most men she knew made it a lifelong profession, not a temporary anything. And even then, he'd been with Colt a lot.

Just not in the evenings, when he'd spent time in other women's beds.

She'd bet her last biscuit that he hadn't slept chastely with any of *them*, not the way he had with her.

After his private talk with Colt, Hogan looked around, searching, she knew, for her.

Violet didn't move from her position near the farthest corner booth where she'd been collecting dirty dishes. She'd planned to deposit them to the washer on her way to her office.

Hogan smiled and came her way. When he reached her, he took the heavy tray from her hands.

"How are you feeling?"

"What are you doing here?"

His gaze searched hers. Then he started away, saying, "You first."

"I'm fine." Violet hustled along behind him. "Why aren't you at work?"

"Liar," he said, almost like a compliment. They were both quiet as he deposited the tray in the commercial sinks where two high school boys worked with awesome efficiency.

It wasn't until they reached her office that Hogan said, "I'll be working from home the rest of the week."

"That doesn't explain why you're here." She headed to the chair behind her desk and sank down to sit.

For too long, Hogan studied her.

She fought off a sigh, a frown and a cough. "What?"

"I wanted to check on you." As if he had every right—and maybe he did after the weekend—he put the back of his hand to her head. "You don't feel feverish."

"Not even a little."

"But you're still pooped."

Given she had both elbows propped on her desk to keep her head from hitting the surface, lying would be pointless. "Pretty much." She forced herself into a more upright position. "But we won't get that busy again until dinner and I can veg here while doing—" she made a face "—paperwork."

To her surprise, Hogan looked uncomfortable. It took her about two seconds to realize why, and with renewed energy she rushed to her file cabinet, but the files were gone, just as she'd known they would be. Slowly turning to glare, she whispered, "What did you do?"

"I brought you into the twenty-first century, for one thing." He took a step toward her, no longer abashed but now righteous. "I streamlined your really shitty records."

"Hogan—"

"And I started the process for some cost analysis."

Throwing up her hands, Violet asked, "When the hell did you have time? You spent all your weekend with me!"

"Not all of it. Most, yes, but—"

God, she felt inadequate next to him. Completely, utterly inadequate. "So you…what? In the random fifteen minutes you had free you updated all my bookkeeping?"

"As I said, I haven't completed it yet, but I've made enough headway to know your old accountant sucked. Good riddance to him."

Violet was barely listening. "I'll pay you."

He stiffened.

"What's your hourly salary? Let me know, and how many hours you spent on it, and I'll—"

Looking more than a little pissed, he took long steps

to reach her, caught her chin and, after scowling fiercely, kissed her.

Oh, he was definitely fired up. Maybe in a good way.

When she didn't fight him, didn't lurch away, he lifted his head and stared down at her. Heat lightened the color of his blue eyes and his breath had thickened.

Violet licked her lips, tasting him. But it wasn't enough. Without really thinking through the obvious consequences, she rested her hands on his chest and leaned closer.

Hogan groaned. By slow degrees he gathered her against his body until they touched from thighs to chests. His attention drifted back and forth from her eyes to her mouth until, finally, his mouth settled on hers again.

Slower this time, more gently.

Far more devastating.

Fisting her hands in his shirt, Violet fitted herself more tightly against him. Oh, she'd known he would be trouble to her senses, but heaven help her, it was even worse than she'd expected. He turned his head, and his tongue touched along her bottom lip. She immediately opened, making her own small, desperate sound of need.

He stroked a hand down her back to her hips, hesitated, then opened his fingers over her backside, cuddling, exploring—

The knock on the door sent them both jumping apart.

Hogan stared at her, unblinking.

"Dad?"

Colt's voice. Dear God. Violet jerked away, pretending to be busy with her file cabinet. Honestly, she didn't know what she was doing. Shuffling something…

Behind her, she heard the door open, and then Hogan said, "What's up?"

"Someone just dropped off a stack of the *Clearbrook Trickle*. What should I do with them?"

"The what?"

Violet cleared her throat. "How can you have been here so long and not know about the *Trickle*?"

"What is it?"

Glad to have something to focus on, but keeping her back to them anyway, she explained, "It's the free community paper. All the various establishments in Clearbrook set them out so the locals can know about any sales, public activities, school calendars and stuff like that. Each week they herald a local citizen for one reason or another, and there's also this newly added advice column. Very delicious stuff."

"Advice column?" Hogan asked.

"Yeah. It's been really fun." She glanced back at Hogan, and with Colt standing there smiling at her in such a knowing way, she had to fight a blush. "It's all worded in a way that you're unsure who is who, you know? You were in it last week. Some lady wanted to know how to convince you to go shirtless."

She watched his face blanch. Then, amazingly, hot color slashed his cheekbones. "You're making that up."

Feeling more herself, now that he was the uncomfortable one, Violet crossed her heart. "Swear it's true."

Colt laughed. "Did you keep a copy?"

Of course she had. She opened a lower drawer of the cabinet and withdrew her saved copy, already folded back to the right page. "Here you go, sugar. Bet you didn't know your old dad was a hottie, did you?"

"Yeah, it'd be hard to miss the way the ladies carry on." Colt shifted the stack into one arm, and with the other, he skimmed the paper. He read aloud.

"Many denizens of the female variety would like to know how to get a certain barbecue chef to tend his meats...shirtless."

Hogan looked aggrieved.

"Ladies, I suggest you ask him. It appears he has few boundaries, if all the gossip is true. Or to be more effective, issue the request to the one who employs him. She seems to be a very competent business owner who won't likely let a promo opportunity go unchecked."

Colt's laughing gaze met hers. "What do you think?"

"I asked him," she said. "So far as I know, he's considering it."

Colt's eyes widened and he guffawed.

"It's absurd," Hogan blustered, and he gave his son a shove, almost making him lose hold of the papers.

Colt caught his balance and laughed all the more.

"It's entertaining," Violet corrected, taking back her copy and storing it in the file cabinet again. "Go read it and you'll see what I mean." To Colt she said, "You can put the new editions on the counter next to the register. They won't be there long."

"Thanks." Colt didn't leave. "I also wanted to let Dad know I'm heading to the creek with friends after my shift ends in an hour. That is, unless you need me to stay longer?"

Well, shoot. Violet glanced up, trying for a bright smile, and said, "Not a problem, kiddo. Go and have fun."

Of course Colt's gaze jumped from hers to his father's and back again. He grinned. "You're sure?"

"Yes." Holding a file in front of her, she faced him. "You look far too much like your dad with that particular expression."

Both father and son blinked over that.

Hogan, bless the man's prudence, stepped out of the office and took Colt with him. She could hear the low drone of their conversation, but not precisely what was said.

Colt's laughter traveled back to her; because of the *Trickle*, or because he knew what they'd been doing?

For a brief second, Violet considered racing to the door and locking it while Hogan was on the other side. But that would be foolish, and besides, she didn't have the energy for racing.

A few minutes later Hogan returned—and he let the door stand open.

Violet stared at him. "You overstepped," she said and wished he'd kiss her again. She wanted him. Worse, she liked him.

The problem was that she very much disliked liking him.

Wanting him was a little easier to take.

"I know I did, but with good intentions." He leaned back against the wall and tried to stare her down. "First, I don't want your money."

"I already pay you!"

"Let me clarify. I don't want your money for helping out a friend and neighbor. For clocking in and standing over a hot grill, yeah, you bet I'll take my pay."

"You don't consider snooping through my records real work? You do that for all your friends?" *Maybe for all the women you lust after?*

He smiled. "You'd be surprised how many people want free advice. Back in Columbus it happened all the time, especially with my wife's…" He stopped, shook his head and frowned.

His wife's what? Her family? Did he see them anymore?

Did Colt?

"Once I have you set up, you'll be able to do the recording yourself. Or you can hire a good accountant to keep up."

"Meaning someone other than you?"

"I'm as good as it gets," he said without modesty. "I'm also expensive. Or used to be, anyway. I meant someone better than the idiot who mucked up your books in the first place."

That idiot had worked for her great-uncle, and since she'd loved her uncle a lot, she'd tried hard to honor all his decisions. Unfortunately, even she knew Uncle Bibb had been out-of-date on many things, especially bookkeeping, and he'd been more interested in making the restaurant a family, rather than a thriving business.

Resenting Hogan a lot, she eased down into her chair. "You mentioned cost analysis."

"Yeah. For instance, you aren't charging enough for the ribs, not with the way they're selling. Same goes for the specialty burgers, the meat loaf and a few other menu items." He came to lean on her desk and spent half an hour telling her his initial assessment, what should be adjusted up and what should be adjusted down. He even suggested she alter her specials based on sales stats.

She didn't like owing him, and now she was more in his debt than she wanted to admit. She was also impressed. "I was thinking the same about the ribs, but until I can offer them through the week, I don't want to tamper with success."

"So let's do a test week. Since I'm working from

home, I can be around enough for you to sell ribs for dinner. We can keep track and see how that goes, plus see what sides sell the best with them. From what I can tell, it's potato salad and leafy salad, but I'm not in the kitchen much, so I can't say for sure. That's just what I see with the customers sitting around me."

Having Hogan around even more would be such a blast of temptation. She was only a flesh-and-blood woman and she hadn't been with a man in too long to count.

But whoever wrote that advice column had recognized an important facet of her personality; she was a businesswoman down to the marrow of her bones. It would be completely stupid to pass up such a terrific opportunity. "You're sure you don't mind?"

"I can get most of my work done in the morning, then swing by to lend you a hand while I get things going."

Disliking him and his unending helpful attitude, she had to fight not to curl her lip. "That's an awful lot for you to have to do."

"True." He briefly touched her cheek. "But I haven't been sick, so I don't tire easily." He smiled and stood again. "I'll go get started, and seriously, Violet, if you need something, ask."

THE WEEK WENT by in a blur of rushed activity, calculations and unending enticement. Between him and Violet, they kept track of menu items, especially those ordered with the ribs, which were an enormous success, just as they'd both assumed they'd be.

At first, Hogan had considered teaching someone to do the ribs during the week for him, for the times when he couldn't be there. But the more time that passed, the more territorial he felt about it.

And damn it, he enjoyed himself. So much time spent in the fresh air instead of an office. The conversation with customers, many of whom had become friends. The freedom of it, being able to laugh and joke even while working.

He loved it—all but the endless, grinding lust for Violet. Lust, but also more.

Hogan didn't mean to, but he continually compared her to Meg. His wife had been, at least seemingly, the perfect partner. He wasn't the only one who'd thought she enjoyed the domestic life, making their home as perfect as she could get it, always clean and orderly and well decorated. She'd loved to cook, stayed involved in the schools and always took pride in her appearance.

Violet, on the other hand, thrived on her business involvement. She would run herself ragged and smile while doing it as long as she was working in the restaurant. By the end of the day her amazing hair was a mess, her subtle makeup smudged and her casual clothes stained, but she never seemed to notice.

He noticed. Hell, he noticed everything about her.

Though incredibly petite, probably weighing no more than one-fifteen, Violet had strength. He'd seen her heft heavy boxes, rearrange picnic tables to rake up leaves and carry platters that weighed nearly as much as she did.

She also handled the occasional disgruntled customer with Southern charm and the take-charge control of a grade school teacher. Far as Hogan could tell, everyone liked her.

Single males flirted with her, but Violet never flirted back, at least not in a way that any guy could take seriously. Her flirting extended to everyone, male, female, young and old.

Except with him. Yet Hogan wasn't sure what to do about it.

Especially since she still denied him.

In no time at all, Hogan fell into an acceptable rhythm. Being away from the office, working from home, made him more productive. He got far more done in a lot less time without Joni constantly trying to get in his pants. And since Colt was still working at the diner, he saw him more often, too.

It made Hogan wonder about opening his own business, a place where Colt could work alongside him. If it weren't for the college expenses...

Damn Meg for throwing away everything they'd worked for, including their son's future.

And for what? Sex with strangers? A few fast good times? Was it a ridiculous midlife crisis, or had she truly, completely stopped loving him to the point that all she felt was disdain?

Hogan didn't like thinking about it, but he couldn't clear the thoughts from his brain. He frowned while standing in the prep area, readying his fully cooked ribs for the grill. He realized he was breathing harder as the old rage and helplessness burned through his blood in a fresh wave.

For far too long that rage had chased him into being someone he hadn't recognized, someone he didn't respect.

Then Hogan felt a familiar hand swat his butt.

Immediately distracted from the choking memories, he glanced up into Violet's light blue eyes. "There's this thing called sexual harassment," he teased, knowing how he felt about her and how he felt about Joni were two very different things.

Grinning, her thick red hair in a loose topknot, Violet said, "But, sugar, you haven't even harassed me...today."

She confused him more than any woman he'd ever known, including his wife. "No, I haven't. You were busy talking to customers."

"A group of young ladies who wanted to know Colt's schedule." She rolled her eyes. "I told them to ask him, and they said he wouldn't share."

"I'm surprised. These days Colt is all about the female attention."

"I think he's a tease, like his father."

He'd like to tease her—in bed. He wouldn't mind toying with her until she squirmed and panted and begged him to—

She bumped her hip to his. "You've got this glazed look in your eyes."

Hogan scowled. "Do you want me to grill or make out with you?"

She pretended to pout. "It has to be one or the other?"

CHAPTER FIVE

SEXUAL INTEREST CLENCHED Hogan's muscles and short-ened his breath. He looked at Violet, wondering if she meant it, if maybe the pressure was building in her the same explosive way it built in him.

The more they'd worked together, the more sexual their banter had become. It left him frustrated and, at times, annoyed.

Regardless of that, he liked seeing Violet every day. He especially liked stealing a kiss here and there— usually when he could catch her off guard.

Her protests were fewer and farther between. In fact, when he didn't steal a kiss, she found a way to provoke him, as she did now.

She'd been nearly herself by Thursday, and today she looked even better—less tired, more refreshed. Recov-ered from her illness.

To be sure, he asked, "You're feeling okay?"

"I feel terrific."

"Not working yourself too hard?"

"No harder than necessary, definitely no harder than you." She tipped her head. "What game are you play-ing now?"

"Game?"

Her look became accusing. "You going to give me that kiss or not?"

Hogan gave it quick thought and decided on a different tack. He held up his hands, now a little messy with seasonings, rub and sauce. "How about you kiss me instead? I believe in equal rights for women. What's good for the goose is good for the gander, or vice versa. If you want a kiss—"

"Are you challenging me?"

More like testing her, but he only cocked a brow and waited.

Giving it some thought, Violet gazed at his mouth until her own expression warmed, and Hogan knew she'd made up her mind.

Anticipation held him still.

Rising on tiptoe, she lightly touched his lips with a fingertip. He could feel her breath, his own suspended. She leaned forward, caught his bottom lip in her teeth and lightly tugged.

Interest keen, Hogan waited.

She soothed his lip with her hot little tongue and slowly, very slowly, fitted her mouth to his in a kiss that made him half-hard.

He held on to the counter behind him; not only were his hands messy, but if he touched her, he just knew he'd get carried away. They had relative privacy in his prep area, yet they weren't alone, not in the restaurant with other employees around, customers coming and going.

For only a moment, her breasts pressed to his ribs and her hands held tightly to his shoulders. *I want to do this again, Violet, with both of us naked and a bed nearby.*

As she eased away she kissed his chin, his jaw and his throat.

In a soft, husky voice, she whispered, "How do you always smell so good?" She brushed her nose along his throat, his collarbone, rested her forehead against his chest for a heartbeat, and then with a sigh, she stepped away.

He was struggling to get his thoughts in order when she said, all brisk business, "I raised the prices on the items we discussed, and so far, no one has even noticed."

Hogan stared at her. "Damn, you're good."

"At kissing? At conversation switches?"

So she'd done it on purpose? He growled. "At making me nuts."

She gave an unrepentant grin. "I've learned from you. God knows you've done it to me enough times."

"Is that so?" Sure, he'd stolen some kisses—and she'd enjoyed it.

Almost as much as he'd just enjoyed it. *Damn.*

Seeing that he understood, Violet laughed. "I like having you around, Hogan. I really do." She patted his abs and sashayed away with her own sexy little swagger of triumph.

He had a lot to think about.

Luckily, an upside to grilling at a crowded restaurant was plenty of time to ruminate.

WHEN NATHAN PULLED into his driveway at 7:00 p.m., grimy from head to toe and still seething, he paid no attention to his neighbors. He had a cloth wrapped around his bleeding hand and an attitude that could spit nails.

He didn't notice Brooklin out front until he slammed his car door, and then heard her call out.

"Nathan? Oh my God, what happened?"

Curt, he said, "Nothing." Which was stupid, given how blood dripped from the soaked cloth and down his forearm. The woman was elusive, but she wasn't blind.

"Are you okay?"

Just freaking dandy. She never wanted to talk to

him, so why now? "Fine," he said, still terse, and kept walking.

It shocked the hell out of him when, before he could reach his front door, she joined him on his porch.

"You're bleeding."

Briefly, he closed his eyes, trying to get his temper under control. "An accident. Nothing major."

"Let me see."

"Shouldn't you be running the other way?"

She pulled her head back, glared at him, then took the keys from his hand and, scowling as much as him, opened his door.

"Go to your kitchen," she ordered, and now she was the one being abrupt. "Do you have a first-aid kit?"

He didn't know what the hell to think, but having her in his house quickly took the heat from his rage. Wondering what she would do, he said, "Under my bathroom cabinet."

"I'll be right back."

As if she invaded the homes of bachelors every day—bachelors she usually avoided—Brooklin went down his hall. Their houses were set up the same. Hell, most of the houses on the street were the same inside, with only subtle differences outside.

Wondering if he'd picked up his dirty clothes after his shower that morning, Nathan went to the kitchen sink and unwrapped his hand. The pad of his thumb on his left hand had already bruised around the two-inch slice. He threw away the cloth and ran water over his hand so he could see how deep it might be.

"Here, sit down." Brooklin showed up with his first-aid kit and pulled a chair toward him. She looked at the blood and bruises, assessing the damage, then began cleaning it with an antiseptic. "How'd you do this?"

She held his large, tanned hand in her much smaller, much paler fingers while she worked. Nathan studied the top of her bowed head. "Stupid cat got stuck in a stupid old air conditioner, and I had to get it out."

"And you stupidly cut yourself on a stupid, jagged piece of metal?"

Her take-charge, sassy attitude lightened his own. "Something like that."

"The cat?"

"Back in the arms of the old lady who owns his mangy ass."

"I trust he fared better than you?"

"Not a scratch."

Once she'd cleaned it, Brooklin carefully prodded. "Since your kit has nylon butterfly bandages, I don't think you'll need stitches."

"I already decided that."

"I'm going to put some medicine on it, okay? Then the bandages, then I'll wrap it."

Nathan was busy noticing that for once she wasn't in running clothes. She also wasn't wearing a bra under her tan T-shirt. Heat ran up his spine until his collar felt too damn tight.

So did his pants.

"Sure," he said. "Knock yourself out."

Instead of activewear, tonight Brooklin wore loose, striped pajama pants. Her thick hair fell free around her face, half hiding her concentrated expression, occasionally brushing his forearm.

Breathing her in, Nathan enjoyed the scents of floral shampoo and sweet, warm woman. She'd broken with her normal routine and that interested him. A lot. "What were you doing before I interrupted?"

She bent closer to his hand. "Waiting for my toe-nails to dry."

He glanced down at her bare feet and saw her toe-nails painted a sparkly purple. For some reason, that made him smile.

"Does this hurt?"

"No." Not his hand. Other parts were starting to strain a little. "You a nurse or something?"

She hesitated, frozen, then shook her head. "No." She wrapped some gauze around the bandages.

With his uninjured hand, Nathan lifted her hair away, then held the thick tresses in a loose fist. Their eyes met. "You don't sound real convinced."

She straightened abruptly. He didn't let go of her hair fast enough and she winced at the tug, but said nothing about it. "All done. I hope you're right-handed."

"I am." This time he brushed her hair back over her shoulder. Her hair was thick and warm and it turned him on. Hell, everything about her turned him on, even her obstinate and secretive attitude.

"Good. Might have been more inconvenient if…" Remembering that she didn't want to engage in casual conversation, she shook her head. "I should get going." But she looked around his kitchen.

Watching her, Nathan stood. "I don't suppose I could impose further and ask you to make some coffee for me while I go change?" He still had blood on his shirt and pants.

Again, she looked around his kitchen. "I suppose I could…"

Not giving her a chance to change her mind, he said, "Thanks," and headed out of the room, already unbuttoning his uniform shirt.

He wouldn't put it past her to make the coffee

and then skip out, so he rushed through changing into a T-shirt and jeans. Barefoot, he stopped in the bathroom and saw that, luckily, he'd left it tidy. He shoved his now-dirty uniform into the hamper and went after her.

Brooklin was in the kitchen, standing at the sink and looking out into the yard, when he came back in.

She didn't hear him enter.

The loose pajama pants rode low on her curvy hips. The T-shirt hugged her narrow waist and proud shoulders.

And even with her back to him, he remembered how the soft cotton material had molded to her breasts, even showing the outline of her currently soft nipples.

Drawn to her, he stepped closer. "So you used to be a nurse, but you aren't now?"

Turning, she braced her elbows on the counter and studied him.

This pose was even more enticing, and he couldn't help but look her over.

She quickly straightened and folded her arms over herself. "You've held back all week and now can't take the curiosity anymore, is that it?"

Nathan had to admit, he loved the way she cut right to the core of things. "Did you appreciate my patience? I jogged with you three times this week, silently, and didn't ask a single question."

"No, you didn't. Your polite understanding of my privacy was a good plan. A solid plan. You impressed me. You should stick with it."

Hiding his satisfaction, he poured the coffee, one for him and one for her. He'd confused her, probably a good thing. "There's milk in the fridge. No creamer, sorry."

"I drink it black." She took the cup, careful not to touch him, and sipped.

"So did you work in a hospital?" He watched her stiffen, her face tightening as if gathering steam. He pressed her anyway. "For a private practice?"

Her eyes narrowed. "No."

"Maybe the military? Though you don't look like any soldier I've ever—"

"I worked in a school, all right?"

Huh. Testy about it, too. "A school nurse. Yeah, that fits." Even firmed in annoyance, her mouth was nice, her lips full and soft. "Was it grade school? High school?"

She shook her head, refusing to answer.

"I take it you've left it behind?"

"Yes." She took a big drink of coffee, burned her tongue, cursed low and set the cup in the sink. "I have to go."

"Because I'm asking too many questions?" He could have told her that the more defensive she got, the more curious it made him. He lowered his voice, almost suspicious now. "Because I'm too interested?"

"Because you're too damned pushy!" She headed toward the door.

Nathan followed. "Thank you, Brooklin, for fixing up my hand." He pretended she wasn't furious. "I really appreciate it."

Uncertain, she glanced at him. "You're welcome. The butterfly bandages should hold, but try not to soak it."

He looked into her unusual golden eyes. "Okay to take a hot shower?"

She swallowed. "Yes." Her eyes went to his chest, then away. "But make it fast."

He resisted the urge to tell her that he preferred things slow. Very slow. "Yes, ma'am. Fast it is." Following her out on the porch, he watched her trot quickly down the steps and all but run away.

Again.

But he was wearing her down and he knew it. She knew it, too, and that's probably what scared her so much.

What the hell was she hiding?

BROOKLIN WAS THOUGHTFUL as she went across the lawns, ignoring Nathan's attention as it followed her.

Without looking his way, she went back into her own home, closing and locking the door behind her. Struck with inspiration—*all kinds of inspiration*—she went straight to her computer and sat down.

Closing her eyes, she pictured Sheriff Nathan Hawley. Over six feet tall, muscular, light brown hair and piercing green eyes. She didn't feel a smidge of guilt; surely every single lady in Clearbrook had, at one time or another, fantasized about him.

Probably the married ladies, too.

Was there anyone, male or female, in Clearbrook who didn't know him? Or at least *of* him?

Being the most imposing man she'd ever met, he would make an impression wherever he went, she was pretty sure.

She'd done her research on him. During the rehab of the neighborhood, he'd been brought in as a result of a special election. His past, working with a SWAT team in Columbus, made him a certifiable badass.

And he knew it.

He knew how damned handsome he was, how he affected people.

How he stirred all the ladies.

Yes, everyone in Clearbrook knew him. There'd be no misunderstandings.

Sometimes, Sheriff, when you push, people push back.

VIOLET HAD EXPECTED Hogan to give as good as he got, and she'd looked forward to it. Their verbal sparring always left her feeling alive and energized. Unfortunately, the weekend was so crazy they didn't have time for teasing. They'd barely had time to breathe.

Even the preceding week was nuts, the usual lulls Monday through Thursday almost nonexistent as families flocked in for the rare treat of ribs on a weeknight.

She couldn't wait to see how busy tomorrow, Friday, would be.

She loved the business; she really did, but clearly she needed to hire more help now. She also needed more picnic tables for outdoor seating. Some of the more regular customers had started bringing their own lawn chairs. Things were awesomely, wonderfully out of control.

All because of Hogan.

Her independent soul rebelled at the idea that he'd been so good for business.

So good for *her*.

But she wasn't a woman who hid from the truth. Before Hogan, the business had steadily grown under her management.

With Hogan, it all but exploded.

If she hoped to maintain the current momentum—and she most definitely did—she needed him.

Blast the man—he'd even done a miraculous job with her bookkeeping.

Did he still want her? Was he as sexually frustrated

as she was? Had he given up on her, or was he just bid-
ing his time?

God, she didn't even know what she wanted, not
where it pertained to an intimate relationship. When it
came to business, she wasn't nearly so indecisive.

Taking advantage of a fifteen-minute break, maybe
the only one she'd get, Violet strolled around back to
see Hogan. She paused just inside the prep area, making note of his organizational skills even here. He'd set
up the area himself, taking it over without a qualm. An
interior door kept the hot summer air from competing
with the air-conditioning inside and allowed him to leave
the exterior door open so that he could easily move inside and still keep an eye on the grills.

A man of many talents.

Something sweet but uncomfortable crowded Violet's
chest, making her heart ache in an odd way. The emotion was unfamiliar and, damn it, unwanted.

Giving herself a moment, she quietly stood there and
watched Hogan, wondering what it was about him, specifically, that affected her in such a startling way.

Gorgeous, yes. No one could deny that. The Guthrie brothers had some amazing genes coasting through
their bodies. But there were others in the area who were
also very attractive, and Violet knew she'd never been
even remotely tempted by any of them. Well, the idea
of sex had tempted her, certainly. But not all the other
stuff, not the confusing emotions that tried to take priority over her restaurant.

And sex, just for the sake of sex, had never really
been her thing. Not in a small town like Clearbrook.
Not with men she'd later have to regard as customers
in her diner. The idea of sex had been nice but, in the
end, just not worth it.

Now with Hogan, the complications would be tenfold, and still she couldn't stop thinking about it.

Standing in front of one of three grills, an apron tied low on his hips, he turned a rack of ribs. The man had an organizational skill that blew her mind. He never looked frenzied or overwhelmed. Even now, under a broiling sun while tending multiple hot grills, he moved with efficiency.

At the table closest to him, his brother, Jason, and sister-in-law, Honor, sat with neighbors Sullivan and Lexie. Hogan laughed at something Lexie said, then shook his head.

Violet could remember a time when she'd thought something might've been going on between Lexie and Hogan. After all, Lexie was an extremely pretty woman with her short, pale blond curls and her very up-front sexuality.

Then Lexie had moved in with Sullivan, and Violet quit worrying about it. Talk about gorgeous—Sullivan, with his inky-dark hair and midnight eyes, killer instincts and ripped body, would keep any woman happy. He was very intense, mysterious and almost intimidating.

He was fantasy material, but not once had Violet been tempted to seek an involvement.

"So admit I was right," Lexie said to Hogan while turning to Sullivan for backup. "He looks blissfully happy, doesn't he?"

Sunlight glinted off Sullivan's black hair as he pretended to survey Hogan. "You know, honey, I think you're right. Hogan looks peaceful."

"She's absolutely right," Honor chimed in, aligning herself with her best friend. "Seriously, Hogan, you *do* look somewhat blissful."

"Peaceful? Blissful?" Jason hugged his wife and said,

"I don't want to be left out, so can I admit that it does seem to suit you, Hogan?"

"It's a gift," Lexie claimed. "A real talent. A man should never ignore the calling of a talent."

Hogan laughed again. "You're all nuts. Yeah, I enjoy it, okay? But it's hardly a calling."

"You're wrong," Lexie insisted. "You were meant to do this."

"This?" Hogan waved his long metal tongs at the grills. "Come off it, Lexie. I can't see myself working in a restaurant for the rest of my life."

That smacked of an insult and Violet decided to announce herself. "Something wrong with working in a restaurant?" All eyes turned to her as she stepped out of the preparation area and into the side yard. "It's not good enough for you?" *Am I not good enough?*

Hogan took in her frown. "I never said that."

"Maybe it's working for a woman that you find objectionable?"

"I work for a woman at the accounting firm, too."

She hadn't known that and it threw her, but only for a second. She squared her shoulders, ignored all the others and stared up into Hogan's eyes. "I think it's out of your hands. The demand now is too high. You've spoiled all the customers—"

Their own little audience cheered at that, sounding very spoiled.

"—and now no one is going to want to give up having your ribs whenever they want them."

The grill hissed and spit, flames licking upward. Turning away, Hogan rearranged the meat and adjusted the heat.

When Violet glanced at the others, she saw they

wore varying expressions of encouragement, amusement, agreement—and worry. The last was from Jason.

Did he expect his brother to bully her? Ha. Not likely.

In front of all those rapt faces, she demanded, "Well?"

Occupied with the grill, Hogan asked, "Well what?"

"Sign on. Agree to work here for a full forty-hour week." She gave that quick thought then amended, "Maybe a little more than forty given how crazy the weekend gets."

He didn't look at her when he said, "What makes you think you can afford me?"

He wasn't saying an outright no? Hope blossomed. Hope and something else. "Let's discuss it." Thanks to Hogan, she not only had a better grasp of her own finances, but she was making more per week. She could give him a bump in pay, no problem.

Finally, he set aside those long sturdy tongs and faced her. "You want to negotiate right now? In front of them?" He nodded toward their friends.

His mood seemed off. The idea of trying to discuss this, alone, made her tingle. Could he keep to business?

Could she?

They hadn't had any alone time in far too long now. And damn it, she missed him. She saw him every day, but not like she had while being sick.

Dumb as it seemed, she missed having him touch her. She missed him holding her while she slept.

At her long internal debate, he gave her a mocking grin. "Having second thoughts?"

"Tonight." Risky. Once she had him alone, or he had her alone—but this was too important. "After we close up."

"Ohhh," Lexie whispered, sotto voce, "to be a fly

on the wall during that meeting." Then she squeaked, thanks to Sullivan's squeeze.

"All right," Hogan said. He turned back to his grill. "If you see Colt, have him come out on his break, okay? I haven't seen him yet today."

Relief flooded through Violet until she almost felt light-headed. Hogan hadn't flat out refused. "If I can pry him away from the girls, sure." While Hogan might be great for her adult customers, Colt was equally great for the younger crowd. And that got her thinking. She needed to do something special for the school, something that would draw in even more young people during the less insane time between dinner and the cocktail hour.

Conversation did not resume.

Hogan busied himself filling a massive platter.

Since he wasn't being totally disagreeable, Violet decided to push her luck. "I was also thinking, maybe you need an apprentice, a trainee of sorts who could learn what you do and how you do it so that if you ever—"

"No."

The abrupt refusal irked her. She put her hands on her hips. "What do you mean no? You won't even think about it?"

"Not right now, no."

"Then when? After you get sick or hurt and I'm left in the lurch?" Only half teasing, she said, "Don't be selfish, Hogan. If you don't want to share your sauce with anyone else, maybe you could just share it with me."

Jason choked and Sullivan snorted.

"Hey," Violet protested. "I'm capable."

Honor and Lexie, both grinning, rushed to agree. With their backup, she decided to take another turn at

Hogan. "You can trust me, you know. I wouldn't share your secrets. But if you teach me, then at least—"

As if much put upon, Hogan sighed, straightened away from the grill and turned to her. They stared at each other, him impatient, her defiant.

Before she could guess his intent, he bent and put his mouth over hers in a firm, no-nonsense kiss that lingered a few seconds too long.

Violet heard the collective breath of the audience, but she couldn't seem to pull away. In fact, she leaned into him. *The cat's out of the bag now.*

Against her now-tingling lips, Hogan whispered, "You may be the boss, but no is still no." And just like that, he gave his attention back to his grills.

Feeling all eyes on her, Violet fought off a blush, turned on her heel and headed back inside.

She heard Hogan say firmly, "Tonight, Violet."

And suddenly laughter broke out. Wow.

So maybe she shouldn't have pushed him after all.

AFTER SULLIVAN AND Lexie left, and Honor went inside to find Colt, Hogan decided it was now or never.

He could feel Jason watching him, though, and as soon as they were alone, he asked, "So you and Violet, huh?"

Since that was what Hogan wanted to talk about, he should have had a better answer, but all he said was "I don't know."

"What does that mean?"

"It means it's complicated." Hogan checked each grill, was satisfied and took a seat next to Jason. "I've been interested since the day I met her. No secret there."

"Definitely not a secret," Jason agreed.

"She's always rejected me."

"You're not one to give up easily."

"No." Hogan looked out over the seating area. Neighbors, friends, people he'd met, people he liked, were all enjoying the day. And his food. He felt a sense of satisfaction over that. "Violet couldn't be more different from Meg."

"True." Jason shooed away a bee. "That's a problem?"

"I don't know. I used to understand what I wanted, but that's all gone now, and this—living in Clearbrook, being close to you, hell, even the sunrises and sunsets—they're all nice." Far nicer than he'd expected.

"I'm glad to hear it. Honor and I love having you and Colt next door. It would break her heart if you moved too far away. You know she never had real family until us, so she takes it very seriously now."

Us. Yes, Honor definitely considered him and Colt a part of her family. "I know." Meaning every word, he said, "Honor is special, not just to you, but to Colt and me, too." He stood to slather more sauce on the ribs, then reseated himself, his legs stretched out in front of him, the sun hot on his back. "Violet is also unlike any of the ladies I've been with recently."

"Amen to that."

Hogan had to grin. "Your disapproval is showing through."

"Not disapproval," Jason protested. "It's just that none of those ladies made you happy. Like you've said, you knew what you wanted and a string of meaningless hookups wasn't it."

"I liked it."

Jason laughed. "I'm sure you did. Hell, you're alive, and a lot of guys envied you the variety."

"Not you."

"No." Still being honest, Jason said, "I was worried

about you, and I was especially worried about Colt. At the time, though, I think the attention was what your ego needed."

Damn, that made him sound pathetic. He laughed. "Meg definitely shredded the old ego, that's for sure."

"No. She just dented it a little. You're okay now."

Was he? As a grown man, Hogan figured he had a right to do as he pleased. But he detested the idea of being weak, and yet that's what he'd been. Weak, hurt and stupidly using sex to bury the pain. "Needing something—" *Someone.* "It's not a good thing."

Jason tipped his head back to stare at the sky. "I need Honor." He straightened and frowned at Hogan. "Hell, I need you and Colt, too. That doesn't make me weak."

Leave it to Jason to cut right through his bullshit. "Maybe." He'd have to think about it, but for now he'd get back on track. "The thing is, I can't look at Violet as a casual one-nighter. Like you said, she's light-years away from those other women. But I won't look at her as a possible wife, either."

"Does it have to be one extreme or the other?"

Again, he said, "I don't know." He was starting to think he didn't know much at all. "It's like this power struggle thing between us. Violet is…independent."

"No kidding."

Hogan glanced at his brother, younger by three years. "And that's another thing." Talking about it was even more uncomfortable than thinking about it. "You know Violet better than most."

Jason didn't pretend to misunderstand. "I do. But I swear to you, Hogan, it didn't mean anything. Not to either of us." He sat forward, his forearms on his knees. "Violet gets lonely, you know? She works around the clock, so I'm sure it's tough for her to date. I think I was convenient. Maybe trustworthy, too. She knew me well enough to know I wasn't psycho, or a stalker."

"So what was your motivation?"

"That's a joke, right?"

The plain speaking put Hogan more on edge.

"Violet's not only nice, smart and sweet, she's also hot. At the time, I didn't need more motivation than that."

Hogan slanted him a disgruntled look. "So she was convenient for you, too?"

"That sounds awful, doesn't it? Just goes to show you that you aren't the only guy to make a knuckleheaded mistake." Jason clapped him on the shoulder. "Luckily, our temporary stupidity didn't mess up the friendship. That's all there ever was between us."

"Honor knows?"

"Knows, accepts it and doesn't worry about it." Jason stood. "If she can handle it, Hogan, then you should be able to, right?"

Sure. Maybe. But that still didn't solve his problem: what to do with his boss, that redheaded hottie who turned him inside out, when the two main choices were both impossible.

CHAPTER SIX

For a Thursday, they'd been positively packed. Realistically, she knew it was the newness of the ribs being available. She couldn't expect every weeknight to bring in the same crowds. But for now, for this day, she felt positively jubilant.

Colt had left hours earlier, after chatting with his dad. She wanted to tell Hogan what an amazing young man he'd raised, but she was afraid that might also dredge up conversation about his wife, and she didn't want to go there. Not tonight.

With new eyes and optimism, she looked around the restaurant. She needed to redecorate. Never fancy, but maybe new paint, new curtains and light fixtures. She felt renewed, so why shouldn't the restaurant, too?

She was standing there staring at a stain on a ceiling tile when she literally *felt* Hogan behind her. Nerve endings went on alert, her senses popping to attention.

Striving for a placid look of mere curiosity, she glanced over her shoulder. "All done?" He'd removed his apron, and from the looks of the damp hair around his forehead, he'd also washed away the sweat from being outside so long.

"Yes."

That led to yet another thought. "I'm going to talk to Jason about building some sort of overhang for you.

You know, for shade. Or maybe I could just buy a big umbrella table for you—"

"Shh." Hogan's finger pressed over her lips. "You're getting ahead of yourself."

His finger, firm on her lips, had her stomach doing flip-flops. Insane. She wanted to bite that finger, maybe lick it.

When he lifted his hand, she smiled. Or tried to. She wasn't sure of her own success. This meant too much to her for her to take it lightly. "We haven't even discussed things yet. You have to allow me to make a pitch before you reject me."

"Let's get the place locked up. Then we can talk in your office."

Kristy, the only employee left besides her and Hogan, laughed. "I promise to hurry."

Violet frowned. "We're talking business."

"Uh-huh." Kristy winked. "Don't mind me." Less than five minutes later, she was gone.

Hogan hadn't teased back, hadn't denied Kristy's assumptions, hadn't really done anything other than look thoughtful, and maybe determined, as he helped to secure the doors.

Alone with Hogan, Violet nervously led the way to her office, rehearsing her pitch in her mind before saying, "Before you say no, let me explain all the reasons why this could be a very good thing for both of us. I've given it a lot of thought, and I think we'd both benefit—"

She was barely inside the door before Hogan caught her arm, turned her to the wall and smothered her gasp of surprise with a kiss that curled her toes in her sneakers.

Violet meant to protest—she really did. But his mouth was hot and, damn him, skilled. The man knew how to kiss. While his tongue stole her thoughts, he leaned into her, his hard body all along the front of hers, his hands holding her face so gently, the kiss devouring.

Thoughts of business fled, replaced by indescribable hunger. She wound an arm around his neck, her hand in the hair at his nape. Her other hand busily stroked the sleek, lean muscles along his shoulders and back, then down the furrow of his spine.

Tensing, Hogan groaned and leaned his hips in against her.

He was hard, and God, she loved it, especially when he caught her hips in his large hands and slowly rocked her against him. The friction… He was pressing rhythmically against her in just the right way, in just the right place, and—

Suddenly leaving her, Hogan stepped back, his breath labored as he stared down at her.

Wilted against the wall, Violet didn't know what had happened. She wanted to pull him close again, to pick up where they'd left off. Every part of her felt alive, too sensitive and needy. "Hogan…"

"This," he said, his voice a growl, "is a problem."

Finally, she saw the look in his eyes and her stomach cramped. For some insane reason, she wanted to slap him. But that would be grossly unfair considering she'd encouraged him.

And she wanted him to continue.

She drew a breath, but with the vise of humiliation around her throat, it wasn't easy. Hogan's expression softened. He even reached out for her cheek—but she quickly ducked away.

Going to the other side of her desk, which she hoped was a safe enough distance, she met his gaze. She tried to sound cold instead of hurt. "So. I presume that was a lesson for me?"

"A lesson? No." He leaned against the closed door, his expression cautious. "I didn't mean to embarrass you."

She laughed. It was a nasty, mean sound. "Well, it doesn't need explanation, does it?"

"I think it does."

"No, I—"

"Violet, *stop*. Let me talk for a minute, okay?"

That almost enraged her. "*Now* you want to talk?" She put a trembling hand over her chest. "Now that I'm turned on and having trouble breathing and I can barely form a thought? Is that a joke?"

"I won't apologize for kissing you." His eyes narrowed. "I've been dying to do it for days."

"You hid it well!"

Surprise showed in his face, then was carefully masked. He watched her like a big cat watches a mouse. "You've been hoping I would—?"

"No!"

His eyes glittered at her. "Fibber," he said softly, making it sound like a come-on. "You know, the way you've been all week, I thought you were giving me payback."

"Payback?"

"Because I've chased you? So you chased me back, knowing I couldn't do anything about it."

Like a life raft, she grabbed it. "That's exactly what I was doing." His indulgent smile told Violet that he didn't believe her. So she wasn't a convincing liar? She wouldn't be further embarrassed about that.

"Violet." He said her name like a damned caress. "We've been busy, too busy to talk much, definitely too busy for me to get you alone the way I wanted to."

"Yes, incredibly busy," she agreed, hoping to change the subject. "That's what I wanted to talk about. The increased business—"

"But even if I could," Hogan said, refusing to be sidetracked, "I knew a kiss or two wasn't going to do it, not for me."

Her gaze got caught in his. "No?"

"Not even close." Pushing away from the door, he moved a few steps toward her. "I don't think it'd do it for you, either, Violet."

No, definitely not. She stared him in the eyes and said, "Maybe I'm stronger than you."

He rubbed his chin. "I have no idea what it is about you, but I want you so damned much I can't think straight. You insult me and I want you." He took another step closer. "You tease me and it makes me hot." Closer still. "You boss me around, and it's all I can do to keep my hands off you."

Well, that was a bit of a balm to her pride. So maybe he hadn't been trying to prove anything to her. And he wanted her? Couldn't be as much as she wanted him, but at least she knew it wasn't all one-sided on her part.

Hogan now stood on the other side of her desk, very near, and yet with a desk between them.

She sighed. "Today, you didn't. Keep your hands off me, I mean. You kissed me in front of several people." Rumors would spread like wildfire. Such was life in Clearbrook.

"You let me. Pretty sure you even participated."

Probably. "What will everyone think?"

"Nothing new."

She frowned in confusion.

"It's not a secret to anyone that we're attracted. The confusing part is why we haven't done anything about it yet."

Violet squared her shoulders. "You are—*were*—so busy chasing everything in a skirt that I—"

"You think I've reformed?"

With no idea what to say to that, she frowned down at a paper on her desk. It was easier than meeting his gaze. "I guess you're probably too busy now, having two jobs I mean, to fit in...extracurricular activities." She hoped that was true.

"Honey, no man is ever too busy for that."

His appalled tone brought her attention up again.

He was smiling.

"I didn't realize you were back on the prowl," she almost snarled.

Watching her, he circled the desk and stopped right in front of her. "Since I was prowling you, it's a wonder you didn't notice."

Violet's heart tried to punch its way out of her chest and she had to fight the urge to grab him. Maybe she just needed to get laid. It didn't have to be Hogan, right? She could— No, she knew she couldn't.

Damn it.

"You see," he said in a rough whisper. "Even now, it's hard to resist. You need to think about this, Violet. Think about having me around so often."

"I have." She'd thought about it far too much and loved the idea.

"We'll end up in bed. You know that."

She hoped so. "Yes."

For a brief moment, Hogan closed his eyes. "Shush a minute and let me finish, okay?"

Wanting him every bit as much as he claimed to want her, Violet nodded.

"I've been trying to figure out what it is about you. I think it's that you're a mix of sweet and sexy, all wrapped up in a gorgeous package."

A wonderful compliment. "Thank you."

"You're also smart and motivated. Often funny, when you aren't torturing me. You have great business sense—no, not as good as me, but good. And whatever you lack in business savvy you make up for with hard work."

Wow. That was an even better compliment since it was on her character, not her looks. She wanted to hug him, but he looked so serious, she held back and joked with him instead. "Are you planning to sleep with me, or saint me?"

"Whether we sleep together or not is up to you. If I work here, for damn sure it's going to happen."

She agreed. And since she wanted it to happen, she didn't see the problem.

"What I won't do," he whispered, "is marry you."

That statement hit like a bucket of ice water. She drew back, stung, startled, speechless.

Hogan never blinked. "That was blunt, I know. The problem is that you're the type of woman most men would beg to marry. I'm just not one of them. I've been down that road and, for me, it…didn't end well."

Still, she stayed silent, caught between a terrible hurt and a spark of anger, between wanting him and being furious.

They stared at each other until she couldn't take it anymore. She had to be rational, had to think about the big picture.

If that reasoning allowed her to indulge her lust, well, it didn't detract from the good business sense.

"I never asked you to marry me, Hogan. I asked you to pump up to forty hours. Oh, and to share the recipe for your ribs, especially the sauce." She paced out from behind her desk, set on how to handle things. "I've been giving this a lot of thought, going over everything I want."

He crossed his arms. "Enlighten me."

"Okay, well, first, I want to remodel a bit. Nothing big and expensive, but the dining room could use some sprucing up. The picnic areas, too. We have plenty of warm weather left. I want to put in some flowers, maybe a fountain, you know, to make the area more pleasing now that it's getting used so much more. Inside I want to paint and change the lights and curtains. Possibly recover the chairs and booth seats."

Hogan's eyes narrowed. "The menus could use an overhaul."

She flashed him a smile. "See, you like the idea of change, too. It's thanks to you that I have so much new revenue coming in. I can hire at least one more person, maybe two, so taking breaks is easier."

"With more waiters, you can serve more guests. Cutting back on wait time should naturally help get more dessert orders."

"I was thinking that, too."

"Now that Colt has half the high school hanging around—"

"The female half!"

He gave one nod. "Which in turn, could be a reason for more of the boys to hang around, I think we need to consider some stylized promo for that age group. Maybe a discount for honors, celebration days when the sports teams win, that sort of thing."

"I was thinking the same things!" Never before had Violet had anyone to share her ideas with. It was fun. "We could play off some of the dances, too, by offering a special menu."

"Get the community and the kids involved," Hogan

said, his arms now down to his sides as he, too, paced while considering various angles. "Maybe we should do a printed poll asking different age groups what they like best for dessert, drinks, sides, main meals—"

"Ha, ribs," she said.

"And given the popularity of that stupid little paper that circulates—"

"The *Clearbrook Trickle*?"

"—I was thinking it might be nice for you to honor whoever receives the citizenship award, or whatever it is the *Trickle* calls it, with a free meal or something."

"That's genius!" Excitement all but made her forget about his ridiculous announcement and innate insult. "Even better, we could name something after the recipient and run it as a special. Like for Charlotte Gains, who was in the *Trickle* a few weeks ago for all her volunteer work at the animal shelter, we could do a Charlotte Burger..." Saying it aloud, it sounded silly.

But Hogan agreed. "I like it. How about a Charlotte Sunshine Burger? We could make up some different combo for it, so it's unique, like maybe add a fried egg, and use a different cheese, or something."

"The Charlotte Sunshine Burger." So happy she wanted to shout, Violet said, "I love that! It's perfect."

They smiled at each other, their combined enthusiasm ripe, until Hogan's eyes darkened and his gaze slipped down to her mouth.

His new awareness sparked her own. Violet knew he was remembering, and she knew he was right. Always, that chemistry would be there, so close to the surface, ready to interrupt.

Her smile wavered, but she didn't give up. "Plotting and planning like this is just one of the benefits for us working together. Will you please admit that you enjoy it?"

Rough, whisper soft, Hogan said, "I enjoy it."

Violet shivered. Could a man be any sexier? Nope. She couldn't quite look at him as she spoke again. "If you insist that sex is another benefit, well, I can handle it if you can."

For the longest time, Hogan was quiet. "Is that so?"

"You don't have to worry about me, Hogan. I'm not weak. You said so yourself. I have a lot on my plate, more than enough to worry about without throwing any sort of commitment into the mix. I want to watch the diner grow. I want to make it the very best that it can be. That's my priority, and I know you can help make it happen." Baring her soul was an uncomfortable thing. It'd be easier to keep things superficial. "Plus, like anyone else, I like the occasional distraction."

He frowned, even while smiling. It was an odd expression that made him look dangerous. "So sex with me would be a distraction?"

"At the very least. That is, I assume it would be." She tilted her head, doing a mock perusal of his very fine physique. "You any good?"

"Like you and your business savvy, what I lack in raw skill I make up for with enthusiasm."

She couldn't help but grin. "Yeah? I like the sound of that."

"It'd be good," he said, his voice rough again, "and you know it."

Given the awkwardness of their conversation, he took it well, even added in some humor—and still managed to make her knees tremble. "So…what do you say?"

"Casual sex is a big enticement. But I still need time

to think it over. I haven't been at the accounting firm all that long. It's a solid job—"

"And this isn't?"

"Violet," he said softly, "I'd be a glorified short-order cook and you know it."

"You cook on those blasted ribs all day."

Shaking his head, he ignored that. "Give me a week, okay?"

A week without sex, now that he'd teased her with it? How could he claim to want her but then just walk away?

Obviously they weren't on even playing fields, and that infuriated her, making her mostly mad at herself. She knew his reputation, knew he'd taken up casual sex as a full-time hobby, that sex meant next to nothing to him, and still she'd let herself get hooked.

Stupid.

She was usually a very even-tempered woman. Usually.

Clearly, that wasn't the case today.

"Tell you what, Hogan. Take two weeks. Take a damned month! I don't care." Rigid, her neck stiff, she stalked past him, ready to make her big exit scene.

The second her fingers closed around the doorknob, his hand flattened hard on the door over her head.

The door didn't budge. "Let go." She was the boss, and she fully expected him to retreat.

Instead, his body pressed hers, his warm breath touching her ear. "Don't think this is easy for me, Violet. It's not."

Bitterness burned her throat. She wouldn't have been able to deny him, yet that's just what he'd done to her. "I'm leaving."

Neither of them moved.

His lips skimmed her ear. "Not yet, okay?"

Something in the sound of his rough, low voice melted her anger. Her eyes half closed. How did he do this to her? She wasn't some young, inexperienced virgin. She wasn't one of those lonely women who had a desperate need for a man in her life.

She wasn't in love with him.

She wasn't. She wouldn't let herself—

"Will you trust me?" His fingertips trailed down her arm, leaving tingles behind.

Violet snorted, but then, her body taut, she whispered, "To do what?"

Nestling a solid erection against her behind, he asked, "How about I just show you?"

Breathing became more difficult, especially when his hands moved from her arms to her waist, around to her ribs and slowly upward.

HOGAN WAS SO turned on, he literally hurt. Not that it mattered, not when all his focus was on Violet. He'd seen her trembling, the flush in her cheeks, and knew she was in as bad shape as he was. He couldn't bear the thought of walking away from her, leaving her like that.

He'd rather suffer alone than have to live with knowing she suffered, too. Especially when he could do something about it. Not what he wanted to do, but he'd make it be enough.

For her.

Going slow in case she objected—after all, she was equal parts pissed at him and pleased with his interest in the diner—Hogan brought his hands up under her breasts. Beneath his palm, her heart galloped. He smiled against her neck. "You're wondering what I'm going to do, aren't you?"

She rested her head back against his shoulder. "Yes."

He liked the already-breathy, strained sound of her voice. "How about we start with this?" He cupped her breasts, and even through her T-shirt and bra, she felt so damn nice, firm and soft, full and warm.

She inhaled deeply. "As long as it's only a starting point."

He liked the way her voice shook. Opening his mouth on her neck, he gently sucked, teased with his tongue... and caressed her breasts.

"Hogan..."

Knowing what she wanted, but also knowing it wasn't easy to give a woman a climax while standing in a small office, both of them fully dressed, he decided a lot of buildup would be best. More torture for him, but with hopefully a nice payoff.

He said, "Hmm?" and moved his erection against her.

Her breath hitched.

Inhaling her scent, loving the taste of her skin, he kissed a slow, damp path from her neck to her shoulder. "You smell so sweet, Violet."

"I've been working all day."

True, she was warm and earthy and musky sweet—more arousing than any perfume could be. "That's why you smell like you, instead of scented soap." With a low growl, he lightly grazed his teeth over the tripping pulse in her throat. "It's a turn-on."

She flattened her hands against the front of his thighs and arched her back a little so that her breasts more firmly filled his hands.

Ever so slowly, he grazed his thumbs over her puckered nipples and felt her immediate reaction. Damn, he wanted to taste her. After toying with her until they were both nuts, he slipped one hand under her T-shirt to stroke the warm, silky skin of her midriff. Reaching up, he dipped his right hand into her left bra cup, and that, skin on skin, her nipple tight against his palm, had them both groaning.

"A front closure," he murmured, feeling the clasp of her bra. "Did you plan that for me?"

"Yes."

Surprised, he looked down at her. With her head resting back against him, her breasts pushed forward, he wished like hell she were naked. She kept her eyes closed, her lips slightly parted as she breathed fast.

Hogan tugged the T-shirt up to her chin and flicked open the bra. The cups parted over her swollen breasts. Her nipples were flushed a dark pink. He filled his hands with her, caressing, enjoying her. The shorts were low on her hips and he could see her from her breasts to her hip bones. She had a beautiful body.

Tugging gently at her nipples, he teased her. "You like that, don't you?" Not waiting for an answer, he said, "I don't want to let go of you."

She made a small, desperate sound of need. "I don't know what you mean."

"Open your shorts for me, Violet."

She went still, then bit her bottom lip.

"Violet," he repeated, "open your shorts. It'll make it easier for me to get my fingers in there. I want to do this—" he carefully worked one nipple, rolling gently, tugging lightly "—to you in other places."

The moan turned into a broken groan. Her nails bit into his thighs.

Hogan didn't let up. He teased and toyed with her until finally, tentatively, her hands went to the snap of her jean shorts.

"Good," he whispered. "Now unzip them, too."

She did, her hands shaking.

It was a heady thing, having bossy, independent Violet Shaw follow his carnal orders. "Push them down a little for me, then open your legs."

"God," she breathed, but did as he told her.

"I love your matching underwear." Tonight she wore pale green with little pink flowers. It was both cute and excruciatingly sexy. "Will you be wet for me, Violet?"

She swallowed, then whispered, "Yes."

Hogan had to lock his knees. He should have known she wouldn't be reserved. Not Violet. "I only have two hands." He took her left hand and brought it up to her right breast, then gave her a kiss on her cheek. He still held her other breast, and now his right hand was free to help her along.

At first, he just traced the tiny crotch of her barely there panties with a forefinger. He could feel the heat of her, the building moisture. Seeing her hand, completely still but against her breast, made him burn. The feel of her soft flesh, her tight nipple and now this...

When he pressed his fingers against her, she gave a sharp cry. Looking at her through heated eyes, Hogan realized she was already so close.

Jason gave this up.

No. *Hell no.* He wouldn't think about that.

Instead, he put his hand into her panties, all while teasing one nipple and kissing her throat and pushing his cock against her backside.

The second he touched her, he felt the wet heat, the slick excitement, and it almost pushed him over the edge.

Knowing he had to end this before he lost control, Hogan stroked over her, opening her, then worked one finger into her.

Violet opened her legs wider, moving sensuously against his hand. It was so damned erotic, so natural, he got lost in her responses, the heat of her and the scent of her arousal.

"Damn, you feel good." He worked in another finger and she groaned, twisting against him. In and out, deeper each time, he stroked her, occasionally pressing the heel of his hand against her.

"Hogan…" she whispered, her voice broken. "No… no more teasing."

She was on the very edge and he loved it. Without meaning to, he thought briefly of Meg, how warm and caring she'd been during sex, but she'd never burned this hot. And the women who had come after her—some of them incredibly bold, some reserved, and the sex had been terrific.

Or so he'd thought.

But this was different. Like a personal fantasy come to life. Violet made him feel things he hadn't before connected to sex, odd things, powerful things.

His fingers inside her were wet from her excitement, her inner muscles squeezing him tight. He pressed higher, heard her long ragged groan and smiled.

"All right." With a deliberate lack of haste, he brought his fingers up to her clitoris and lightly teased over it. Her body jerked and she gave him another deep groan. Against her smooth jaw, he murmured, "Tell me what you like."

"You," she gasped. "I like you."

Almost in pain, Hogan smiled. "I like you, too, Violet. I especially like the way you let go." She wasn't shy or overly modest. God knew, as a natural beauty with a slim but shapely figure, she had no reason to be. Maybe it was her naturalness that affected him.

Gauging her every reaction, he found a rhythm that made her cry out, and as he felt her tightening, he tightened, too. She wanted to come, needed it badly; he sensed her straining toward release. When it didn't happen, her frustration grew.

"Shh," he told her. "Take it easy."

Pulling his hand away, Hogan turned her to the wall and kissed her hard. She looked dazed, confused, even desperate—until he went to his knees.

Her panties were around her thighs, her shorts dropped down to her ankles, her T-shirt rolled up under her arms and her bra cups open.

Looking at her gave him a lot of pleasure. "You are the hottest fucking thing I've ever seen."

She stared down at him, her breath ragged.

After kissing her smooth belly, the top of each slim thigh, he cupped her ass in his hands and drew her forward to his mouth.

"Hogan…"

"Shush." At the first stroke of his tongue, her fingers tunneled into his hair, holding tight enough to sting. But her small cries, the scent of her, made everything inconsequential except for her release.

Hogan licked over her, in her, tasted her, nuzzled against her, teasing more until her desperation grew—then he drew her in for a soft, devastating suck.

Less than a minute later, she stiffened, her thighs shaking, her hips riding with the rhythm of his tongue, every breath a sharpening gasp. As she came, she groaned long and deep.

Hogan groaned with her.

Slowly, very slowly, her pleasure subsided and she sank back against the wall, using his shoulders to hold herself up.

A little devastated, Hogan looked up the length of her small, mostly bare body. How she got more beautiful every damn day, he didn't know. Feeling ridiculously proud—and remarkably tender—he eased her panties back up, then her shorts.

Cheeks damp, her eyes closed, she continued to struggle for breath.

Standing, he smoothed back her hair, smiled and lightly kissed her parted lips. "Damn, Violet, that was nice."

She didn't open her eyes but she did hum some vague reply.

It wasn't until he fastened her bra and tucked away her breasts that she cracked open one eye. "Hogan?"

"Hmm." He straightened her T-shirt.

"What the hell are you doing?"

Lassitude kept her voice light, husky. He fought off a triumphant smile. "Don't get mad or offended, but I need a couple of weeks to think about your job offer."

"Weeks?" she repeated.

She seemed to be struggling, Hogan thought, and he wanted to hug her. "We can start working on all the things we discussed, but I need time to think about making any switch." Employed full-time at a restaurant? He didn't even know if he could make that work financially.

"So," she said, visibly sorting her thoughts, "you did this to me, but you're taking that—" she pointed at the very visible erection in his jeans "—home alone?" Her gaze searched his. "It *will* be alone, right?"

"The only woman I want right now is you, so yes, definitely alone." When he pulled her to him, she put her arms around him and rested against him, limp. Hogan smiled now that she couldn't see him. Damn, he felt good.

"That hardly seems fair," she murmured.

He shrugged. "I'll take care of me when I get home."

Leaning back, she gaped at him. "You'll take care of...?"

"Don't act surprised, Violet. We're both single. We've both—"

Eyes wide and her cheeks now red, she smashed a hand over his mouth.

His smile broke into a grin. "At least one of us will sleep soundly tonight."

She tucked her face against him, hiding.

Pleased with her, Hogan brushed his mouth over her temple. "You're okay?"

"Mmm. If I wasn't so completely sated, if my body wasn't still throbbing in a very nice way, I'd probably want to smack you. But after that, after what you did, I suppose I should try to be understanding." She tipped her face up to see him. "You're waiting for me, right? Because you want me to have all my options?"

Glad that she'd figured it out on her own, that she hadn't jumped to condemning conclusions, he touched her cheek. "You should know the...circumstances of our relationship, personal and in business, before you make any decisions."

"You're a pretty good guy, Hogan Guthrie, you know that?"

He hoped that was true. He wanted it to be true.

Now if one very sexy little redhead would stop defining temptation, he just might make it so.

CHAPTER SEVEN

KNOWING BROOKLIN HAD altered her routine just to throw him off, Nathan settled back and waited. She obviously didn't know his routine well at all because on Fridays, he didn't have to be into the station as early. He had two more hours, and knowing Brooklin as he did now, he couldn't see her waiting until the afternoon to get in her run. She'd wait only until she assumed he'd left for work.

Then she'd come out.

The woman did like her exercise. Maybe she found it cathartic. Maybe she was prone to gaining weight, unlikely as that seemed. He didn't know her reasoning, only that she ran nearly every day, rain or shine.

He stayed back on his porch, out of her view if she took a quick look, and drank his coffee. From his days in SWAT, he'd learned patience. He could wait her out, no problem.

Finally, fifteen minutes later, his attuned ears heard the closing of her front door. He pictured her in his mind, her toned body, that thick, honey-colored hair, and his anticipation built.

When she reached the bottom of her walkway she glanced up—and their gazes held.

Nathan set aside his cup, stood so she'd see his running shorts and shoes and smiled.

Her attention went over his bare chest, then over the rest of him.

In the next second she slipped on those ridiculous large sunglasses and, her mouth set, started by.

He trotted down to join her. "Good morning, Brooklin."

Through stiff lips, she snapped, "Morning" and kept going.

Keeping pace beside her, he asked, "Sleep in, today?"

"No."

Those clipped responses amused him. She could be the prickliest woman ever, but for bizarre reasons, that attitude only drew him more. "Want me to drop back a few feet? I don't mind trailing behind if you'd prefer to jog alone."

"If you're right behind me, I'm not alone!"

"You could pretend," he offered, his tone good-natured in comparison to hers. When her stride lengthened, he matched it. "Put in your earbuds. You won't hear me." But he'd have the nice view of her long legs and firm butt.

Rolling her eyes, she glanced his way. "How's your hand?"

It was the funniest thing for her to be so annoyed and yet still solicitous. "Nearly good as new." He held it out to show her. He now had only two small Steri-Strips over the cut, which was almost completely closed.

Looking at his hand, she visually examined it, then nodded. "Good." She glanced up at him and away, easily going past a large crack in the sidewalk.

He watched her profile. "Your eyes are unusual."

She frowned behind the glasses and finally said, "I know."

Testing her, wondering if his hunch could be correct, Nathan said, "Bet they make you easily recognizable."

She stopped.

Taken by surprise, Nathan went two steps past her and then had to backtrack. By the time he got to her, she was jogging again.

With an exaggerated sigh, he caught up to her again. "I don't suppose you want to talk about it?"

"Do you ever concern yourself with what I want?"

Damn. Her reaction had to mean that his suspicions were correct. So who was she afraid of? "I'd very much like to concern myself—"

"Good. Then leave me alone."

For only a second, her "fuck off" attitude bothered him. But he had good instincts, damn it, and his instincts told him there was a lot going on here. "I used to be SWAT. You know that, right?"

"Yes." Using the back of her wrist, she brushed a bead of perspiration from her temple. The morning got rapidly more humid and hot. Her hair, now in a fat ponytail to keep it off her neck, bounced behind her, swishing side to side. After a moment, she said, "The town loves you, always bragging on you like they have their own personal hero."

Nathan knew that, had heard it many times himself. It used to embarrass him, then annoy him. Now he just accepted it, like he accepted the laid-back feel of the town, the occasional crime, the quirky denizens and their sometimes bizarre requests. "My point was that I have resources."

Brooklin put her head down and picked up the pace.

Trying to outrun her problems? Could be, but regardless, she couldn't outrun him. "I have no intention of snooping into your past, Brooklin. I just wanted you to know that, if you need something, I could probably help."

With a deep breath she slowed, her gait now easy,

more of a long-legged lope. He could see her thinking, but he had no idea what conclusions she'd drawn.

"You won't snoop?"

He did his own thinking, trying to find the right words to reassure her. "I have the ability to find out things. Friends and resources most people don't have. But it wouldn't be right for me to use those resources without legal reasons. It would feel like… I don't know. A violation of your privacy. Sort of stalkerish."

Brooklin's eyes widened in disbelief, and then she laughed.

"Hey." He smiled, liking the way she looked when more lighthearted. "A background check is different from jogging. I understand that difference. That's all I'm saying."

She was silent for a minute. Then she nodded. "Thank you."

"You're welcome." Deciding to press her—again— he said, "Will you have dinner with me on Saturday?"

She laughed again, this time with less sarcasm. "You are the most persistent man."

"Will you? It doesn't have to be a romantic date. We could go to Screwy Louie's. Grab some of Hogan's famous ribs. Hang out. Talk." It was the talking that interested him most. Well, and looking at her. Damn, but she was nice to look at.

She nearly shocked him senseless when she said, "Okay."

He forgot to jog. "Really."

Two steps past him, she stopped, too. "Why not?"

"Exactly." Grinning now that he'd gotten his way, Nathan realized they'd circled the block and were in front of Hogan's house. A woman knocked at his door.

He and Brooklin both looked as Hogan opened the

door wearing only jeans. He looked surprised, then stiffly polite.

"Wonder who that is."

Brooklin elbowed him. "I'm sure it's none of your business."

"Hogan and I are friends."

"And in a small town, everyone notices everything, I guess."

"That's about it." Nathan looked again, saw Hogan finally let the woman in and wondered about it. "It's odd," he said, "because Hogan never takes women to his house."

"Oh?"

"His son is there, and that's just not something he'd do." Nathan decided he'd ask Hogan about it later. "I have to go shower for work. How about I get you at seven on Saturday?"

"How about," Brooklin said, "I meet you there at eight."

He didn't want to, but Nathan agreed. *One step at a time*, he told himself. But after he'd left her, he wondered if she'd show up.

And if she didn't, then what would he do?

HOGAN HAD AWAKENED Friday morning earlier than usual, especially considering the night he'd had. With the taste and scent of Violet still on him, he'd had a hell of a time sleeping—and didn't care. He couldn't get her out of his thoughts, just as he couldn't stop smiling.

It was nine in the morning when he peeked into his son's room. Clothes, pizza boxes, shoes, papers—mess was literally everywhere, over the floor, the bottom of the bed, and on every surface.

God love him, Colt lived like a pig. Hogan could

still remember Meg's endless lecturing to their son. She would threaten, complain, beg, ask, demand, and still Colt would keep his room tidy for no more than a week. So often she'd give up getting him to clean it and would tackle it herself.

It was one of the few memories that didn't tear at him, and Hogan shook his head. For the most part, he didn't worry about Colt's disorderly room. He figured when Colt needed to get it together, he would. Long as he kept the destruction contained to only his room, and not the rest of the house, Hogan was content to let it go.

For the past year, both he and Colt had had bigger fish to fry.

He saw Colt stretched out on the bed, on his stomach, sound asleep in only his boxers. Across the bottom of the bed, Diesel snored, and occasionally his legs would flicker as if he dreamed of racing around the yard.

Hogan couldn't help but grin. His son's room was now half the size of the one he'd had in Columbus, but he still had the same amount of mess—with a big furry dog added in.

The note near the coffeepot had said to wake him up at nine, but he looked so sound asleep, Hogan hated to disturb him.

He tapped his knuckles against the door. "Rise and shine, Sleeping Beauty."

Diesel lurched up, a bark already forming. He saw it was Hogan, gave him a reproachful look from his dark eyes and flopped back down. Colt only groaned and pulled a pillow over his head.

"Classes start late today?"

A mumble came from beneath the pillow.

"What's that?"

"My phone died, so I couldn't set the alarm." He cocked open one eye. "Thanks for waking me."

Hogan smiled. "I'll give you five more minutes."

"I'm awake," Colt muttered and flopped onto his back, both eyes closed again. Diesel shifted and did the same.

"Uh-huh." Leaving the door open, Hogan headed back for the kitchen and another cup of coffee. He wanted to get his accounting work done so he could get to the diner extra early. He was anxious to finalize some plans with Violet, especially concerning new menus. The current menus, encased in cracked plastic, were old and faded, with ancient font and prices that desperately needed an overhaul.

He'd just sat down at his PC when the knock sounded on the door. Diesel came charging out, always caught between an ecstatic welcome and furious suspicion.

"Down, Diesel." On his way to answer the door, Hogan yelled down to Colt, "That was your five minutes."

"Be right there," came the sleepy reply.

Grinning, Hogan got the dog to sit, opened the door and found his boss—*one* of his bosses—standing there, a wide smile on her face.

Diesel hated her on sight.

Quickly shrugging off the surprise and hopefully hiding his disconcerted unease, Hogan thought to say, "Ms. Jeffers?"

She laughed at the formality. "Good morning, Hogan. For heaven's sake, call me Joni."

Diesel rolled his lips, snarled and tried to sniff her crotch.

"Ack!" She pushed him away. "Down! Get away from me." She tried to scurry behind Hogan.

He pasted on a formally polite, businesslike expression. "Diesel, out you go." The dog was reluctant, but he finally went out to the yard to do his business.

Hogan stepped back, but still blocked the entrance. "Sorry about that. We weren't expecting anyone."

"I hope you don't mind." She swatted dog hair away from her slacks. "I wanted to stop in and see how your work is going."

What a huge lie. He'd turned in all his reports, all his accounts, every damn day. She had no reason to be here, except for the obvious.

"It's going well, Joni, thank you. No problems at all." He didn't invite her in.

Of course, that didn't bother Joni.

"I'd love to see your work area."

He'd bet his last dollar that wasn't all she wanted to see. "Has there been a problem with my work?"

"No, of course not. In fact, you're more efficient than anyone else at the office. I'm extremely pleased."

He'd known his work was top-notch. Nice that she didn't lie about it. Holding the door a little wider, he indicated the desk in the living room with the shelf behind it. "I work right—"

"Oh, what a charming house." She stepped in around him.

Shit. Seeing no hope for it, he said with only a modicum of sarcasm, "Come in."

Her gaze slanted his way, and her lips curled. "Thank you. Do I smell coffee?"

Her hint had the subtlety of a sledgehammer.

More than anything, Hogan wanted a shirt. Joni kept staring at his chest like she planned to make him her next meal. "Sure. I'll get you a cup. You can make yourself at home in the kitchen and I'll just go finish getting dressed."

Her hand closed over his forearm. "Don't bother on my account."

The way she licked her lips made him want to bolt.

Then Colt stepped out of his room, stretching, still in his boxers. "Hey, Dad, is there any coffee—" he looked up and saw Joni "—left?"

In the two seconds it took Colt to dive back into his bedroom, Joni's gaze went all over him in a most inappropriate way.

"Who," Joni asked, "was that?"

Hogan freed his arm none too gently. "My son, who also didn't realize we'd have unexpected company this early." Doubting that Joni had taken note of his clarification that she was, absolutely, unexpected, Hogan walked away without giving her a chance to say anything else. He left the front door open so Diesel could return on his own.

In his bedroom, he yanked on the first shirt he saw and stepped into sneakers without socks.

No way in hell did he want his son alone with that woman.

He and Colt met in the hallway, each stepping out of their rooms at the same time. Colt, now dressed in shorts and a rumpled white T-shirt and carrying other clothes, flashed him an apologetic grin and detoured into the bathroom.

Joni still stood where he'd left her, but now she looked panicked as Diesel returned and, once again, inspected her.

The shower came on.

Make it quick, Colt. His son could prove a welcome buffer this morning. Being sure to stay out of reach, Hogan headed into the kitchen. Patting his thigh, he

called the dog to his side, saying, "I'll get you that coffee." *Then hopefully I'll get you back out the door.*

With other plans clearly in mind, Joni joined him.

Unfortunately, Diesel saw a ray of sunshine coming through the side kitchen door. Apparently deciding
Joni wasn't a real threat, he strode over to plop down,
groaned, smacked his chops and went back to sleep.

While Hogan got down another mug, Joni stepped
too close. So close, in fact, his elbow almost bumped
her boob while he poured.

"Your son is very handsome. How old did you say
he is?"

Ignoring her leering tone, Hogan stressed, "He's *seventeen.*"

"He looks older, more like a grown man." She
touched Hogan's arm. "Obviously he got his looks and
muscular build from you."

"He's taller." Hogan sipped his coffee and added,
"He's also leaner, but then, he's still a kid."

Hair damp, Colt came into the kitchen and, with a
smile at Joni, said, "Sorry about that. I didn't know we
had company." He headed for the fridge.

Again, Joni's gaze went over him. She murmured,
"No problem at all."

"Colt," Hogan said, "this is my boss, Ms. Jeffers."

He said, "Ma'am," in a ridiculously proper way.

Joni smiled. "Colt."

Colt dug through the refrigerator and then, standing
in the open door, finished off the orange juice straight
from the carton.

It was such a kid thing to do, Hogan applauded him
for it and didn't say a word.

Proving he wasn't a dummy, Colt closed the fridge,
crushed the carton and threw it away, then said to

Hogan, "Don't forget, you're driving me to school this morning."

"Oh, right," Hogan said, and he glanced at the clock. "We should leave in two minutes."

"Just gotta brush my teeth," Colt said. To Joni, he added, "Nice to meet you, ma'am."

Joni stared after him, the look on her face very disturbing. Then she caught herself and said to Hogan, "I thought you were working."

"I am. It'll only take me a few minutes to drop him off. Then I'll be back at it." For good measure, he added, "I want to finish up the Hardesty file before the end of the day so I won't be brewing on it over the weekend." He'd rather brew on Violet.

"I thought we could do breakfast."

"Ah, sorry. Maybe another time."

"Dinner, then?"

Had he ever been that pushy with a woman? God, he hoped not. *He really needed Diesel to come sniff at her again.* "I already made plans."

Her gaze narrowed as she searched his face, looking for a lie.

But he *would* be busy. Very busy.

Working with Violet.

"Come back into the office Monday. I think a group meeting is in order."

Group meetings usually only meant one thing. "New account?"

After sipping her coffee, she nodded, then broke into a huge smile. "Logistics Unlimited liked your presentation." This time when she clasped his arm, it felt like an all-business, satisfied-boss gesture. "It's a huge coup for us, Hogan. You did well."

Satisfaction welled up. No, he wasn't at the old prestigious firm, but he was making a difference. He was making his mark.

He was advancing.

Smiling back, he said, "I'll be there Monday."

Colt returned, the straps of an enormous backpack slung over one muscular arm, filled with heavy books. "You ready, Dad?"

"Sure."

Unfortunately, Joni didn't leave until they did, and she didn't pull away until he and Colt were in his car.

Colt shoved the backpack to the rear seat and hooked on his seat belt. "Sorry. It was all I could think of."

"You did great, thanks." Hogan glanced in the rearview mirror. "I wonder if she'll follow me."

"I wouldn't be surprised," Colt said. "Talk about work pressure…"

Hogan shook his head. "You could tell—"

"That you weren't interested? Yeah. I'm not stupid." He lounged comfortably in his seat, his long legs stretched out. "Plus, you never bring women to the house. Uncle Jason said you don't want to corrupt me."

"What? Jason said that?" When had they had that discussion, and why?

"Not exactly that," Colt said, "but close enough. It's what he meant. And for the record, I don't feel corrupted, okay? If you ever want to invite someone over, it's not a big deal."

The last of that completely threw Hogan. His son giving him permission to actually date? Not permission for random sex, but to have a relationship?

Because he wasn't sure what to say or think, Hogan asked a question instead. "How'd that even come up?"

"We were talking about Violet."

Another staggering thought. "What about her?"

Colt glanced in the side-view mirror. "That lady is waiting."

Damn. Just as Hogan started to pull away from the curb, Joni finally drove past them, waving.

Colt tapped his fingers on the dash, then gave in to a laugh. "I have another half hour, so do you want to drive around the block or something, just in case she circles around?"

Shit, shit, shit. "Yeah, I probably should." Instead he drove toward the diner. It was dark inside, no one there. Since he had Colt alone… "I have a question for you."

"Sure." Colt nodded in a sage way, put on his serious face and said, "Violet is nicer, hands down."

"What?"

Grinning like a nut, Colt said, "Your question. You weren't going to ask me my opinion on the ladies?"

Hogan snorted. "No." *But Colt liked Violet?* "Joni is only my boss."

"Yeah? Did you tell her that?"

His hands locked on the steering wheel. "I've made it as clear as I can."

"So maybe you want to introduce her to Violet?"

Damn, why was Colt harping on her? He didn't see Joni anywhere, so he headed back toward the house so Colt could get his own truck. "Violet is also a boss."

Colt studied him. "But she's not *only* a boss, right?"

Feeling like he was slogging through quicksand, Hogan wondered what to say.

"You know, Dad, it's not a big deal."

But in Hogan's heart, he knew it was. A very big deal. Colt had lost his mother, his home, his friends— and while he'd been trying to deal with all that, Hogan had been out acting like an adolescent ass.

Feeling his verbal way carefully, Hogan said, "Joni is only a boss. I'm not involved with her in any other way."

"I figured."

"Violet…she's a friend first, a boss second."

"Uh-huh." Shifting in his seat so that he faced Hogan, Colt said, "I'm not a kid, you know? I'm not blind, either. And like I said, I like Violet."

"She and I aren't—"

Colt held up a hand. "I was just saying that I wouldn't mind if you were."

Somehow, that mattered a lot, probably more than Colt realized. "I appreciate that, son, I really do. But as I told your uncle Jason, it's complicated." He waffled, but maybe it was past time he and Colt had a talk. "Things have been rough, for both of us, I know. But I'm finally getting back on an even keel. I'm not anxious to get involved again. Seriously involved, I mean."

Colt, too, changed his tone. He looked out the passenger window and said, "You loved Mom."

Without hesitation, he said, "Very much." Even at the end. If he hadn't loved her, none of it would have hurt so much.

"What she did was wrong."

Hogan ached for Colt. "But she was still your mother, and I promise, I'm never going to forget that."

"I know."

Hogan couldn't let it go there. "The problems, Colt… they were strictly between Meg and me. They didn't have anything to do with you, okay? It's important that you know that."

He was quiet for a long time, even after they'd parked back at the house. When Colt did speak, his voice was low, painfully serious. "It's never felt that way. When someone cheats, it's like cheating on the whole family."

Hogan's heart clenched. "Your mother loved you a lot."

"Not enough to think about how torn up our lives would be." He laughed, a raw sound of hurt. "She sat with me at the dining room table, going over colleges, helping me to decide... Then she stripped away my college fund like none of it had ever been real."

Hogan wasn't sure what to say about that. He settled on the truth. "I'm not sure what your mother was going through. Maybe a midlife crisis, maybe something more." A small breakdown? Hogan just didn't know. "She wasn't herself there at the end."

Colt's hand fisted on his thigh. "Whatever it was," he whispered, "she did it to both of us. I still love her. I'll always miss her."

"Of course you will. She was a good mom." He squeezed Colt's shoulder. "Look at how terrific you turned out."

Colt shared the barest of smiles. "I don't blame you, Dad. I saw what happened, I heard the fights and I don't blame you. I just... I thought you should know that."

Hogan stared at this amazing young man who was his son, astounded all over again. His eyes burned and his throat felt tight. He nodded, swallowed hard and managed to say, "Thank you."

Suddenly Colt turned to him. "So what were you going to ask me?"

It took him a second to adjust to the shift and to remember. Then he gladly accepted the change. "Violet is thinking about doing some before or after party stuff at the diner for school dances or sports events. What do you think? Would enough kids your age show up to make it worthwhile?"

Colt frowned as he gave it some thought. "That's a

great idea, actually. There aren't any nice places nearby and not everyone wants to drive an hour to downtown."

Hogan wasn't sure he'd call the diner "nice," but in comparison to the nearby fast-food restaurants, it was preferable.

"Violet could do something outside, if the weather holds." Colt gave it more thought. "You know, I was upstairs once. She's got half the upper floor empty. If it was cleaned up, maybe painted, it could work out great for a party."

Hogan had never even thought about the upstairs. "What's up there?"

Colt shrugged. "Storage mostly, I guess. A few of the rooms are used to keep holiday decorations for the diner. There's another room where she stores extra tablecloths and stuff, and some old booths that I guess she replaced. She sent me up there to get some spare fluorescent bulbs when one blew in her office."

Huh. "I'll check it out." In fact, he'd get to the diner early so he could look it over. "Thanks for the idea."

"No problem." He reached into the back and hauled out his schoolbag. "I have to go or I'll be late."

"You aren't already?"

Colt shook his head. "I got a couple of classes free because I'd already aced the tests. Others were doing some makeup work. I'll see you tonight at the diner, okay?"

Hogan rarely got mushy. It just wasn't something done between a father and an almost-adult son. But this time he couldn't resist. "Love you, Colt."

Colt gave a lazy grin, but it turned into a laugh. "Yeah, sure. Love you, too, Dad."

Why it was funny, Hogan didn't know, but damn it, he was grinning, too.

FOR THE FIRST time in a long time, Colt felt like life was getting back to normal. His mom had been one to hug him and tell him she loved him every single time she saw him, all the time, coming or going, for just about any reason at all.

In the end, she'd loved other things, other people, far more.

His dad, though, he was all about *showing* love, quiet and controlled, unwavering, through thick and thin. Colt knew his dad had been hurting a lot, but not once had he turned his back on him. He'd uprooted them, yes. He'd been majorly pissed, understandably. But he'd always been there.

The thought that he might not be had never crossed Colt's mind. His dad was dedicated.

Sure, his dad loved him, but sometimes love wasn't enough. His mom had proved that. But dedication with a sense of responsibility—his dad had it. Big-time.

Colt wondered if he'd been so pathetic today that his dad felt the need to say the words as well as show them. He hoped not; he wanted to make things easier for him, not harder.

He needed his dad to know that he understood, that he knew just because he was a father, he wasn't impervious. He was allowed to grieve, and he was allowed, finally, to enjoy life again. Colt wanted him to be happy. He didn't want to do anything to get in his way.

His mom had taken a lot from his dad, but she wasn't going to take everything. Colt wouldn't let her.

Thoughts of his mother left him hollow with a hurt he wanted to deny. He was still mad at her, but she'd never know.

Dead people didn't have to deal with the messes they left behind.

Lost in dark thoughts, Colt didn't see Charish until he literally ran right into her. Her petite body bounced back from the impact with his, her arms flailing, books and papers falling, and at the last second Colt managed to drop his own bag and catch her by the upper arms.

He hauled her in close to keep her from hitting the floor.

In a single heartbeat his thoughts went from ugliness to feelings a whole lot hotter. Damn, he wanted her.

She stared up at him, her big dark brown eyes unblinking, stunned probably. Then her small hands settled against his chest and her attention went to his mouth.

Charish often looked at him in that way.

Usually it made it hard for him to think, but other times it made him uneasy.

She was new to the school, and as his dad had said, she needed a friend more than anything else. Wasn't easy, but he'd have to remember that.

Especially now that he knew more about her.

He liked her, but there was something about her... A lot of the other guys liked her, too. The girls, not so much. Jealousy, maybe. He wasn't sure.

"You okay? I'm sorry." Colt laughed at his own preoccupation with problems a year old. "I didn't see you."

"I didn't see you, either." She glanced down at spilled books and papers.

They were alone in the back hall, on their way into school. Colt still had hold of her arms. For such a slim, small girl, she was chesty in a way that made him sweat. Her top wasn't really low-cut, but no matter what she wore, if it fitted her overall, it hugged her boobs real tight.

He took a breath, let her go and knelt to pick up the mess.

"I can do it," she said, her voice low.

"I don't mind." He still had a few minutes before he had to get to class. His attention shifted to her legs. Really pretty legs, long and slim. Kneeling in front of her, with her wearing a short skirt, he had an up-close view.

He remembered being in his truck with her, kissing her, touching her naked thigh, testing the waters—

Charish shifted, cocking out a hip.

Had she caught him staring? Colt looked up and saw her smiling slightly. He'd only kissed her that once, but it was enough for him to remember how soft her lips felt, how she'd breathed faster, the taste of her.

And her inexperience.

He surged to his feet and handed her back her stuff. "On your way to class?"

"Yes." When she turned her head, her long, dark hair spilled around her shoulders and over her chest. "Opposite direction of you, though." She wrinkled her nose. "Chemistry."

He remembered her hair, too, the silkiness of it. He didn't consider himself a noble guy, but not taking advantage of her was, in his opinion, noble as shit.

Charish was interested. He knew it, but part of her interest could be loneliness, and that stuck in his throat, because he'd been lonely for a long time, too.

Besides, he wanted to make life easier for his dad, not tougher. That meant added income and paying his own way for college. If he kept on the current track, he could graduate this quarter, then work full-time.

Virgins, no matter how sweet they might be, would only complicate things.

Charish looked up into his eyes. "Colt, what's wrong?"

"Nothing." *My life. But no, it was getting better. A lot better.* He shook his head.

She stepped closer to him. "You going to Marley's party tonight?"

He'd forgotten all about Marley's party. "I'm working at the diner."

With a half smile, she accused, "All you do is work."

"Not really." He put in maybe twenty hours a week at the diner. What he made gave him spending money, with extra to put toward college. He didn't work so much that it interfered with school. He juggled it all, and he tried not to complain.

"You do lawn work, too, right?"

"Yeah, in my spare time."

She laughed. "What about spare time for dating?"

"I date," he said, smiling at her. "Just not this weekend." He picked up his backpack.

She touched his arm to keep him from leaving. "Colt…did I do something wrong?"

Damn, he hated stuff like this. There'd been enough drama in his life lately to choke a horse. He didn't want to add more. "No."

She shifted nervously, readjusting her books. "I thought you liked me."

"I do."

"When we were in your truck… Is it because I said no? I mean—"

Colt cupped the side of her face. Not kissing her was suddenly really hard. "I like you, Charish. I really do. And no, it's not because you didn't want to have sex. It's because I don't think you've *ever* had sex." He watched her face and saw the heat crawl over her cheeks. "I don't want to talk you into anything. That wouldn't be fair." Because she looked agonized, he dropped his hand. "We could be friends if you want."

Staring down at her feet, she nodded. "Only friends?"

It gnawed on him, that nearly impossible urge to put his mouth on hers, but they were in school and a teacher could show up any minute. Plus, kissing her would destroy that whole "friend" bullshit he'd just given her. "I have to get to class. I'll see you around, okay?"

Without meeting his eyes, she nodded.

As he went down the hall, Colt felt her staring at him. At least she'd distracted him from memories.

CHAPTER EIGHT

VIOLET HADN'T SLEPT as soundly as Hogan predicted she would. How could she when she kept thinking about him "taking care of himself"? Oh, how she'd love to watch. Until he'd said it, though, she'd never much thought about a man doing that. When she fantasized, and of course she did, it was about her playing an active role with a man, not a man on his own.

Hogan had added all kinds of new dimensions to her fantasies, and he definitely had the starring role.

She really wanted to talk to him about it, to do more of that incredible sexual teasing and touching—she could barely think of anything else—but just as she'd predicted, the weekend was a madhouse. A wonderful, insane, nonstop madhouse, and she loved it.

The place stayed so packed, she didn't get a chance to talk to Hogan alone Friday night or most of the day Saturday. He'd no sooner set up the grills than customers surrounded him in the outdoor area. Other than idle chit-chat and a few long looks, they'd been forced to behave.

Around eight on Saturday, Nathan showed up and joined a woman new to the area. Fascinating. Violet found herself wondering about Nathan "taking care of himself." Then she wondered about Jason, too. She glanced around at all the different customers, better than half of them male, and given the train of her thoughts, she felt like a pervert. Of course she'd known they did that; she knew *everyone* did it. She was a normal adult and she wasn't stupid. But she'd never specifically thought about it.

Good grief, Hogan had rotted her brain. She bit her lip, but still laughed.

Around eight thirty, she finally caught time for a break. She grabbed a cold tea, a salad and the latest *Trickle*, which was now days old. Colt had left a copy of the paper in her office, but she hadn't yet had a chance to read it. Maybe catching up on neighborhood news would get her brain out of the gutter.

She took an empty stool at the counter and dug in, both to the food and the news.

She read about the passing of Mrs. Berger, a very sweet ninety-year-old woman whose niece brought her to the diner once a month for dinner. Since Violet hadn't read the paper, she hadn't known about her passing. Already she'd missed the funeral. Feeling terrible for the niece, she made a mental note to send her flowers and a card.

She also read about a new science class offered to grade school children at the local college. Nice. It sounded messy and fun and kids would probably love that.

A nearby boutique, one of her favorites when she splurged, which wasn't often, had a terrific sale going on for a few more days. And at the beginning of the month, the flower shop would offer a free carnation to the mothers of active military, just as a thank-you to those who served.

She skimmed through the rest of the news on neighbors and businesses, and finally, with her salad almost gone, she went to the advice column that grew ever more popular every day.

Some weeks there was only one question answered, and others there were two or three. The first one this time was about a neighbor who cut his grass too late in the evening. The noise coming through the open windows, the complainer said, made it impossible to hear her evening shows.

The advice was to politely talk to the neighbor first, to explain that it was disruptive. If that didn't work, close the windows and turn on the air-conditioning.

Violet grinned. Good common sense, but nothing fun until she read on to the next request for advice. As she took in the words, her eyes widened.

Good God, it was about Nathan, and it was *delicious*.

A hand touched her shoulder and she jumped a good foot, feeling both guilty for what she'd read and titillated by it.

Twisting, Violet found Hogan standing there, one brow up, a half smile in place. She pressed a hand over her pounding heart. "You just took a year off my life."

His gaze went over her face in an intimate, affectionate way. "Didn't mean to startle you."

"Are you on break?" she asked at almost the same time.

"Sort of. I came in to get food, but I can take it back out with me. Colt is watching the grills for me until then."

Her eyes widened. Colt, his son. Of course. Mentally jumping ahead, she said, "He'd make the perfect apprentice."

"No."

"You are the most stubborn man." Gorgeous, too. His jeans weren't tight, but they did fit his tight butt and muscular thighs. His T-shirt stretched over those beautiful broad shoulders, then fell loose over his flat stomach. Now, after what he'd done to her, she looked at him differently.

She wasn't sure she could ever look at him the same again.

Seeing her scrutiny, Hogan's brow went a little higher. "I was going to ask you about seeing the upstairs, but now you've got me interested." He peered over her shoulder at the paper she'd spread out on the bar. "Reading gossip again, huh?"

"Yes." Grinning, Violet snatched up the paper, grabbed Hogan's hand and dragged him down the hall.

"Uh…where are we going?"

"My office."

"Seriously, honey, I only have five minutes."

Violet choked. *Oh, what she'd give for ten more minutes.* "I want privacy enough to tell you something, that's all."

"Okay, but people are watching us go."

She glanced back, and sure enough, half the customers and all the employees made note of them holding hands. Violet rolled her eyes. "Let them wonder. It'll keep 'em sharp."

"Hold up." He yelled back to the cook, "Put together a loaded burger for me, will you? I'll be back in one minute."

Jerry, the cook, gave an absent wave while juggling three things on his griddle.

"One minute, huh? Well, that ought to kill any thoughts of us doing anything."

Near her ear, Hogan said, "In one minute, I could be kissing you with my hand inside your shirt, or maybe in your shorts—"

"Don't!" She dragged him into the office and closed

the door. "I finally got my brain on something else, so don't get me thinking about that again."

He gave her a long, heated look. "So you've been thinking about it?" His gaze moved over her. "About me?"

He honestly had to ask? "That's rhetorical, right? After what we did? How easy it was for you? Yes, I've thought about it, and you, a lot."

He smiled. "I'm glad I made an impression."

Oh, he'd made an impression all right.

"Come to any conclusions?"

Definitely. But saying so right now might scare him off. Her personal interest in him as a man wasn't the only factor to consider.

She also needed his expertise with ribs and restaurant planning. She wanted Hogan in her bed—and she wanted him to work full-time for her.

Frowning at him and her own mercenary thoughts, Violet put some distance between them, then snapped open the *Trickle.* "Listen to this." She read aloud.

Dear Advice Anonymous,
What's the best way to get the attention of a sexy, sandy-haired, green-eyed alpha without seeming too forward? Between his work in law enforcement and performing with the band, he almost never dates. I can't get him to look at me twice, so I need a subtle way to get his attention. Advice?

Signed, "Hungry for a Hottie."

She looked up to see that Hogan was as astounded as her. Satisfied with his reaction, she said, "That's Nathan, right? I mean, it has to be."

"Sounds like him. Who else around here is in law enforcement and in the band?"

"And a hottie."

Hogan's eyes narrowed.

"No one that I know of." She grinned, knowing she'd tweaked him. "Want to hear the reply?"

"Yeah." Hogan came to stand next to her, again reading over her shoulder. "I do."

Already his body heat touched her, and she could smell his sun-warmed skin and hair. Violet cleared her throat.

Dear Hungry,
Perhaps the gentleman doesn't deserve your attention. From what you've said, he's probably arrogant and cocky, well aware of his hero status to the community and his own good looks. I suggest you try ignoring him. Men like him feed off attention and if you deny it, he'll begin to seek it out.

    Also, it's possible he's not into women.
My best,
Advice Anonymous.

Violet glanced up at Hogan. His mouth was right there, so close. She thought of his mouth, what he'd done to her, what else she'd like him to do—

"Holy shit." Oblivious to her sexual musings, Hogan laughed but quickly cut it short, almost in sympathy for a friend. As he stepped back, he said, "Nathan's going to lose it."

Half her brain remained on the idea of kissing him, but the other half caught his statement. "Who do you think the woman is?"

"The gossip columnist?"

She waved a hand. "No, the one who's after Nathan."

Hogan shrugged, his expression thoughtful. "He's out there right now with that new neighbor of his. She'd seemed pretty resistant the first time I met her, but who knows with women? Looks like she's being friendly enough with him now, so maybe she already got her wish."

"I saw them sitting off alone."

"Yeah. She got here before him and took the farthest table away. When he got here a few minutes after her, Nathan barely said hello, he was in such a hurry to join her." Hogan gave an evil grin and snatched the paper from her. "I think I'll go share this with him. See what he says."

So much for sympathy. "Wait." Violet grinned. "I'm coming with you."

On his way out, Hogan grabbed his hamburger and some chips, and Violet got him an iced tea.

"Before I forget," he said, "I talked to Colt about the ideas you had."

Violet frowned at his back. "I was going to do that." She'd looked forward to it, damn it. New ideas excited her, and like a kid with a new present, she wanted to untie the ribbon and pull back the paper herself.

"He's my son."

He had a point, but still… "You're trying to take over."

Hogan paused, and Violet almost ran into him. He turned to face her.

She waited for him to apologize.

Instead, he said, "When we close up tonight, how about you show me the upstairs?"

Pasting on a sassy smile, she asked, "Is that a euphemism for something?"

His white teeth flashed at her. "You really are focused on sex today, aren't you?"

Yes, damn him.

He actually laughed. "I meant that I wanted to see the upper floor."

Disgruntled, Violet shrugged. "There's nothing much up there."

"I'd like to see for myself. Colt thinks it might work for parties."

Parties? Hmm… "It's just storage."

"Storage can become usable space." He started on his way again.

Definitely trying to take over, Violet thought with a frown. She'd show him the upper floor, no problem, and maybe while she had him alone, she could engage him in an encore. A tug of warmth low in her belly made her breathing quicken.

Keeping her voice low, Violet asked him, "Have you thought about me?"

"I'm alive, aren't I?"

That sultry reply came with no hesitation and made her feel better. "Did you…you know. Take care of yourself?"

Hogan laughed again, but didn't reply as they stepped through the prep area and then outside.

A wave of heat slapped her in the face. "This humidity is killer." And of course, his grills were directly in the sun, not a bit of shade reaching far enough to offer any relief. A canopy of some kind would have to be a priority. Guilt made her frown. "I'm sorry, Hogan."

"For prying?" He smiled as he asked it, then whispered, "I don't mind, especially since I told you what I'd do."

So he *had*… Violet's knees weakened, and she had to

shake her head. "No," she said, her voice thin and a little too breathy. "I meant for keeping you out here broiling in this awful heat." It was early evening, but probably still hovered near ninety. The sun stayed high in the sky, a bright yellow ball in a pure blue, cloudless sky.

She looked away from Hogan's piercing gaze to the surrounding seating. Not more than four feet away, tall trees cast long shadows. "Feels like it's gotten hotter as the day went on, instead of cooling." At least the various picnic tables were nestled under long-branched trees, the harsh sunlight dappled by the leaves. Those that weren't under trees had broad umbrellas. She saw that despite the sweltering day, every seat was taken. She needed more.

"Don't worry about it," Hogan said. "It's just the angle of the sun as it sets that makes it seem so bad." He paused to check on the grills, spoke briefly with Colt and then continued on.

As Violet passed Colt, she said near his ear, "Think you could do this? I mean, if I got your dad to share the recipe?"

"I already know it." Colt chuckled at her shock. "And yeah, I can handle it. But Dad would have to agree."

Just then, "Dad" snagged her arm and dragged her along with him. Taken by surprise, Violet almost tripped over a tree root. "Hey."

He righted her, helped her past a picnic table filled with a rowdy family that included four kids, then said, "Don't try bribing my son."

"Bribing?" Violet imbued as much umbrage into her tone as she could, but damn, she had hoped to bribe him. "I only asked him if he knew—"

"And then you were going to work on him." Hogan

gave her a look. "Colt puts in enough hours as it is. I don't want him losing even more free time."

"We could just shift the hours he has. Shoot, he could possibly work *less* hours if he filled in for you sometimes instead of all the other stuff he does."

Hogan took a big bite of his burger, chewed while looking at her, then swallowed. "I'll think about it."

He acted so autocratic, Violet wanted to trip him, but they were already too near to where Nathan and the woman sat opposite each other at a picnic table.

The area was very green, the grass thick and soft. Leaves shifted overhead, and a butterfly played around the end of the table. The scents of food and summer hung in the air.

And it was all hers. Sometimes, pride made her want to burst.

"I'm still the boss," Violet reminded Hogan, low enough that no one else would hear, but the way Nathan grinned at her as he stood, she wasn't sure.

As if seeking patience, Hogan looked up at the sky for a count of three before giving his attention to his friend. A devilish smile split his face. "Nathan, how's it going?"

Nathan eyed him. "What are you up to?"

When Hogan just stood there, eating his hamburger and trying to look innocent, Violet stepped forward. "Nathan, introduce me to your friend." She put on her most engaging smile.

"Sure." Nathan gestured between them. "Brooklin, this is Violet Shaw, the owner and the brains behind the excellent food and service. Violet, my new neighbor, Brooklin Sweet."

The very pretty woman seemed hesitant. Then she returned Violet's smile and offered her hand. "It's nice to meet you, Violet. Nathan isn't exaggerating about the food, or the service. I can see why your diner is so popular."

"Thank you." *Oh,* Violet thought, *I like her.* "This is Hogan Guthrie, my barbecue master. Have you tried his ribs yet?"

"I need that on a shirt," Hogan said. "Barbecue Master. It has a nice ring to it."

Nathan rolled his eyes.

"We met the other day," Brooklin said, nodding to him.

"I'm glad you remember." Hogan tapped the rolled-up paper against his thigh. To Violet, he said, "She's a salad eater, but I won't hold that against her. Nathan ate enough ribs for the two of them."

"I tried a bite of his," Brooklin said, "and it really was delicious."

Pleased with that praise, Hogan said, "Thank you."

"She's a health nut or something," Nathan teased. "Jogs every day and eats a lot of rabbit food."

"How do you know she jogs?" Violet asked.

"Because I jog with her." He bobbed his eyebrows.

"I used to be a nurse," Brooklin said, moving past Nathan's innuendos very quickly. "Being healthy has become a habit."

Pretending shock, a hand to his heart, Nathan sagged against the table. "You just offered that up. They didn't even have to pry it out of you."

She ignored him to talk to Violet. "How did the diner get its name? Screwy Louie's is pretty different. Fun and unique, but different for sure."

Violet took the seat opposite her, nudging Nathan out of the way. "My great-uncle had a hand in raising me. Uncle Bibb—a nickname for Billy—named the diner after his longtime military friend, Louie, because he said Louie was the one who inspired him. Uncle Bibb loved him like a brother. I inherited the diner when my uncle passed away."

Hogan stared at her. "You never told me any of that."

Violet ignored him. "For the longest time, I didn't want to change anything, you know? There are so many nice memories wrapped up in this place. Changing anything felt like losing a part of Uncle Bibb."

Hogan sat down beside her, consternation on his face, his food almost forgotten.

"But it's time to update," she said, hoping to put Hogan at ease. "More than anything, Uncle Bibb wanted the place to thrive and that requires change." She shoulder-bumped Hogan. "Even the record keeping was ancient. But now that my uncle's bookkeeper isn't with me anymore, Hogan has everything modernized. It's been an amazing switch."

Brooklin smiled at Hogan. "A man of many talents."

"That's exactly what I told him!"

Hogan leaned close to her ear. "That could go on the shirt, too."

Violet stole one of his chips, saying, "You better eat up while you can. Colt can only man the grills so long."

Hogan frowned and dug in.

With the two of them now taking up Nathan's seat, he moved to sit next to Brooklin instead of across from her.

Violet knew Nathan well, and she saw that he was more than casually interested. The poor man could barely take his gaze off Brooklin. Violet could see why. Brooklin had beautiful hair; a slim, toned body; and a very pretty face with a full mouth, narrow nose and the most unusual eyes she'd ever seen. "You said you used to be a nurse. What is it you do now?"

"Total career change, opposite side of the spectrum."
Brooklin half laughed. "I make custom jewelry."

"Wow, really?" Violet said.

Nathan's brows went up. Then naturally he looked at
her hands and throat.

She laughed. "Everyone expects me to wear my own
stuff, but I only do when dressing up. Like Nathan said,
I run every morning, and after that I work at home. I
changed one of my bedrooms into a studio and I keep
all my supplies there, along with a big desk and comfortable chair. Seems silly to put on nice jewelry for
that, you know? But I have a website if you're curious."

"I am, yes."

Brooklin dug a business card from her purse.

Nathan stared as she handed it over and Violet knew
before a day passed, he'd ask her for the website url.
Hiding her amusement, she asked, "What type of stuff
do you make?"

"Mostly I like working with sunstone and amber,
tourmaline and raw gemstones, like citrine, garnet and
amethyst. Customers can have their pick of the metal
and the stone, and then I create it either with or without
their suggestions."

Nathan watched her, riveted by her every word, but
Hogan only finished eating, the paper beside him.

"You sell online?" Violet asked.

"I do. But some of my pieces are also sold through
various kitschy shops, like that little boutique near here."

Violet gasped. "I love that boutique! They're having
a sale soon. Will your jewelry be included?"

Brooklin nodded. "I agreed to twenty percent off."

"I don't freaking believe this," Nathan grumbled.
"How many times have I tried to get a single bit of info

out of you, and you acted like I was plowing through your privacy."

"You," she said, "had different motives."

He threw up his hands. "How do you know Violet's motives aren't the same?" Soon as he said it, he shook his head. "Never mind."

Violet laughed. Nathan clearly wanted something altogether different than mere friendship.

Now that he'd finished eating, Hogan started grinning again. "Read the *Trickle* lately, Nathan?"

Distracted, Nathan glanced at him and snorted. "No." He realized Hogan had the paper with him, and he saw the page he'd opened it to. "God help me. Are you into that stupid advice column now, too?"

"Not usually, no. But Violet pointed out that the person mentioned last week sounded familiar."

Without much interest, still scowling at Brooklin, he said, "Yeah? Who is it?"

Hogan spun the paper around in front of him. "Maybe you should read it."

Suspicious now, Nathan put a forearm on the table and leaned forward to read.

Because Violet could barely take her attention off Brooklin's very light brown eyes, she noticed the way the other woman quickly looked away, along with her small smile. So maybe she was the "hooked on a hottie" local.

Nathan didn't give Hogan the reaction he wanted. Instead he laughed.

Nonplussed, Hogan asked, "You think it's funny?"

"You don't?"

"You read *all* of it, right?"

"Yeah." Nathan turned to Brooklin. "For the record, I'm definitely into women."

"Good to know," she murmured.

Fascinated with their byplay, Violet asked, "Any idea who it might be?"

"Probably a joke. You both know Stan is gay." Again, he turned to Brooklin. "He's the drummer for the band. He hit on me when I first got to town. I explained I was straight, so he asked me to join the band instead. He's a good guy, but a real comedian. Smart, too. I wouldn't put it past him to be the voice behind the 'Advice Anonymous.'"

"The person admiring you," Violet pointed out, "isn't Stan, though, right? So who is?"

"No idea." Nathan stretched, not in the least concerned.

"Anyone been flirting with you?" Hogan asked.

"Sure." He shrugged. "It happens." He leveled a look on Hogan. "You know it as well as I do."

Hogan smiled.

"Oh my God," Violet complained in a long, drawn-out way as if pained. "You're both insufferable."

"Not me," said Nathan. "I can't help it if women and men alike are attracted to me."

Brooklin narrowed her eyes at him. "I thought you said it was a joke?"

"The column is, for sure. The rest? Who knows."

Propping her chin in a fist, Brooklin stared at him. "So you don't put any credence in the column?"

Nathan barked a laugh. "No. Who would?"

"A lot of people, apparently."

"Right. You know, I hope it is Stan writing the column. It'll give me ammunition to harass him for a year. I just hope the person writing about me isn't old Mrs. Carlton." He shivered. "She's eighty, only wears her dentures half the time and always wants to pet on me whenever she gets close."

Brooklin cracked a reluctant smile. "I hope you're kind to her."

"Me, kind?"

Violet laughed. "He is *very* kind, always."

"It's not easy," Nathan insisted. "Kindness encourages her. I have to struggle for that right balance of authoritative figure and friendly neighbor."

"That's probably the lure, though," Violet said. "Women love an authoritative guy, especially in uniform." She gave a deliberate shiver.

"Some women maybe," Brooklin said. "Not all."

Nathan grinned at Hogan. "Looks like you really need that shirt, pal. Maybe it could pass as a uni."

"Probably depends on what I wear, or don't wear, with it."

Knowing her face was now hot, Violet stood. "I need to get back to work, but, Brooklin, I'll definitely look you up. Thanks for the card."

"Thank you for the wonderful meal. I hope I'll be seeing you around."

"I'm always here, so I'm sure you will." She looked expectantly at Hogan. "Well? Are you done?"

Doing his best to look like a martyr, Hogan followed along, groaning, "Sometimes, the boss is so damn bossy."

HOGAN LOOKED AROUND the upper floor with keen interest. Dust motes floated in the air, visible beneath a bare flickering bulb. It was warmer up here, almost stifling. He saw air ducts but assumed they were closed, likely to save on the bills.

The finished ceiling slanted with the roof, but was plenty tall enough in the center. If they moved out all the boxes and junk, seating could go along the walls under the windows.

Lots and lots of windows. Ratty blinds covered them, but he'd already checked and they seemed solid, in good shape. Filthy, but then, no reason to clean this part of the place.

It wouldn't take a lot to refinish the floor. A sander, some polish.

Aware of Violet watching him, he walked from one side to the other, determining when the roof got too low. Yes, more than enough room.

Overall, the area needed a good cleaning, paint, some fresh lighting, but it could add an all-new facet to the business. If they did the work themselves, the cost would be minimal in comparison to the probable income.

"What are you thinking?" Violet asked.

"What a great area this could be."

"Really?" She peered around as if she didn't see it.

"Come here." He reached out a hand, and when she took it, he led her to a big box of old pots and pans that he'd shoved toward the window. "Sit there and imagine everything clean, some nice lights. Pretend you're on a date with a high school sweetheart, and you're getting ready to dance."

Laughing, she said, "That'd be tough to do. I didn't attend many dances in school."

Sitting there like that, she looked sweet and young and far too enticing. "No?"

She shook her head. "I worked with Uncle Bibb."

Hogan thought about what she'd said to Brooklin, a past he'd known nothing about, and instead of going over the imagined floor plan, he came to stand in front of her. "When did your parents die?"

"My sophomore year." She turned her face up to his,

her blue eyes large in the dim light. "A stupid house fire. They weren't burned. But by the time the firemen found them, they'd died of smoke inhalation."

"What caused the fire?"

"Faulty Christmas lights."

Though she'd told it without much emotion, Hogan hurt for her. He took in her straight but fragile shoulders, shoulders that had carried a very big burden—and turned it into a successful business.

She'd caught her mass of fiery hair in a messy pony-tail and somehow, even that made her look vulnerable.

Or maybe it was his own perspective that brought about those feelings.

He knelt in front of her. "Where were you when it happened?"

She half smiled, her gaze slipping away from his to look around the room. "Uncle Bibb had taken me to a Christmas play downtown, then out to dinner. We got home really late."

More than anything, Hogan wanted to hold her, but he didn't trust himself, knowing that once he got his hands on her he wouldn't want to let go. Not until he'd crossed every line that existed. Besides, the hurt was years old now—it had to be.

"I remember," she whispered, "being lost, you know?"

"Yes." He knew very well.

"Uncle Bibb didn't let that last very long. He took me home with him and said I'd live there and we'd work out everything else. It was awful, losing them so suddenly like that, but he made it better as much as he could. He kept me busy, giving me chores at home and a job at the diner. He talked to me nonstop and...just filled the silence so I couldn't dwell on it too much."

Had he given her time to grieve? *Probably*, he thought, *when she should have been sleeping*. He knew that was the time memories crawled in on him. Memories, regrets and anger. "We don't have to change anything."

The half smile widened until she had dimples in her cheeks. "You're sweet, you know that? But honestly, Hogan, Uncle Bibb talked a lot about using the space up here. He never got around to it, but I remember sitting with him on the front porch, snapping green beans and listening to him make plans. Back then, he wanted to use this area to host private dinners, like for a birthday party or anniversary. But if he was here, still, I know he'd love the idea of doing stuff with the high school."

The picture she painted, of an older man and a young girl, sitting on a porch, breaking beans and dreaming of the future, was a nice image. He wished he could have met her uncle. "The house you're in now, it used to be his?"

She nodded. "Everything I have is because of Uncle Bibb."

"Not true." He stood again, but brought her up with him. "I can't think of anyone who works any harder than you."

She twisted her mouth to the side. "You can't, huh? What about you? Shoot, what about Colt? Between the three of us, there's a lot of hard work and long hours going on."

The three of us.

His heart lurched and his brain shied away from the implication of grouping them together that way. He released her and turned, pretending to study the layout again while he quieted his unease.

As if she belonged there, Violet stepped up to his side. "I worry about Colt, too, you know." She also stared out at the floor, at the dust and grime and so many boxes. "He and I were talking the other day. He's a straight-A student."

"Yeah. I often wonder how I got so damn lucky."

"Good genes," she teased, and then more seriously, "plus good parenting."

Hogan shook his head. He'd screwed up several times in the parenting department. Luckily Colt wasn't the type to rebel or act out. No, he just got better, more damned perfect.

At some point, that high standard had to break.

"He'd asked me about more hours," Violet said softly.

"What?" Startled from his thoughts, Hogan scowled. "He already works too much. I've tried to tell him—"

She rested a hand on his arm. "He loves you. And he wants to go to college." Her blue eyes locked in understanding with his. "I think he's looking for a way to pay for it."

"Yeah." Hogan stepped away from her hand, because seriously, even that simple touch pushed him. Then he ran a hand through his hair. "He has the grades and the drive to go to the best schools, but—"

"But it's not feasible. He understands that."

"He shouldn't have to."

In that familiar, playful way of hers, Violet shouldered him. "No, he shouldn't. Colt is a great kid who deserves the best of everything. But kids are resourceful and adaptable, and if anyone can handle reality, he can. Besides, in the big scheme of things, he has everything he really needs, which is mainly a father who loves him like crazy and is always there for him."

Talk so personal left Hogan rigid. Any minute now she'd ask about his wife, and he didn't want to go there. The room that had just recently felt large and full of possibilities now felt far too small and strangling. "It's late. We can talk more about the space later."

She looked at him, her expression quizzical and then accepting. "Sure. We'll hash out the plans in all our free time."

An obvious joke, given the hours they put in, and he grinned with her as they headed for the stairs. The narrow staircase was another thing that would have to be addressed. The lighting sucked and she needed a new handrail, as well as some slip-proof treads.

In his mind, he tallied the to-do list, while also thinking about working side by side with Violet. One thing for sure: she always entertained him.

She was close behind him, and halfway down she softly said his name.

Going still, Hogan glanced back at her.

She gave him a wistful smile. "Two weeks is going to feel like forever."

CHAPTER NINE

VIOLET SPENT MONDAY morning doing laundry, cleaning her house and then shopping, first at the boutique where she bought a beautiful blue druzy necklace made by Brooklin, and then for some type of shade for Hogan. She loved the necklace, its delicate lines, the uniqueness of it and the vibrancy of the blue stone, which the saleslady had sworn was the same color as her eyes. She planned to wear it as soon as she had a chance to dress up a little.

As for the shading device, she wasn't entirely sure of what she wanted, just that it needed to protect Hogan from the sun.

While she looked around, she called Jason and asked him if he could give her a price on adding an awning or something to the area where his brother worked. Something more permanent that wouldn't be a fire hazard over the industrial grills.

Sounding a little smug and far too teasing, Jason promised to get right on it.

Did he think she had too much concern for Hogan's hide? Was she giving away her interest?

Nonsense.

Hogan was an employee. Currently a highly in-demand employee who kept her customers coming back with hungry looks on their faces. Of course she didn't want him abused by the summer sun. It took her another hour to find exactly the right thing, or things really, that she thought would work.

By the time she got to the diner, she didn't have long before other employees would begin showing up.

Hogan, she remembered, would be going into his office. She hated to admit it, but she missed him already.

It wasn't a lie—two weeks would feel like an eternity waiting for his decision.

Once he came to work for her, she could also have him in her bed. At least, that seemed the logical conclusion, the reason he wanted her to wait and be sure. She liked the idea that he couldn't be around her so much without wanting her.

Unfortunately, she didn't need proximity to make her want him. She did. All the time. Whether he was right next to her or home with his son.

While her thoughts spun this way and that, she got the small wrought iron table and massive umbrella into place by the grills. She put a fat, comfortable cushion on each of the two chairs that came with the set, then used the printer in her office to create a sign that read: Reserved for the Barbecue Master.

Snickering, she fastened it to the table so customers would know not to use it.

It was Hogan's table, with two chairs for the times that Colt joined him.

As soon as she could, she'd get that shirt made for him—and then, even though she knew he'd been joking, she'd coerce him into wearing it.

She smiled while greeting her employees, while opening up the diner and welcoming customers, but the time dragged. It never had before, but now, waiting for Hogan, it did.

Would he get there at six? Later? She wasn't sure.

The man had a regular, respectable, white-collar job and he obviously liked it. Why, she didn't know, because despite what he said, Hogan was not a stuffed-shirt accountant.

Oh, he was terrific at numbers, no doubt about it. But the job didn't fit him, not the way... What? Violet groaned and dropped onto a stool.

Did she really think Hogan could be content working morning to night in a small-town diner?

Why not? She was. Uncle Bibb had certainly loved it, too.

She'd never be rich, but she was comfortable. She had a retirement plan, money saved, a small but nice house.

When the *Clearbrook Trickle* arrived, Violet took a copy into her office and sat down to stew. They wouldn't get really busy for another hour or so, and she wanted to see if there was another mention of Nathan inside.

The first bit of advice *was* about him and Violet sat forward, the paper opened on her desk, anxious to read.

Dear Advice Anonymous,
A certain gorgeous "man of the law" jogs without a shirt! Merciful heavens, he looks fine in a uniform or out of it. Should I tell him I think so, or continue to peek from my window as he goes past? It doesn't matter that he sometimes has a woman with him. It's easy to ignore her when he's there looking so fine. But I wouldn't want to make him uncomfortable. I wouldn't want him to take a different route.
To speak, or not to speak?

A man in a uniform. Of course that had to be Nathan. And he'd mentioned something about Brooklin jogging with him, so she had to be that other woman who was supposedly easy to ignore.

The reply was even more entertaining.

Dear Speak,
Don't be shy! Let him know how you feel. I suggest you join him jogging. Wear something sexy to get his attention. All's fair in love and war.
Advice Anonymous.

Violet laughed out loud. Poor Nathan! He was about to be accosted by every interested woman in the county. She couldn't wait to show Hogan!

The next bit of advice took her by surprise.

Dear Advice Anonymous,
What could be sexier than a man who grills delicious food and looks good doing it?

Violet frowned, her back stiffening.

He has a great sense of humor, too. But he's always working. Not that my friends and I mind ogling him at the grill, but how do I get him away from the job, and away from his kid, long enough for us to have a little fun?

Since I know other ladies are thinking the same, I have to make my move quickly.

Signed, Ready to do some cooking of my own.

Ha, Violet thought, her mouth pinched and her brows down. *He may not be officially mine, but I'm the one scheduling all those hours.*

It was one thing for women to want him shirtless,

though she definitely nixed that idea now. But to try to take him from his job?

Her gaze dropped down to the reply, curious as to what advice would be given. Maybe she'd even pick up a tip or two that she could use herself.

Dear Ready to Cook,
I appreciate your position, but I suggest you think twice about this one. Something tells me he could already be involved with another. You see, he's very recently had a lady to his house, and that indicates she's more than a casual date.

After all, there's no place like home.

Exploding from her chair, Violet stared at the paper, trying to deny what she'd just read.

Hogan had a woman over? Very recently?

Who? When?

Surely not the other night. He'd left her late, and he'd promised—he'd made that outrageous claim that he'd take care of himself!

Fury buried the possibility of hurt—until she stopped to think. It was a gossip column, for crying out loud. Written by an anonymous person, and everyone knew you couldn't believe anonymous rumors. It was for entertainment, not meant as fact.

Still, she'd ask Hogan about it as soon as she saw him.

While she waited, she went over it in her head again and again, determined to be calm and cavalier. She wasn't the type to fly off the handle, to make assumptions or act clingy.

She waited for him to show up, constantly checking the door where he usually entered. When he did show up, he went straight to Colt to talk for a moment, then got caught up in greetings from neighbors and customers.

He headed for the prep area, but Jason was right outside that door, doing measurements for an overhang. That entailed lots of questions from Hogan and no real answers from Jason.

"I wanted to give you some shade," Violet said, stepping into the mix.

Hogan gestured at the table. "And that? That's not enough shade?"

She grinned at the rainbow-striped umbrella, large enough to shield three men. "It'll do until something more substantial is built. But if we get any wind, you'd be in trouble. So something better—"

"There are other renovations we'd talked about besides this."

Feeling mean, Violet slowly turned to glare up at him and folded her arms over her chest. "Yes," she said, in a soft but deadly tone. "We discussed things, but I'm the boss and I make the final decisions."

Hogan stared down at her, his gaze speculative, as if he knew she reacted for reasons other than the obvious.

Damn him, how did he read her so easily.

"So," Jason said, "I'm done here. I'll get together some options and prices and be in touch."

Hogan said, "You're talking to the boss, right? Not to me? Just because this is where I work, I wouldn't have any say in it."

No, she would not let him make her feel guilty. "It's *for* you, damn it."

With a nasty smile, Hogan said, "But I love my very colorful table so much, why would I want anything else?"

Violet threw up her hands and walked away.

From behind her, she heard Jason say, "Good going. Real smooth. Way to show appreciation for her consideration."

Exactly, she wanted to shout, but she didn't.

Then she heard Hogan add with a note of surprise, "The table really is nice, right? Did you see my sign? Barbecue *Master*."

The men laughed.

Violet was ready for a distraction, and she found it with a surly trucker who'd been in before, but wasn't a regular. The man grouched fiercely about his burger, claiming it was overdone. She had the cook prepare another for him, but after eating most of it, he claimed the bun was stale.

He wasn't quiet about his displeasure, either.

"Consider it on the house," Violet said and made a mental note to wait on him herself from now on—if he ever returned.

But the surly brute wasn't done. "It took too damn long for me to get it, too."

"Which one?" she asked politely. "The first burger or the second?"

"Both of them! And there's too much ice in my Coke. I shouldn't have to pay for that, either."

Odd, but now that she was close to him, Violet smelled alcohol. She glanced out the front window and saw his truck.

"If you wanted less ice in your drink, you should have said so. Now that you've drunk it all—"

"All of two slurps!" He slapped the drink away, knocking it over, the mess going off the side of the table and onto his pant leg. He roared as if someone had set him on fire, causing an enormous scene.

As she quickly cleaned up the mess, Violet saw Colt

out of the corner of her eye. He was striding toward her, his dark expression identical to his dad's. With a stern frown, she waved him away. The last thing she wanted was for the man to insult Colt. She'd put up with plenty from awful customers in her lifetime, but that'd be crossing the line for her.

Luckily, Colt halted several feet away.

Most everyone in the diner watched as Violet knelt down to clean the mess from the floor, too.

"My pants are ruined!"

Never mind that it was his own fault. Violet said, "Why don't I make it up to you with a cup of coffee and some pie?"

"You think I'd pay for more shitty service?"

She straightened back to her feet. "I'll get it for you myself, and it'll be on the house."

He scowled, blustered and finally said, "Make it quick. I need to get going."

"Of course." After gathering up all the soppy napkins, she darted around to the kitchen area, washed her hands, then cut a large slice of apple pie and placed it on a plate.

Kristy was there, mostly hiding from the conflict, and Violet said, "Call Nathan. Tell him we have a very drunk truck driver who will be driving out of my lot in five minutes. Tell him I said for you to call him specifically. He'll know what to do."

Kristy nodded and pulled a cell phone from her pocket. She realized what she'd done and blanched. After all, cell phones weren't permitted on the floor—that was one of Violet's strictest rules.

She said only, "We'll discuss that later. Make the call." Next she hurriedly filled a cup with steaming coffee.

As she headed back toward the man, she saw that Hogan now stood in Colt's place. Had Colt gotten him? Probably. And that meant Colt now watched the grills.

She bent the same stern look on Hogan that she'd given to Colt, but he looked unimpressed with it. To reinforce her decision for him to stay out of it, she gave a small shake of her head.

And Hogan, the ass, winked at her.

Oh, if she didn't have a situation to deal with, she'd… What? He stood close by, but so far, he didn't appear inclined to interfere. As long as he minded his own business and let her deal with hers, they wouldn't have a problem.

At least, not a new problem.

Hoping that Hogan understood her responsibility as the owner and boss, she went back to the man. "Here you go. The coffee is hot and strong, and the pie is fresh. Hope you like apple."

Cross, the man glared up at her. "I do."

"Excellent." Violet stayed beside him, even when he made it clear he'd rather be left alone. She didn't trust him not to start another problem, and if he did, she wanted to handle it herself. "You pass through here often?"

"None of your goddamned business."

She tsked. "You've been drinking."

Red eyes pinned her. "That's none of your business, either."

"Ah, but I see your truck out front. That is your truck, isn't it?"

"So?"

His words didn't overly slur, but she saw the vagueness in his bloodshot eyes, how he weaved in his seat, how his hand shook. "I assume you expect to leave the way you arrived? Driving?"

"Go bother someone else."

By the minute he looked less aggressive and more lethargic. Pie and coffee—coffee he didn't drink—couldn't make him more inebriated. Then she saw the flask half sticking out of his pants pocket. "Is the pie good? You seem to be enjoying it."

"It's all right."

"My name is Violet."

"Good for you."

"And you are?"

He gave her an uncertain look, rubbed his head and muttered, "Wilbur."

"Do you drink often, Wilbur?"

He shook his head, then caught himself and shouted, "Go away, damn you!"

Instead, Violet sat down across from him. "The problem, Wilbur, is that you're drunk. It's not safe for you to drive."

"Bullshit." He almost fell over. "I'm fine."

"I know people who will be in their cars. Family men and women, some of them with kids."

He pushed aside the empty pie plate and, with her watching, lifted out the flask for another drink. Belligerent, he stared at her as he stuck it back in his pocket.

Or tried to.

"I'm leaving."

"You haven't touched your coffee."

Looking ready to explode, he made a fist—and Violet quickly left her seat. "Wilbur, I called the sheriff. He'll be here any minute. I'm sorry, but I can't let you drive."

"You bitch!"

"I have a feeling," she said low, "you'll thank me tomorrow."

He heaved, impotent fury on his face. Then he shoved out of his seat, holding on to the tabletop to keep from falling, shouting rank curses that caused quite a stir in the seating area.

Hogan never moved, but Violet knew he was there, primed and ready.

She appreciated his restraint.

Then finally Nathan came in. Casual as you please, a man in control, he strode directly toward her. "Sorry, Violet, I was in a meeting. I'll take care of it now." When the man almost toppled over, Nathan caught his arm and eased him into his seat.

Fifteen minutes and a lot of shouts later, the man was arrested for disorderly conduct. The second he was out of the diner, Violet escaped to her office. Good Lord, the day was going downhill fast.

She wasn't surprised when Hogan immediately joined her.

He knocked once, opened the door and stepped in. "Hey, you okay?"

She felt just contrary enough to say, "Of course. You?"

Rather than take the bait, he gave her a crooked smile. "I'm a little shook-up."

Violet stared at him.

Holding out a hand, Hogan said, "Still shaking, mostly because I'm so pissed. I really wanted to level that guy."

"You're shaking?"

"Yeah. Adrenaline, you know?"

Amazing. "You didn't interfere."

He shrugged. "You had it under control." Then his

brows leveled. "But honest to God, honey, if he'd tried to touch you, I'd have—"

"Interfered," she finished for him, not really wanting to know what dire thing he might have done, while also appreciating the endearment. Since he'd admitted his own reaction, she blew out a breath. "I'm a little shaken, too, but thank you for not getting involved."

"You're welcome."

"I have to say, though, I'm surprised at your control."

No longer content with the distance between them, Hogan moved closer and drew her against him. "You made your feelings on it loud and clear with that death glare you sent me. And I get it. It's your place—your employees and customers watching. Optics matter."

Well, there was that. But mostly she hadn't wanted things to escalate, not if she could keep the situation calm. "Thank you again."

"You want to thank me?" He tipped up her chin…

And another knock sounded on the door. Colt, not so very different from his father, stepped in without waiting for her to answer.

She and Hogan didn't have time to step apart, and Colt grinned. "Just seeing if you're okay."

Pressing out of Hogan's arms, Violet asked, "Are you talking to me or your dad?"

Laughing, Colt said judiciously, "Both?"

"I'm fine," she assured him, then waved a hand toward Hogan. "But he's shook-up."

Colt came on in. "Yeah, me, too."

Surprised, Violet stared at him. "You're…?"

Colt growled, "Man, that guy needed a beat-down!"

Hogan agreed.

The two of them stood there, side by side, both

twitching for violence, and she had to laugh. "Like father, like son?"

"He was rude as hell and raising his voice at you," Hogan said.

"Being drunk isn't an excuse, either," Colt added.

Suddenly it occurred to her and her eyes widened. "Who's watching the grills?"

"Uncle Jason showed up. He's spelling me."

Hogan put an arm around his son's shoulders. "And you were spelling me, so I guess we both better get to work."

"Wait a minute," Violet demanded. "Are you saying your whole damn family knows your secret recipe?"

"Nah," Colt said. "Jason is just making sure nothing burns."

When the door closed behind them, Violet dropped into her seat. She'd wanted to ask Hogan about that piece in the *Trickle*, but not in front of Colt. And now his brother was out there, too.

She'd have to wait until the evening, when she could finally get him alone. Which meant she had a lot more hours to stew.

Or so she thought.

HOGAN STARED AT the paper Jason held, denying what he said. "No."

"Yup."

"But she's my boss, not a woman I'd date, and she was only in my house for half an hour!"

Jason shrugged. "Advice Anonymous knows all about it."

"Damn it, it was bad enough when…"

Honor perked up. "When what?"

Lexie laughed. "You didn't see?" She bobbed her

eyebrows. "The ladies want your brother-in-law to do his magic, sans shirt."

"Can't you shut her up, Sullivan?"

Sullivan grinned. "I wouldn't even know where to start."

"Will you do it?" Honor asked.

Jason snorted. "You know he's not."

"At least that whole thing was a joke. But this…" Furious, Hogan turned to adjust the ribs on the grills, added more sauce to one slab, then snatched the paper away from his brother and dropped onto the very padded cushion Violet had put in his wrought iron chair.

At his table. With the sign.

Under the massive rainbow umbrella.

As he read, he could feel the stares of Sullivan and Lexie, Jason and Honor. Had Violet seen the stupid column with the very inaccurate account of his supposed "date"? Who the hell dated at nine o'clock in the morning?

If she'd seen it, Violet hadn't said anything. Did that mean she trusted him?

Hogan shook his head at his own thinking. Their relationship was so open-ended as to be nonexistent. They didn't have an understanding, so trust wasn't involved. He'd stupidly offered her two weeks to think about things, and while he'd expected to suffer celibacy for that entire time, would she know that?

His reputation hadn't been the best, not since coming to Clearbrook. How many times had Violet teased him about chasing from one woman to the next? One-night stands, a string of them, didn't exactly make him trustworthy material.

Honor said softly, "Your ribs are on fire."

"Damn it." Tossing the paper aside, Hogan jumped up

and used his water bottle to douse the flames. A quick check and he announced, "Nothing burned. Thanks, Honor, for letting me know."

She came closer. "You okay?"

"What? Oh, yeah. Fine." Annoyed, definitely. He didn't like being the topic of gossip in a local paper. But he'd explain to Violet. She wasn't unreasonable. Hell, in most cases she was amazing.

The way she'd handled that drunk earlier made him ridiculously proud. He started to smile, remembering it.

Suddenly Jason cleared his throat and said low, "Incoming."

Hogan looked up—and there was Joni bearing down on him, a fat smile on her face as if he were a long-lost friend. He stared at her, surprised at seeing her in skintight jeans and a top so low-cut it looked like she might spill out. Wondering if he could still escape, knowing he couldn't, he almost groaned.

It needed only this.

"Hogan!" She rushed right up to him, grabbing him in a hug that squashed her boobs to his chest. Taken off guard, he didn't block her or move away quickly enough.

Quickly Hogan set aside his tongs, and then eased her back a few steps. "Joni. You're here."

"As are you." She laughed. "I didn't realize you ate here. I saw the place the other day when I visited you and it looked…interesting."

At her mention of the visit, his small audience went more alert. He could almost hear them piecing things together, deciding that she was the one in the *Trickle*.

Joni's gaze went over his face, his chest, then more slowly, his apron and the grills behind him. Her expression stilled. "What are you doing?"

Damn, damn, damn. He turned, saying, "Joni, this

is my brother, Jason, and his wife, Honor. Our friends Sullivan and Lexie."

Everyone stood, taking a minute to say hello, chatting to her, making quick conversation—mostly giving him a chance to get his thoughts together.

It wasn't happening. His brain was blank.

Dismissing the others in her usual pushy, single-minded way, Joni faced off with Hogan. "Tell me you're not working here."

He racked his brain, still came up blank and shook his head. "Can't."

"Can't *what*?" she demanded.

"Can't tell you I'm not working here, because obviously I am." Almost laughing at the absurd situation, he gestured at the sign Violet had affixed to his table. "I'm the Barbecue Master."

The others immediately jumped in, praising him, bouncing back and forth from his skills with accounting to his skills with the grills.

The entire situation felt bizarre and ridiculous, and he knew it couldn't get much worse.

When Violet showed up, Colt in tow, Hogan threw up his hands.

"What's going on?" Violet demanded, looking all kinds of suspicious as she took in how close Joni stood to him.

Joni gave her a single glance and dismissed her as unimportant. "You work for me," she said to Hogan. "You can't moonlight."

"I don't recall you mentioning that in the interview."

"Because I never would have guessed…" She put her hands on her full hips. "But it's a fact," she snapped. "An accountant does *not* take a second job, not in a diner, for God's sake."

Very deliberately, Hogan avoided Violet's gaze. "Why don't we discuss any conflicts tomorrow in the office? I can even come in an hour early."

"I think we should talk right now." She took hold of his arm, ready to lead him away.

Hogan held his ground. "Tonight I *am* working here, and I can't just leave."

"You could quit," Joni pointed out. "Who would care? You don't need this job."

"Now, wait just a minute," Violet said. "I would care."

"This isn't the place to talk." Hogan tried giving Violet the same look she'd sent to him earlier, a look that said "butt out," but she completely disregarded it.

"Hogan can't walk off right now." She flapped a stack of small papers in the air. "We have orders to fill."

Joni didn't even acknowledge her, and she didn't release Hogan. "If it's for the extra pay, I can take care of that." Leaning closer, she whispered, "Come with me now. I'll give you a raise."

Hogan caught her hands and set her away from him. "Joni—"

"A raise," she stated, "plus more benefits."

Violet gasped.

Damn. He wanted to know the details of the benefits, but as he'd said, this wasn't the place to talk, so instead, he asked, "Why now?"

"It was already in the works after you brought in Logistics Unlimited. That account has opened doors to others."

Hogan crossed his arms. "I was at the office all day today and you never mentioned it."

"I wanted it to be a surprise." She smiled, reaching out to stroke his shoulder. "Let's go to dinner now and we'll discuss it."

Again, Hogan set her away. "Joni—"

She latched on again. "Seriously, Hogan, lose the apron and let's go." She reached for the ties, ready to take it from him.

With a low growl that startled Hogan, Violet warned, "Get your hands off my employee."

Disbelieving, Hogan stared at her. Her voice was so mean, he half expected her red hair to stand on end.

Joni was bigger, thicker, but Violet looked ready to jump her.

Trying to reason with her, he said, "You dealt with a drunk, disruptive guy earlier and never raised your voice."

Violet kept her gaze locked on Joni. "The guy never touched me—but she's all over you!"

"Now, Violet," Hogan soothed, aware of everyone in the yard staring, including his son and brother, "you're causing a scene."

"*She's* causing the scene," Violet snapped, "by trying to steal you away."

Curling her lip, Joni laughed with derision. "Steal him away from *what*?" Her gaze dipped over Violet with contempt. "A job as a cook in this dive? I doubt anything I could do would reflect worse than the place itself."

Violet's hands curled into fists. "You're insulting my diner?"

"Yours?" Joni laughed. "Seriously, Hogan, the joke is over. Now let's go."

This had gotten way out of hand. "Listen," he tried to say, but Violet cut him off.

"You have two seconds to get off my property before I call the sheriff and have you arrested for indecent… groping!"

Joni huffed, her chest swelling until he thought for

sure she'd pop free. She turned on Hogan with narrowed eyes. "If you don't leave with me now, right this very second, I'll be forced to fire you."

Again he tried to speak, to find a compromise, but again Violet beat him to it.

"You aren't foolin' anyone, sugar. It's not the job you're offering him, but yourself."

Red faced, Joni snarled to him, *"Well?"*

"We will talk tomorrow," he insisted. "First thing. I can get there at eight—"

"Forget it." Joni thrust up her chin. "Remember that you signed a contract. The clients are mine, not yours— you can clear out your desk in the morning."

Stunned, Hogan watched her walk away. Or more like stomp away. *He'd just been fired.*

In front of half the damn town.

"Good riddance," Violet called after her.

Several groups cheered. He heard a few people shout, "Go Violet!" and "You tell her!"

Breathing hard with fury, Hogan reached out and grabbed Jason, shoving the tongs into his hand. "Don't let the meat burn."

Jason said, "Uh—"

But Hogan already had Violet by the arm and he was two-stepping her past his son, who just stared, and into the prep area.

When Violet realized what was happening, she jerked free, turned and slammed the door on everyone's gawking faces.

So numb with shock he could barely think, Hogan asked, "Do you have any idea what you've done?"

She threw up her hands. "I've *saved* you."

No, she couldn't be that damned obtuse—she

couldn't be that blind to what it meant for him to be fired. "I didn't need to be saved! *I needed that job.*"

Her eyes flinched, and then she muttered, "If you're going to bellow like that, we should have just left the door open. Everyone can hear you anyway."

Her cavalier attitude rubbed him raw. He laughed, but not with humor. "Jesus, it took me forever to find that job. You know that, Violet." He shoved his fingers through his hair, still too numb. "I have a house payment, insurance… I was saving for Colt's college."

Silent now, Violet put a hand to her forehead.

He saw she was shaking. All over. "You should have stayed out of it."

On a slow breath, she nodded. "Maybe."

"No maybe to it. I'm fucked." He had no idea what to do now. None. Closing his eyes, he tried to get his rage under control. He could talk to Joni in the morning, but she'd been humiliated, and women were funny about things like that.

Hell, he was humiliated, too, and the last thing he wanted to do was to try to talk her around. Joni was a pain in the ass on a good day, but if she thought she had the upper hand—

"Tell me what she paid you."

His eyes opened. "What?"

"What did you make a week?"

Folding his arms, Hogan named his weekly salary. "Plus benefits."

Her shoulders drooped. "Oh." Then she rallied. "I can come close to that, I promise."

"I wouldn't ask you to." He'd seen her books. He knew her income. There was more potential, yes, but she wasn't there yet.

Looking utterly miserable, Violet started to pace. "I know this isn't where you wanted to work—"

"Wrong."

"—and I know you liked the more respectable suit-and-tie job."

Hogan scoffed. "I haven't worn a tie in ages."

Earnest now, she stared right into his eyes. "But I promise you, Hogan, you have my solemn vow, you will like it here."

Unbelievable. "You aren't even listening to me."

She sucked in a breath. "Please tell me you aren't going to quit."

"Quit the only job I have now, thanks to you?" Somehow her desperation finally kicked his brain into gear. Possibilities began rushing through him, dozens of them. He wasn't optimistic—he wouldn't go that far, and there would be some definite challenges. But he could see a light, a faint glimmer of a light, at the end of the long, dark tunnel. "No, I won't quit."

She collapsed back against the prep station and got sauce on the seat of her pants.

Hogan caught both her arms and drew her forward again, away from the mess. "We'll have to make some changes."

Oblivious to the "secret sauce" soaking into her shorts, she asked suspiciously, "We?"

"Forget it, Violet. You can't be territorial, not when you booted out my boss. Not when this is now the only income I have."

"I wasn't being territorial, exactly…"

"Yes, you were. You always are. I understand it and we'll work around it. You'll remain the boss—"

"Gee, thank you."

"—but I need to be the manager."

Her mouth opened, then closed. "Beth is my assistant manager."

"Assistant, yes. But Kristy said Beth isn't even sure if she wants to come back. She likes being a stay-at-home mom."

Violet drooped. "I know. She told me if she does come back, it won't be for months."

"If she does, she'll be an assistant manager, but I'll be the manager."

The suspicion grew. "To manage *what*?"

"Damn near everything." And before she could explode, he added, "With your input and approval." *But with his input and approval, too.*

She thought about it, but now that she'd gotten her way, Violet bit back a smile. "I think that sounds doable. We can discuss the finer points tonight." Her fingers toyed with the neckline of his T-shirt. "When we're alone."

It seemed a million emotions, previously bottled up, exploded all at once. Without giving it too much thought, Hogan hauled her in, ignored her gasp and took her mouth in a deep, hard kiss that only left him primed for more. She softened immediately, her hands clutching his shoulders, her belly pressing against him.

He'd told her what would happen if they worked together full-time.

She seemed to be in complete agreement.

The second he released her, Violet plopped back against the messy station again.

Trying to still the furious drumming of his heart, Hogan said, "You've ruined your shorts."

She looked over her shoulder at her butt and shrugged. "But not your life?"

He agreed with a smile. "I think my life is going to be fine." Complicated as hell, but altogether fine.

He walked out to the grill, truly the Barbecue Master.

CHAPTER TEN

At NINE THIRTY THAT NIGHT, shortly after closing, Violet stood upstairs in the musty room, watching Hogan move a massive trunk, then another. They each held items of sentimental value. She'd go through them when she was alone, without an audience, in case she got a little weepy with nostalgia.

After he'd cleared the spot, Hogan stopped and stared at the warped door. He lifted the heavy lock. "What's this?"

"A lock."

"I can see that. But what's behind the door?"

"The stairs."

"*What* stairs?"

So he was still testy? Apparently. Since that obnoxious woman had left and they'd made their future plans—*she loved the sound of that*—Hogan had waffled through many different reactions. She could understand, though. Likely every time he thought of the challenges, it weighed on him. Unlike her, he had his son to think about, too.

Although she did a lot of thinking about Colt, as well. As a terrific young man, a valuable employee and an extension of Hogan, how could she not?

Every so often, guilt pierced her, but she couldn't regret what she'd done. No way could Hogan have enjoyed, or even been content, working in that atmosphere. Colt had told her about Joni Jeffers's visit to their home, how the woman had leered at Hogan. It wasn't even close to a date, not when the former boss had forced her way into their house.

"Violet, did you check out? Or are you as surprised by the door as I am?"

Surprised, no. She was excited. But not about the door, or expanding the space. She wanted to kiss him again.

And other stuff.

She shook her head. "I was just thinking."

Looking skeptical, he cocked a brow. "About?"

Hogan wanted only to talk business. Okay, so she'd tamp down her carnal urges and they'd talk business. If he could keep it under wraps, then she could, too.

Maybe.

"There's a back entrance to this floor," she said, striding closer. "You've never noticed it in the back lot? Rickety metal stairs that lead up to an equally rickety door? That's why I have it double locked. I always thought someone could force their way in otherwise, and I didn't like the idea of getting here and finding an unwelcome, um, visitor."

"I'm glad you thought to secure it." He stared at the door. "I can't believe I never noticed."

She shrugged. "It was there when Uncle Bibb bought the business, long before I can even remember."

"Another entrance," he murmured, fascination in his expression. "Come on. I want to see it." He took her hand and tugged her along with him.

"So we're done exploring up here?"

"For now." Even going down the narrow stairwell, he kept her hand enclosed in his. "I want to get home early enough tonight to actually visit with my son. He has to have questions."

Guilt, damn it. She tried to shake it off. "Given what he told me about that woman, he's probably relieved."

"*That woman,* huh? Her name is Joni Jeffers and she is—*was*—my boss. She actually runs a good, solid business. She's respected. The agency was respected."

He was respected? Violet wanted to hug him and tell him… What? They reached the landing, and as they turned the corner to the main room, she said, "My diner is not a dive."

With a short laugh, he said, "No, it's not. You've done well with it. I think I can finesse things a little more, though. Now that I can dedicate all my time to it, we'll put it on the fast track."

A shiver of dread mixed with affront went up her spine. Fast-track changes? She looked around as they went through the dim interior to the back door. "Uncle Bibb poured his heart into this place. I see him everywhere. He chose the booths and tables himself, you know. Even repaired them a few times."

Hogan nodded, somewhat distracted. "He was a handyman?"

"Yes. But see that nick in the wall, right there by the storage room? He was carrying a ladder to change a light, accidentally hit the wall, knocked himself over, bumped a waitress who sent her tray flying, and the noise scared half the customers." She couldn't see that nick without smiling.

Glancing at her, Hogan said gently, "We'll leave the nick," and drew her outside with him after he'd unlocked the door.

"I remember when he replaced the Screwy Louie sign, taking down the old wooden one and putting up the neon. He was so damn proud of it."

"With good reason." Again holding her hand, Hogan

led her around to where a longer section of the brick building met a shorter section, and in that space was the stairs. "Huh."

The heavy metal bin for trash sat beneath the stairs. Broken chips of concrete, dried leaves and a bottle cap filled the corner.

Violet had never much minded the random debris that got in that corner, but now, with Hogan seeing it, she wished she'd had it swept. "It's not a pretty sight, is it?"

"Not like it is, no. But it could be." He released her to run his hand along the rail of the stairs, giving it a couple of tugs. "It's not actually rickety."

"It feels rickety if you walk on it."

Taking that as a challenge, Hogan bounded up the steps, his tread deliberately heavy. "No, they're solid. It's just that they're metal, so they make a racket. We'd have to have them inspected, but I think they'd be okay."

The glow of a tall security light reflected on Hogan's dark hair and sent interesting shadows over his body, showcasing the width of his shoulders, making the cut of his muscles more defined. "Okay for what?"

As he came back down, the clanking of his shoes on metal echoed over the lot. "If we get the upstairs set up for a younger crowd, you don't necessarily want them tromping through the restaurant, disturbing people who only want to eat. They could use this entrance, instead. You'd have more capacity without all the chaos."

Violet pictured it, somewhat liked what she saw, but it was so much change it still bothered her. "You're moving at light speed," she grumbled.

He tweaked her chin and smiled down at her. "Have to. Some little redheaded wonder ensured I got fired, so now we need to make this work."

They were alone in the lot, the printing business next

door to them closed, no one around. Even the street was quiet. The scents of sunshine and grill smoke still clung to him, mingling with the scent of *him*.

Staring up at him, Violet saw his eagerness, as if maybe she hadn't totally screwed up his life.

She licked her lips, then softly said his name.

His gaze went from teasing to awareness in a heartbeat. His thumb released her chin and instead brushed over the corner of her mouth, then drifted up her cheek until his fingers played with loose tendrils of her hair, tucking them back behind her ear.

When his hand cupped her nape beneath her ponytail, she almost melted. It was such a guy thing to do, especially with the way he drew her in closer while lowering his mouth.

Lord, she was lost long before their lips touched.

This kiss was nothing like the one earlier in the prep area. He'd been hungry then, devastating, hard and fast. Now he only played with her, nipping her bottom lip, licking her upper, settling his mouth gently over hers with almost no pressure.

Wanting to feel the warmth of his big body, the strength of him, she moved closer. For so long she'd been tackling everything alone, and now there was Hogan, and somehow, in such a short time, he'd infiltrated every part of her life.

Almost every part. She'd work on the rest very soon.

Holding her, he turned until her back was pressed against the brick wall of the building. He leaned into her, his hips pinning her in place. Both of his hands now held her face tipped up to his so he could kiss her as long and slow and deep as he wanted.

As he eased up, she felt his hot breath on her mouth. "Violet."

The way he said her name, all raspy and rough, was incredibly sexy. "Yes." Yes to anything he wanted. He could change the diner; he could take her to bed. *Yes.*

She felt his smile. "You are such a contradiction." He leaned in closer, using a hand on her behind to keep her snug against him, his other hand braced on the wall above her head. Tilting his head slightly, he fitted his mouth to hers, moving so that her lips opened and he licked in.

A Barbecue Master with a magic tongue. Maybe that's what she should put on his shirt—when she got around to getting him a shirt. He knew how to kiss. He knew how to use that tongue to make her toes curl.

Pulling back, he kissed the corner of her mouth again, then her jaw and her neck. He put his forehead to hers. "I shouldn't have started this."

"You could try finishing it."

"Definitely. That's at the top of our growing to-do list." He put some space between them. "But I really do need to talk to Colt tonight."

This time the guilt that swamped her actually hurt. "I'm so sorry. Damn, I completely forgot. I shouldn't have, though. It's unforgivable. I know how confused he must be and you already said—"

To quiet her, Hogan touched his finger to her lips. His eyes looked midnight dark and aroused, but still, he was such a responsible parent. "Colt's not a baby, and he's probably not all that confused."

Violet clasped his wrist and pulled his hand away. "Maybe not confused. That's not the right word. But like you said, he has to have questions."

Nodding, Hogan said, "Since it's just the two of us now, I don't like making decisions without him. Not big decisions like this. At least not without talking to him about it."

Dropping her head back against the brick, Violet groaned. "The truth is you didn't make the decision. I did, and I'm really sorry."

"It's done. I'm not going to regret it too much. In the future, though, you might try holding that temper under wraps."

"Temper?" She laughed at herself. "We both know it was jealousy. Mostly, anyway." In her defense, she said, "She did insult my diner, too."

Hogan went quiet, staring at her thoughtfully, even a little warily.

God, now she was scaring him off. Trying to backtrack, she teased, "I can't have her getting what I haven't even gotten yet." She figured Hogan could handle sexual jealousy. It was just the emotional stuff that worried her.

So she'd hide all emotion. Somehow.

"Trust me, she won't get anything like that from me." He looked up at the sliver of a moon. "I have to see her tomorrow."

"Yeah, I know."

In an enormous understatement, he said, "It's going to be awkward."

Hating to think about it, Violet growled, "It's grossly unfair of her to put you in this position." Conveniently exonerating herself for her part, she added, "She's such a…witch."

His mouth twitched. "Nice edit. Too bad you didn't show more discretion earlier."

Shoving aside the pesky guilt, she glared at him. "Seriously, Hogan, are you really regretting it so much? She was awful. You couldn't possibly have liked working with her."

"When it comes to responsibility, liking something has little to do with it." Again he took her hand. "Come on. Let's lock up so I can get home. If I stand here talking any longer, Colt will already be in bed when I get there."

"You really think so?"

"No." He led her back into the diner so they could set the alarms. "Actually, I'm positive he'll be waiting up."

THE WHOLE GANG was waiting on Jason's porch when Hogan pulled into the drive. Diesel was the only one who rushed to greet him. He stroked the dog as he headed across the lawn for his brother's house.

Jason gave him a long look. "Get everything worked out?"

"For the most part, yeah."

Honor stood and wrapped her arms around him, squeezing tight. It always amazed Hogan how different it felt to hug a woman who was now a relative. Honor was very pretty, maybe even sexy in an understated, cute way, but he could have been hugging an actual sister. Instead of the deep heat and stirring of his blood that happened when he held Violet, this felt like a sweet, comforting warmth.

He hugged her off her feet, then kissed the top of her head. Diesel still stood beside him, tongue lolling out, tail swatting the air. Jason watched him. Colt looked worried. And Honor didn't want to let him go.

Hogan barely stifled a laugh. "I really am fine, you know. I'm not going to curl up in a ball or anything."

"We know." As Diesel headed over to Colt and Jason tried—but failed—to look reassured, Honor patted his cheek. "You're an incredibly strong man and I'm so proud of you and I'm glad you're my brother-in-law."

"All that?" he teased.

She nodded. "Plus, even though you probably didn't need the hug, it made me feel better."

"Why are you feeling bad?" He ruffled her honey-blond hair. "I'm the one who got fired."

She wrinkled her nose. "Will you be mad if I tell you I'm a *little* bit glad?"

Had everyone wanted to see him employed full-time with the diner? It seemed so. "I could never be mad at you, hon."

Next he turned to his son. Diesel was practically in Colt's lap, his head and both front paws stretched out over his long legs, luxuriating in the way Colt scratched his scruff. "What about you?"

His son looked up with a grin. "I keep picturing Violet yelling at that woman. Man, she was fired up."

"A redhead's temper," Jason said, then dodged his wife's hands when she tried to smack him. He finally caught her, pulled her close and gave her a firm kiss and a smile. "Violet's usually calm about everything. She handles customers like a grade school teacher with an unruly class. Instead of attacking, she firmly reasons things out."

"Like that drunk guy," Colt said. "She never lost her temper with him."

Honor, who obviously knew all about that now, said, "That's the Violet I know. Very easygoing. Always smiling at everyone. But today. Whew. She did look ready to attack."

Someday, Hogan thought, he'd look back and laugh about it. But he wasn't there yet. Every time he thought of the god-awful scene, he wanted to growl in embarrassment.

Would he ever have real privacy? He sure as hell

hadn't had it in Columbus. Now he didn't have it Clear-brook, either. Dodging the uncomfortable knowledge, he said to Colt, "You ready to head home?"

"Yeah." As Colt started to stand, Diesel lumbered to his feet, wagged his tail at Colt and Hogan, then headed for Jason's front door.

Hogan shook his head. "Staying here tonight, Diesel?"

For an answer, the dog ignored Hogan and continued to stare at the door, waiting for it to open.

Honor laughed and went to let him in. "He does like to play fair, visiting us occasionally to let us know he loves us, too."

"I don't think he's made up his mind yet where he lives." Hogan knew Jason and Honor didn't mind. The dog had started out as hers, but then had bonded to Colt. Occasionally, he just crashed wherever he was nearest.

Jason gave Colt a one-arm man hug, clapped Hogan on the shoulder and said, "Let me know if you need anything."

"Thanks." Not that long ago, he'd lived with his brother while getting back on his feet. He didn't want to ever do that again. Jason had been terrific about it, but he was a grown man, damn it. He would make it on his own.

Honor hugged each of them again, lingering over Colt, who always seemed to enjoy her attention. Then she and Jason went inside together, a happy couple completely devoted to each other.

There'd been a time when Hogan thought he had the same. Hell, back then, Jason had razzed him about having the perfect life with a loving and dedicated wife, a smart, responsible son, a big house and prestigious job.

Amazing how quickly life could change.

As they crossed the dark yard, Hogan looked up at

Dear Reader,

IT'S A FACT: if you answer 4 quick questions, we'll send you **4 FREE REWARDS!**

I'm not kidding you. As a leading publisher of women's fiction, we value your opinions... and your time. That's why we are prepared to **reward** you handsomely for completing our mini-survey. In fact, we have 4 Free Rewards for you, including 2 free books and 2 free gifts.

As you may have guessed, that's why our mini-survey is called **"4 for 4".** Answer 4 questions and get 4 Free Rewards. It's that simple!

Thank you for participating in our survey,

Pam Powers

To get your 4 FREE REWARDS:
Complete the survey below and return the insert today to receive 2 FREE BOOKS and 2 FREE GIFTS guaranteed!

"4 for 4" MINI-SURVEY

1 Is reading one of your favorite hobbies?
☐ YES   ☐ NO

2 Do you prefer to read instead of watch TV?
☐ YES   ☐ NO

3 Do you read newspapers and magazines?
☐ YES   ☐ NO

4 Do you enjoy trying new book series with FREE BOOKS?
☐ YES   ☐ NO

YES! I have completed the above Mini-Survey. Please send me my 4 FREE REWARDS (worth over $20 retail). I understand that I am under no obligation to buy anything, as explained on the back of this card.

194/394 MDL GMYP

FIRST NAME	LAST NAME

ADDRESS

APT.#	CITY

STATE/PROV.   ZIP/POSTAL CODE

ROM-218-MS17

READER SERVICE—**Here's how it works:**

BUSINESS REPLY MAIL

FIRST-CLASS MAIL   PERMIT NO. 717   BUFFALO, NY

POSTAGE WILL BE PAID BY ADDRESSEE

READER SERVICE

PO BOX 1341

BUFFALO NY 14240-8571

NO POSTAGE
NECESSARY
IF MAILED
IN THE
UNITED STATES

his son, who, at six foot three, stood above him. "Did you grow another inch?"

Colt grinned. "Nah. Maybe you're shrinking?"

"I'm not *that* old." At thirty-five, he still had his physical strength and stamina—but he shouldn't have been starting over. *Again*.

They stepped into the house, and while Hogan closed and locked the door, Colt beat him to the punch, asking, "You and Violet worked it out, huh?"

"Sure." Somewhat. He wasn't entirely confident on how things would go, but the last thing he wanted was for Colt to have to worry.

"You let her off the hook, right?" Colt censured him with a frown. "You didn't make her feel bad for losing her cool, did you?"

He had, but not excessively. Honestly, he still wasn't sure how he felt about it. *Humiliated, yes. Irate, definitely. Marginally, insanely grateful? Could be.*

After all the damage his wife had done, deep down it had felt good to have a woman care enough to defend him.

Hogan twisted his mouth. "She said she was jealous."

"That was pretty obvious." Grinning ear to ear, Colt said, "She likes you. Everyone knows it."

And that, Hogan thought, was a problem, too. He had no intention of ever marrying again. So where did that leave his relationship with Violet? Business and casual sex? Somehow he couldn't see her being content with that.

He looked at his son. "Do you like her?" *What the hell kind of question was that?*

"Yeah, I do." Colt sprawled on the sofa. He was so long limbed, he overflowed everywhere. "She's different from Honor, you know? I mean, she's not always hugging me and stuff. She talks to me more like I'm an adult." He gave it quick thought and amended, "Like an equal. And when I talk to her, she listens."

Concerned, Hogan sat on the edge of the chair. "I don't listen?"

"You do, sure." Colt seemed amused by his worry. "But you listen because you have to."

"No, I listen because I love you."

For a second there, Colt flushed. "Right, I know that, but it's different with Violet. She's not a relative. She treats me the same as she does Jerry or Kristy."

"She respects you."

"I think so, and I like it."

So Violet won Colt over by treating him like an equal and showing him respect? Knowing his son was at the tipping point to being a man, a really good man, he understood that. Respect, of course, was a very important thing.

"Plus," Colt said, "I'm comfortable with her."

"Me, too." Hogan's thoughts jumped ahead. "There's something about her—" *Another thing he hadn't meant to say.*

Picking up a throw pillow, Colt tossed it into the air a few times. Then he crammed the pillow onto the couch and spoke quietly. "I know you're worried, Dad. There's been a lot of stuff happening and I wasn't crazy about moving at first. But I really like it here, now."

"We're not going anywhere."

"I know." Colt stared at the pillow. "And I know you want me to be happy."

Chest tight, Hogan nodded. "More than anything." His son needed to know that. Secure, but happy.

With a slow breath, Colt looked up and met his gaze, man-to-man. "I want you to be happy, too, Dad. You deserve it. When you're working with Violet, you seem to be happier than I've seen you for a really long time, so I'm good with it. Better than good. Everything else, we can work that stuff out, right?"

Emotion gripped Hogan's throat, but this was important, so he got it together. "Right." While they had this uncommon heart-to-heart, he added, "We have each other. We have our health. Those are the most important things." He tightened his mouth. "But I want college for you, too, Colt, and a decent house—"

"Are you kidding? I love this house." Grinning again, Colt added, "And I really like living next door to Uncle Jason and Honor. With college, well, I have an idea."

Worry gnawed on Hogan, but he tried to hide it. "You're still going." Not a question.

"Definitely." A solid statement.

Relief loosened his muscles and Hogan even managed to smile. "Want to share?"

"Not yet. It's complicated school stuff and I'll tell you about it later."

Hogan didn't like the sound of that. "Colt, somehow I'm going to make it work. I want you to understand that. I'll find a way—"

"I know. Now roll that back to the mushy stuff. Let's focus on that right now. We're both here and healthy and that's good, right? Like you said, that's the important stuff."

"Agreed."

"Just don't hurt Violet's feelings, okay? I have a feeling she needs to focus on the important stuff, too."

Thinking about her background, the loss of her parents and her uncle Bibb, Hogan nodded. "You may have a point." Which, of course, only added more complications.

THEIR FIRST FULL official week together went amazingly well and they accomplished so much, Violet was left in awe. Having a partner of sorts, well, she was still very unsure about that, but it had gotten things moving, and now that the upstairs was cleared, she started to see the potential.

Hogan had moved the important stuff, the trunks, a few memorabilia signs and possibly some collectors' items, into Jason's garage until they had time to go through it. Anything that could be refurbished to use in the room once it was finished was also in the garage.

Everything else had been donated.

Unfortunately, from Monday to Friday they'd been so busy working, she hadn't been able to coerce Hogan into more than a few stolen kisses.

The man slowly drove her insane.

Also, she didn't want to be like *that woman* who'd pressured him to the point of harassment. She wanted him, wanted him to know that she wanted him, but she didn't want him forced to dodge her.

"So what do you think?"

Lost in thought, Violet had no idea what Hogan had asked her. "Hmm?"

With a bucket of drywall mud beside him and a joint knife in his hand, Hogan laughed at her. "You do tend to go off into your own little world."

Because that's the only place where she was getting any. She sighed. "You look great messy—do you know that?" He had a dollop of mud in his hair, a smudge of dirt on his jaw, and he looked as much in his element as he did while grilling.

Confidence on a man was so damn sexy.

Hogan shook his head. "You're demented." Nodding

toward the paint samples, he repeated, "Have you settled on a color?"

Every day, a few hours at a time before or after their shifts at the diner, they'd worked upstairs, first clearing the space, then while she'd washed the cobwebs off the windows, he'd patched the walls.

"You're only giving me five choices."

"Because," he argued for the tenth time, "those are the most appropriate colors."

To him, anyway. To *"Mr. In-Charge."* She wrinkled her nose. "They're all…blah." She looked around again, thinking how big and open the space seemed now that it wasn't packed to the ceiling with junk. "You know what would be great?"

"Given the umbrella you chose for me, I'm half afraid to ask."

No, he was afraid because he really wanted to take over. It was in Hogan's nature, that of an alpha, to make all the decisions. He tried to resist those inclinations, or at least conceal them. After all, he had given her five choices. Five choices of bland colors to paint the upstairs of *her* diner.

It was only that persistent guilt that kept her from rolling her eyes.

Well, guilt and his enthusiasm for the job. He'd tackled the cleanup work without a single complaint, and he was now full-time. She'd won at least half the battle, so she tried to be gracious.

He watched her, waiting, patient as she'd again gone off into her own little world. She put up her chin and said, "I want to paint it yellow."

"Yellow?"

"Not some drab, faded yellow, but a nice bright yellow—like the school colors. That way, when one of the sports teams is playing, we could hang up banners and stuff and it'd look great for spirit day, right?"

Hogan stared at her, and slowly he smiled. "Actually, that's a great idea."

Did he really have to look so surprised? Straight-faced, she muttered, "Thank you. I manage one every now and then."

"Given the success of the place, and the fact that you hired me, I'd say you've had a lot of great ideas."

She bit back her smile. Now that he agreed, she couldn't wait to tell him the rest of her ideas. "At first I thought about green for the curtains and stuff, you know, really going all out. But then I remembered myself in school. I wasn't all that into school things, so I don't want to overwhelm the place, just make it accommodating to our plans, whatever our plans might be."

"Brilliant."

The compliment warmed her. After her uncle Bibb had passed away, honest feedback on her hard work had been tough to come by. Customers were always nice, but it wasn't the same thing, not by a long shot. "So how about something more neutral, but also sturdy and easy to clean? Like rattan blinds. Well, fake rattan, not the real thing. Fake is cheaper and probably more durable. They'll look nice with the floor, once it's polished up."

Slowly, keeping his gaze on her, Hogan set aside the mud knife and cleaned his hands on a rag.

When he started in her direction, Violet's heart jumped into her throat. "What are you doing?"

"What I've been wanting to do for a while now."

Optimistic, she asked, "Sex?"

That stalled him, even made him shake his head and laugh. "I was thinking about a kiss, and an agreement on how good things are going since we're compromising."

She did most of the compromising—well, not really. It was just that he thought of things before she could, and she agreed with him, so there was no reason to insist they did anything a different way.

It just burned her butt a little that he didn't give her a chance to be the director.

Stopping in front of her, his gaze searching hers, Hogan murmured, "But your idea has merit, too."

She repeated, "My idea of…sex?" Her hopefulness made him cocky.

And damn him, that cockiness made her hotter.

"Sure. Why not?" He pulled her in close, his big hands open low on her back, and bent to nuzzle her neck. "You realize that all we have up here is the hard floor?"

Urgent now that she got his agreement, Violet tunneled her fingers into his hair and kept him close. "I don't care." It'd take ten minutes to get to her house, and since he was on board *now*, she didn't want to take a chance on him changing his mind by giving him too much time to think about it.

He leaned back, his expression tender. "You're great for my ego."

"I doubt your ego needed much help. But what did you expect? After what we've already done, the past week has to count as the longest bout of foreplay in the history of mankind."

A smug, very masculine smile appeared, and his gaze heated. "Have you been frustrated, honey?"

"Very."

"So imagine how it's been for me." He leaned in near her ear and whispered roughly, "I know how you taste, and how you sound when you let go." His mouth touched her temple. "And then to be here with you all week, constantly surrounded by people… I could teach you a thing or two about frustration."

Violet grinned in relief. "I'm glad I'm not the only one suffering."

"Tease." He kissed her hard and fast, and just as she was getting into it, he stepped back. "Let's cover that window first, okay? There's enough gossip about me going on already. I don't want to put on a show."

Breathing wasn't easy. "You don't have to get home to Colt?"

"He knows I'm here working. I told him I might not get in until after midnight. He's probably going to bed right about now."

So they had uninterrupted time. "I would never want to interfere with—"

"I know, but I wouldn't let you anyway." He softened that rebuke by adding, "Anytime it's a problem, I promise I'll let you know."

Nodding in acceptance, she grabbed up the sheet that would serve as a curtain until they finished the remodel. They definitely didn't want to be seen if anyone happened to be out there.

Going on tiptoe, she got it tacked back up into place over the window, and when she turned back, Hogan was shirtless.

It was an amazing thing when a man so wonderful on the inside also had the perfect, very masculine wrapping on the outside.

Without conscious decision, Violet walked to him, her hand already lifted to touch what he'd exposed. He didn't move as she reached up to put her palm on his sleek, hard shoulder. *So warm to the touch, his muscles firm, flexing under her palm.*

Fingers spread, she slowly trailed her hand down over

his collarbone and into his crisp, dark chest hair, over the bulge of a pec muscle, then down over his flat abdomen. That downy line of dark hair that bisected his body and disappeared into his jeans was about as sexy as anything she'd ever seen. "You look nothing like an accountant."

He snorted a short laugh. "You're stereotyping?"

With a shrug, she said, "Honestly, you don't look like any man I know."

"What's that supposed to mean?"

Violet pulled in a much-needed breath. "Every part of you stirs every part of me."

He lightly caught her waist in his hands and drew her nearer. "I'm glad." Then his mouth was on hers, immediately nudging her lips apart, his tongue licking over them before invading for a long, hot, wet kiss that left them both breathing harder.

He drew back enough to say, "I need to see you," between kisses, and quickly pulled her shirt over her head.

Violet flushed. "Damn."

With his gaze glued to her body, Hogan asked, "Problem?"

"My underwear doesn't match."

The side of his mouth quirked. "No?" He reached for the snap to her shorts. "Let me see."

"I dressed in a hurry today," she rushed to explain, "and we've been so busy I haven't had a chance to do laundry. So—"

He pushed her shorts down, cutting off her lame excuses. Once they got past the flare of her hips, they fell easily to her feet.

"Step out," he said, holding her hand and looking at her body from below her chin to above her knees.

She did, kicking off her sandals at the same time.

Hogan studied her so thoroughly, she couldn't help but fidget. One of these days she wanted to be dressed up a little for him, wearing more makeup than just mascara, her hair fixed in something other than a ponytail, her clothes better thought out than shorts and a T-shirt. It would be nice to smell like perfume instead of French fries or chili.

And certainly, she wanted to wear some of her sexier underthings.

"They coordinate," Hogan said. "A white bra with white-and-pink-flowered panties." He kissed her temple, her jaw, while opening the back closure on her bra and taking it off her.

"You're far too good at that."

"Shh." His large, rough hands held both her breasts, softly kneading while his mouth played over her skin.

Violet closed her eyes to the overwhelming sensations of being touched and kissed with the knowledge of what was to come.

No more frustration, not tonight.

"God, you smell good," he whispered, making her rethink the perfume. Sliding an arm around her back, he brought her up so he could nuzzle her breasts.

In an agony of anticipation, she waited, her body on fire, and finally, *finally*, his mouth reached her nipple, his soft tongue laving, circling, and then he closed his firm lips around her, drawing her into the incredible wet heat of his mouth.

Groaning, Violet sank her fingers into his hair, keeping him right there. She felt the rhythmic pull of his mouth all the way to her womb.

While he suckled on her nipple, he also stroked her behind, squeezing each cheek, fondling her over her panties, then suddenly sliding his big hand *into* her panties, against her bare skin.

Arching forward even more, she heard him murmur husky encouragement as he touched her from behind, his fingers hot, a little rough, unhesitating in their exploration. He idly traced her sex, each pass opening her more, easing the way. Then he pressed a finger in.

A raw groan tore from her throat. She'd been waiting so long, forever it seemed, that she needed him now, right this second. He continued the alternate touches, lightly, then deep, tormenting her until she said, "Hogan, *please…*"

Taking away those amazing fingers, he whispered, "You're already wet," and went to a knee to strip her panties off her. He looked at her, completely naked, and slowly kissed his way up her body, starting with her inner thighs, her hip bones, her stomach, ribs and each breast, until he stood. With his gaze on her breasts, he reached for his zipper.

"Let me." *Pretty please.* She'd thought about it so many times, pictured the scenario in her mind until she couldn't wait to get him naked.

Hands shaking, Violet reached out, but instead of unfastening his jeans, she stroked the solid erection straining against the denim.

He put his head back, his hands tight at his sides.

Nice as it was to see him like this, impatience drove her.

Violet kissed his throat, lightly bit his shoulder and deftly opened the snap. After slowly sliding down the zipper, she reached into his boxers and closed her hand around his pulsing shaft.

Hogan breathed deeper. Then, his forehead to hers, he watched her stroking him.

He felt big in her hand, exciting her unbearably. She

brought her thumb up and over the head, felt the warm slippery droplet there and heard his choked sound of suffering.

"I won't last," he groaned. "Not if you keep doing that." His hand covered hers, tightening for only a moment before he pulled her away. After a few strained breaths, he smiled at her. "You still have those condoms?"

"Yes." Bare assed and not caring, she hurried over to where she'd left her purse by the stairs. "I'm also on the pill, so you don't have to worry."

"The back of you is as beautiful as the front."

"Is that so?" She put a little more sass into her walk and heard him laugh.

It was an awesome thing to be with a man who turned her on like no other, drew her admiration as a dad, shared her work ethic and made her laugh. Those things, she decided, were a perfect combo.

This time when she turned, a condom in hand, Hogan stood completely stripped, his shoulders against the wall, his hands lax at his sides, one leg bent.

Lord have mercy.

She stopped and just stared. He wasn't a muscular hulk, but rather naturally strong, his body lean and hard from everyday work and probably a generous donation from an excellent gene pool. Much as she wanted him, she could be happy to look at him for an hour.

Eyes hot, Hogan smiled at her. "Don't go shy on me now, honey. If I don't have you soon, I'm a goner."

She knew just what he meant. "Death from lust?"

"Something like that."

"You are an incredibly gorgeous man, Hogan." She couldn't keep her gaze off him, looking him over from his wide shoulders and well-developed arms, his hairy chest to narrower hips. He was fully erect, his strong legs casually braced apart. Even his feet looked sexy to her. "I've been thinking about this since the day I met you."

"Hussy," he teased, then searched her face. "You hid it well. More often than not, I thought you disliked me."

"I disliked things you did. A lot." She licked her lips. "But I still wanted you."

"What things?"

She waved the hand holding the condoms. "The way you looked at women, sometimes with contempt, how you chased after everything in a skirt."

He didn't deny the accusation, saying only, "We barely knew each other then."

Shrugging, she stepped close and looked up at him. "Maybe even then I was jealous. Maybe," she whispered, "since I'd wanted you at first sight, it burned my butt a little that you ignored me."

"You know why I…" Hogan shook his head. "Let's not go there, okay?" He held out a hand.

Because she'd once dated Jason? Was that the biggest reason he'd ignored her? She didn't want anything to ruin the moment, so she didn't press him.

As he rolled on the condom, she touched him, lightly holding his testicles, kissing his biceps, breathing in the rich, masculine scent of him.

"You're playing with fire." He abruptly turned her against the wall, and his mouth took hers, the kiss consuming even as he stroked her left thigh, lifting it high against his hip. With his other hand, he readied her.

Violet could have told him that it wasn't necessary; she was so close to the edge, she only wanted to feel him, all of him.

She wanted to feel him deep inside her.

Maybe he was the same because he growled, "I can't wait, honey. Tell me you're ready."

Eyes heavy and body burning, she whispered, "I've been ready for a month."

He smiled against her cheek. "I love your country accent, especially when you're hot and bothered. It's even more pronounced."

Deliberately drawling her words, Violet said, "Then how 'bout you get on with it, darlin'?"

"Hell of an idea." He opened her with his fingers, guided himself to her, and after slowly gliding against her, ensuring they were both slick, he filled her with one long, firm thrust.

She cried out, her fingertips digging into his shoulders.

He groaned, crushing closer against her.

For a minute, they stayed like that, relishing the newness of it and, at least for Violet, the rightness of it, too.

"Hold on to me." Hogan hooked both her knees in his elbows and lifted her against him, opening her legs wide, supporting her weight with his arms.

He was so deep that Violet couldn't seem to catch a breath, but she didn't care. She kept her arms wrapped around his neck, thrilled when he kissed her again, excited even more as he began a slow, steady rhythm while also moving her against him with his hands. She tightened around him, squeezing him inside her, and heard his broken groan of pleasure.

Between her legs she felt an answering rush of heat and dampness. She knew he felt it, too, and her skin heated and tingled, every inch of her body so sensitized that she already strained for release.

Hogan seemed in less of a hurry, content to kiss her lazily, touch her, fill her while riding so easily against her… That damned alpha male control made her a little insane and she tried to encourage him to haste with her own movements.

She wanted it harder, deeper.

Faster.

"Not yet," he whispered against her mouth, pressing in all the way, grinding against her, then withdrawing until he almost left her, only to slowly sink in again. "Not just yet."

She tried to stay with him, she really did. But the pressure was building, twisting inside her. *"Hogan."*

"Easy," he whispered. "Easy, Violet. Let it last."

On a shattered breath, she gasped, "I can't," and then she was coming, her whole body taut, twisting, her head back against the wall as she cried out with the intense sensations clenching inside her.

She vaguely felt Hogan's surprise, then heard his deep guttural groan, and finally, as he lost control, she got what she wanted.

Just as her climax had started to fade, he drove into her hard and fast and brought her right back there with him again. She locked her ankles around the small of his back, her fingers behind his neck, and trusted him to keep them both upright during the release.

CHAPTER ELEVEN

BECAUSE NATHAN KNEW her schedule well, he realized right away that something was off. Brooklin hadn't come out to the porch to read early evening, as she so often did. But more than that, her lights hadn't gone off at ten, as per her usual pattern. In fact, damn near every light in her house blazed.

He'd gotten home late and had expected to see her house dark and quiet, except for the porch light she always left on.

Tonight was different.

He was beat, a hot shower and a soft bed uppermost in his mind. At least until he'd seen her house and felt the uneasiness. Through much of his life he'd learned to never discount his instincts. They'd served him well in SWAT—for the most part. Clearbrook was quieter, calmer, but still, occasions arose where he had to trust those internal alarms.

For only a moment he argued with himself about all the reasons why Brooklin might still be up. A party? Doubtful.

A date? Hell, he hoped not.

Trouble? That seemed his best guess, so he headed over to her porch, cutting across the lawns instead of going out to the sidewalk and up her walkway.

They were on friendlier terms now, but she hadn't let him kiss her good-night after their "date," which wasn't much of a date since she'd insisted on buying her own food and they'd only gone to Screwy Louie's, sitting with other neighbors and indulging nothing more than very casual conversation. But it was a start, never mind that they hadn't really seen each other since.

Through the drawn blinds, he saw no shadows. So she wasn't moving around? Maybe she'd gone out and hadn't returned yet, and she'd left on the lights so she, a woman alone, wouldn't be entering a dark house. It was late, after eleven, but with all those lights on, she wasn't likely to be asleep.

To hell with it. He'd rather apologize for bothering her than to ignore her if she needed him.

He knocked, then waited.

No answer.

He stewed a minute more, but his instincts insisted something was off. Pulling out his cell, he called her.

On the very first ring, she answered in a whisper. "Hello?"

Even with her voice so soft, he heard the uncertainty. "Brooklin? It's Nathan."

With less of a whisper, she asked, "How'd you get my number?"

She didn't exactly sound angry, but definitely thrown off. "You left it with the boutique and their books were open and I saw it."

Still very distracted, she said, "Oh God. I'll have to talk to them about that."

Now that she spoke more normally, he heard it in her voice. Something was definitely wrong. "I already did. I told Phillis, the girl that works the day shift, that it was a terrible practice and she promised not to let it happen again."

After a slight hesitation, she said, "Thank you."

By the second, Nathan grew more concerned. "Let me in."

That perked her up. "What?"

"I knocked, but you didn't answer the door. Let me in."

The curtain on the small rectangular door window moved, and one eye peeked out. Then both eyes. She frowned.

He heard the locks clicking—*multiple* locks—and finally she cracked the door open enough to say, "What are you doing out there?"

"Checking on you." Trying to look as casual as a very horny, overly protective man could, Nathan propped a shoulder on the door frame and didn't make a move to enter. "Everything okay in there, Brooklin?"

Her eyes narrowed. The knuckles on the hand holding the door turned white. "Why do you ask?"

"Your lights were on," he explained gently. "And now, seeing you, I know you're spooked about something."

She jerked back. "No. I'm...fine. Thanks for checking, though."

When she started to close him out, Nathan stopped her with one hand flattened on the door. "Okay, here's the thing." Damn, he didn't want it to happen this way, didn't want to insist and force his way in, but in his gut, he felt she needed him. "I'm not just an interested guy, you know? I'm also the sheriff. And as the sheriff, I can tell that something is wrong. You can't ask me to ignore that."

To his surprise, she accepted his explanation. The door widened a little more, enough for him to press in, and so he did.

Clearly that hadn't been her intent because she just

stared up at him. She'd probably hoped for more of a conversation, not an invasion.

Trying to make it easier, he smiled and said, "Hi."

She blinked. "Hi." Looking around her own house as if unsure of what to do, she said, "Everything really is fine, I promise."

Needing to touch her, Nathan cupped the side of her neck. "Okay, now this is just the interested guy part of me. Sorry that you're getting hit with both tonight. But, Brooklin, I know you. Not as well as I'd like to, but well enough to know you're jumpy." He, too, glanced around the house. "Since you're not the hysterical type, I'm concerned."

His hand was still on her neck, and rather than complain or move away, she'd stepped closer. Spooked? It seemed so. "You can see nothing's wrong."

He nodded, but asked, "Mind if I have a look around?"

Her laugh was short and disbelieving. "I guess you can if you really want, but there's no one else in here."

"I won't invade your privacy, okay? I'll just look around real fast."

"Fine." But she went ahead of him, moving first to a desk area, closing a laptop, stacking a few papers and sticking them into a folder. Putting the folder under other things.

Hiding stuff.

No, he wasn't an idiot. But whatever she had on the laptop was a mystery for another day.

Aware of her sticking close behind him, Nathan glanced into the kitchen and dining area, and checked that the back door was locked and the windows secure. He noticed not only that she was a neat freak, but that she had the outside lights on all the way around the house.

That was new. He was used to seeing her front porch light and a smaller light over her back door. But not the floodlights.

Next he went down the hall, peeked into her immaculate bathroom, even looked behind the shower curtain and in the linen closet, then went into a guest bedroom. She had it set up for making jewelry with a craft table, high swivel chair, two gooseneck lamps, tools and various containers. A cabinet made up of many small drawers sat against one wall, and on the other a variety of hooks held chains in different thicknesses and metals, along with some completed pieces. He would have liked to look at the jewelry more closely, but the inspection came first.

Lastly, he stepped into her bedroom. He should have taken only a quick look, checked the closet and maybe under the bed, then gotten the hell out of there.

But he lingered.

It was a hell of a lot more feminine than he'd expected. A fluffy, snowy-white comforter topped a full-sized bed over a pale blue pin-striped sheet set. Two fat ruffled pillows were at the top, with coordinating blue striped throw pillows. Abstract flower art in soft pastels filled one wall, and blue patterned curtains covered the only window.

He didn't need to look under the bed. He could see beneath it from where he stood and there wasn't even a speck of dust.

Striding ahead of him, her jerky movements giving away her nervousness, Brooklin opened the white slatted closet door. "See? I'm all alone."

But she didn't have to be. Chest expanding, Nathan

nodded. "I see." *Get the hell out of her room.* "So why are you edgy?"

She gestured at him. "You're here."

"I make you edgy?" Okay, so he knew he did on some level, but not like this.

Brooklin shook her head. "No. I mean, you poking around is unsettling." In defiance, she said, "I wasn't expecting company."

"I'm hardly that. I'm a sheriff and—"

"And a man. I know. You've explained it."

Yeah, he had. Seeing her standing five feet away from him, not getting any closer—not in her bedroom—he knew what he had to do.

He turned and walked out.

Going only as far as the living room, he sat down on the edge of a padded chair, legs apart, elbows propped on his knees, his fingers steepled together, and he waited.

Without a word, she joined him, sitting on the sofa opposite him. She didn't look at him, but instead stared down at her feet and bit her lip.

Until then, probably because of his concern, he hadn't noticed what she wore—or didn't wear.

He did now.

Her feet were bare—slender, feminine feet, with smooth, shapely calves and her thighs… He saw that she kept her knees and ankles pressed together.

It was dangerous to his libido, but he took in the rest of her in a loose, short-sleeved nightshirt that landed midthigh. The shirt wasn't snug, but he could still see her breasts, soft and full, beneath the thin material.

Her hair hung over one shoulder, she wore no makeup at all and he felt such a grinding lust it almost leveled him.

"I thought I heard someone outside."

Nathan had gotten himself so mired in sexual thoughts, her words jolted him. "What do you mean? You heard someone, or you thought you heard someone?"

She shook her head and whispered desperately, "I don't know."

Dredging up his flagging sheriff mode, he said, "Tell me exactly what you heard."

She swallowed, nodded. "I saw shadows first."

"In back or in front?"

"Front. By my picture window. I... I don't know. I was just heading to bed, but when I saw it, I froze, and by the time I got to the window to peek out, no one was there. But then I heard a noise at the back of the house. Like..."

Seeing she was truly shaken, Nathan left his chair, went to the couch and sat beside her, his arm around her shoulders. "Like?"

Her gaze locked on his. "Like someone was trying the door."

Don't think about kissing her. Never before had it been such a struggle to stay professional. He looked away from her mouth and back to her incredible eyes. "Turning the doorknob?"

She nodded.

"I'm going to go take a look, okay? Sit tight and I'll be right back." He stood.

She shot up after him. "But it's dark out there now."

Who was she running from? Someone bad, given her reactions. Nathan took her hands, all the while telling himself that she was a woman alone, a woman suddenly frightened, and he was the freaking sheriff, one of the good guys, so he absolutely would not take advantage of her.

"It is. But, Brooklin, it was dark when I walked over here. It'll be dark when I have to go home." *Unless she wanted him to stay?* He shook his head. "I'll be all right. You can lock the door behind me, okay?"

The offer left her divided. He could see that she most definitely wanted the door locked—but she didn't want him on the other side of it.

He smiled to reassure her, briefly cupped her face, then went out the front door before he gave in to inappropriate urges that had no place in the moment. She didn't lock it behind him.

Instead she followed him.

Sticking close.

He looked around the porch, but there wasn't much to see. It hadn't rained lately, so no mud had been tracked up onto the concrete. Her porch was as tidy as the inside of her house.

Far as he could tell, no one had tried to mess with the window. In the night with only the porch lamp, he didn't see any fingerprints on the glass. "I'm going around back."

She nodded, grabbed a fistful of his shirt at the small of his back and followed.

No denying it, it turned him on the way she trusted him. And getting to be the big bad protector fed some basic nature in most every guy.

But it also infuriated him that someone had scared her, had apparently impacted her life enough to leave her feeling threatened. More than anything, he'd love to run into some punk right about now, just so he could remove the worry from her eyes.

He didn't need a flashlight to see around the house, not with all the outside lights on.

When he spotted the trampled flower in the landscaping, very near the back door, he paused.

Brooklin stared at it in horror.

"Could have been a dog, or even a raccoon or possum," he said, though his damned instincts were going crazy, mostly because of her reaction. Around the back of the house, he found nothing amiss. Maybe some displaced mulch, but again, that could be a critter.

"Someone was here," she whispered.

Since he couldn't prove that, and no one was around now, his only thought was to reassure her. "You know there's still some crime in the area. It's a lot better since the revitalization program. Lots of new homeowners fixing up houses, new businesses moving in, more community involvement. But petty things still happen." And some not-so-petty things.

"Yes, I know. I read all the literature before moving here."

Of course she had. Unfortunately, there was nothing petty about her suspicions. Nathan took her arm and led her back to the house. Once inside, he said, "You're not worried about a random break-in or burglary, are you, Brooklin?"

She frowned but didn't meet his gaze. "Of course I am. Anyone with a brain worries about it."

"So I guess I'll rephrase that. You're not *only* worried about a random act. You think someone has specifically targeted you." He saw her face, the way she flinched, and knew he'd hit the mark. "The reason you relocated here… Someone was bothering you? Or worse?"

Because he'd pushed, she shut down on him. "Thank you so much, Nathan. As a neighbor you went above and beyond and I really do appreciate it." She made a show of looking at the clock. "It really is late now—"

"Come to my house tonight."

Her mouth was still open, midsentence, but after his blurted request, nothing else came out.

Getting closer, but not too close, Nathan stared down at her. "Not being alone would help. I promise."

For a second, he thought she'd cry. Her mouth trembled, and she got that extra-soft look in her eyes, eyes that went a little glassy. But instead she smiled and even leaned against him for a moment, totally taking him off guard.

Before he could get his arms around her, she'd stepped back again.

"That's a very nice offer, Nathan. But I don't think it's a good idea."

He thought it was a great idea. "You're worried about me jumping past the sheriff mode, maybe even the neighbor mode, and going straight into interested guy mode, aren't you?" This time he drew her in, not in an embrace, just nearer, his hands on her shoulders, which were hopefully safe ground. "I want you, Brooklin, you know that. But I'll control myself. I won't even hint that we should do more than get a good night's sleep. You can have the bedroom and I can camp out on the couch."

"I wouldn't kick you out of your own bed."

She hadn't said an outright "no," so it was his turn to smile. "You're not willing to share it with me, either." When she stayed quiet, he said, "Fine, you can take the couch. You'll fit better than I would anyway."

"Then what about tomorrow? And the day after that? I'll be coming right back to the same ridiculous worry where I overreact and impose on a neighbor."

"First," Nathan said, "I'm more than a neighbor. Remember, I'm also the sheriff, and an interested guy. We've jogged together. We even ate at Screwy Louie's."

She almost laughed. "True, but that doesn't really change anything. Not about tomorrow."

"*Second*," he said, stressing the word since she hadn't quite let him finish. "Tomorrow you can buy alarms for the windows and doors. Then you'll rest easier. If anyone tried to come in, you'd know it before they got one foot over the threshold."

She looked uncertain, and very tempted. "Alarms?"

"You met Honor. I know you don't know her well, but she had a similar situation. Hers really was random and petty crime, but she was plenty spooked. Around here, neighbors help neighbors, so Jason, Hogan and I, with Colt's help, secured her place a little better. You could stay with me tonight. Then tomorrow I could pick up what you need."

She started to protest, so he gave her a squeeze.

"You can pay me back. It won't be a lot of money."

Giving it some thought, she stared at his chest. "That's probably not a bad idea."

"I can help you get things installed. Or Colt could help you. He's handy like his uncle, and being a high school senior, he's always ready to earn a few bucks."

Wanting to give in, but fighting it, she shifted, hugged herself, looked around her empty house, and then finally up at him again. "You really wouldn't mind?"

"No, of course not." But he was wondering, *Which part?*

"Thank you. I promise I'm not usually so jumpy. It's just that…" The explanation trailed off, and instead, she gave him a quick, self-conscious smile. "Just let me put on some yoga pants and flip-flops. Then I'll grab a pillow and quilt."

Nathan watched her go down the hall. It wasn't the best of circumstances, but still, it felt like he was making great strides.

Sᴘʀᴀᴡʟᴇᴅ ɴᴀᴋᴇᴅ ᴏɴ the floor, Violet tucked in close to his side, Hogan thought about life. "Not since high school have I sneaked in a quickie in such an awkward place."

She snuggled closer, one of her slim legs over his, her fingers toying with his chest hair. "Two quickies," she clarified. "And honest to God, Hogan, I'm not sure I could survive anything longer." She pressed her warm mouth to his chest. "I don't mean to sound melodramatic, but that was…" Her breath teased over his skin. "I'm not sure I have words."

Yeah, she was definitely good for his ego. "Given my past history—"

"Your history with women?"

"I meant sex, but yeah, with women. It has to be you." Teasing her, he said, "You're just easy."

She lightly bit him, then licked the spot. "Not usually."

He couldn't deny that it had been somehow special, far more combustible than usual. Everything he did, she loved. And vice versa.

She moaned and he got harder. She squeezed him and he had to fight not to come. She made those breathy little sounds during her release, and he'd completely lost it.

"I wish we had another condom."

Hogan grinned. "Easy, and greedy."

Rather than laugh with him, she looked up, her eyes luminous in the dark room, her hair, now out of the ponytail, very messy and somehow sexier because of it. "I'd like to do this about a million more times."

The words were light enough, undemanding, but still they stole his contentment. "Not tonight, I hope. I have to recoup."

"Tomorrow, then?"

Why did she have to try to nail him down right now? He frowned, then closed his eyes. "I imagine we'll have a hard time staying apart. Tomorrow might not work, not if we're going to get all this work done."

He felt her stillness, the reluctant way she settled against him again, this time without all the ease and comfort.

"I want to ask you something, Hogan. And I don't want you to assume I'm pressing for more or anything like that. I'm not and I won't. I'm a big girl and I've been taking care of myself for a long time. You don't have to worry that I'll get all needy and clingy, okay?"

Hogan opened his eyes and stared at the ceiling. Jesus, she'd said a lot there, all of it some sort of prelude to whatever she planned to ask him, and he was just supposed to say, *Go ahead*? Even though he sensed an emotional trap of some kind? Frustration rolled over him, and damn it, he did want her again. Hell, he wanted her right now.

With a grave sigh, Violet squeezed him. "See? You're already doing it. Just forget it, okay? Pretend I didn't say anything."

"I wish we had another condom." If they did, he could kiss her and she'd forget the stupid question, whatever it was.

"Me, too. I'll remember to put more in my purse."

Un-freaking-believable. He'd never known a woman like her. She wasn't insulted that he didn't want to talk, and she was even willing to let him distract her with sex.

Or maybe she hoped to distract him with sex. When it came to Violet, he could never tell for sure.

She patted him. "We'll rest a few more minutes, and then we can head home—to our respective homes, I mean. You can just let me know when you want to get together again."

She made him feel like a complete ass. To cover that, he stroked a hand down her side, past the dip in her waist and then to the rise of her hip. "We'll be together tomorrow."

"But like you said, we'll be working. It's okay. I understand."

Well, damn it, he didn't. The silence stretched out, and he knew, any second now, she'd decide it was time to go. Thoughts chewed on his peace of mind, more turbulent by the second, and even though he didn't mean to, he spilled his guts.

"Everyone in my acquaintance—family, friends and coworkers—they all knew about my wife, what she'd done before she died."

Violet went still, then very deliberately soft against him. "What did she do?"

"She cheated. Not with just one guy. Hell, maybe with more than two. But two for sure." He could feel Violet's heartbeat, strong and steady against his ribs. "She cheated, I found out, and before I could even show her how pissed I was, she died."

Her fingers, small and soft and so damned competent with everything she did, whether it was working the diner, cleaning or making him insane with lust, teased over his abdomen. "How did she die?"

"She was leaving to meet a guy. We'd had a big fight and she just walked out. I knew where she was going, but I didn't know what to do about it." He shrugged, trying to sound unaffected by discussing the most miserable night of his life. "It was storming and she caused a wreck with three other cars. Luckily no one else was seriously hurt, but Meg wasn't wearing her seat belt. They found her body in the street."

It was so silent in the big empty room he heard Violet's strained breathing.

"It was in all the papers, on the local news stations, lots of people asking too many questions. The guy she'd been going to meet fell apart, like maybe he'd been in love with her." Hogan didn't say *too*. "He knew he wasn't the only one, but unlike me, he didn't seem to care. The entire thing, all of it, was just pathetic. My ignorance, Meg's lying, the way she died, and this other bozo who was content to be...not her husband."

Violet hugged him and whispered, "I don't really know what to say, except that I'm sorry."

"I want you to understand, Violet. I came here, supposedly to a quieter life, and just when things seem to be falling into place, I get caught up in another massive scene where everyone knows my business, knows that my boss wanted in my pants, and that I ended up fired." That wasn't entirely fair and he knew it. He was likening the two situations when the similarities were light-years apart.

But he wanted to make a point. What point, he couldn't say for sure. Or hell, maybe he'd just wanted to talk about it.

Violet squeezed him tight, her face in his neck. Then slowly she sat up. She pushed her hair back, and in the shadowy room he saw that her face was a mask of misery.

Damn. "I didn't mean to say all that..."

"It's what I was going to ask, so thank you for telling me." After a shuddering breath, she managed a halfhearted smile. "You're right, too. I really shouldn't have gotten involved between you and that woman."

"Her name is Joni—"

"I don't care what her name is!" After that small explosion, she got herself together. "It wasn't my place to get involved and I'm sorry. Really sorry. I can't fix it now, except to try to make things work." Her gaze flashed to his. "With the diner, I mean."

"I knew what you meant." Concentrating got more difficult. So did hanging on to the resentment from the memories. Violet was here in front of him, naked, her pale skin visible in the dark room, and he was starting to get hard again.

"I don't know what happened with your wife, why things fell apart, but I'm sure everyone who knows you understood—"

"Understood what?" He wrapped a long lock of red hair around his finger. "That I wasn't enough for her? That I was too blind to realize she was fucking two other guys, practically under my nose? That she'd bankrupted me, even robbed my son of his college fund? What could anyone have understood?"

Horror filled her eyes, and for a second he thought she might cry. It was the last thing he wanted. Hurting her would hurt him, too, and after reliving that god-awful humiliation, he already hurt enough. He whispered, "Violet… Don't, honey. I'm sorry. I should have just answered your question, not gone off on a rant."

"You did answer my question, but it was worse than I'd ever imagined." Anger stiffened her shoulders, brought color into her cheeks and even brightened her beautiful eyes. "I'm sure anyone who knew you understood that your poor wife had ruined the very best thing to ever happen to her. And that's really sad, Hogan. No one should be remembered for cheating and lying. She destroyed herself."

"Yes."

Violet flattened a hand on his stomach. "But she didn't destroy you."

For a while there, it had been a close thing. But now, he could agree. "No, she didn't."

He grunted when Violet dropped onto him, kissing his face all over from the bridge of his nose and his jaw, to his brow and the side of his mouth. "You're a wonderful person, Hogan Guthrie. I'm so glad Colt has you."

He took her shoulders and levered her back. "And I have him."

"Exactly." She gave him one more smooch, then wiggled her belly against him. "You're hard again."

No wonder. Her breasts were against his chest, her nipples once again puckered. He could feel her pubic hair on his hip, and her hair hung around him like a silky curtain. Cuddling her backside, he smiled and asked, "You're sure?"

"Yes, most definitely. I'm totally impressed, too."

"You should be."

"I'd love to take advantage, I really would, but two mind-blowing climaxes, topped with heartbreaking disclosures, are more than I can take in one evening."

"You probably needed to know."

She nodded. "And I definitely needed the sex. But now I'm kaput and I think I need some sleep so I can keep up with you tomorrow."

Amazed, Hogan swatted her on the butt. "I like how you did that."

"What did I do?"

How could she look so innocent? He had half-moons in his shoulders from her nails, and his legs were still shaking from her enthusiasm. "You were you."

She tried lifting a brow, but then laughed. "Am I supposed to understand that?"

The fact that she could laugh right now, and that she had him smiling because of it, was a wonderful thing.

"I'll explain." Hogan brought her down for a longer, softer kiss. He tangled a hand in her hair, tasting her, wanting her again, but able to show some restraint since, as she'd said, he'd just come twice.

Her small, soft body felt so perfect against his. But he knew the softness was a disguise, because Violet had an inner strength that awed him.

"Was that an explanation," she teased, "or more of your torturous foreplay?"

"That was me unable to resist your mouth." He kissed her again, briefly this time. "I told you about my humiliating past, and you didn't look at me like a loser. You didn't launch into more questions, or pity me, or get emotional—other than for a second or two. Instead, you were as you always are, very sweet and open and honest, and that steered me away from the morbid. You, Violet Shaw, are not only good for my ego… You're also good for my frame of mind."

"I have an idea."

Hogan grinned. "I just bet you do."

She folded her arms over his chest. "Maybe you could just always think about sex with me when those awful memories start to intrude."

Pretending to consider it, Hogan slowly nodded. "That sounds like a very workable plan." Truthfully, though, he'd probably be thinking about sex with her around the clock, awful memories or not.

CHAPTER TWELVE

TWO DAYS LATER, Brooklin went out to her porch to read, just as she did most evenings. The sun still hung in the sky, painting the horizon in vivid hues of red, orange, yellow and purple. The hazy evening air filled her lungs. Off in the distance, someone mowed a lawn. When she listened closely, she could hear children playing the street over.

Life filled the area, but soon it would be dark, and then the fear would creep back in on her.

After crashing on Nathan's couch only twice, getting back in her own place felt oddly depressing.

With the security system installed, covering every window and door, she was safer now. No reason to worry about bogeymen from her past sneaking into her present.

Still, for the first time since moving here, she felt alone.

Odd, because until recently she really had been alone and she'd liked it. Alone meant no one to judge her, whisper about her, or worse, threaten her.

Despite her best efforts to remain alone, that had changed. Not only had she met a lot of new people at Screwy Louie's, she now knew Nathan much better. Knew him and liked him. Probably too much.

Her time on his couch had been a revelation. Not once had he made a move. In fact, he'd barely looked at her, as if having her on his couch didn't affect him at all.

She could have been a guy friend for all the personal attention he gave her. Though she hadn't wanted to get involved, it was still a little deflating to accept that he hadn't been that aware of her as a woman.

Because she'd definitely been aware of him as a man.

Had he given up his pursuit of her?

Brooklin shook off that thought. It had taken a full day to get the things she needed for the security system, so Nathan had offered his couch a second time, and it had been a repeat of the first.

Zero teasing. Zero recognition of her as a woman.

It was almost a relief when earlier today, Jason and Colt had shown up, tools and supplies in hand to get all the security stuff installed.

Nathan had gone on about his day.

While the two guys had worked, she'd watched the process, learning about the upkeep and how to set or reset a sensor. In between instruction, they'd chatted.

Jason adored his wife and mentioned her often while telling her stories about her many neighbors and the local businesses. They were both pretty terrific, and after her time spent working in a school, she especially related to Colt. Such a conscientious, mature young man.

She knew now that Colt had very specific plans about college, but he was anxious to finish high school—early if possible. He wanted half of the year to work and save to help offset the costs.

Admirable. She told him about a special program that had been at the school where she'd previously worked. It was just what he'd been looking for. Soon he would check with his counselor to see if his school offered something similar. He certainly had the credits to finish up, if that's what he and his father wanted.

His uncle, she'd noticed, hadn't appeared overly keen

on the idea. Not that Jason had complained, because he hadn't. Jason Guthrie had a quiet, calm demeanor, somewhat different from his more outgoing brother, Hogan.

And Nathan was different from them both. He had more macho presence, at least in her opinion.

Damn it, she didn't even like macho men.

Trying to force Nathan out of her head, she thought about the sensors instead. What would she do if one of them went off? Would she have the wherewithal to defend herself? That is, if she could get herself off the ceiling?

Before considering the job done, Jason had tested the sound for her, wanting her to be aware of it. The shrill, earsplitting noise had nearly stopped her heart. He'd shut it off quickly, but—wow. It was enough to wake the dead. No way would she sleep through an intruder.

Reassuring, but still she worried.

Why hadn't Nathan at least talked with her more while she'd been at his house?

Knowing she wouldn't read tonight, Brooklin set the book aside and thought about her life. She had a story to finish typing, and jewelry commissions that weren't quite done. Plenty to keep her busy.

Yet she sat there wasting time while repeatedly checking the street, waiting for Nathan to get home.

Annoyed with herself, she stood to go inside.

Of course, that's when he arrived, and since he'd already seen her, it would be rude to leave now.

And just when had she started making excuses just to see him?

As usual, Nathan looked irascible as he exited the official vehicle. His sandy-colored hair stood on end, as if he'd raked his fingers through it more than a few times. His uniform shirt, unbuttoned to the waist, had a blue stain, still wet, soaking the right side.

Brooklin braced her arms on the porch railing and called out, "What happened to you?"

He made no pretense of going to his own door. Nope, he made a beeline for her, and as he crossed the lawns, he shoved his reflective sunglasses to the top of his head. "It's been a real bitch of a day."

She could tell. "You're not hurt?"

"No." He kept coming. "It ended with a four-car fender bender when Bingo let out. No one hurt but it was a test in patience."

Mouth twitching, Brooklin asked, "And that turned you blue?"

His gaze narrowed on her, not really with irritation, but with something far more intense. "Three seniors blamed each other, all of them loud, threatening each other with me."

"You said four cars?"

He nodded. "The fourth was a single mom. She had a three-year-old with her and he didn't like the confusion, especially with his mom on the phone, freaking out to her cousin, so I took the kid out of his car seat— and he dumped his juice on me."

Picturing Nathan dealing with all that, Brooklin smiled. "Is it sticky?"

Now that he'd reached her, Nathan stood close, clasped her wrist and flattened her hand against his bare chest.

Voice rough, he said, "You tell me."

Yup, sticky. But what she noticed most was the heat of his skin, the light covering of hair and the undeniable strength. *You do not like macho men*, she reminded herself. But without meaning to, her fingers contracted in a gentle exploration of his muscle.

"Brooklin."

She looked up and got caught in his gaze.

Slowly, very slowly, Nathan leaned down until his mouth touched hers. When she didn't pull away, he turned his head a little, making for a better fit, and kissed her in a way she hadn't been kissed in far too long.

Well before she was ready, he lifted his head. "I'd have you real close right about now if I wasn't a mess."

She still didn't know what to say. Confusion swamped her. *Talk about sending mixed signals.*

"Will you stay with me tonight?"

Trying to deny the disappointment she felt, she explained, "I don't need to. Your friend Jason, and his nephew, Colt, got everything installed."

"I know. I talked with Jason earlier." He released her wrist and took a step back. "I wasn't asking you to camp on my couch, though you're always welcome to do that. I meant that I wanted you to stay with me, as in right next to me, preferably in my bed, but I can make the couch work if you've gotten attached to it."

But... Brooklin scowled at him. "I was there for two nights and you barely noticed."

"That's a joke, right?" He laughed, his attention on her mouth. "I've chased you since the first day I met you. I thought I'd made my interest plain enough."

"I thought so, too."

"So you honestly believed you could be that close, sleeping all soft and warm on my couch, and I wouldn't be aware of it on every level, for every damned second that you were there?"

The way he watched her mouth caused Brooklin to

lick her lips in nervousness. His gaze sharpened, then came up to her eyes.

She let out a breath. "I don't know."

He touched her cheek. "You slept at my house because you were worried. You don't need to be anymore, so I don't feel like I'm taking advantage by making myself clear."

Her heart swelled. "So the reason you didn't talk to me, the reason you went straight to bed, was because you were being considerate?"

"Trying my best." He tipped up her chin. "It wasn't easy, Brooklin. But because of the circumstances, you were off-limits."

"I thought…" Brooklin shook her head. "When you didn't show any interest, I wasn't sure what to think."

"Think that I'm a saint if you want." He smiled. "But now you're fine, your house is secure, and if you come to me, it's because you want to, not because you're worried about being alone."

Actually, she was still worried, which was ridiculous. Her problems and all the danger were long behind her.

Nathan scrubbed a hand over his face. "I'm rushing you, aren't I? We've only had one date, if Screwy Louie's even counts."

"It counts," she said softly. "And yes, I'd like to stay with you tonight. That is, part of the night. I really do need to be in my own place in the morning for my routine—"

Nathan kissed her. He kept a hand on the back of her neck, but still didn't hold her close. Honestly, she didn't care about his sticky shirt, but again, he ended the kiss before she was ready.

"You're welcome all night, but if you decide you need

to head back over here, just let me know and I'll walk with you."

It was a wonderful offer—and Brooklin accepted.

NATHAN TRIED TO maintain his persona of a calm, in-control guy, but the second Brooklin agreed, he got semihard. "You don't need a pillow and blanket tonight. I have them on my bed."

"I don't plan to sleep there anyway."

So how much time would she give him? An hour? Two? He wasn't sure a week would be enough, but he only nodded.

"Let me grab my keys and lock up."

When she started in, he followed her, then drew up short at the sight of a .38 revolver on her desk. "You have a gun."

Startled, Brooklin looked at the weapon, flushed and then lifted her chin. "Yes, I do."

"When did you get it?"

"Before I moved here." Defiantly, she stated, "I have my conceal carry."

"You don't carry it when you're jogging. I would have noticed."

"No."

His thoughts continued. "You had it at Screwy Louie's?"

"Yes."

Damn. *What, or who, had scared her so badly?* Nathan picked up the gun, found it fully loaded and saw it had a laser. Cocking a brow, he asked, "Need the laser for your aim?"

"I don't know. I've done plenty of practice, but I've never had to use it when I was in trouble. I figured if I was a person who panicked, the laser would help ensure I hit what I aimed at."

"Which would be…what? Or should I ask who?"

"Actually, you should just mind your own business."

Nathan eyed her militant stance, the rigid way she held herself and the rebellion in her eyes. She considered him the law, assumed he would harass her for arming herself and prepared to defy him. "Would you mind if I took you shooting sometime? I could offer some tips."

Her face went blank, then flushed with relief. "I'd like that a lot."

"Good." Still treading carefully, he asked, "You feel like you need to bring this tonight? Or could we leave it here?" He resisted the urge to tell her he'd keep her safe. She was an independent woman who'd taken measures to ensure her own safety against a threat he didn't yet understand. She didn't need a caveman undermining her efforts.

"I'll leave it here." She took it from him, handling the gun safely but with confidence. "I have a box I lock it in."

Without being invited, Nathan followed her down the hall and into her bedroom. From her nightstand drawer she removed a sturdy metal case with a fingerprint lock. Inside it he saw a box of additional ammo, along with pepper spray. He watched her lock it away, put the box back in the drawer and cover it with a book.

"I already showered and brushed my teeth." She headed out past him, went to the kitchen and grabbed her keys from a decorative hook on the wall. She pocketed her phone and turned to him with a smile. "Ready if you are."

Very ready. "Let's go, then. I'll need five minutes to shower." *And to cool down so I can show some finesse.*

She turned on the porch lights outside each door, stepped out and locked up securely.

"You added the extra locks to the doors?"

"Yes." Her gaze didn't meet his. "Seemed like a good idea for a woman living alone."

"I agree." Putting his arm around her, Nathan led her to the yard. The houses were close together and it took less than a minute to get to his front door. He only had one lock and he got it open quickly. They stepped into darkness.

Brooklin went still beside him until he turned on a lamp.

"I like your house."

He glanced around. "Thanks. I haven't done much with it except to make myself comfortable."

Smiling, she, too, looked around. "The furnishings are a lot like you. Big and sturdy and strong with no fuss."

He'd never thought of furniture that way, but he did have an oversize recliner, and the couch was twice the size of hers, taking up one entire wall. "I'm a bigger guy, so—"

"Yes, you are." She reached for the last two remaining buttons on his shirt.

"Brooklin." He caught her wrists. "I need a shower."

"Yes, you do." As she stripped the shirt off him, she looked at his chest and arms and abs. Idly, she touched him, her expression fascinated. When she looked up at him, her golden eyes were glowing. "Think you can make it a very fast shower?"

"Fastest in the history of mankind."

"Good. I'll wait in your bedroom." She peeked down the hall. "This way, right?"

Would she wait for him in bed? "Same setup as

yours." He led her halfway, then detoured into the bath-room while she went on. Since he was already hard, he didn't bother grabbing clean clothes or waiting for the water to warm. He stepped under the cold spray, scrubbed from head to toe and dried with the speed of light—all while telling himself to get a handle on his lust.

Brooklin had been reluctant enough that he didn't want to rush her now.

As he lectured himself, he stepped into his bedroom, a damp towel wrapped around his hips. He was just in time to see her climbing up into the bed. Naked. Her back to him.

He'd never seen anything sexier or more exciting.

While he soaked up the sight of her, she settled her-self in the middle of the bed, noticed him and smiled. "That was fast."

"Not exactly what a guy wants to hear the first time with a woman."

Laughing, she half turned toward him, resting on an elbow, one leg bent. Her thick hair hung over her shoulder, a silky hank loosely curled around her breast.

"Jesus, you're beautiful."

She bit her lip, then said, "Drop the towel and I'll see if I can return the compliment."

No problem dropping the towel; he wasn't a modest man. But he snorted over the rest of what she said. "Men aren't beautiful, especially not with a face like mine." He sat on the bed beside her.

Slowly her smile faded. She came up next to him, lightly touching her fingertips to his mouth, his nose, then over the scar that cut from his temple to the side of his mouth. "I think your face is amazing." Leaning in, she kissed him.

Not the way he wanted to be kissed, not on his mouth with lots of tongue and wet heat.

No, she kissed a feathery path down that damned scar. "You're incredibly handsome, Nathan."

Ill at ease with the soft talk, he bore her down to the bed and rested over her on his elbows. "If you say so." He took her mouth the way he'd dreamed of doing it, open and hot, his tongue sliding over hers, deeper and hungrier by the second.

Her breasts against his chest felt indescribably good and he had to touch her, first gently, just learning the shape and feel of her. Her nipples thrust against his palms and he used his fingertips to roll them, to pluck until she was panting and moving against him.

He kissed her jaw, her throat, then dipped down to take her nipples, one by one, into his mouth. He thought he was doing okay, keeping a firm hold on his control, until she reached between their bodies and took his dick in her hand.

Nathan forgot what he was doing. He'd been too long without a woman, plus he'd wanted this particular woman for a while now.

She seemed to understand because she said, "Do you have a condom?"

He had a whole box. "Yeah." Letting her continue—he didn't have the strength to stop her—he moved to slide next to her, giving him access to her body, too.

Such a beautiful body, all lean and strong from running, but still soft and supple, too. He bent to her breast, sucking gently on one nipple while dipping his hand between her legs.

Wet. Hot.

"It's been a while for me," she said shakily.

He didn't mind admitting, "Me, too."

As he worked two fingers into her, her breath shuddered out. "So get the condom."

Nathan half laughed, half groaned. "Yes, ma'am."

She touched him, over his shoulders and chest and down to his thighs, while he found the box in the bedside drawer, tore the condom open with his teeth and rolled it on. Soon as he moved over her, she opened her legs and he fitted to her perfectly.

At first, he just rubbed himself against her, his eyes closed as he absorbed the feel of her under him.

Glad that she'd left on the lights, he looked at her, seeing her hair spread out around her on the pillow and her eyes, those amazing eyes, glittering with need.

They both groaned as he pressed into her, the fit at first excruciatingly tight until he got past the initial resistance. Then her body eased to accommodate him.

"A very long time," he murmured, loving the snug grip around his erection.

"Too long," she agreed. She shifted under him, groaned softly and said, "I'm so glad you're my neighbor, Nathan."

Hell, from his perspective, he was already more. But there was still so much he didn't know about her, especially about her past.

Right now, at this moment, he really didn't care. "Me, too."

Lacing his fingers with hers, he stretched her arms up high over her head and, starting slow, rocked deep into her again and again.

He wanted to savor this first time, to enjoy her to the fullest, but she wrapped her legs around him, lifting her hips to hurry him along. He felt her stiffened nipples against his chest and watched her face twist with pleasure.

When she bit his shoulder, moaning softly, he gave up. Scooping an arm beneath her hips, he lifted her into his heavy thrusts and soon they were both lost.

Fifteen minutes later, with Brooklin held tight in his arms, Nathan was thinking that he'd like to start all over again.

Then Brooklin said, "It's late." She kissed his chest, nuzzled her nose against his chest hair and announced softly, "I need to get home now."

WHEN VIOLET RUSHED into the little boutique on South Street, she almost ran into Brooklin. The two women, narrowly avoiding a collision, stepped back, laughed and greeted each other.

"I'm sorry," Brooklin said. "I was on my way out, thinking about…" She shook her head. "Obviously I wasn't paying attention."

Thinking about what? "My fault," Violet insisted. "I was hoping to get to work a little earlier today—" She wanted a few minutes alone with Hogan, enough minutes, hopefully, to have an encore. "But I wanted to come by here first."

"Busy as you stay, I imagine you're often in a rush."

"Very true," Violet said. "It's a hazard of running my own business. But I don't mind." She smiled. "I came in to buy more jewelry, but I didn't expect to find you here."

"Really?" Brooklin gestured toward the display case, now completely filled. "I had a few more necklaces to drop off."

"That's what I bought," Violet said. "I think it's called a druzy necklace. I'd never heard of that before, but it's beautiful and unique, so I was hoping to find matching earrings."

Brooklin gave her a knowing smile. "Dressing up for someone in particular?"

"That's the plan. So far Hogan has only seen me in work clothes. Mostly because, as you said, I'm always working. And while my shorts and T-shirts aren't exactly a uniform, they're not very pretty, either. I can't get too dressy—it wouldn't be appropriate and I'd probably end up ruining whatever I wear. But I did have a new pair of skinny jeans and this very pretty top and the blue of the druzy stones goes perfectly with it."

"You got the natural druzy agate? I hope so. It'd be perfect with your eyes."

"I did! And it's beautiful, so I'll take that as a compliment."

"That's exactly how I meant it." Other ladies sidled in around them, but they didn't pay much attention as they naturally scooted to the side to get out of the way. "So you and Hogan are a couple? You know, I thought so, but I wasn't sure—"

Oh crud, Violet thought, knowing good and well that Hogan didn't want her starting any other rumors. "We're not a couple. Not the way you mean. Did you know Hogan is a widower?"

"Nathan's never mentioned anything about it. I only knew he was single."

Aha. So she was with Nathan. "You didn't ask?"

"I value my privacy so much that I don't think it would be fair for me to pry."

"With me, you don't even have to pry. I'm an open book." Hogan, not so much. "The thing is, he's such a gorgeous guy that I'd like, just once, for him to see me fixed up just a little."

Proving she was a very nice woman and not at all nosy, Brooklin nodded. "I completely understand." She hooked Violet's arm and drew her outside to the sidewalk, saying low, "The earrings in there are overpriced. Why don't you let me show you some that I haven't yet brought in? They'll match the necklace perfectly, and you'll get them for half the price."

"Oh, but I don't want to cheat you—"

"You wouldn't. I love that boutique, but she marks up all my jewelry by almost fifty percent. It sells, so I'm not complaining. But we're friends now, right?"

"I hope so," Violet said. She'd liked Brooklin the moment she met her. The lady was smart, beautiful, talented, and best of all, she hadn't given Hogan the time of day. No flirting from her. She was as far from Joni Jeffers as a woman could get.

"Good. I met Honor and Lexie, but I haven't really gotten to know them yet. And I know Nathan, of course, since he's my neighbor."

"And he's been chasing you."

Brooklin laughed. "True. I wasn't really running away all that hard, though."

"So he finally caught you?"

"Yes, and it was pretty wonderful."

Violet couldn't help but grin.

"I'm not yet sure what it means, if anything. I'm just trying to take it one day at a time."

A wise woman. "You know Jason and Colt, too, right? They're Hogan's brother and son."

She nodded. "They came over and installed some security stuff for my house, so I got to know them a little better. So far everyone in the town, even Mr. Westbrook, who's almost seventy and cuts his grass in his Speedo, has been super nice. But I don't know... I felt like you and I clicked."

"I thought so, too," Violet said. "It helped that you weren't flirting with Hogan."

Brooklin laughed. "He overwhelmed me. I was trying to stay low-key, and at the time, I was also dodging Nathan. Hogan wouldn't let me. He can be… Let's call it pushy."

"When it comes to attractive women, he's very pushy." Apparently Nathan could be pushy, too. Or maybe *persistent* was a better word. Whatever, Violet liked Nathan a lot; he deserved to be happy.

"Trust me," Brooklin said, "every word Hogan said to me was for Nathan's benefit, and I knew it." She shook her head. "Your Hogan is funny, very handsome, and I'm betting he's a handful."

Your Hogan. Thinking very carnal thoughts, Violet sighed. "He is." A wonderful, caring, sexy handful.

"He's also all yours. Anyone with eyes can see it." She nudged Violet with her shoulder. "Don't worry. I won't say anything to anyone. Just let me give you the earrings at cost, okay? I'll enjoy knowing you have them."

"Since you insist, that would be wonderful. But then you'll have to let me reciprocate with some free meals or something."

"Maybe when you're taking a break? We could chat more."

"Deal." Without having realized it, Violet saw that Brooklin had led her toward a parking lot used for all the kitschy little shops in the strip. "Your car is here, too?"

"Yes." Brooklin started to point. "I'm that little—"

The loud revving of an engine cut her off, and two seconds later a dark green minivan with tinted windows gunned out of the lot, coming right for them. Violet tried to scream, but nothing came out.

Brooklin grabbed her, and together they fell between parked cars, crashing up against a railing, a brick wall and the concrete floor.

Never slowing down, the van sped away.

Stunned, Violet caught her breath, took one look at Brooklin, and when she saw she was bleeding, she gasped. "Oh my God, are you okay?"

Her elbow was scraped raw, blood trickling down her forearm.

"Yes," Brooklin said, her voice clipped, almost angry, as she carefully sat up. "You?"

"I'm—" Violet gasped. When she put pressure on her ankle, it hurt. "Oh, hell." She looked down and saw that her foot and ankle were turning a ghastly bluish purple, already swollen.

"Sit still." Ignoring the blood on her arm, Brooklin drew out her phone, scrolled through her recent calls, clicked to connect, and a moment later she said, "Nathan. I… This is Brooklin. Are you busy?"

NATHAN COULDN'T REMEMBER the last time he was so pissed. Brooklin's elbow had stopped bleeding and Violet was now on her feet and both of them were so damned stubborn, he wanted to howl.

He'd have liked to take them to the emergency room. In fact, Brooklin encouraged Violet to do just that. But they both decided that they not only didn't need medical care, they didn't need help of any kind.

For the tenth time, Brooklin said, "I don't need you to drive me home. I just… I reacted without thinking."

"We were both pretty rattled," Violet said, and then she checked the time on her phone. "Seriously, I need to get going now. Mondays are always a little crazy. Actually, lately, every day is crazy."

Nathan didn't like it, but what could he do? "You're sure you're okay to drive?"

"Yes." Gingerly, Violet put her weight on her now very swollen, black-and-blue left foot. "If it was my right, I'd be in some trouble. But I promise I won't cause a wreck."

"I still think I should call Hogan."

"There's no reason. He's probably already at the diner right now, and there's no one else to fill in for me. Besides, I really do feel fine." She winced as she took a hobbling step.

"Right," Nathan growled. "Perfectly fine." He pointed at her. "I wasn't talking about having Hogan fill in for you, and you know it. You should call him."

She turned even more stubborn. "Should I call Jason and Sullivan, too? What about my cook? My next-door neighbor? You're not making any sense, Nathan."

Did she hope to hide her relationship with Hogan? Apparently so. "It's not my place to—"

"No," she agreed quickly. "It's not."

"Fine, then I'll just…" He looked around and saw that while he'd been debating with Violet, Brooklin had almost slipped away. "Don't do it," he shouted to her from across the lot.

With her back to him, she froze, her shoulders coming up in an exaggerated flinch.

"I mean it, Brooklin. Give me one more minute to get Violet in her car and—" He looked back to see Violet sliding behind the wheel. His gaze shifted back and forth between the two women, but Brooklin still stood there, and Violet now waved.

"I'm fine, Nathan, just as I told you I'd be."

After another quick, critical glance at Brooklin, he went to Violet. "You're going straight to the diner?"

"Yes. As it is, I might be late, though, so can we wrap this up."

"Yes, we can." He bent and kissed her forehead. "Take it easy, okay? Get some ice on that ankle."

"I will."

With nothing else to do, he headed for Brooklin. She hadn't budged an inch, so he stepped around in front of her. She looked guilty, angry and pale. "I suppose you're fine, too?"

"Of course."

He nodded. "Come on, then." He walked the rest of the way with her to her car, but instead of getting inside, she walked around to sit on the fender.

She didn't say anything, and he didn't yet trust himself to speak.

"I'm sorry I bothered you."

That was definitely the wrong thing to say, he decided, when his head nearly shot off his shoulders. "Why did you call me? And so we're clear, that's the sheriff asking."

She shook her head. "Gut reaction. I was…at first afraid. But the car left and didn't come back, so—"

"Minivan. You said it was a minivan, not a car."

"Yes."

"Dark green, but neither of you saw the plates."

"I told you, I wasn't exactly looking."

"And," he said, still fuming, "because of dark tinted windows, you have no idea who was driving it?"

"We couldn't see a thing."

"But that's not what I asked you." Nathan had a feeling she knew damn good and well who was behind the wheel of that van.

Almost proving his assumption, she looked away, staring out at the street.

Nathan tamped down his temper. Trust, he knew, was a fragile thing that had to be earned. But damn, she didn't make it easy.

"Can you admit," he said, trying to sound reasonable, "that me being the sheriff had nothing to do with you calling?"

"Yes," she whispered. "I can admit that." Then she glanced at him. "But I'm still sorry for bothering you."

Nathan felt downright mean. "I shouldn't be surprised. After all, we had sex two days ago, you left immediately after and you've dodged me since."

Looking cornered, Brooklin fretted with the edge of the bandage wrapped around her elbow. Mr. Marson, from the pharmacy right next to the lot, had walked it out to her, saying someone had told him she was sitting there bleeding everywhere.

Brooklin had assured him that it was fine, just a scrape and that she'd clean it and put on a fresh bandage when she got home. Nathan had thanked Mr. Marson, and then the arguing had begun.

He didn't want to argue with her. He wanted... What? To pamper her? She wasn't a woman who enjoyed being pampered. To protect her? How could he when she wouldn't even tell him the threat?

Though he'd asked around, no one else had noticed any more than Brooklin or Violet had. The van had nearly run them over, then disappeared. Of course, he'd alerted his deputies and the local police, but there were a lot of green vans in Ohio.

Unable to stop himself, Nathan touched a tendril of her hair, half in and half out of a fat braid. He trailed his fingers down her shoulder to the edge of that bandage. "Brooklin..."

In a sudden rush, she pressed herself against him.

He could feel her trembling and he hated it. Folding her in close, lifting her onto his lap, he whispered, "Shh. I've got you."

Her hand fisted on his shoulder. "But that's just it," she said, agonized. "I can't lean on you."

"Sure you can." He rubbed his hands up and down her back, his thoughts racing. "Is that why you ran off in such a hurry? You don't want to lean on me?"

"No." She nodded. "Yes."

Trying for a little levity, maybe to make up for his overbearing anger a moment before, he asked, "So it wasn't that I'm a lousy lay?"

She sat back, horrified. "Is that what you thought? Oh my God, *no*. You were amazing. You are amazing."

The grin tugged at his mouth, and when her eyes went wide, then narrowed in suspicion, the laugh broke free.

"Jerk," she said, trying to shove away from him.

He held on. "I was teasing you—that's all." Lower, he added, "I am confused about why you booked, though."

Giving up, she dropped her forehead to his chest. "You scare me, Nathan. Not like my past scares me or that van scared me. But I like you, and I don't want you to get the wrong impression."

Piecing together the things she said proved challenging, but he gave it a shot. "So if you tell me who you think is bothering you, who you're afraid of, you think I'll get the wrong idea?" Meaning, she thought he'd... What? Think badly of her?

"Don't sound so incredulous. It's possible."

Since he didn't know her background, she could be right. "Do you have a criminal record?"

Her mouth flattened and she shook her head.

"You haven't gotten away with murder or armed robbery?"

"No. Don't be ridiculous."

"You're not married?" Damn, don't let her be married. He could take armed robbery easier than that.

"No, I'm not married and never have been, but I was engaged once."

Once, but not anymore. "I'm glad you're not still engaged." He kissed her nose. "Nothing else could be all that important."

Briefly, she closed her eyes, then opened them to give him a direct stare. "Okay, if it's not that important, will you give me a little more time to tell you?"

He didn't want to. He wanted to insist she tell him right now. But insisting would just make her withdraw and he knew it. "You *will* tell me? Soon?"

"Yes. I just need to put my thoughts together."

What could he do but agree? "All right."

She touched the buttons on his shirt. "Could I come over tonight?"

So once again she was afraid, and that made him a slightly better choice than being alone? Not that it mattered, because he'd never turn her down. "Sure. What time?"

"What time will you get home?"

"If all goes well, around six."

"Six works for me." She looked at his mouth. "I could fix you dinner? I'm actually a decent cook."

He'd rather take her straight to bed, but again, he had to take things slowly. "Sounds like a plan." Ignoring the few people gawking at them, Nathan drew her in for a kiss. "You'll take care of that arm when you get home?"

"Yes. Remember, I used to be a nurse." This time she leaned in and kissed him. "I'll see you at six."

CHAPTER THIRTEEN

HOGAN STAYED BUSY till damn near eight o'clock. Weekdays were easier than weekends, so once the dinner crowd died down a little, he shifted everything to one grill and started cleaning the others. With any luck he'd be able to grab some alone time with Violet after the diner closed.

It surprised Hogan when Mr. Marson, a pharmacist in his early fifties, usually distracted and brusque, deliberately caught his eye. The man rarely gave him more than a passing greeting. But now, his hands tucked deep in his pockets and his gaze concerned, he looked ready to settle in and chat.

Curious, Hogan said, "Mr. Marson, how are you?"

"I'm fine. How's Violet?"

That threw him. "Busy, I suppose. I haven't seen her much tonight." And it bugged the hell out of him. Since that night they'd had sex, she'd teased him endlessly. Subtly, so that others never caught them. He wanted her nonstop, and yet today, she'd stayed out of sight. It had been busy, sure, but they both knew she could have spared a few minutes to visit, or at least to say hi, if she'd wanted to. Most nights she came to the prep area to at least steal a kiss. Often she was the one to hand him an order for ribs.

Today, she hadn't come anywhere near him, or anywhere near enough to where he grilled for him to even get a peek of her. Why would she decide to ignore him now?

"Busy?" Marson said. "What do you mean, she's busy? I told her she should keep that ankle elevated with ice on it. When I didn't see her inside, I hoped she was at home resting."

Hogan stared at him. Violet had hurt her ankle?

"That other one," Marson continued, "the new lady, her elbow was bleeding enough that I'm not sure she didn't need stitches. I know I'm not a medical doctor, but I'm also not an idiot."

"No, of course not." What the hell had happened?

Like it was somehow his fault, Marson glared at Hogan. "It's a wonder both of them weren't killed, and she's still on her feet? Not a good idea. Not at all."

Killed? Jesus.

"Told them both to go to the ER to get checked, but even the sheriff couldn't convince them."

"Nathan was there?"

"He's the sheriff. Of course he was there. Wouldn't you call the sheriff if someone tried to run you down?"

Hogan stared at him. By the second he had more questions than answers. "You're saying someone deliberately tried to hit Violet and Brooklin?"

"I didn't see it myself, but the way it was told to me, that's exactly what happened. Doesn't make any sense, but you know how stories grow and get more dramatic. I was curious, though. So what do you think?"

Since this was the first he'd heard of it, Hogan didn't know what to think. He didn't want to admit that to Mr. Marson, though, so he asked, "What did Nathan think?"

"He was plenty irate—I know that. And he put in some calls. But the van was gone, so what could be done?"

"I don't know."

"What did Violet say?"

"Not much." As in, nothing at all.

"Ah, she's still upset. She did look ready to cry. Not because of her ankle, though. I think she was just shook-up."

"I'm sure you're right." Hogan barely knew Marson, but apparently he loved gossip. Maybe working at the pharmacy was like working as a bartender. He got to hear everyone's stories. "If you'll excuse me, I'll get my son to watch the grill and I'll go check on her."

"You'll make her take it easy? Get her off her feet?"

If the whole thing didn't sound so serious, Hogan would have laughed. He had *no* control over Violet. But he said, "Yes, I will."

"You make sure she's got it propped up, okay? And discolored as it was already, if she doesn't keep ice on it, it's only going to bruise worse." He picked up a pair of tongs. "Go on and get your son. I'll keep an eye on things until he gets here."

Divided, Hogan eyed him. "You grill?"

Marson snorted. "Of course I grill. What red-blooded man doesn't? Go on. I won't let anything burn."

"Thank you." Hogan found Colt first. He was on a break, sitting with a tableful of friends, including that supercute girl, Charish, who was new to the area. He decided not to bother him, but somehow Colt sensed him and looked up. As soon as their gazes locked, he was on his feet.

When Colt reached him, he asked, "What's wrong?"

"Who said anything was?"

Colt frowned. "You know Violet was hurt, don't you?"

Well, hell. Did everyone know except him?

Colt nudged him toward the kitchen as he explained, "She didn't want you to know. No idea why. But she said I wasn't to bother you. I'd have told you tonight anyway, after work, but since you already know, will you check on her? She's been rotating things, working the floor for an hour, then disappearing into her office for an hour. I've tried to help out, but you know how she is."

Yes, he knew. Stubborn, determined and sweet. "How's her ankle?"

"I swear, Dad, it makes my ankles hurt to look at it."

Hogan nodded. "I hate to drag you away—"

"No big deal. You want me to watch the grill?"

"Just for a few minutes."

"Got it. Take your time."

Hogan watched him go—then he saw Colt's friends at the table, all of them laughing, half-empty plates in front of them, not a care in the world, no real responsibilities.

He also saw Charish's face as she watched Colt go. Damn.

When he walked into the office, Violet was sitting on the floor, her back against the wall, a plastic storage bag of ice on her ankle and a puddle around her foot.

She looked up at him and said, "Um…"

Hogan closed the door behind him, then squatted down by her foot and lifted the ice pack. Colt had warned him, but still it nearly took his breath away. Swollen, black and red and blue, it had to be broken. "You need to go get an X-ray."

She groaned, squeezed her eyes shut and whispered, "I am not a weak person."

"Definitely not," he agreed.

"First that stupid pneumonia, and now this. I never get sick and I've never been hurt before. Then you show up and…this is ridiculous."

Hogan heard the note of tears in her voice and it almost destroyed him. "Is it hurting that much?"

"No, and don't talk all sweet to me. I'm sappy enough already."

"Sappy?"

"Sitting in here, feeling sorry for myself and wondering if you're going to think I'm one of those women who always has an issue."

First things first. "This is leaking everywhere. Don't you have a real ice pack here?"

"No."

"Then at least let me get you another bag."

"In the cooler. Colt's been refilling it for me."

A picnic-sized cooler sat beside her desk. Inside were two more individual bags of ice. Hogan sat back on his heels. "My kid is amazing."

"I know. He's the one who got me all sappy, babying me and being so sweet. I had to threaten to slug him if he didn't quit."

"Perfect reaction to kindness."

"I told you, that stuff makes me sappy!"

Shaking his head—and grinning—Hogan got a new bag and, as gently as possible, placed it on her ankle. "I'm sure he didn't mean to upset you. He's worried about you—that's all."

"But I'm used to taking care of myself. I don't want him to worry. I don't want you to worry, either."

On that last word, her voice broke. Hogan sat down beside her, same position with his back against the wall, and took her hand. She squeezed his fingers hard. He wanted to kiss her, but he didn't want to do anything to make those tears spill over.

"Will you tell me what happened? All I know from

Marson is that you could have been killed, and a van was somehow involved."

With a new focus, she nodded. "It was the craziest thing." More animated and less teary, she told him about the speeding van, how Brooklin had reacted and how Nathan had looked like he could chew nails. "Nathan's dangerous. If that idiot driver wasn't already gone, I think our good sheriff would have had him for lunch."

"Brooklin called Nathan?"

"Yes."

Hogan looked at her small hand, at the short, unpainted nails, and asked quietly, "Why didn't you call me?" It was a weird thing to admit, but he was both insulted and maybe a little hurt that she hadn't.

She tried to laugh that off. "Right. If I was going to call anyone, it would have been Kristy. She's less vital to the running of things here than you or Jerry."

"I'm different from Jerry or Kristy."

"True. But I'm paying you to cook ribs, not listen to my hysterics."

Though the insult grew, he kept his voice calm. "Were you hysterical?"

"Maybe for a minute." Her head dropped forward. "This stupid floor is not comfortable."

"No, it's not." He brushed his thumb over her knuckles. Her small, slender hands were delicate but strong. She'd had a lifetime of working, pushing past adversity. But when he thought about her doing this all day, serving customers on that hurt ankle, then coming in here to suffer alone, it bothered him deep down to his soul.

Damn it. He didn't want things going too fast or getting too serious. But he also didn't want this, her cutting him out and dealing with things on her own when she clearly needed someone.

He wanted to be that someone. At least for this. And for the diner.

And for sex.

Angry at himself, and at the idea that she really could have died, Hogan asked, "You can stand on it?"

"Of course. I can wiggle my toes and flex it and everything. It's uncomfortable, but I can do it."

"Obviously, since you've been working."

"You can stow the sarcasm, Hogan. There was no one else to fill in for me, and things had to get done."

Frustration ripped through him. "You're the boss."

Incredulous, she stared at him. "More sarcasm? Colt is a lot nicer than you."

"Thank God."

She gave him a cross frown. "I was joking. You're very nice." Then she added, "I honestly don't think it's broken. I just twisted it."

"It looks bad, honey."

"I bruise easily." Settling back with a sigh, she leaned her head on his shoulder. "I would have bet money that Colt wouldn't tell you. I made him promise he wouldn't."

"He didn't."

She turned her face up to see him. "Then how did you know?"

"Mr. Marson. He said your foot should be elevated."

"That old snitch." She sighed. "It's hard to prop it up in here. When I get home, I can—"

"Violet." Hogan knew he had to tread carefully. She wasn't unreasonable, not usually, so hopefully she'd do the right thing. But he had to inch carefully around her pride. "Don't you think you should head home now?"

Her groan was long and dramatic, ending with a disgusted but resigned "Yes, I guess so."

"Thank you." With her agreement, Hogan released some of the tension in his shoulders. "Maybe I could—"

"No." She cut him off with a scowl. "I can drive myself, okay? I'm not incapacitated."

"Still…" His brain scrambled on ways to make it work. Maybe Colt could stay on the grill. One of the dishwashers could serve, and—

"No, Hogan. If it was that bad, I promise I'd say so. Besides, it's my left foot."

"So you won't need it to brake the car. But getting to the car, and out of the car into your house—"

"Are you serious?" She rolled her eyes. "I've been working all night. Going to and from the car won't be a problem."

Hogan cupped her chin and looked into her eyes. "You're one hundred percent sure about this?"

Being snide, she asked, "Gee, Dad, want me to call you when I get home safely?"

He kissed her mulish mouth and said, "As a matter of fact, I do."

FIRST THING ON Tuesday morning, Hogan headed out to track down Nathan. He hadn't slept much, mostly because he'd spent the night fighting the urge to go to Violet's house and take care of her. Or *try* to take care of her. The woman could be difficult when it came to her independence.

His concern, apparently, was something she didn't want.

She'd made it clear, in no uncertain terms, that she wouldn't be missing any work. Violet had the notion that he wanted to take over.

Not true. Or rather, not entirely true.

For the most part, Hogan had no problem at all working for her. She was a fair, funny boss.

Other times, he resented the hell out of the fact that
she got to call the shots.

This was one of those times.

Knowing Nathan left the house early, Hogan went
up the porch steps, raised his hand to knock—and it
opened before he could.

Brooklin almost ran into him.

In one cursory glance, Hogan took in her dishev-
eled nightshirt over shorts, sleep-rumpled hair and still-
slumberous eyes. He also saw the bandage on her arm.

So she'd been hurt, had called Nathan, then spent
the night.

But Violet hadn't even planned to let him know.

At the moment, Brooklin looked as startled to see
him as he was to see her.

"Hogan," she gasped, her voice thin.

With embarrassment—or something else?

He couldn't help it. He grinned. "Morning, Brooklin.
It's nice to see you again."

"I was just…" Her voice trailed off. "Yes, nice to see
you. I'm sorry, but I need to go. Nathan's in the kitchen."

"No," Hogan said. "He's right behind you."

She jumped, turned to Nathan and said, "You have
company."

"So I see."

Hogan watched Nathan's eyes narrow and saw Brooklin's widen in reaction. Then Nathan brought her close
and kissed her on the mouth.

Whistling, Hogan looked down at his feet—but he
listened.

"I'll get home earlier tonight," Nathan said. "But it's
practice night."

"Practice night?"

"For the band. You know I'm part of a band, right?"

"Yes. Hogan mentioned it when he first introduced himself."

Hogan whistled a little louder.

Ignoring him, Nathan said, "We practice in my garage every Tuesday, but we've missed a few weeks while some of the guys took their vacations." He drew her close again. "You're welcome to come over anyway."

"I don't want to interrupt."

"We finish up around nine, otherwise the neighbors complain."

"I promise not to complain," she said. "I'm actually curious to hear you."

"Feel free to listen, and after it breaks up, you and I have some talking to do, right?"

Feeling the tension, Hogan wisely stepped away to lean on the porch rail. He heard whispered protests from Brooklin, smooth insistence from Nathan.

How nice would it be to have Violet spend the night, to wake up with her in the morning—even to debate with her on the front porch?

Not that long ago it would have been an appalling thought, yet now he envied Nathan for it.

A few seconds later, Brooklin brushed past him as she left, hurrying over to her own house.

"You want to come in?" Nathan asked. "I still have some coffee left."

Hogan grinned, but said nothing until he and Nathan were behind a closed door. Nathan, freshly shaved and dressed for work but with his shirt still untucked and unbuttoned, headed back for the kitchen.

Hogan followed him. "Well, that was interesting."

Stopping at the coffeepot, Nathan returned his grin.

"Hope you enjoyed it, because you probably just set me back. She's prickly as hell, and twice as private."

"Probably why she and Violet get along." He thought of Brooklin's reaction at seeing him and asked, "I couldn't tell if she was embarrassed because I saw her here, or if she was maybe… I don't know. More than startled?"

Nathan turned grim. "Finding a guy standing there might have alarmed her before she realized it was you."

Did that mean she really was in danger? Sympathetic to Nathan's mood, Hogan stated his concerns carefully. "I heard they were together yesterday when they both got hurt?"

"That's why you're here?" He handed Hogan the cup of coffee.

"Yeah." Not needing an invite, Hogan pulled out a chair and sat at the table, waiting for Nathan to join him. "What the hell happened?"

Nathan thoughtfully sipped his coffee. Rather than answer, he asked a question of his own. "Did you talk to Violet?"

"Yes." Hogan didn't give the frustrating details of how she'd tried to keep him in the dark. "She told me that someone in a van almost ran them over. She seems to think it was deliberate."

Nathan frowned. "Yeah."

"Yeah, what?"

Nathan rubbed the back of his neck, then met Hogan's gaze. "Are you and Violet involved?" He shook his head. "I mean, for more than convenience or whatever."

Drawing himself up, Hogan scowled. "What the hell does that have to do with anything?"

"You're putting me in a bad spot, Hogan. Brooklin is private, so I don't want to talk to just anyone."

Yet Hogan could see that he *did* want to talk. "I work with her. I like her. We're…friends."

Nathan snorted. "Look, I can either give you the report I filed, or I can tell you what I really think is going on. But if you aren't involved with Violet, if you don't care a hell of a lot for her, then I'd say it's none of your damned business."

Hogan stewed for about three seconds, then said through his teeth, "We're involved." He pointed at Nathan. "But we're still working it out, so keep it to yourself."

Nathan sat back in his chair. "Violet's not a woman to play games."

He gave him a dry look. "Since we're involved, don't you think I already know that?"

"Maybe."

Not a woman to play games, no. Violet was a woman to respect, to admire and to desire. Somewhat reluctantly, Hogan admitted, "I care about her, and if she's in trouble, I need to know."

After gulping down the rest of his coffee, Nathan stood. "Fine. But I've only got five minutes before I need to head out the door, so I have to make it short and to the point."

Hogan stood, too. "I'm listening."

"Brooklin is hiding something from her past, something that happened before she moved here. I have no idea yet what it might be, but she's afraid and my instincts tell me there's danger. Hopefully soon she'll tell me everything. I can't very well protect her if she doesn't."

Hogan soaked that in. "That's why she hired Colt and Jason to set up the security on her house?"

"From my suggestion, yeah. I don't think she's a woman who spooks easily, but she saw some shadows on the front porch, then heard someone trying to open her back door."

"Hell, that'd unsettle anyone, man or woman."

"Agreed. I get the feeling, though, that Brooklin is afraid of someone specific. You can't repeat any of this, but now that Violet is involved, I suggest you keep an eye out, especially if she's closing up the diner at night."

Without thinking of how telling it might be, Hogan said, "I'll make sure I'm always there with her." Then it hit him and he looked at Nathan, who only stared back as if he'd expected nothing less. Moving on, Hogan added, "Violet should know about all this, too."

"Agreed. I think Brooklin will tell her on her own. She's not the type of woman who'd want to see anyone else get hurt if she could help it. But tonight when we talk, I'll bring it up."

Hogan stated it as a fact. "If she doesn't tell her, I will."

"I'd do the same. Just let her know it's private." Nathan looked at the wall clock behind the table and began buttoning his shirt. "I don't mean to throw you out, but I have to get going."

Until that moment, Hogan had been too concerned with the situation to joke. But now he said, "Got a late start this morning, huh?"

Nathan barely bit back his smile. "That's private, too."

After clapping him on the shoulder, Hogan said, "I'm glad you won her over."

"I'm not entirely there yet, but I'm making progress."

At the door, Hogan got serious again. "If you find out anything else…"

"I'll let you know. Until then, just be a little more on guard."

WEARING THE ONLY pair of bootcut jeans that she owned, which hid her colorful ankle, and thick-soled walking sandals that made being on her feet a little less painful, Violet made her way slowly down an aisle in a local department store. Just as she reached the folding chairs, Hogan came around the corner. He, too, had been looking at the chairs, and he did a double take when he saw her.

His surprise quickly shifted to annoyance. "Why the hell are you shopping?" Before she could answer, he added, "How's your ankle?"

Damn, he looked good in the mornings. Then again, when did the man *not* look good? He, too, wore jeans, but with running shoes and a well-worn KISS T-shirt. He'd shaved, but his hair looked a little mussed, as if he'd done that macho frustrated thing of running his fingers through it.

Skipping his questions, she said, "You're up and about early."

He frowned at her a second more, then stepped close, tenderly touched her cheek and bent down to press his mouth to hers for three heart-melting seconds. Softer now, he said, "Let me try again, okay?"

She nodded.

"Good morning, Violet. How are you?"

With her heart pumping a little faster, she smiled. "I'd curl my toes if I could. But I can't. And no, my ankle isn't worse. In fact, some of the swelling has gone down. But it's now mostly black, like a sickly eggplant."

"You shouldn't be on it."

With a shrug, she said, "I iced it off and on all night."

His brows pinched with concern. "Which means you didn't get any sleep."

Rolling her eyes, she laughed. "Lighten up, Hogan.

I'm not going to perish. I promise I'm fine. In fact, I'm determined to be a very good patient today." She gestured at the shelf. "I was looking for one of those folding chairs with a foot thing that comes up. You know? I've seen them during the community picnics at the creek. Usually it's the elderly using them, but I thought it could work for my office."

Hogan's mouth tipped in a crooked smile. "That's what I was looking for, too."

So sweet! "You were, really?"

"Yeah. Thank you in advance for agreeing to be a good patient. Hope you don't mind if I hold you to it."

After a quick glance around to make sure they were alone in the aisle, Violet walked her fingers up his chest. "We could make a deal."

His gaze went intent, hot, and he murmured, "I'm listening."

"Will you come to my office…let's see, at least twice? You should be able to manage that, right? And while you're there, will you kiss me?" She put both hands on his thick shoulders. "God, I've missed kissing you."

"Two trips to your office? Yeah, I think I can handle that." His expression looked so absorbed, she held her breath, hoping… Then he whispered, "I could come by for a little while tonight after work."

Warmth spiraled through her. "A booty call," she breathed dramatically. Batting her eyelashes, she said on a sigh, "Be still, my heart."

His expression changed. "I didn't mean—"

Violet laughed. "Yes, you did, and I'm glad." Rushing past that so he wouldn't withdraw the suggestion, she asked, "It won't be a problem with Colt?" Almost as quickly, she shook her head. "No, never mind. Forget I asked. You already told me that you wouldn't let…

well, *us* be a problem with him. And I'm glad for that, too." She really was. The last thing she ever wanted to do was make Colt's life any harder. She cared for him a great deal and figured he'd had enough turmoil in his young life.

Hogan looked away. "I'm starting to feel like a real bastard."

Fisting her hands in his shirt, she pulled him closer and regained his attention. "Listen up, Guthrie. I *want* that booty call, okay?" She gave him a hard, fast kiss. "Truthfully, I need it. It reassures me that you make Colt your priority. That's how it should be. And then I don't have to worry about being a problem."

His gaze moved over her face until he was satisfied. Then he nodded. "You're never a problem, believe me."

A woman with two noisy kids moved into the aisle.

Hogan took a chair off the shelf, then her arm. "Let's go." He adjusted his long-legged pace to match hers, aware of her slight hobbling no matter how she tried to hide it.

"I was going to get some real ice packs, too." She grinned at him. "Last night I used up all my bags of frozen vegetables, and the freezer bags at the diner leak."

"I grabbed some from my house. They're already nice and cold and in a cooler. I also looked it up on the internet and you should have wrapped your ankle."

She waved that away. "I tried it, but the only way that worked is if the wrap went around the bottom of my foot, and that made it so bulky, walking would be impossible." Pausing, she lifted up the hem of her jeans on the left leg. "My big concession today is these hideous sandals, which are a godsend or I wouldn't have conceded to them, and the chair so I can elevate my foot and ice it occasionally. Other than that, I'm treating this like any other day."

He frowned down at the spongy, thick-soled sandals. "I suppose it's better than nothing."

"Mostly I'm worried about Brooklin. But she's coming in today for lunch, so I can see how she's feeling then."

"Good." Hogan gently led her to the checkout line behind two other people, then lowered his voice so no one would overhear. "Maybe while she's there you can test out your chair." He looked down at her, his expression far too solemn. "And you know, it wouldn't hurt to find out who the hell would want to run her over, with you as collateral damage."

Shivering with the reality of what could have happened, Violet moved closer. *Collateral damage.* Yes, she'd wondered about that at least a hundred times. "Last night, I kept wondering if I'd imagined that part." She stared up at Hogan. "If it was deliberate, wouldn't that make it attempted murder?"

"I'd say so." With one arm, Hogan drew her closer and kissed her forehead. "But it could have been someone high or drunk, or just stupid."

She tried to believe that, but had to admit the truth. Someone was after Brooklin.

Danger had come to Clearbrook, and by pure accident, she'd been drawn in.

CHAPTER FOURTEEN

BECAUSE COLT HAD the day off, Hogan relied on Kristy and Jerry to let him know when Brooklin showed up. Kristy proved to be the most accommodating, informing him of her arrival, that they'd ordered turkey-and-veggie pitas and that they'd gone to Violet's office to eat.

Because it was important—at least it felt that way to him—Hogan got ahead on ribs then left a panicked Kristy keeping watch over them while he went to talk to the ladies. To make up for the loss of Kristy on the dining room floor, he pulled one of the dishwashers to wait tables. It was quite a shuffling of staff, but at their slowest time of the day, so he felt it was safe to take advantage.

Instead of barging in as he usually did, Hogan tapped politely on the door and waited. A second later Brooklin opened the door.

He peered around her and saw Violet in the chair, the leg of her jeans rolled up and an ice pack on her ankle. He nodded in satisfaction and stepped in without an invite.

"Ladies."

Sitting forward, Violet demanded, "Why aren't you on the grill? What's wrong?"

"You're both injured, that's what's wrong."

"But the grill—"

"I've got it covered." He turned to Brooklin, saw she

avoided his gaze and took in the bandage on her arm. "How badly are you hurt?"

"It's fine," she said, her attention on the wall to the right. "A deep scratch, but nothing a little antiseptic ointment and a few suture bandages didn't fix."

Deciding to get to the point, Hogan crossed his arms and watched her. "I heard someone deliberately tried to run you down."

She swallowed loudly.

Violet tossed aside her ice bag and swung her leg off the chair. "Hogan…"

"No, don't get up." In two big steps he reached her, urging her back to a comfortable position.

"I was getting up to throw you out." Her look stern, she said, "Brooklin and I are talking."

"So I came in too soon?"

She growled, "And you'll go out even faster!"

"No," he said, meaning it. "I won't."

Violet looked ready to blast him.

Brooklin interjected before she could. "It's okay, Violet. He may as well hear it, too." She faced him with the same enthusiasm she'd give a firing squad. "I was just telling Violet that, yes, I think it was deliberate, but I can't know for sure. I thought…" Her voice faded off.

Hogan's first concern was Violet, but what man could be immune to a woman distressed? Gentling his voice, he said, "You thought you were safe here?"

"Yes." Folding her arms around herself, she cupped the thick bandage on her elbow, almost as if it gave her courage. "There is someone who may have found me here. I don't know how. It doesn't make any sense…"

No, so far, it didn't. "Who would want to hurt you?"

Hugging herself tighter, she turned away. "I'm sorry, but I think I should talk to Nathan about that first."

With more questions than answers, Hogan asked, "Because he's the sheriff?"

"In part." Her gaze lifted to meet Violet's and then resolutely moved to Hogan's. "I never wanted anyone else hurt. If I'd thought there was any way—"

"We know that," Violet said.

Hogan agreed with a nod. "As I told Violet, she was likely collateral damage."

Brooklin winced, took a deep breath and straightened. "As long as I stay away, I don't think anyone would bother her."

Violet almost shot out of her chair. "Forget it! I have no idea what's going on, but I'm not about to let some thug choose my friends for me. Next time I'll be ready. Next time I'll—"

Incredulous, Hogan turned on her. "What the hell are you talking about? You both need to be more careful, not go around offering challenges."

"I'll be careful," Violet said, her eyes mean as she figuratively dug in. "But I won't let you dictate to me, and I *like* you, Hogan. What makes you think I'd let some vicious dick push me around?"

"God help me," Hogan muttered. How would he convince her not to be reckless? He couldn't risk her like that, definitely couldn't lose her—

Surprising him, Brooklin was the voice of reason. "I understand, Violet, I really do. Of course you're right. But tonight I'll talk to Nathan. Until then, if I see you, it should only be in a big setting like this. Not alone. In fact, you shouldn't be alone at all." She looked at Hogan. "In the evenings—"

"I'll be sure to close down the place with her."

Flopping back in her seat, Violet grumbled. "I've

been running this business alone for a very long time without a babysitter."

Brooklin's devastation showed through her brave front, despite her slight smile. "That was before me, though."

Neither Hogan nor Violet had anything to say to that. It'd help if he knew what they were dealing with.

Soon. If Nathan didn't get in touch tonight, he'd track him down again tomorrow.

On her way to the door, Brooklin said, "Please be careful, okay? Both of you."

"Are you leaving alone?" Hogan asked, and he saw Violet beam at him as if he'd just done something wonderful. Hell, it was only a question.

"I was able to park closer this time."

"I'll walk you out anyway." He pointed at Violet, taking in her beautiful tumbled hair, the body-hugging tank she wore, the makeup and the jewelry. "Stay put, okay? I have a lot of compliments to give you soon as I get back."

Her smile widened even more. "You noticed."

She had to be kidding. "I'm not blind, honey. I just prioritized." He closed the door on her delighted laugh.

A laugh.

After receiving confirmation that someone had likely tried to—

"I like Violet a lot."

Hogan glanced at Brooklin. "Yeah, me, too."

She didn't look at anyone as they walked through the restaurant. "I really will stay away from her."

"Why? If you can make it here without harm, then it's the perfect place to visit, right? Lots of people around. Safety in numbers and all that." He opened the front door, searched the area, saw nothing but the usual sluggish traffic, sunshine and neighbors, then stepped out ahead of her. "I appreciate that you kept her off that leg for a while today."

"I needed to apologize."

"Knowing Violet as I do, I doubt that. She wouldn't blame you."

"No, she didn't." Brooklin pointed to her car. "This is me. I found a spot at the curb this time."

"Lucky."

"I circled the block three times."

Hogan laughed. "Okay, then let's call it smart." He waited while she unlocked the door with a key fob, then opened it for her. When she was in, he said, "Mind if I ask where you're headed?"

"Straight home. I have some work of my own to get done. And yes, I'll be watching the area, same as you just did."

"Still doesn't feel right. I'm surprised Nathan isn't dogging you."

"He tried." She put the key in the ignition. "You interrupted a bit of a disagreement this morning."

"With Nathan insisting and you refusing?"

Brooklin fell quiet, then gave a soft laugh. "Odd how you have me spilling my guts. Nathan could tell you that I rarely do. But for some reason, here I am, sitting here and telling you things."

Not enough things. Hogan smiled. "Since I'm not Nathan, maybe sharing doesn't bother you as much."

"I didn't want to get involved." She frowned. "Or maybe it's that I didn't want to involve anyone else. Know what I mean?"

"I do."

She dropped her head back against the seat. "But now I've involved Nathan and Violet both."

"I'll watch out for Violet."

"I'm glad."

"And you," he said, "should trust Nathan." Then more softly, he added, "You don't want to be looking over your shoulder your entire life."

"No," she agreed. "I don't." She turned her face up to his. "Go and give Violet that flattery now. She's waiting for you."

Hogan returned her smile. "It's nice, you know?"

"To have someone waiting?"

He nodded.

"My thought exactly."

He watched her drive away, then headed back inside. He went to Kristy first, to see how she was managing.

The second she spotted him, she almost collapsed and tried to hand him the tongs. "What took you so long?"

You'd think he'd asked her to create magic, the way she acted. "It was only a few minutes." When she started to leave, he caught her arm. "Hold up. I'm not quite done yet."

"Hogan!"

Keeping his fingers wrapped around her wrist, he peered at the ribs, then proclaimed her an expert. "Terrific job. You've kept basting them, right? They look perfect."

Now instead of straining away, she eased closer and smiled. "Really? They're okay?"

Using a fork, he pried off one small bite and tasted it. "Mmm. Better than okay."

While Hogan removed the ribs and put on more to cook, she beamed. "Keep up the great work, and I promise only ten minutes more."

Cockier by the second, Kristy agreed. "Sure. This

is easier than waiting tables. Lots of nice people stop by to talk."

"Maybe you can be my official fill-in when I need time away."

Alarm set her eyes wide. "Wait a minute. Helping now and then is fine, but I don't know about doing this for an entire shift."

She squeaked when he gave her a quick, laughing hug. "Ten minutes more. Fifteen tops. I'll be back before things get busy. Just watch for fire and slather on more sauce every so often."

As he left her, Hogan saw Kristy concentrating hard on the ribs, her tongs at the ready.

He was still smiling when he rapped on Violet's door and stepped in. She'd left the chair and was busy returning the ice packs to the cooler.

"Let me." He took it from her, knelt more easily than she could and finished in seconds, the cooler once again secure.

"I could have managed," she said, her tone nettled.

Hogan didn't debate it with her, not when he had other, more important things on his mind—such as getting his mouth on hers.

Like a starving man, he caught her close.

"What a—"

The second her lips parted, his mouth covered hers, his tongue sliding in as he shifted for a better fit. When she melted against him, he lowered one hand to her ass so he could pull her in tight.

"Mmm," she whispered.

Kissing a path to her throat, he breathed in her fragrant skin and felt his muscles knot in reaction.

A hint of perfume curled around his senses, and he smiled.

Breathless, Violet said, "If I'd known a little makeup and loose hair would cause this, I'd have gotten to it sooner."

"You look amazing, honey, but you always do." While palming her perfect ass, he nipped her earlobe and whispered, "But I'd be all over you regardless."

"Really?"

He drew in her skin, careful not to mark her, then soothed the sensitive spot with his tongue. "I've missed you. That's all."

She drew back to stare up at him, her gaze wide with delight. "That's *all*?"

Framed with mascara, her eyes looked even bluer than usual. Skin flushed, mouth wet from his kiss, she was the hottest, most appealing woman he'd ever known, special in ways he only just started to realize.

To help him concentrate, he shifted his hands off her luscious behind. "It doesn't matter what you wear or whether your hair is up or down." He stroked his fingers through the long, silky waves. "Though I admit, you do have gorgeous hair." He thought of it drifting over his body as she kissed him and nearly groaned.

A slow smile curled Violet's mouth—a naked mouth, without lipstick, and he was grateful for that.

"So," she teased, "the fact that I'm wearing my sexiest underthings wouldn't affect you at all?"

Now he did groan, drawing her closer as the heat built beneath his skin. "How sexy?"

Her small, hot tongue touched against his throat. "Barely there," she whispered.

Hogan crushed her against him. "Okay, that's tempting." He gave her payback, saying, "But not more so than having you naked." Finally, with no real choice, he stepped back. "And that's enough of that or Kristy will be stuck on the grill for longer than ten minutes."

Sensuality dropped away and alarm stole her soft expression. "You left Kristy on the grills? Hogan, you know she can't cook!"

"She's not cooking," he said as he caught her, keeping her in front of him. "She's minding the grills. That's all. I got her set up before I came in to talk to you."

"But she—"

Hogan kissed her again. She resisted for about two seconds before giving in with enthusiasm.

The second he lifted his mouth, though, she demanded, "Who's waiting tables?"

"I pulled one of the washers." And before she could explode, he again sealed his mouth over hers. He stuck with it a little longer this time, teasing her lips with his tongue, his teeth. *God, he loved her taste, the heat of her.*

He eased back slowly with kisses to the corner of her mouth, her chin and her nose.

Eyes still closed, Violet breathed, "I'm going to kill you, damn you. You can't just take over."

Unable to help himself, Hogan grinned. "Before you rush off to rearrange things I *haven't* messed up, will you promise me something?"

"Depends." On a sigh, she got her eyes open. "If it's to let you meddle so much, the answer is no."

Still grinning, Hogan said, "You're a tyrant, and no, I don't need to interfere with your business."

"Needing to isn't the point. You enjoy it." She rested against him, winced when she did so and readjusted so that she had less pressure on her foot.

"Two promises, actually. First, will you try to take

it extra easy today? We can manage without you being on your feet too much."

"I promise to use my own good sense to know when I should rest. How's that?"

Not good enough, since pride dictated her actions more so than good sense. But pressing her further wouldn't change that, not today. Besides, he liked her proud and stubborn and capable.

"I guess it'll have to do. So, let's move on to the second thing. Will you let me stay the night?" He curled his fingers over her jaw, let his thumb brush over her bottom lip. "Not just for sex. We both need to sleep at some point. But I'm worried, whether you are or not. Until we learn more about Brooklin's problem, I don't like the idea of you being alone."

"What about Colt?"

That she'd think of his son first endeared her to him even more. He couldn't hold back his expression of satisfaction, or the tenderness swelling in his heart. Crazy that Violet did that to him, turned him on until he thought he'd catch fire, all while making his brain foggy and his thoughts gentle. It was an amazing contradiction, sometimes unsettling, sometimes perfect.

"Colt can stay with Jason and Honor."

Taking only a few seconds to consider it, Violet nodded. "I don't mind. Truthfully, I'm a little spooked, too. Having company will be nice. But aren't you worried about the whole town knowing?"

"Jason and Honor won't gossip. No one needs to know but us." Then he thought of how he'd caught Brooklin coming from Nathan's house and he knew anything was possible.

It didn't matter. Violet was the priority right now.

Violet—and keeping her safe.

He didn't want to dwell on that, so he lifted the small oval necklace she wore. "This is beautiful. Brooklin made it?"

"Yes. You really like it?"

"It's pretty, and it matches your eyes."

She smiled. "That's what Brooklin said, too."

"I also like this shirt. Maybe too much." The lacy tank hugged her body like a second skin and showed more cleavage than usual.

"If it wasn't for my stupid foot, I'd have on sexier jeans, too." She walked her fingers up his chest. "I wanted to get your attention."

"You always have it." He briefly cupped her breast, groaned low and made himself step away before he said too much.

Or did too much.

Violet didn't object; she just watched him as if waiting to see if he'd touch her again.

"You're dangerous."

Her lips curled.

Pointing at her, he said, "Stop that before you find yourself bent over the desk."

Her lips parted. "Seriously?"

Groaning, Hogan turned away and headed for the door in a move of self-preservation. "I'll check in with you later." Over his shoulder, he said, "Or if you find the time and want to visit me at the grills, feel free."

Pleased with that invite, she nodded. "Will do." She shooed him away. "Now go before Kristy burns something and we have to take a loss."

Hogan laughed on his way out. Always, Violet kept the success of her diner and turning a profit at the forefront of her mind.

He admired that. He more than admired *her*.

How the hell had that happened?

WHEN BROOKLIN HEARD the music start, she went to the window to look out. Nathan had his garage door up and she got her first glimpse inside.

It was unlike any garage she'd ever seen.

The band had set up half in, half out, with two guitars, an elaborate set of drums, a keyboard and a tall microphone. Large speakers were stationed near the doors. Behind them, finished walls, a bar, a comfy couch, a table and chairs filled the space.

She wasn't sure, but she thought Nathan might have created a man cave for himself that served the dual purpose of being the perfect space for the band to practice.

Drunken Monkeys, she remembered. What a name.

None of the guys looked remotely like monkeys or drunks, but none of them were as handsome as Nathan.

While playing one of the guitars, he sang "Born on the Bayou" and, mesmerized, her heart swelling, she realized he was really good.

And he looked incredibly sexy.

Slipping her shoes on her feet, she hurried out the back door and across the lawns to join them.

When he saw her, Nathan smiled, but he didn't miss a single note. The other guys grinned hugely and poured their hearts into the music.

As the song ended, she broke into applause. "That was fantastic!"

One of the members, a guy with longish hair and a porn-style mustache, elbowed Nathan and said, "She expected us to suck."

"Seems like," he agreed, teasing her. Nathan turned

to another one of the members. "Stan, you want to grab her a chair?"

The infamous Stan, she thought. He winked at her, fetched her a lawn chair and presented it with fanfare.

"Thank you." He was a handsome guy, but again, not as handsome as Nathan.

"No problem." He folded his arms. "So you and Nathan, huh?"

Handsome and bold, she decided. Aware of Nathan nearby and the other two guys listening in, she leaned closer and said as a confidence, "It's possible, given we're neighbors, he's gorgeous and apparently talented, as well."

Stan snorted a laugh. "So you're after convenience and care about looks. At least you're discriminating enough to care about talent."

She held up two fingers close together. "I have a smidge of integrity."

Laughing again, Stan said, "I think you turned it all around. You're the gorgeous one, but Nathan isn't too much of a dolt, so I'm betting he's been hot on your heels."

"True," she agreed, playing along. "He completely wore me down."

"Glad to hear it." Stan turned to Nathan, fashioned a ridiculously mournful face and said, "I guess this takes me out of the running?"

"You were never in the running," Nathan said. "Not my type."

Brooklin laughed with them.

The other two guys came to introduce themselves, Kurt and Mike, also teasing her, razzing Nathan, and finally they got back to work.

For hours Brooklin curled up in the chair and listened. During one break, Mike-with-the-porn-mustache, but also beautiful green eyes, brought her a cola. In between songs, Kurt moved a stool out of the garage to the front of her seat so she could get more comfortable. Mike was a little more reserved than the others, maybe a few years younger, too, and very sweet.

They were charming guys, very entertaining and loaded with talent.

Lost in the enjoyment of their music, Brooklin forgot about the accident, her aching arm, the possible danger lurking in the unknown. The setting sun bled over the sky in vibrant colors as the air cooled a little. Crickets began to sing. Lights inside the garage sent long shadows over the lawn.

Not until almost ten o'clock did they wrap it up, and when Nathan realized it was so late, he winced.

"We're bound to get a few complaints," he said. "We're supposed to be done by nine."

"I don't understand why. I could have listened all night long."

"Bless your heart," Stan said. "She's a keeper, Nathan."

While Brooklin stammered over that, Nathan smiled at her as if in agreement.

Keeper? She wasn't a keeper—was she?

In an obviously practiced routine, the men returned the instruments to the garage. Brooklin wandered in to look around, amazed at the highly organized and functional space. The refrigerator and bar looked new, but the sofa and two chairs were well-worn and comfortable. The painted floor gave the space a functional finish.

"This is really nice," she said. She especially liked how a large gazebo sat so close. On a hot afternoon, it'd provide shade and a little privacy.

One by one, the men bade her farewell. Stan even pulled her in for a surprise hug. Near her ear, he whispered, "Nathan's a keeper, too, just so you know."

Teasing him, she asked, "Did I really steal him away?"

"I tried," Stan admitted. "You never know until you ask, right? But even though, until now, he didn't do much dating, he's straight as an arrow. I forgave him because what we needed most was a singer for the band. Since Nathan joined in, it's been a perfect fit. We're lucky to have him."

She felt pretty lucky to have him, too.

When they were finally alone, the sun completely gone and a bright moon in the sky, Nathan locked up the garage. The sudden lack of light added a quiet ambience to the area.

The night air felt fresh and clean with a soft breeze that rustled the trees.

She loved Clearbrook, everything about it. More and more she loved the attention from her hunky neighbor, too. Was it possible for her to start over in all ways?

Or would the imminent threat do her in?

Nathan took her arm and led her toward her house.

Uncertain of his intent, Brooklin asked, "Are you sending me home?"

"Yeah." Far too serious, he stared down at her, then gently touched her cheek. "To get your toothbrush and whatever else you need to stay the night."

Oh, good. Because suddenly, more than anything, she wanted to stay with him.

THEY HAD TALKING to do, serious talking, but that could come after.

Nathan wanted this time to be slower, more deliberate. He wanted to undress her, unveiling her little by little. He wanted to kiss every inch of her.

He'd thought about little else lately.

Once in his house, he locked the door, smiled at her, then scooped her over his shoulder.

Surprised, she reared up, laughing. "What are you doing?"

"Taking you to bed." With one big hand opened wide on her backside, the other cupped around a sleek thigh, he went down the hall and into his room, flipped on the overhead light, then lowered her to her feet near the unmade bed. Before she could say anything, he was kissing her.

He kept on kissing her as he stroked her breasts, her firm ass, her belly and between her thighs. When he finally stripped her shirt off over her head, she was frantic—and he loved it.

The shirt, then her bra, landed on the floor at their feet. Neither of them cared. He managed to strip off his own shirt in between soft, sucking love bites to her throat, her shoulder, down to her breasts.

Her nipples were taut and she arched up to his mouth. With his forearm beneath her ass, Nathan lifted her then leisurely drew on her, idly switching from one nipple to the other, his tongue rasping, his teeth gently tugging, until she groaned and whispered, "Nathan… *I need you now.*"

Getting a little desperate himself, he lowered her to her back on the bed and stripped off her shorts and panties.

Eyes heavy and lips parted, she trailed her own fingertips down her body from her breasts to her belly.

Nathan growled, shucked off his jeans and came down beside her. Watching her, their gazes locked, he wedged his hand between her thighs. She was wet and hot, and as he fingered her, making them both hotter, he kissed her again.

He couldn't get enough of her mouth, of the sweet taste of her, but she was soon so close to a climax, her hips twisting against him and her breaths choppy, that he knew he'd lose it if he didn't get inside her.

After rolling on a condom, he came down over her. She wrapped her legs around him, urging him to her. "Nathan…"

Her hair was spread out on the pillow, tangled around her face. Her breasts heaved. "You're beautiful," he said, needing to slow down but unable to stop touching her. He coasted a hand down to her slender waist, then her belly, savoring her warm, silky skin.

She was his. One way or another, he'd make it true.

Her heated golden gaze never wavered. Voice shaking, she whispered, "Now, Nathan. Please."

"I want to kiss you everywhere."

"No," she whispered fast. "I can't take it. Not now." She squeezed her eyes shut as if regaining control, and when she opened them again, he saw so much in her gaze, it moved him. "I'll enjoy that, later, I promise. And I want to kiss you, too."

Damn, he hurt. He knew it wouldn't take much convincing on her part, not when the pulsing beat of need kept pounding through him.

She touched his jaw. "Right now, I just want to be a part of you."

Since he wanted that, too, he nodded. "Later, though. I'll hold you to that promise." They'd have plenty of opportunities, he told himself.

Hopefully a lifetime.

Nathan opened her with his fingertips, then posi-

tioned himself against her, watching as his cock pressed
into her body, seeing how her sex opened around him...

Lost, he lowered himself to his elbows and began
stroking deep.

Groaning, Brooklin clutched at him, her head back,
her body already shivering. Far too soon, she cried out
as she came.

He watched her, enthralled, until she quieted. Then
he let himself go.

Yeah, he loved her. No doubt about it. Whatever her
secrets, no matter her past, he couldn't deny the overwhelming emotion he felt for her.

He was wondering if he should tell her or if a dec-
laration would scare her away, when suddenly a shrill
sound, slightly distant, penetrated the quiet.

They both froze, alert. At first he assumed it was a
siren and wondered why it didn't sound familiar.

Two seconds later, he realized the truth and the meaning of that sound fully registered.

"Oh God," Brooklin whispered, her eyes flaring with
sudden fear. "Someone is breaking into my house!"

Nathan rolled to his feet, jerked on his boxers, opened
the nightstand drawer and retrieved his gun, then rushed
from the room.

Brooklin, hastily wrapped in the blanket, chased after
him. *"What are you doing?"*

Knowing it to be a rhetorical question, he didn't
slow. At the front door, he said, "Stay here. Lock up
behind me." He silently closed the door behind him,
heard the lock click into place, then took the porch steps
in one leap. Pissed, beyond furious, he quietly circled
her house, going around to the back first. The noise
continued and one by one porch lights came on up and
down the street.

There was no one around.

Whoever had set it off was long gone. Still, he searched, going two doors up, then backtracking.

Not until sixty-year-old Mrs. Blankenship said, "Sheriff, you're in your underwear!" did he remember that he wasn't dressed.

Her gaze, her husband's gaze and half the damn neighborhood's went over him as if they'd never seen a man in shorts before. His boxers were dark, thank God, and fitted like swimming trunks. Still, it was awkward as hell.

Resisting the urge to cover himself with his hands— because one of his hands held his weapon—he addressed them all. "That's an alarm you're hearing. I'll get it shut off in a minute. Someone has been stalking the neighborhood, attempting to break in. This was probably another attempt." He didn't specify that it was only Brooklin's house bothered so far. "You all need to be careful, okay? And let me know if you see anything shady."

That, he knew, would garner him a dozen calls at least, because many of the denizens found everything to be shady.

"Go on home now. It's under control."

Reluctantly, people departed.

He stood there, chewing on his anger, until he realized Brooklin was walking past. She'd dressed, her face was white beneath the moonlight, and her posture was resigned.

Saying nothing, he fell into step beside her.

Using her key, she went into the house and straight to the alarm. When she shut it off, the silence fell around them like a suffocating blanket.

She kept her back to him and whispered, "I was accused of inappropriate conduct with a student."

Nathan stared at her. Hell, he hadn't seen that coming. Still he waited, and when she said nothing else, he prompted her with "And?"

"I didn't do it."

"I know that."

She jerked around to face him, her expression so hopeful it nearly crushed him.

"You would never hurt a kid. Not in any way." Down to the marrow of his bones, he believed that. "Who accused you, and why?"

Drawing in a shuddering breath, she groped for a kitchen chair and dropped into it. Tears welled in her eyes and choked her voice. "I've been so afraid."

"Of me judging you? Jumping to conclusions and believing the worst?" Damn, he felt a little choked, too. "That's just foolish." He pulled out his chair, drawing it close enough that their knees touched.

With a shaky smile, she slapped away the tears, swallowed hard and looked him in the eye.

CHAPTER FIFTEEN

"TEACHERS HAD SENT a girl, Elle Ivers, to me several times for supposed accidents when they would notice bruises or cuts. I knew in my gut something was very wrong. She was quiet and reserved—not unlike many girls in high school. But Elle… I looked at her and I knew she was wounded. I just didn't know what to do about it."

"You tried to get her to talk to you?"

That Nathan wasn't doubting her meant more than she ever could have asked for. She so desperately needed someone to believe in her, without the painful proof laid out, without the conclusion of the court as backup.

"I tried a lot, but it's a tricky thing. I couldn't flat out ask her if someone was abusing her, if the bruises on her arms were caused deliberately instead of being from the many excuses she gave." When Nathan took her hand, she squeezed hard, so glad for the human contact. "It's a terrible thing to see someone being mistreated and not be able to do anything about it."

"I can't imagine."

No, he couldn't, because he was a doer, strong and capable. First in SWAT and now as a sheriff. He was amazing, and she didn't want to lose him.

Another deep breath helped give her voice strength. "When I found out Elle was dating Mike Muller, a top-notch jock, I wondered. He was so much bigger than her, obviously tough to play all the sports, strong in the way young men can be. I tried to watch them together, but if anything, he seemed extra protective of her." Her gaze lifted to his. "Then one day Mike came to see me. He said he could only talk to me if I could promise it'd be private, that I wouldn't tell anyone."

"A tough situation to be in."

"At the time, I didn't even think about that. I just knew something was wrong and I wanted to help." She stroked Nathan's knuckles, the fine hair on the back of his large hand that entirely engulfed hers. "Mike told me that Elle's father was abusing her. He didn't know what to do. Elle had missed three days of school and didn't answer when he called."

"Damn."

She nodded. "There's a protocol we're supposed to use, but Mike made me swear I wouldn't contact children's services. Elle was ashamed. The things her father did to her…she didn't want the whole town to know."

Maybe because that was too painful to talk about, Nathan asked quietly, "You were helping Mike when someone got the wrong idea?"

A close enough guess. "Not just anyone—Elle's father." Remembering left her shaken. "I confronted him. I left Mike and Elle out of it and just said that as the school nurse, I'd noticed things and I wanted to know how she'd gotten hurt so many times."

"That took guts."

"Honestly, I was so angry I could have beaten *him* to death."

Nathan smiled, a sad smile, and said, "I understand that."

"He was smug when he denied it, saying his daughter was just clumsy and I should mind my own business. Of course, I couldn't." The words came faster, as if she needed to rush to make Nathan believe her, rush before he had time to make terrible assumptions. "I worked hard to find a way to free Elle. Mike said she was afraid because she didn't have anywhere else to go, and there were months of school left. Her father had her so cowed that she still didn't want to confide in me, and she definitely didn't want to report her dad. It took almost two weeks to finally convince her." She closed her eyes. "And in that two weeks, I'd met with Mike several times, advising him, helping him find the right words to convince her and helping him plan for what to do."

Nathan waited, patience personified.

"Without me knowing it, Elle's father had skulked around and taken photos of me with Mike. Sitting in his car—not touching or anything, but just being with him was damning enough. There was one of us out back of the school, talking close so no one would overhear. Photos of us meeting on the side of the road." She groaned at her own stupidity. "Those photos were sent to my school, and I was immediately let go while they investigated."

"Did you explain?"

"I couldn't. I'd given Mike my word. I was afraid if I told the truth, it'd get Elle in more trouble." She pulled away from him and folded her hands in her lap. "I had a fiancé. Remember I told you that? Well, he was a biology teacher at the school, and he dumped me fast enough, too." It almost made her sick to admit it. "He believed the worst. Before I could even explain, he ranted and told me I'd shamed him and made him look like a fool."

"He sounds like a fool."

She let that go. Thinking about Russell only got her

riled. "The entire community condemned me—until Mike and Elle went to the police. He'd convinced her to tell the truth about her father."

"I like this Mike," Nathan said.

She nodded. "I do, too." Her gaze jumped to his. "I mean—"

"Shh. I'm not your idiot ex. You don't need to explain."

Relief left her weak. "Thank you."

"Thank you for helping Elle, even though it nearly cost you everything. It was a heroic, selfless thing to do."

Did he really feel that way? She'd been reviled for so long it'd be a novel thing to be seen as a hero to someone other than Elle and Mike. "It took a long time," she admitted, without going into the grueling day-to-day grind of the trial, "but finally Elle's father was sentenced to ten years in jail."

"When was that?"

"Only three years ago."

"You've been moving around since then?"

"Yes. Few people would recognize me. But I get… restless. Sometimes it's like it all comes back to me and I just need to get away."

Nathan curved a hand around her neck. "Not anymore, okay? Clearbrook is your home. You have friends here now." He frowned a little. "You have me."

Brooklin started shaking all over. "Don't say that yet. You have to know everything first."

"I'm still here, still listening." He leaned in and pressed his mouth to hers in a brief, firm kiss. "But it won't matter."

Best to finish it, she decided. "Before he was convicted, Elle's father told me he'd kill me. He said I wouldn't see him coming, but one day he'd be there and he'd make me pay. He was...graphic about what he'd do to me." She shuddered. "What if he's out of prison now? What if—"

"Shh." Nathan drew her into his lap and held her close. "Will you let me look into it?" He put a finger under her chin and tipped up her face. "Understand, Brooklin. Not because I need to see any facts. I trust you. But I can find out where he is, if he's still in prison, when he's likely to be let go if he is."

It would be such a relief to know for sure. "Yes, of course. I'll give you all the information you need."

Nathan hugged her. "Whatever happened with Mike and Elle?"

Because that was one of the few good memories, she smiled against his throat. "After Elle got her GED, they married and Mike took a job with his father's company in Texas. Neither of them wanted to stay in Ohio, not after the trial. We exchange Christmas cards each year and they always include a little note, so I know that they're still together and still happy. Last Christmas they said Mike is going to school part-time and will get his bachelor's degree soon. Then he'll be able to take a promotion in the company. Elle works from home."

"That's a happy ending for sure."

"Elle struggles sometimes, but Mike is always there for her. I think I knew, even when they were high school seniors, that they were the real deal."

"I'm glad."

Brooklin put her hand to his face. "It means a lot that you didn't assume the worst, that you trust me."

"Enough that you'll trust me, too?"

She didn't need time to think about it. "Yes."

"Then stay with me until we get this figured out."

It wasn't a romantic request. He wasn't asking her to move in with him. But he cared—she was sure of it.

Teasing him, she said, "I'll stay if you tell me your secrets, too."

"I don't have any secrets."

"Nathan." She kissed his face, his brow, the bridge of his nose and the scar that cut across his right cheek. "Will you tell me about this?"

He didn't want to, she could see that.

He asked, "Does it bother you?"

"It keeps you from being too beautiful."

Laughing, he stood her on her feet and picked up the gun from the table. "Beautiful, huh? Do you need contacts?"

She stopped him with a hand on his chest. "You are beautiful. Ruggedly beautiful. And that mark doesn't detract in any way. I only asked because it looks like it was painful, and I hate that for you."

For the longest time he waffled, undecided, then finally said, "Let's save that for tomorrow, okay? Right now I want to get hold of Hogan. Since whoever is after you is also aware of Violet, I think—"

"That they should know everything." God, how she hated the possibility of losing Violet as a friend. Or worse, the whole town finding out. She'd been detested enough to last her a lifetime. "Of course. You'll tell them?"

"I think the sooner, the better, so yeah, I'll clue them in tonight." He took her shoulders. "Don't look like that, Brooklin. They're both good people, I swear. You don't have to worry about them knowing."

She wasn't convinced. After all, her own fiancé had bought into the worst of the accusations. But it wouldn't be fair to keep it private, not anymore, not with the level of risk.

For now, she'd count her blessings that Nathan understood. Once he dug into the records, he'd have all the details before him, so if he did harbor any doubt it'd be put to rest.

For now, that had to be enough.

THANKS TO A large group that came in half an hour before closing, then continued talking and laughing long after they'd finished their meals, Hogan and Violet, but also Kristy, were late closing the diner. Violet refused to show any rudeness to customers, Hogan agreed with her, and Kristy decided it was her job to see it through to the end, so they did what they could around the party and waited.

The customers were nice, using the diner for a reunion of sorts, and once they realized it was past closing time, they quickly packed up, leaving behind a very hefty tip for Kristy.

They were about to walk out the door when Nathan called Hogan. He recognized the number, realized it was late for a call, and even as he answered, he saw by the look on Violet's face that she expected bad news.

Hogan did as well—and he wasn't wrong.

It was obvious Nathan condensed a complicated story, but the crux of it all was that Brooklin had been falsely accused by an abusive asshole while helping kids the same age as Colt.

Far as Hogan was concerned, that made her a hero. When he told Nathan that, the sheriff said, "My thoughts exactly. And I know she'll appreciate it. You know, she wasn't sure what you and Violet would think."

"Tell her we think we need more people like her."

Hogan heard whispering on the other line and assumed Nathan was putting Brooklin at ease.

When he came back, he asked, "You'll keep Violet with you?"

"Yes." He watched Violet and saw her slightly favoring her foot as she sat in a booth, her gaze trained on him, waiting to find out what had happened. "We'll be at her house. Colt will stay with Jason." Until everything was settled, though, they'd need a longer-term plan. "We've had our fair share of crime in the area, but this feels different. I don't like it, damn it."

"I'll find out what I can tomorrow. Until then, be careful."

After pocketing his phone, Hogan sat across from Violet in the booth and, in low tones, explained what had happened.

Violet took his hand. "Poor Brooklin. I'm worried about her."

Because Violet had a huge heart. She cared about Brooklin already. She definitely cared about Colt.

Did she care about him?

Did he want her to?

"What is it, Hogan?"

He lifted her hand and kissed her knuckles. "Nothing." But it was something. Something that scared him half to death.

Surely he wouldn't get roped back in? Only with Violet, it didn't feel like that.

Hadn't he learned his lesson about women... He cut off that thought with alacrity.

His wife had taught him plenty of lessons, but Violet was nothing like her.

She was far more genuine.

But then, he'd once thought the same about Meg.

He could no longer trust his own judgment—that was the problem. He knew he wanted Violet, pretty much around the clock. He detested the idea of another man touching her, and the urge to personally protect her, to keep her safe, thrummed through his blood.

She made him laugh. She had his respect, his admiration.

Yet she never asked for more than he was willing to give.

Did *he* want more?

Kristy, who'd been getting her things from her locker, came in and gave them both a wary look. "Uh-oh. You guys look like something terrible has happened. What's wrong?"

Violet rushed to reassure her. "Everything is fine."

"Then why does Hogan look like he might kill someone?"

Violet turned to stare at Hogan. "He does look ferocious, doesn't he?"

Rolling his eyes and hopefully ridding himself of the "ferocious look," Hogan said, "Everything done?"

"If you're not going to tell me what's going on, then yeah, I guess everything is done."

Hogan shook his head and lied through his teeth. "I had to deal with a grumpy customer today, that's all. It's soured my mood."

"Odd that your mood seemed okay fifteen minutes ago." Kristy shrugged her shoulders. "I'm ready to collapse in my bed, so I'm out of here. I'll see you both tomorrow."

Within fifteen minutes, Hogan and Violet locked up the diner. Following her to her car, he said, "I wish we were riding together."

Without any animus at all, she replied, "That'd draw

too much attention, and since you want to keep our 'thang' private, it's better that we drive separate."

Their "thang"? Hogan let that go, since he didn't know how to define the myriad and confusing things she made him feel. He just wanted to go on feeling them. "You're limping."

"Just a little. It's been a long day." She looked up at him. "You can make it feel better very shortly. All I need is time to take a quick shower."

Beneath the security light, her hair glowed, showing different shades of red. Her eyelashes left long shadows over her cheeks, and her mouth—God, he loved her mouth—smiled at him.

Hogan touched her cheek. "I'll shower with you, okay?"

Pressing a hand to her breast, she said, "Lordy, sugar. Talk like that will stop my heart."

He had to smile. "I'll be right behind you."

Her mouth pursed, and after shifting her gaze around the area, ensuring they were utterly alone, she whispered, "Behind me, huh? You know, I think I just might enjoy that."

Hogan groaned. "Now I have to drive with a boner." He bent for a quick kiss, got her into her car and, pushed by heated urgency, all but jogged to his.

In only a few minutes they were at her house.

They were barely in the door when Hogan began stripping off her clothes. Wanting to take care with her foot, he tempered the urge to rip her clothes away like a maniac.

It was insane, maddening, but he'd needed her so much…

Oh God. He stepped back to stare at her. Her lingerie was indeed mind-boggling.

Violet took in his expression, shook back her hair and struck a pose. "You like?"

That had to be a rhetorical question.

He nodded. "What there is of it." The same rosy color as her flushed skin, the filmy bra cups lifted her breasts while barely covering her nipples. Her panties were no more than a decorative thong.

He could see her through the near-transparent material.

"Should I take it off?"

"No." He drew her to him. "Let me."

He forgot about her foot—his focus was on everything between her knees and her chin. Minutes after he had her stripped, Hogan had them both in the shower, and he had his soapy hands all over her.

VIOLET, HER HAIR hastily pinned up atop her head, flattened her hands against the shower wall and concentrated on staying upright.

Not easy with Hogan determined to drive her insane. The shower spray hit her side; Hogan's hot mouth was against her nape.

And his hands, slick with soap, played over her breasts, her nipples, her thighs and her belly, over and over again.

When he suddenly turned her, she expected a kiss, but instead he took his time rinsing her, and that was a new torture all its own.

The man was oh-so-thorough.

Her eyes stayed closed until he sank to his knees. As she stared down at the top of his wet head, seeing the way he looked at her with such absorbed concentration, her heart skipped several beats.

"Hogan?"

He kissed her belly and slid a hand between her legs. "Keep the pressure off that foot, honey." Two fingers pressed into her, going deep. "I want you to come for me now."

She braced her hands on his shoulders, sucked in much-needed air and whimpered, "Okay." It wouldn't take much and she knew it. Just thinking about his mouth on her was nearly enough.

First he nibbled on her inner thighs, his fingers very still inside her, not moving, just *there*. In reaction, her muscles squeezed against those invading fingers, and she felt his smile against her hip.

"I like that. Hold me tight, honey. Real tight."

She squeezed again, then groaned because it felt so incredibly good.

With his other hand, he parted her, still looking at her, his expression sharp, focused, and as he leaned forward she held her breath, her fingertips digging into his shoulders.

The first touch of his tongue, stroking over her, in her, wrenched a groan from deep in her throat.

But that was nothing compared to the way he drew her clitoris between his lips, how he sucked so gently, his tongue laving rhythmically.

The water started to cool, but it didn't matter. With each firm stroke of his fingers, each soft pull of his mouth, she twisted closer and closer to release until, with a sharp cry, she came—just as he'd requested.

Minutes later, still lethargic, Violet smiled as Hogan placed her in the bed. Leaning over her, he freed her hair, smoothed it out and bent to kiss her mouth.

She didn't have the wherewithal to pucker. He'd pushed her, drawing out her climax until her legs had begun to buckle. Then he'd caught her, turned off the water and even dried her from head to toe.

Such an amazing, attentive, sexually charged man. She'd never known anything like it, or anyone like him.

She loved him. How could she not?

It was a secret she'd happily keep since sharing meant she might lose him.

How long would it last anyway?

Her heart ached as it answered with: *surely not long enough.*

Sighing, Violet stared up at Hogan, watching as he finished drying himself. By the second, she regained her wits and her desire.

"You look satisfied with yourself," he remarked, coming down over her, his damp body still taut with need. "I take it you like me on my knees?"

"I like you any way I can get you." The second those words were out, she worried. Had she said too much?

Hogan surprised her with his own look of satisfaction. "You taste good, Violet."

She pushed against his shoulders, and after a brief, unspoken question, Hogan went to his back. She straddled his hips, her hands braced on his shoulders. He stared at her breasts, very near his mouth.

"I think I owe you some payback."

Lust tightened his face. "Yeah?" He held her by the waist, his gaze reluctantly rising to meet hers.

"Oh, yeah." His big body pleased her so much, and it was her turn to explore him in minute detail. She started with his mouth, kissing him long and deep the way she liked. Her breasts pressed against his hairy chest, making her nipples tighten again. His hands went down her hips, cupped over her bottom, then curved in to touch her.

With her position, her knees spread out on either side of his hips, she was open and available to him.

He took swift advantage.

She was swollen and so very sensitive from her recent orgasm. As he toyed with her, her back arched, but as good as that felt, Violet didn't let herself get distracted with her own pleasure.

This was Hogan's turn.

Trying to ignore his tantalizing fingers, she nibbled her way down his chest, teased one flat male nipple. His hands fell away from her. Triumphant, she slid farther down to his ribs, his stomach, the tops of his muscular thighs.

"No other man could smell as good as you." She brushed her nose against him, lower and lower, his musky scent filling her head.

His body went rigid as his anticipation built.

Holding his erection in both hands, she feathered her lips over him, relished his groan, then licked her tongue up the length of him.

He threaded his fingers into her hair, urging her closer.

She smiled up at him, lightly pressed her lips to the head, then slowly took him deep into her mouth.

His hips lifted off the bed, his hand fisting in her hair in reaction.

Wow, she liked that, liked affecting him so strongly.

Did he realize how, together, they were uniquely explosive? Or what if it wasn't the same for him? No, when she looked up the length of his powerful, straining body, she saw the agony of pleasure on his face.

He felt it—and she relished her sensual control.

Locking his gaze with hers, he softened his hold on her hair, gently stroked his thumb over her hollowed cheek, then curved his hand around her nape and encouraged her to take his length again.

In total agreement, Violet worked him with her hands and mouth, accepting all of him while sucking, then sliding back with her tongue teasing, only to repeat it again.

His breathing grew ragged, his heels pressing into the mattress, his testicles tight. She felt him throbbing in her mouth and knew she wouldn't be able to enjoy him much longer.

Suddenly his hands closed over her shoulders and he pulled her away, up and onto her back.

"Hogan—"

His mouth covered hers, voracious, wild, his hands all over her, a little rougher than usual, but she loved it. Just as quickly he left her, grabbing for the condom and rolling it on in record time.

"This is going to be fast," he warned. "And hard."

He came over her, his mouth once again on hers, and then he was inside her, taking her in long, deep thrusts, bringing her back to the edge of a climax in a blinding rush. The second she let go, he did, too, his head back as he pumped heavily into her.

Through the haze of her own release, Violet watched him. She had to bite her lip to keep from stating her love—words he didn't want to hear.

Words, feelings that might push him away from her.

When the rage of pleasure waned, he slowly sank down to her, his head beside hers on the pillow, his strong heartbeat thundering against her breast. Violet held him close, her lips brushing his damp shoulder.

He didn't fall asleep. Not Hogan.

No, he gave himself five minutes, and then he took care of business, getting up to remove the condom and turn out the lights before returning to the bed and smoothing the covers over them both.

Violet couldn't speak around the emotion choking her, but then, she didn't need to.

Hogan pulled her against him, kissed her forehead and said, "If you need anything tonight, let me know. I don't want you straining that foot more than it already is."

She couldn't even feel her legs, much less her foot. She snuggled in, closed her eyes and enjoyed the novelty of having Hogan all to herself for the entire night.

BY MIDDAY, COLT was anxious to get out of school. With a definite goal in mind, he'd been putting aside his money and looked forward to the tips he'd make at Screwy Louie's on a busy Friday night. He'd found a lot of satisfaction in earning his keep and building his savings. Since he wasn't dating, and he usually ate dinner at the diner, he'd had very few expenses. Gas for his car, insurance—his dad covered everything else.

When he thought of his dad, he also smiled. It'd been so long since he'd seen him this happy, this comfortable with life. The strain Colt had gotten used to seeing in his face and the set of his shoulders had disappeared.

As to that, he realized that he, too, was more relaxed and undeniably more prone to grinning. Violet did that to a guy. She had such an easy way about her that you couldn't be around her and not be happy. She liked to tease Hogan, which gave him a whole new focus—away from the problems that had once weighed him down.

For Colt, she mothered in the most subtle of ways while also showing respect and caring. He liked her a lot.

She was perfect for his dad.

Colt wondered about that, trying to decide if Hogan had accepted what he felt for Violet, while hoping he wouldn't mistake her casual attitudes for lack of intensity.

She was nuts for his dad, no doubts about that at all. Colt knew he was young, but he wasn't blind and he saw it plain enough, along with most everyone else. He'd even talked to his uncle Jason about it.

Jason had told him that above all else, his dad was a responsible guy. On top of that, he was now far more cautious. Hogan liked to study all angles, figure out all possible scenarios. With a new love interest, there would be a lot of things to mull over.

Jason didn't say, but one of the main things his dad considered was Colt.

Colt hoped he didn't mull them so long that he lost Violet. That would devastate his dad—and it would bother Colt a lot, too. Already, Violet seemed a part of them. The diner was like a second home.

He liked his world now, damn it. Liked it a lot and he wanted it to continue, not come to another abrupt halt.

Walking down the school hallway toward the back door, his thoughts tumbling, he almost plowed into Charish.

She sidestepped with a laugh, saying, "You on a mission, Colt?"

He looked up and stared. She always looked so pretty to him. "Charish. Hey."

"Hey, yourself." Her gaze moved softly over his face, and her voice lowered. "You okay?"

"Yeah. I was just thinking." He moved to lean a shoulder against the lockers. "I got some news today. I'm pumped about it."

She seemed happy that he was happy, her smile sweet. "What news?"

"I'm going to graduate early."

The smile slipped and her face went blank. "You're… what?"

"I'll be out of here in January." Once he started talking, Colt couldn't contain his enthusiasm. "It's a new program Ms. Decker told me about."

"You saw the counselor?"

"Yeah. I wanted to go half days so I'd have more time for work to save for college, so we went over everything. But since I have all my credits, I can actually just graduate in a few months. I've already met all the requirements. That'll give me months to save up for college."

The hurt in her eyes surprised him.

"I'm not leaving right away or anything," he said, wondering at her expression.

Her teeth bit into her bottom lip, but she rallied and gave him a nod. "That's terrific, Colt." Her smile trembled. "I'm happy for you."

He studied her face. "You don't sound happy."

She didn't deny it. "Will you be at the diner tonight? A bunch of people are meeting there."

"Yeah, but I'll be working."

Charish deflated.

"You'll be there?" he asked, wanting to see her smile again.

She stared down at her feet. "Mack invited me to go."

Immediately, Colt stiffened but tried to play it off as if he didn't care. "Yeah? Like a date, you mean?"

Her gaze flickered up to his. "Yes."

"What'd you tell him?"

She shrugged. "No one else is asking me out, so I agreed."

Colt shifted, tried to talk himself out of saying anything, but the words erupted anyway. "You know what he wants, right?"

She looked up at him, silent, almost daring him to show it mattered.

But he couldn't. "He has a rep, Charish."

"Does it matter?"

More than she realized. More than he'd realized. Her being friends with the group, that he could handle. But damn it, he didn't want to take advantage of her, so he sure as hell didn't want some other dude to do it. "You tell me," he challenged. "Is that what you want, Charish?"

"I want you. I told you that."

Wow, talk about flooring a guy.

Her mouth firmed and her eyes went a little glassy. "But you're not interested, are you, Colt? And I'm tired of wishing for things that aren't going to happ—"

Before giving it much thought, Colt bent down and kissed her, and of course he quickly lost his common sense. She felt good, tasted good.

Not want her? She couldn't believe that.

Without breaking the kiss, he moved her to the lockers and pressed her against them with the length of his body. Still with his mouth moving over hers, he shouldered off his backpack and dropped it to the floor.

She did the same with her purse.

While touching her from chest to knees, her small body soft and sweet and so tempting, Colt felt lost.

Intruding voices, thankfully still distant, helped him to get it together. He eased up. They were both breathing hard.

It had been a while since he'd kissed anyone. He'd been so set on his future that he'd missed some of the present. He'd missed girls. And kissing.

He'd missed Charish.

He felt on fire from the inside out. He looked at Charish, seeing her bewilderment, her willingness. Her innocence.

Colt groaned. "I want you."

With her fingertips, she touched her mouth.

"Tell Mack to forget it."

Nodding, she whispered, "Okay."

Damn it, she was too agreeable and it bothered him. "You know I'm not available often. I have two jobs, sometimes more. I need the perfect grades for college, especially since I'm using the program to get out of here early."

Her gaze lowered. "You'll go away to college?"

"No. I mean, I wanted to, but things change. I figured I'd go local." The way her hair fell over her shoulders, how her chest still moved with deep breaths, made him almost desperate to touch her again. "If we do this—"

Her gaze shot up to his. "This?"

Needing a second to get himself together, Colt locked his molars. What guy could be immune to those big dark eyes? Not him. "If we're together."

"Oh." Those eyes went dazed—and hopeful.

Colt tipped up her chin, soaking up the sight of her. *She had to understand.* "I won't be able to keep my hands off you, Charish, and you don't exactly say no."

Soft with sincerity, she whispered, "I trust you."

Those three small words pushed him over the edge. "Okay then."

She frowned slightly. "Okay what?"

"I don't want you with any other guy."

Her chin went up. "Well, I don't want you with any other girl, either."

Despite all his misgivings about getting involved, Colt grinned. "Sounds fair."

The smile bloomed on her mouth. Then she launched herself against him. *There was only so much a guy could take*.

"Ahem."

They looked up to see the counselor wearing a tolerant expression, though she said, "Sharing your good news?"

"Yes, ma'am."

"I'm glad you're happy, Colt. But no celebrating in the hallways, please."

He said again, "Yes, ma'am." Then Colt smiled down at Charish. "I'll see you tonight at the diner?"

She nodded. "I'll be there." Her lips twitched, and she added, "With *friends*."

CHAPTER SIXTEEN

FRIDAY HAD ROLLED around quickly, or so it seemed to Hogan. Maybe it was because he'd enjoyed himself so much despite the threat of trouble.

For days they'd stayed on guard, yet nothing more had happened. While Colt and Diesel only stayed twice with Jason, Hogan continued to spend at least part of each night with Violet, and he enjoyed it a lot. He made love to her, or she made love to him, he thought with a grin, and they'd steal a few hours to sleep together. But to keep up appearances, mostly for his son, he hadn't stayed till morning again.

Even staying that long would have been a problem except that Colt had assured him that he knew how to lock doors, and he did have Diesel with him. Diesel loved everyone, unless they came to his house unexpectedly.

Hogan thought of himself at seventeen—with a pregnant girlfriend and a hasty marriage. Not once had he considered himself too young to deal with anything that came his way.

He owed Colt the same respect, so he tried to be more understated in his protectiveness.

That protectiveness now extended to Violet and it hurt every time he had to leave her. If Violet felt the same about him going, she never let on. Instead she'd hug him tight, kiss his mouth thoroughly enough to rev his engine all over again, then remind him to lock up as he left.

Violet liked to torture him, but he had to admit, he enjoyed her methods.

Repeatedly, far too often in fact, he thought about moving her into his house. For a variety of reasons, the idea nibbled on his brain. It'd be nice to have her, Colt and Diesel all together. She'd be safe, and he'd have her next to him the entire night, waking with her in the morning.

Sharing everything.

But he wasn't far enough gone to do that, not to Colt. His son had been through enough changes for a while.

Colt had also seen his father at his worst not that long ago. Hogan wanted to be a man Colt could look up to. He wanted to be a good influence on him.

Hogan sighed. After the past week, he'd gotten so used to looking for trouble he did it now by rote, scanning the street whenever he left her house, occasionally even circling the block once or twice. His gaze searched everywhere whenever Violet was out in public.

There'd been nothing.

Even when Violet and Brooklin had met up, expanding their new friendship, there were no issues. Nathan still had fits about them being out alone together, but the women claimed they were careful.

Currently Brooklin all but lived with Nathan—and Nathan seemed more than pleased. Hogan envied them the freedom to do as they pleased, not that he regretted his son. Never that. He just regretted that he'd been a blind ass for so long.

If he'd have realized what Meg was doing, if he'd been the one to call quits on the marriage instead of being discarded, would it have all been different? Was it his pride as much as anything that had flattened him so badly?

He wondered what Violet would think if she knew the direction of his thoughts. Did she want more from their relationship?

He knew she appreciated the sex; the woman had an insatiable appetite. Just thinking about it, about her and how she enjoyed him, lightened his mood.

"What?" Violet suddenly asked, coming up behind him where he stood in front of the big front window, blinded by the afternoon sunshine. "I saw that wicked smile, Hogan. What were you thinking?"

He turned to her, appreciating her snug tank top that fitted her breasts perfectly, and trim-fitting jeans. Her hair hung in a fat, loose braid over her left shoulder. It looked romantic and sexy and messy, perfectly suiting her.

His shift would start in only a few minutes. It was just past the lunch hour and a small crowd remained in the diner, but no one too close to them. Propping a shoulder on the wall and looking down at Violet, he hedged the truth, saying, "I was thinking about you."

Splaying a hand to her chest and ramping up her drawl, she said, "Little ol' me? Why, sugar, I'm flattered."

Hogan noted that she barely limped now. The bruises were fading, but still, she had enough vanity to keep them covered, preferring concealing jeans over her usual shorts.

"Specifically," he said, happy to tease her, "I was thinking of your legs."

"My legs?"

"How nice it feels when you wrap them around the small of my back. Or when they're over my shoulders and I'm—"

Smashing a hand to his mouth, she silenced him. With raw sincerity, she said, "Don't do that to me, not while we're stuck here without an ounce of privacy. We've got too many hours ahead of us yet."

Hogan bit her finger, surprising her, because now they were drawing attention. "I miss your shorts, too. I liked seeing your legs all day while I worked. I considered it a perk of the job."

"One more week," she said, seeming somewhat boggled by his public display. "Then all those nasty colors will be off my ankle."

"It'll give me something to look forward to."

"How about looking forward to this?"

Until she flagged an edition of the *Clearbrook Trickle* in his face, he hadn't noticed that she had it in her hand. Knowing this had to do with the stupid advice column, he asked on an aggrieved sigh, "What now?"

Leaning in next to him, shoulder to shoulder, she snapped open the paper and, sure enough, flaunted the newest "Advice Anonymous" column. "You," she said. "Shirtless."

"Me, shirtless?" he repeated, disbelieving that anyone still pushed that particular idea.

"It's what the public demands. See here? It says there have been *numerous* requests and that this is just one of many. It's a movement, Hogan. A movement among the women of Clearbrook."

Two ladies at a table lifted their drinks and shouted, "Hear, hear!"

Violet gave him a lift of her brows that said, without words, *Told you so.*

He shook his head, turned his back on the women and said, "We already talked about this, remember?"

Ignoring that, Violet read the piece aloud.

Dear Advice Anonymous,
What would be the odds of success if a group of us (ladies) petitioned Violet Shaw to have her barbecue chef attend to his grills shirtless? I know, I know, it's a bold request. But he works outside and it's hot, so it'd make sense. Maybe we could make it a ladies' night out feature? Violet is a businesswoman, so she'd have to go for that, right?
Signed,
Ready to be brazen.

Violet grinned at him expectantly.
Feeling his ears go hot, Hogan said, "No."
"Don't you want to hear the reply?"
Yeah, he had to admit, he did. "Go for it."
She cleared her throat, then continued reading aloud.

Dear Brazen,
Keep in mind that a petition would require you to sign your name. Your real name. All of your many curious friends would also have to do the same. However, I'm sure if you followed through, if there were enough names on that petition, Ms. Shaw would present your request to the barbecue master, maybe even with a little persuasion. He strikes me as the type who might like to flaunt his wares. What have you got to lose?
Advice Anonymous.

Even before she'd finished, Hogan started walking away.
Laughing, Violet snagged him by the back waistband of his jeans, pulling him up short. "I'm trying to utilize a little persuasion here, Hogan."

"No."

"But don't you want to see the petition?"

Groaning, he tried to pry her loose, but she just fell into step beside him.

It was then that Hogan realized a lot of ladies were watching.

As in—an unusual amount of ladies.

Well, hell.

How had he not noticed that the after-lunch crowd was largely female?

Preferring not to look like a fool by running away, he stopped, gave a short laugh and stared at Violet. Only Violet. He did his best to pretend no other ladies were present, despite their rapt and amused attention.

Like a magician pulling a rabbit from her hat, Violet whipped out the damned petition from behind the *Trickle*. "Voilà! Thirty-five names, Hogan." She slapped the paper against his chest, giving him no choice but to take it.

Reluctantly, he glanced down at the names—then snorted. "I see Honor and Lexie on here. And Brooklin." His gaze snared her. "And *you*."

She rolled one shoulder. "I didn't want to be left out."

There were several names he didn't recognize, but too many that he did. "This is a joke."

"Nope."

"But some of these women are in their sixties."

"News flash, darlin'—being sixty doesn't make you blind."

Hell, he was a man and it flattered him to get so much attention. He didn't flaunt, no. That was just stupid. But it wasn't like he was ashamed of his body. In fact, given how Violet reacted to him, he was starting to think…

He shook his head. No, he wouldn't let this turn him into a vain ass. "This is insane. You know that, right?"

Violet could barely fight off her grin. Her lips kept twitching to the point that he wanted to kiss her and to hell with anyone watching.

It also told him that she was having fun at his expense.

Violet didn't want him grilling shirtless; she just wanted to tease him. Again.

He'd have to give that some thought.

She said, "I forgot to look at the paper last week. There was so much going on." Her voice lowered even more. "Remember, that's when someone tried to get into Brooklin's house and we found out everything."

"I remember." How could he forget? He'd been on edge ever since.

"Then when I got the petition, I realized what it was and grabbed the *Trickle*. There it was, all spelled out."

Giving himself time to think, Hogan chose avoidance for the moment. "I need to get to work." He handed the paper to Violet, but as he stalked away, he heard a sudden roar of laughter.

Feminine laughter.

A smile cracked, yet he kept on walking.

His narrow view of females, once tainted by his cheating wife, was now much more open. He had to admit, these ladies were nuts, Violet especially. But God love them, they were fun.

What they didn't yet realize was that, finally, he could be fun, too.

And he could turn it all around on them.

FRIDAY AND SATURDAY evening crowds were always a little rowdier than the workweek. Not in any drunken or destructive way. Just a little louder, more packed, added chaos from the sheer volume of people coming and going. For the first time ever, Hogan resented that Violet was in the diner while he was stuck outside.

If he couldn't see her, how could he protect her?

Around seven o'clock, Nathan stopped by the grill with Brooklin, both of them looking very cozy together. After a glance around to ensure they weren't heard, Nathan said, "The cretin I told you about?"

"Yeah?" Hogan's gaze skipped to Brooklin, and he realized she looked tired, maybe a little defeated. "Bad news?"

"Not really." Nathan frowned. "He's still in prison."

"But…" Damn. Hogan didn't know what to think.

Brooklin turned her face up to Nathan. "I'll go find Violet. It'll give you guys a chance to talk while I update her."

Nathan stopped her. "If you see anyone suspicious at all, let me know."

Her smile was sad and fleeting. "I will."

Soon as she was gone, Nathan pulled up a chair under Hogan's rainbow umbrella. "She's stoic, but this is getting to her. We thought for sure it'd be Elle's father, Richard. But no chance. Given his track record in prison, I don't know if that bastard will ever get out."

"Troublemaker?" Hogan asked, then laughed without any humor. "You know what I mean."

"Yeah, I do. He's caused enough problems that he's been transferred twice. They got him to the new location only it wasn't ready, so he got moved again. That's why it took me a little longer to track him down. But he's definitely behind bars and likely to stay there."

"So who's threatening Brooklin?"

"That's the million-dollar question." Nathan sat back, his expression strained. "I love her."

Hogan's surprise didn't last. He smiled. "I figured."

"I have no idea who's bothering her or why, but someone is, and gut instinct tells me it's serious."

"Could that be emotion slanting things?" Nathan's reaction amplified his own. Uneasy, Hogan gave his attention to the grill. "You caring more for her could make the problems seem bigger, right?"

"No. At least, I don't think so." He pinched the bridge of his nose. "Never been in love before."

Hogan understood his confusion. He *had* been in love before, but things with Violet were different. Somehow…richer. Bigger. More confusing.

Could be his age, too. He was no longer a kid rushing into life and assuming it'd all work out. Older, and hopefully wiser, he knew things didn't always go as planned.

Sometimes they even went horribly wrong.

He said to Nathan, "Trust me. Having been there previously doesn't make it any easier."

That sharpened Nathan's attention and gradually he smiled. "You know, I was starting to think you were too damn stubborn, or else too stupid, to admit the truth."

"I hope I'm neither, but I am admittedly reluctant." And unlike Nathan, he wasn't about to make a public announcement on his relationship.

Nathan wasn't the pushy type, so he only said, "Don't be so reluctant that you miss out on something good," then slapped Hogan on the shoulder and went back to brooding while he awaited Brooklin.

Minutes later, Jason and Colt showed up with Honor. They went through the usual greetings. Then Hogan took Colt aside to fill him in, just as he'd done every day since the incident. Hogan wanted him aware of everything so he could be on guard.

When he finished, Colt's scowl was as dark as Nathan's. "I don't like it."

"No," Hogan said. "Nathan and I don't, either. But for now, there's nothing we can do except stay alert."

"Is it possible it was a fluke? Maybe the bozo moved on already..."

"I'd like to think that," Hogan said. "But since someone tried to get into her house, I can't."

"Yeah." Colt frowned, then put a hand on Hogan's shoulder. "I'll be inside, so I'll keep an eye out."

That both reassured and alarmed Hogan. "Don't take any chances."

"It's a crowded diner. No one would try anything in there."

"We don't know that. Remember, someone tried to run them both down during the middle of the day in the busiest part of town."

Colt's expression darkened even more. "We could be dealing with a nut."

"We could—so promise me, Colt."

His smile went crooked. "You think I'll try to be a hero? I'm not stupid."

"No, you're not." Hogan started to relax.

Until Colt added, "But you also can't expect me to stand by if someone tries to hurt Violet." He eyed his father. "I like her a lot. More than a lot. And I like how things are between the two of you."

Thrown by that casual statement, Hogan said, "You do?"

"Yeah. Everything is starting to feel... I don't know. *Normal* again." Colt shook his head, troubled, then asked, "Would you prefer for me to go away to school? I mean, you and Violet would have the house to yourselves then and—"

"Violet has her own house." And they didn't have the money for him to live away on campus. Not yet, anyway. Choosing his words carefully, Hogan said, "If all things were possible, what I'd prefer most is for you to have choices so you could decide what it is *you* want."

"I already know what I want." He shifted, looked at the people not that far from them, then to Hogan's face. "I was going to talk to you about something tonight, but I don't know… This feels like the right time."

Alarm slammed through Hogan. He said over his shoulder, "Jason, watch the grills for me."

Jason, who'd been talking with Nathan, said, "Sure," and without breaking the conversation went to poke at the ribs.

Hogan stepped aside with Colt, not far enough for serious privacy but it was all they had. "What's going on?"

Colt tried for a strained smile. "Nothing life or death, or even all that serious, so relax."

Hogan didn't think he could relax until he knew what had put that particular look on his son's face. He tried his own smile, and for the most part, managed. "I'm all ears."

Colt drew a breath, visibly girding himself, and said, "I'm going to graduate early."

All the tension fell from Hogan's shoulders, making him almost limp. No girl was pregnant, Colt hadn't been in a wreck, no mentions of drugs or any number of other things that he always took for granted because Colt was that type of young man, as honorable as good men twice his age.

"Jesus…" He laughed. "You had me there." Now able to draw a deep breath, Hogan said, "So, what's this about graduating early? What does that mean?"

Colt's smile went crooked. "What were you thinking?"

"That maybe I was going to be a grandpa early."

Snorting, Colt said, "No, I'm careful."

Hogan stared over that unintended admission, then shook himself. He wasn't obtuse. Colt was a good-looking kid, big, fit. Of course... He shook his head again and said, "Good. Not that you couldn't tell me if anything like that ever—"

"Relax, Dad, seriously. I'm not a drug addict, haven't robbed a bank, and I definitely haven't been careless with a girl."

Sharing the truth, Hogan said, "I couldn't really imagine any of those things. But in all seriousness, for any problem, ever, I'm here, okay?"

"I know, thanks. But it's nothing like that. There's a special program at the school. I can graduate in January, which will give me half the year to work and save for college, and then—"

"January?" That hit Hogan like a ton of bricks. "Graduating early is about working more?" His guts cramped. His son already worked too much. Maybe not as much as Hogan had at his age, but Colt didn't have a new wife with a kid on the way.

"It's about me getting on with my life. I'm acing school, you know that."

"You're freaking brilliant and it unnerves me. I have no idea where you got all those smarts."

Raising a brow and giving Hogan a look, Colt said, "I know exactly where I got my brains."

Damn, it was nice to be admired by his son. Really nice. Hogan took his shoulders in both his hands. "Then you're smart enough to know that high school isn't only about study. It's about social stuff, too."

"Out of school, I'd have more time for dating." Then he dropped another bombshell. "I've decided the local college would be better, too. Remember, we checked into it—"

"I know there are choices here, Colt." His son wanted to be a mechanical engineer. For two years, he'd talked about more prestigious colleges. MIT and Stanford were out, so he'd been focused more on the University of Michigan—which still would have been a financial stretch.

But now he was ready to settle for sticking closer to home?

"They have a decent program."

Hogan shook his head. "But it wasn't the choice you wanted."

"Not at first," Colt agreed. "But things changed."

Yeah, they had. Colt's mother had died, Hogan had lost his job, they'd moved—

"I don't mean the past," Colt said. "The more I've thought about it, the more I like the idea of sticking around. I like it here now." He shared another crooked grin. "And you know you'd miss me."

"A lot." He'd gotten used to having Colt at the diner with him. He valued the extra time they had to chat.

That didn't mean he wanted his son to give up on his goals.

"I've been thinking, too," Hogan said. "I could take a second mortgage, and—"

"You said it, Dad. They're my choices. Right?"

Hogan didn't want to, but he nodded. "As long as you're making those choices for the right reason."

"I am. I've given it a lot of thought, and I'm pretty pumped about it."

Damn, but Colt seemed dead set on things. "I want to meet with the counselor, hear about this program, and we have to talk about it more."

"Sure. I got you some literature on it. It's on the kitchen table at home."

Home. Did Colt truly feel like Clearbrook was now home? Hogan hoped so, because for him, it felt more like home than anyplace they'd ever been. "All right. I'll look at it tonight."

"I better get to work."

Stopping him, Hogan harked back to their original conversation. "If you see anything at all suspicious tonight, come get me."

"Sure. If there's time." He slung his arm around Hogan's shoulders, reminding his dad that while he was a whole lot leaner, he was now a few inches taller. "I won't play hero, but I'm also not going to hide in a corner, okay?"

Hogan put him in a headlock, they both laughed, and then he heard Sullivan say, "You're not burning my share of ribs, are you, Jason?"

Hogan released his son and glanced at his grill. "Damn it." He quickly shouldered Jason aside and hit the dancing flames with a spray bottle of water.

Both Sullivan and Lexie had joined the growing crowd outside. Sullivan explained, "We were going to sit inside, but it's jammed. Friday nights are getting busier than Saturdays."

"I know," Hogan said. "We'll have the upstairs ready soon. Then hopefully the younger crowd will fill that space and leave the main floor more open." In a town the size of Clearbrook, plans were seldom kept quiet. Most everyone knew about the expansion of space.

"I better get in there," Colt said. "But don't worry, Dad. I'll crawl out, my head covered, and get you if anyone looks at me funny."

Hogan threw a dish towel at him, grinning as his son ducked inside.

"You've done a great job with him." Sullivan stared after Colt. "I wish all young adults were that well-adjusted."

Lexie wrapped an arm around him. "Thanks to you, more of them are."

"She's right," Hogan said and saluted Sullivan with the water bottle. Being a true badass, Sullivan ran his own karate school for kids with behavioral issues. Hogan respected him a lot.

He was also in prime shape. If the ladies wanted to see someone without a shirt, they should be after Sullivan. He could make them all blush.

Then again, few people other than Lexie felt comfortable hassling Sullivan. From the first meeting on, Lexie had deliberately provoked him, flirted outrageously and eventually chased him down. They were yet one more happy couple to view as an example.

Hogan frowned at himself. An example of *what*?

He didn't feel like figuring it out, not at the moment, because another idea had just crowded his brain.

Ladies' night. Could he possibly convince Sullivan to take part? What about Jason? Nathan?

He was considering things when Jason brought up the awning that would go over his area.

"Violet wants two walls as well, to help shelter you from inclement weather."

The way his brother said it, Hogan knew those were her words. "When did she decide that?"

"She called me Wednesday so I could reconfigure my plans."

Hogan grumbled. "You'd think the rainbow umbrella and table would be enough."

"She's locking you in," Honor said.

The men all looked at her. "What do you mean?" Jason asked. "Why would she want to lock Hogan in?"

"Figuratively, I mean." Honor glanced at each of them, apparently amazed that they didn't understand. "Come on, guys. Violet's a businesswoman, and Hogan is good for business."

"He's good for *her*," Lexie added, apparently in agreement with her best friend. "That factors in, too."

Nodding, Honor said, "So of course she wants him as comfortable as possible. I mean, Screwy Louie's wouldn't crumble if Hogan walked out, but look at all the recent changes. Things are on the uptick, and they both look happier. Violet doesn't want to backtrack."

"She has the hots for him," Lexie insisted with bobbing eyebrows. "And honestly, Hogan, I think you owe me some gratitude for suggesting you work here." She managed a haughty expression. "I feel instrumental in this whole business and personal relationship."

"Agreed." Straight-faced, very sincere, Hogan said, "Thank you, Lexie."

The guys grinned, but both Lexie and Honor *oohed* in astonishment.

"You realize how lucky you are?" Lexie asked in disbelief.

"Yup."

Her tone cautious, she said, "Wow."

Honor pressed a hand to her heart. "Oh, Hogan, seeing you happy makes me happy for you."

He drew back. "You're rushing ahead, hon."

"Let her rush," Jason said.

When Honor pulled him into a big hug, her head on his shoulder, her arms tight around him, Hogan went with the suggestion and let her. Honor always had a funny effect on him, making him feel valued. He grumbled near her ear, "I'm not eloping or anything."

"I know," she said, just as quietly. "But you are getting on with your life."

Huh. Yeah, maybe he was.

With one more squeeze, Hogan released Honor. "It's a nice thing, having a sister-in-law."

"Almost as nice," she said, "as having a brother-in-law."

Jason, pleased with that exchange, smiled at them both, then led his wife away so they could eat.

When Hogan thought of Meg this time, when he thought of all she'd taken, what hit him was that her actions had put him here, right where he was this very minute, surrounded by very genuine people, working a no-stress job he loved, alongside a woman who matched him in nearly every way.

He'd loved Meg—he couldn't deny that. If she hadn't cheated, hadn't died while walking out on him, he'd be with her still, a faithful, dedicated husband to the bitter end.

But what he felt for Violet was as different as night to day. He and Meg had each accepted their designated roles. Until she'd changed, they'd taken on their responsibilities without question, without much complaint.

But with Violet, everything was shared.

Everything.

And that made it so much better.

Ten minutes later, Hogan was still standing there, staring at the grill, breathing harder under the weight of realization, when Violet slipped out to visit him.

"My," she said, giving him a hip bump, "with that blank stare on your face, I don't think it's my legs occupying your thoughts this time."

Hogan turned to see her, *really* see her, and felt his heart expanding. She did look happy. And beautiful.

She looked like *his*.

"Hey."

She cocked her head to the side. "You okay?"

Actually, he was better than okay. He felt at peace. "You visited with Brooklin?"

"I did. I feel so bad for her, Hogan. She thinks she's somehow responsible, but she has no idea what's happening or why."

"Nathan will figure it out." He glanced over at them where they sat alone beneath the shade of a tree. "He's in it for the long haul."

"Brooklin is, too. But with this big mystery, she's afraid Nathan could get hurt."

Hogan scoffed. "He's the sheriff. Before that he was SWAT. Pretty sure he can take care of himself."

"That's what I told her, but she reminded me that Nathan had been hurt once, and once was more than enough."

Huh. Yeah. Hogan looked at Nathan, at the scar on his face that now just seemed a part of him, like his hair and eye color or his height. But thinking of it, he had to agree. "Maybe it was a fluke."

"How Nathan got hurt? No, I don't think so. He wouldn't take it so personally if that was the case."

"Probably not." Had Nathan's gut instinct once failed him? If so, that'd explain why he was doubly determined to keep Brooklin from harm.

Violet sighed. "We'll all be careful and eventually we'll find the jerk who's giving her a hard time."

Hogan brushed away a few tendrils of dark red hair that had escaped her braid. He saw the dampness across her cheekbones and the flush in her cheeks, proof that she'd been rushing to keep up with customers. "How's your foot?"

"What foot?"

He slid his hand around to her exposed nape. "The foot that's still bruised and tender."

"It's on the bottom of my leg, right where it belongs." She tipped back her head to stare up at him, her tone casual but her expression probing. "Hogan, since when did you start all this familiar touching in front of people?"

Looking at her mouth, he asked, "What people?"

Her lips curled. "You can be so funny." She rested against his supporting hand for just a moment. "Okay, so you no longer care if folks around here see you getting cozy with me. You gotta know, sugar, I'm fine with that."

"Yeah?"

"It was never my problem in the first place."

True, he'd been the ass. But ever since she'd gotten hurt, he'd had the urge to show everyone the truth.

Now was a good time to start.

"Good." He bent to kiss her nose, her chin, then briefly brush his mouth over hers.

Violet blinked at him. "I'm starting to think there's something in the air today. You know, Colt just told me I was one of his favorite people, and I needed to promise him I wouldn't hesitate to tell him if I saw anyone fishy. Then he gave me a hug. Like…a four- or five-second hug."

Hogan grinned. "I hope you promised him."

"Not exactly, no. If I did see someone suspicious, the very last thing I'd want is for Colt to get involved. He's young, your son, an employee, and one of *my* very favorite people, too. All reasons why I'd want to protect him, not drag him into harm's way."

That gave Hogan something new to chew on. "So you two get along that well?"

"We do. He's mature beyond his years, but still with all that boyish charm. And he's a real sweetheart. I'm going to miss him something awful when he goes off to college."

"Did you tell him that?"

"Not tonight, but I have, yeah." She gave a wistful sigh. "He said he'd miss me, too."

Lots and lots to think about, Hogan decided.

Kristy came out, needing more ribs to fill her orders. Hogan loaded her platter full.

Violet sniffed the air. "Even though you've been serving those for a while now, they still make my mouth water. I don't suppose you have any other specialties to share?"

"I grill a mean steak."

She shuddered. "Too expensive."

"Huh. Well…" He pretended to search his mind, then offered, "I'm good in bed. Does that count as a specialty?"

She opened her mouth, closed it, then laughed and patted his chest. "I'd sure count it, but I don't want it on the menu."

His inclination was to kiss the sassy smile off her mouth, which would require something more than a peck, maybe some tongue, too. Unfortunately, too many customers sat around them, enjoying the balmy evening while dining with friends and family. Honor and Jason were at a nearby table, with Honor glowing at them like a proud mama. Lexie and Sullivan sat with them, Lexie once again bobbing her eyebrows.

Nathan and Brooklin were farther out, seated across

from each other, leaning in close to talk, their body language intimate.

Knowing they were being watched, Hogan said, "When I get you alone…" He left it open-ended enough to entice.

"Oh, I hope it's something good." Violet propped her hip against his rainbow-covered table and held out a gift bag.

"What's this?" Hogan eyed the colorful tissue paper.

"It's a little something for you." A wicked light glittered in her blue eyes, and she couldn't suppress her smile. "Go on. Open it."

Curious, he set aside his tongs and pulled the puff of tissue paper off the top of the bag.

Inside was a shirt.

He knew exactly what it would be. Grinning, he withdrew it and shook it out.

Sure enough, Barbecue Master, in a special flame font, blazed across the front of a supersoft black T-shirt.

"Look at that," he said, flattered that she'd had it made for him. "I like it."

"It's your size, right?"

He checked inside the collar, saw it was a large and nodded. "Yeah." He smiled at Violet's expectant expression. "Now it's official. Thank you."

"Put it on."

Pausing, wondering what she was up to, Hogan repeated, "Put it on?"

Violet nodded.

He glanced around, recognizing many familiar faces, some of them not well-known to him but he'd dished up their food many times.

Fortunately, he didn't see any strangers who could be a threat to Violet or Brooklin.

But he did have everyone's attention. In fact, ladies had crowded out of the building and were now watching from around the front wall. "You mean…now?"

"Yes." Her mouth twitched with suppressed hilarity. "I want to see it on you."

"Violet—"

She leaned in and whispered, "I was encouraged to ask. But as your boss, I certainly don't expect you to—"

"I'll do it."

Her eyes went comically wide. Two beats of silence passed before she demanded, "What do you mean, you'll do it?"

Hogan almost laughed. So, she'd thought he wouldn't? She'd come out here to razz him, fully knowing women would watch? Violet was quirky, and he adored that about her.

Trying to pretend confusion, he asked, "Why not?"

Her mouth pinched.

"Do it," Honor said, starting a chant. "Do it, do it, do it."

Others joined in, proving they'd all known what was happening.

"Hogan," Violet said, fresh color on her cheeks, "you don't have to—"

"Oh, I don't mind." Funny, the more she protested, the more he wanted to call her bluff. He lifted a hand, said loudly, "You're all about to be disappointed." Then he stripped off his shirt.

Raucous cheers rang out from the ladies, while the men booed him.

Colt stood in the doorway from the prep area, an ear-to-ear grin splitting his face.

Someone, probably Lexie, gave a loud wolf whistle.

Mrs. Arbuckle, at least eight-five, playfully shouted, "Oh, my heart!"

"Here." Violet shoved the new shirt at him. "Put it on already before you kill someone."

Fighting off a laugh, Hogan bent and kissed her mulish mouth before pulling on the shirt and smoothing it down. The kiss was to let everyone know that he'd done this to tease Violet, not for any other reason.

Not for any other woman.

Holding his arms out to his sides and doing a slow turn so everyone could see, he called out, "What do you think?"

More cheers filled the air, scaring birds out of the trees.

Hogan snagged his arm around Violet and hugged her close. He knew without a doubt, here, with Violet, with all the crazy neighbors and family, with his smiling son, was exactly where he needed to be.

CHAPTER SEVENTEEN

AFTER THE LAUGHTER died down, Nathan turned back to Brooklin and found her smiling as she watched Hogan and Violet. "You look happy."

She took his hand in both of hers, emphasizing the contrast in their sizes. "I am."

"I'm glad." The setting sun cast a halo around her hair. The air smelled thick, as if it might rain. A breeze teased past.

Nathan drew her hand to his mouth and kissed her knuckles. Her skin was so soft, her nails short but glossy with polish. "I never would have imagined Hogan doing that, but I'm glad he did." He'd gotten used to seeing the strain on her face, but for the moment it was gone. "I like seeing you like this."

"Like what?" Brooklin could barely contain herself. Then she started snickering.

"Lighthearted, I guess." He didn't want her to worry. He wasn't about to let anything happen to her. But this hilarity? "What's going on?"

The snickers turned into full-blown chuckles.

His own mouth twitching, Nathan said, "What? It wasn't that funny."

She tried a deep breath, but couldn't get the amusement off her face. Leaning in, she confided, "I orchestrated most of that."

"Yeah?" Nathan had no idea what she was talking

about, but her mood was so carefree, he wanted it to last. "How's that?"

Her golden eyes searched his. She leaned closer still, whispering. "I'll tell you something no one else knows, if you'll tell me how you got hurt."

"Hurt?"

With one fingertip, she lightly traced the scar on his face. "This." She ended by moving that finger over his bottom lip. "You had promised to tell me, but then you didn't and I didn't want to press you."

"Pressing me now is okay?"

All the past wariness flooded back into her face and she withdrew. "No. I'm sorry. I shouldn't have—"

"No, it's fine." Nathan circled the table, then sat down close beside her. Keeping an eye on the surrounding area, at all the different people there, he said, "I don't mind telling you. I just forgot." A lie. They both knew it. "Besides, once I tell you, you're going to share some awesome secret, right?"

"Yes." She cautiously smiled again. "It truly is awesome."

He nodded, wondering where to start. "Truth is I screwed up. We were executing a search warrant for a drug bust. We used some flash bangs—"

"Flash bangs?"

"Explosions that disorient the occupants." He stopped, remembering, then looked away. "I was first in. There were four occupants, but they were down, cowering. Everything seemed secure in the main rooms. I called it clear. Then Officer Johnson tried to force open an interior door. Soon as it budged, two men came out shooting. Johnson wore his helmet, but he got struck in the back of the head."

Brooklin covered her mouth. "You got hit, too?"

"The gunfire shattered a mirror. My eyes were mostly protected by the visor, but not the bottom of my face. The glass…" He could almost feel again the pumping adrenaline, the frigid anger. "It jammed inside my helmet. That's how I got cut. Wounded, but not down."

"What did you do?"

"I killed them both." Just not in time to spare Johnson.

Eyes big and soft, Brooklin whispered, "Did Officer Johnson survive?"

He shook his head. "He was young. Newly married." Nathan's throat felt tight, but he ignored it. "He died later in the hospital."

"I am so, so sorry."

He picked up her hand and kissed her wrist. "You had a right to know."

Just like that, she melted into his arms. "I'm not sorry for asking. I'm sorry that you were hurt and that you lost a friend."

Nathan hugged her close. Damn, she felt good in his arms.

"Thank you for telling me."

He nodded. "I got out of SWAT after that. At first I couldn't decide what I wanted to do, and somehow I ended up in the area. Didn't take me long to decide this was home."

"And then you became the sheriff."

"It seemed the perfect fit."

"I understand why. Clearbrook is a special place." She stroked a hand over his chest. "Small enough to be quaint, with a variety of characters in it. Large enough to have all the conveniences within a short drive."

Did she realize what that innocent touch did to him?

He flattened his own hand over hers, then said, "Will you officially move in with me, Brooklin?"

She froze.

Nathan set her back to see her face, to make her understand. "Eventually we'll find the guy bothering you. But it doesn't matter. I want you with me whether there's any overt danger or not. Always."

She searched his face. "You love me?"

How the hell had he forgotten that part? He gave a crooked smile. "Yeah, I love you. I think I lost it for you the very first time I saw you. Everything after that was just buildup."

That brought her right back into his arms. "I love you, too. But there's something else I need to tell you."

Since she'd agreed, she could tell him anything she wanted. It wouldn't matter. "Your exciting secret?"

"Yes." She looked around as if to ensure no one could hear her. In a barely there whisper, she said, "You know that advice column in the *Trickle*?"

Suspicion crowded in. He remembered the columns with questions about him, and the disparaging way the columnist had replied. "Yeah?"

"I'm Advice Anonymous."

Nathan stared at her. "No."

"Yes. I'm sorry about those first few. I think my replies came from both a touch of jealousy and a little spite."

"Just a little?"

She gave him a shameless grin. "Okay, I was spiteful. You were pestering me...and I liked it. Only I thought that was dangerous, because if we got involved—"

"You'd have to explain. But now you know it doesn't matter."

"No, because you're so wonderful. Still, I wouldn't

have told, except that if I move in with you, you're bound to see the pile of mail I get, and you'll see me working on the weekly piece, so—"

His burst of laughter cut her off.

People looked their way. Brooklin bit her lip.

Once he'd caught his breath, Nathan said, "You were the one who accused me of preferring men."

She winced. "Guilty. I'm so glad Stan wasn't offended."

"Stan thought it was hilarious, especially when you insulted me. And Hogan."

"That was before I knew you both well."

When she'd wanted to stay distant—only he hadn't let her. She'd tried her best to make him lose interest. Good thing he wasn't a quitter. "Now that you know Hogan—"

She gave him a beautiful smile. "I honestly get a lot of mail from women asking questions about both of you. Recently, since I didn't want to share you, I decided to focus on the requests about Hogan."

"And it brought him and Violet closer together."

Brooklin nodded. "And now you see why I'm so pleased."

"Yeah, I do." He kissed her, lingering longer than he should have, but unable to pull away. Against her mouth, he murmured, "You are one multitalented lady."

"And you love me?"

He took her mouth again. "Yes."

She put her forehead to his. "The past, those awful accusations… I was so ashamed. It seemed everyone believed the lies, even my fiancé. I couldn't see trusting anyone else, definitely not a man." She sat back and touched his face again. "But now there's you."

"And you love me, too?"

She nodded. "Everything about you." Tears sheened

her eyes. "I went from being so alone to feeling so blessed. Thank you for convincing me to let you in."

He touched away the tear from her bottom lashes. "Sometimes I'm a pretty smart guy." Nathan breathed in the scent of her, stroked her soft hair, felt her toned body against his.

They would put an end to the danger soon. Very soon. Somehow he'd figure it out.

IT WAS NEARING the end of the day, the crowd mellower, the servers wearing down. Giving Kristy a break, Violet waited tables. She'd just finished serving a family of four when she saw a familiar face go past the front window.

Oh, hell no. *Joni Jeffers*.

Moving quickly, she cut through the diner to the prep area and then outside. She got to Hogan seconds before Joni did. He looked up at her to smile, saw Joni and went still.

A second later he gave Violet a stern shake of his head, no doubt an implicit warning to behave.

Ha! Okay, yeah. She couldn't, wouldn't, cause another scene. But if Joni hoped to win Hogan back, she could forget it.

As usual, Joni was dressed to kill in a fitted sundress appropriate for the warm evening. She even wore heels and she came directly to Hogan.

He said, "Joni, hi. How are you?"

"That was my line to you." She flicked a cautious glance Violet's way.

"Ms. Jeffers," Violet said, her smile all but forcing the woman to be cordial.

"Ms...." Joni shook her head, impatient. "I'm sorry. I don't know your name."

"You can just call me Violet," she drawled. *Or you can go away.*

"Violet." Her teeth showed in a strained smile. "Pretty name."

Oh ho, now what was that? An attempt at *niceness*? Violet crossed her arms. The woman was up to something.

Hogan stepped in. "Did you come for dinner?"

"Actually, I have some business I'd like to discuss with you."

It took everything Violet had not to protest. If she was superpolite, she'd step away and give them privacy.

Not happening.

"How about I watch things for you?" She snatched the tongs out of Hogan's hand and planted herself—all of two feet away—at the grills.

Joni said, "Could we talk somewhere private?"

"Sorry, I can't. You probably saw that we're slammed tonight. I'm betting Violet has a dozen other things she should be doing. But I can take a few minutes real quick, right here, if it's important."

Keeping her back to them, Violet curled her mouth in a satisfied smile. *Take that, Joni.*

"Fine," Joni said. "I'll get right to the point. A few of the companies who had you handling their books... well, they want only you."

There was silence, and then Hogan asked, "How many companies, Joni?"

"Three. Okay, maybe four. They're big accounts and I don't want to lose them."

"That's a tough spot...since I don't work for you anymore."

"Yes, well..."

Violet literally *felt* Joni's glare against her back. She didn't budge.

Joni cleared her throat. "Since I don't want to lose them, I thought maybe we could work out something."

"Something like what?"

She inhaled sharply. "How about you continue with their books for a commission?"

"I have very little free time. It'd depend on how big the commission is."

She named the size of the account and a percentage for the commission. Violet, quickly trying to do the math in her head, almost whistled. That would put a nice chunk back into Hogan's budget.

But he said only, "I'll give it some thought."

"You're serious? That was a more than generous offer!"

"And I appreciate it. But my time is limited, so I have to consider it carefully before I take on anything else."

Joni stewed, then snapped, "Eight hours a week. Surely you can eke out that much time from your social calendar."

She was so damned snide, Violet's hand tightened around the tongs. They were good and heavy—but no, if she did, Hogan would be embarrassed again.

And he'd lose the very nice offer.

Striving for patience, Joni sweetened her tone and said, "Very well. How much time do you need?"

"I'll let you know on Monday."

"That'll be fine. Thank you." She stepped closer to Violet. "Those ribs really do smell delicious. Could I get an order to go?"

"Certainly." Violet turned to Hogan, a brow raised.

He rolled his eyes. "I'll get Kristy and a take-out container."

"Thank you, sugar." She gave her attention back to Joni. "I gather those are some important accounts?"

"I would not have come here otherwise."

Violet took her measure, then admitted, "It took guts."

"I have guts," Joni confirmed with some obvious pride. "I run my own accounting firm."

"I run my own diner." It was Violet's turn to flash her teeth in the semblance of a smile. "Just think, we actually have something in common."

As Hogan came back out, Joni watched him and said, "Maybe more than one thing?"

The smile turned to a snarl. "Only if you mean admiration, because, honey, he's hands-off to you."

Joni rolled one shoulder. "Sadly true—and I accept it."

Like she had a choice, Violet thought. But she decided to be gracious in her victory.

Minutes later, Joni was gone with her dinner, and Violet really wanted to stamp her claim on Hogan to avoid all further assumptions by women like that.

He beat her to it, looping his arms around her hips and nuzzling her throat. "I'm proud of you, Violet. Other than glaring just a little, you held it together."

Seeing no harm in the truth, she confessed, "It wasn't easy, not with that woman."

"I know. I could tell." He pressed his mouth to hers in a soft kiss that felt both tender and possessive. "Thank you."

That made her roll her eyes. "You don't have to thank me for not behaving like a lunatic."

"Where *that woman* is concerned," he teased, mimicking her, "I think I do."

Violet punched him in the stomach, but she was too

close to put much strength behind it and he only laughed at her.

Feeling strangely emotional, she traced a fingertip over the words on his shirt. Barbecue Master. True enough, he was a master. But she should have put Screwy Louie's Barbecue Master.

Because damn it, he *was* hers.

She'd add the correction to the next shirt she got him.

Picking up on her mood, Hogan lifted her chin. "You know you don't have to worry about Joni, right? Even if I take the offer—"

"You have to. I know that."

He gave her a long look. "It'd solve a lot of problems, true, but there's nothing between Joni and me."

She couldn't resist one more grouching comment. "Not for lack of her trying."

He pulled her in for a longer, deeper kiss, then whispered, "She could run naked in front of me, and it wouldn't matter. I only want you."

Her heart did a double beat. As sincere as she could make it, without seeming too clingy, Violet said, "That's probably good, since I only want you."

His gaze went hot. "I've thought about it a lot. About you." He put his mouth to her ear, whispering, "How you taste, the way you sound when you're getting close. How tight you squeeze me when you come, and how wet you are—"

Shaking, Violet pushed his back. "You're doing it again! Blast it, Hogan, we can't get out of here yet."

He grinned. "Soon, though. And now you have something to think about."

She fried him with a cross frown. "Wasn't like I needed help with that." Knowing she'd been gone too long, she turned away with a huff and strode into the dining area.

She found Colt hustling to keep up without her.

Poor kid. After a quick apology to him, she told him to take his break and dived back in—but Hogan was right.

He'd certainly given her something to think about.

To MAKE A POINT, Colt went right up to the table where Charish sat with a few of their friends, two other girls and two other boys, including Mack.

He bent and brushed his mouth over hers.

Everyone stared.

Charish beamed.

"I've got fifteen minutes. Let's go outside."

Accepting the hand he offered her, Charish left her seat in a rush.

Mack said, "Hey!" around a fat grin.

With his arm behind Charish, Colt subtly flipped him off, then heard the group laughing.

Earlier, he'd told Mack the way of things, and there were no problems.

Colt led her out the front door. His dad was around back, along with two dozen customers at least. He wanted time alone with her. Now that he'd made a move, his body was telling him to make a few more.

At least at the front of the building it was quieter, any passersby on the move.

They strolled down the sidewalk to where his truck was parked at the end of the block. It was nearly deserted here at the narrow one-way side street that got little traffic.

Charish looked up at the sky. "It's pretty tonight."

Colt kept his gaze on her profile. "The sunsets are always great. Honor loves them." In case she didn't know, he explained, "She's my aunt."

"I've met her," Charish said. "I go to the salon where she works."

Colt admired her hair, long and dark and currently bone straight down her back, swishing just above her hips. She changed it up a lot with ponytails, braids, straight or wavy, up or down. No matter what she did with it, it always teased him with the need to touch it.

Now he could, and so he stroked his hand through it, bunched it in his fist and enjoyed the silkiness of it.

Starkly aware of her as a girl who wanted him, a girl who hadn't taken a nice "no" as an answer—thank God—Colt lowered the back gate, took her tiny waist in his hands and easily lifted her up to sit.

Before he could pull back, Charish wrapped her arms around his neck, keeping him from stepping away.

"Colt?"

Those big dark eyes stole any self-proclaimed control. Unable to resist, he leaned in and kissed her.

She immediately opened her mouth, scooted closer until her breasts were against his chest, and he knew he just might lose it.

This wasn't the school where touching was off-limits, but still they didn't have complete privacy, so he forced himself to end the kiss. "What time do your parents expect you home?"

"I have another hour."

She'd be gone before he got off work. "How about I come by tomorrow? I have a few hours in the morning. We can take my dog, Diesel, to the creek." And with any luck, the parklike area wouldn't be too jammed. He wanted his mouth on hers, and more.

"I'd love that." She kissed his face, his nose, his jaw, his chin...

Smiling, Colt cupped her face and said, "Hold still." Then he took her mouth the way he liked, the way she apparently liked, too, given her soft moan.

He let his hand travel to her shoulder down to her waist again, and then to the flare of her hip.

She wore a denim skirt, and refusing to think of possible consequences, his palm coasted over her bare thigh.

They both breathed harder.

She's not telling me to stop, Colt realized, and of course that sent his thoughts reeling into different scenarios, all of them impossible on a truck bed at the curb of the street with him having only ten minutes left for his break.

But he couldn't leave her, not yet, not this time.

It wasn't until someone bumped into him that he came back to the here and now.

He looked up and into a pair of mirrored sunglasses.

"Sorry," the guy said absently. He tugged a ball cap lower, stuffed his hands deeper into his loose cargo pants, stepped up to the sidewalk and continued on.

The guy's distracted gaze stayed glued to the diner, which was probably what caused their collision in the first place.

Colt watched him stride toward the diner, saw him pause and study the building.

Alarm bells went off in his head and he pulled Charish from the truck, his hand tight on hers. "Come on."

"What's wrong."

She sounded startled and uncertain, so he paused to reassure her. "Not a thing with you, except that I shouldn't start things I can't finish." He brushed his knuckles over her rosy cheek. "When we're alone, though…" He left that thought unfinished.

Squeezing his hand, she sighed and said, "I can't wait."

Colt breathed a little harder. Her agreement was almost more temptation than he could take. If he didn't get his brain elsewhere, and fast, he'd end up embarrassing himself.

When he looked back up, the guy was gone. Into the diner? Oh, hell. "Let's go." He picked up the pace, causing Charish to almost jog beside him—which made her breasts bounce, and *damn*, he *really* needed to focus.

When he burst into the diner and looked around, he saw the man wasn't there after all. Violet had just left the dining room with a tub full of dirty dishes. A large group was in the process of getting their seats, another group leaving.

Everything was as it should be and finally he started to relax.

"What in the world was that about?" Charish asked.

"I thought I saw someone…" What could he say? It was private business and he wouldn't break his father's trust by speaking out of turn. "Never mind. It's not important."

"You're sure everything is okay?"

"Yeah. But I have to get back on the clock now. Tomorrow, okay? I'll call you when I'm on my way."

She went on tiptoe to brush her mouth over his. "I'll be ready, Colt."

Damn, the way she said that with so much promise… Colt watched her walk away, her hips swaying, her expression content, and knew he was a goner. Good intentions only took a guy so far.

As Violet started back into the room, loudly humming, Colt stopped her. "Okay if I take two more minutes?"

"Sure, honey. Take ten if you need them."

Violet called everyone "honey" or "sugar," but he still liked it. No one had ever treated him with quite the same combination of respect, affection and familiarity.

He'd have told his dad by now that he not only adored Violet, he loved her, too. He wanted her in their lives. But his dad needed to make that decision on his own—while also knowing it would never be a problem for Colt.

Going through the diner and out to the prep area, Colt found his dad cleaning one grill while the last of the ribs sizzled on another. "Got a sec?"

Hogan looked up, saw his face and put everything else on hold. "What's up?"

It had always been that way, Colt thought. His dad seemed to know his moods, always picking up on any trouble or worry, no matter how trivial it might be.

"How do you do that?"

"What's that?" As usual, Hogan played down his concern so Colt wouldn't feel pressured or put on the spot. He cleaned his hands on a towel, occasionally giving Colt a searching glance while he waited with extreme patience.

Colt felt a reluctant grin tug at his mouth. "You're the best of dads. You know that, right?"

Taken aback, Hogan spiked up his brows. "What brought that on?"

"Just saying. You're always telling me what a good son I am, right? Figured I'd return the compliment."

Abashed, Hogan nodded. "Thank you."

Moving on before that all got too serious, Colt said, "Anyway, I wanted you to know about something. Probably nothing. But I don't know... It didn't feel right."

"Then we don't want to dismiss it."

Exactly Colt's thoughts. He explained about the man and how he'd watched the diner.

"You'd know him again if you saw him?"

"Not sure. He wore reflective glasses and a Reds ball cap."

"Hmm." Hogan looked toward Nathan, caught his eye and with a lift of his chin called him over.

Colt wasn't sure what to think. He didn't want to make a big deal out of nothing, but he'd also rather look like an alarmist than have the guy be an actual threat.

After he'd heard everything, Nathan clapped Colt on the shoulder. "My rule is to never discount instinct. If it felt wrong to you, then it likely was. We don't have much to go on, but can you guess age? Hair color? Height or weight? Anything like that?"

"Maybe a few inches shorter than Dad. Thin. Definitely older than me, but not *old*. Maybe your age. Somewhere in there." He shrugged. "I'd say brown hair, but that's just a guess. Mostly I looked into those reflective glasses. Oh, and he wore really baggy tan cargo pants."

Suddenly Violet came out dragging Kristy in her wake. She almost stumbled over her own feet when she saw Nathan, Colt and Hogan in close conversation. Surprise quickly shifted to irritation.

Colt knew she thought she'd been excluded. She was such a take-charge woman she wouldn't like being left out.

Hogan separated from them, taking a step closer to her. "Everything okay?"

"What's going on here?"

Hogan said, "You first."

"All right, fine. I wanted you to hear this yourself." She pulled Kristy forward.

Obviously confused, Kristy looked around at everyone, shrugged and said, "I was putting trash bags in the Dumpster around back by the stairs, and someone came by to ask about Brooklin. At least, I think it was Brooklin. The way he described her, especially her eyes, and saying she was new to town... What?"

Colt watched in awe as Nathan banked the fury, as his dad calmed his expression.

Something was happening. He *felt* it. Instinct, Nathan said. Was it the same guy?

"When was this?" Nathan asked.

"Just a few minutes ago. I thought you and Brooklin were gone. I told him to check back here but he said he already had and he couldn't find you."

Hogan said, "Can you describe him?"

Kristy rolled a shoulder. "He wore a hat and sunglasses..." She frowned and said again, more strident this time, *"What?"*

Violet quickly spoke up. "There's a guy who's been hanging around pestering the ladies. If you see him again, get away from him, okay? And then let me know."

"Or better still," Hogan said, "tell me."

Violet pinned him with a look of umbrage.

Colt, not wanting them to clash, asked Kristy, "Was he wearing cargo pants?"

"I think so. Honestly, we're so busy right now I wasn't paying that much attention."

"What exactly did he say to you?"

She smiled at Colt, liking his calm and easy tone more than the tempered tones of Nathan and Hogan.

"He said he was a friend of hers, knew she was new to town and wanted to hook up with her again. He described her and asked if I knew where she lived. I told him Clearbrook wasn't that large, but that I wasn't sure.

Anyway, I told him to talk to the sheriff." Her expression turned sly. "I figured Nathan would know where she lived."

Ignoring that, Nathan asked, "He was on foot?"

"Far as I know."

"Anything else?" Hogan asked.

She shook her head. "Why so much interest? The guy didn't seem dangerous. I thought he had a nice smile."

Violet stepped in. "No, he's probably not dangerous at all. But it's a little creepy how he keeps approaching all the women. Like I said, steer clear of him, okay?"

"Sure, no problem."

"And from now on," Colt said, "I'll be the one to take out the garbage."

Soon as Kristy went back to work, Violet said, "All right, tell me quick. It's slowed down some, but Kristy can't handle it on her own."

"I'll go," Colt offered, but Hogan shook his head.

"I want you to describe the guy to Brooklin." Then to Violet, he explained what had happened.

Her horrified gaze shot to Colt. Voice a bit shrill, she said, "I want you to stay away from him, too. You understand?"

"Yes, ma'am."

"Don't you *'yes, ma'am'* me, Colt Guthrie. You're all agreeable because you plan to do just as you please."

He said, "Uh…"

"I want your promise."

Colt was stuck. He didn't like seeing Violet upset, but no way could he make that promise, not if the guy might bother Kristy or Violet. He glanced over at Brooklin and included her in his thoughts. He couldn't let some jerk bother *any* woman. "I, ah…"

Hogan handled the issue, putting his arm around

Violet and steering her away. "I'll talk to my son, okay?"

She didn't want to—anyone could see that—but Violet gave in. "Fine."

"Now I need Colt to describe the guy to Brooklin."

"I would love to be in on this conversation, but I really do have to go." She pointed at Hogan. "You won't keep anything from me."

He grinned at her, said, "Yes, ma'am," then pulled her in for a lingering kiss before she could blast him.

Colt loved the look in his dad's eyes, as well as the surprise on Violet's. She glanced at Colt and blushed, then hustled in.

"Nicely played, Dad," Colt said, giving his approval. "You've got her confused."

Hogan nodded. "She'll figure it out soon enough."

She would, huh? Colt figured things were moving right along, with all the pieces falling into place.

There was only one exception.

When they all turned to Brooklin, they found her watching like a deer in the headlights. She knew something was happening.

Colt sympathized with her as Nathan fetched her over.

Tense with uneasiness, she asked, "What's happened?"

Nathan put his arm around her. "Someone asked about you. I want to know if you recognize the guy at all."

Colt gave the description again, watching Brooklin closely as he did so. He saw the fear disappear and a look of relief take its place.

"Well," she said, leaning into Nathan, "I don't think

that's a tragedy at all. In fact, the guy you described could be Russell."

"Russell?" Nathan asked.

"My ex-fiancé. Remember, I told you he was a teacher with me?"

If Nathan had looked pissed before, it was nothing like the thundercloud that surrounded him now. "Your ex-fiancé? Here?"

She shrugged. "Could be. I've never seen Russell in a ball hat or cargoes. But the height sounds right, and he was always slim."

"We'll hang around a little longer," Nathan decided with grim anticipation, "just in case he comes back." Not fooling anyone, he fashioned a mean smile and said, "I'd like to meet him."

The show of jealousy amused Colt, but he coughed it away so he wouldn't offend the sheriff further. "I better get in there now. I can tell Violet what's happening if you want. That way you can finish up out here."

Hogan agreed, but said, "If you see him, Colt, let me know."

"I will." He grinned at his dad. "And I'll do what I can to keep Violet away from him."

CHAPTER EIGHTEEN

VIOLET DIDN'T NOTICE her foot the rest of the night. How could she? She wasn't sure her feet had touched the ground.

Multiple times, Hogan had publicly kissed her. To anyone observing it'd be clear they were a couple. Even the idea of Brooklin's idiot ex hanging around wasn't enough to dampen her happiness.

She wanted to ask Hogan what it meant, but at the same time, not knowing was nice. She could imagine anything.

And everything.

But at least now she knew they were making progress. She'd been more than willing to give Hogan time. After everything he'd been through, after all the upsets in Colt's life… Well, she loved them both enough to be as patient as necessary.

She hadn't heard Colt approach until he said, "What a day. That had to be the biggest Friday yet."

Smiling, she turned from cleaning a booth. "I think it was. Your dad is doing inventory right now, to see what sold best with his ribs. I'm guessing it was a banner night."

"Everyone's gone now?"

"Kristy just finished up and left. Last I saw them, Brooklin and Nathan were still out back, but I imagine they'll go before we do."

Colt's smile stayed in place, and he kept looking at her.

"What?" She touched her now-very-messy braid, wondering if she'd gotten a French fry caught in it, or a pickle or something. Some days, when she ran from cleanup to serving, to carryout and back again, she ended the day a real mess.

He shook his head, looked down at his feet, drew a breath and finally met her gaze again. "I like having you in our family, Violet. I really do."

"In your family?" *Oh, how nice that sounded.* "But I'm not—"

"Yeah, you are."

Colt wasn't the type of kid to dance around something. He was more mature than that, more confident. She wouldn't insult him by pretending she didn't understand. "I would truly love that." Then she held out a hand. "But I wasn't rushing things. It'd only work for me if it's what you and your dad want."

"I do. And from what I've seen, Dad does, too. He wouldn't stake a claim like that otherwise."

"Stake a claim?"

Colt laughed at her. "You know what I mean. All the PDAs."

"Right." Those *public displays of affection* were new for him. She wrinkled her nose. "I didn't want to make too much of it."

"You two will work it out. I just wanted you to know I'm happy about it."

Well, he just about melted her heart. "Thank you, Colt."

"I know it's been a long day, but I wanted to ask you about something else, too, if you have a few minutes."

She would always have time for him. "Sure. What's up?"

In short order, he explained an early graduation program. "I'll be out in January, and I was wondering if you'd have some full-time work for me. I could learn from Dad at the grill, since I know his 'secret sauce.' But I wouldn't mind doing whatever."

Devastated, Violet drew him into the booth and made him sit down. "Out in January, you said?"

"Yes."

"Colt, when I was your age, I worked full-time. At the time I didn't mind it, except that I missed all the dances and parties and all the fun stuff." Which, of course, meant on some level she'd minded very much. "I don't want you to miss it, too."

"I don't care about all that."

"Of course you do. I saw you talking with that girl tonight."

"Charish." He said her name with a good dose of pleasure. "She's my girlfriend."

"A girlfriend?" That was news to Violet. "Well, you little sneak. How come I didn't know anything about that?"

"It's a new thing." He drew his finger over the damp surface of the booth top she'd just wiped down. "Since I'll be out of school and can save for college, and I decided to go to college locally, I…" He paused, seeming at a loss for the right words.

"You decided you had time for Charish, too?"

"Something like that."

Pleased that Colt would confide in her, Violet asked, "You like her?"

He gave her a rascal's grin. "You saw her, right?"

"I did." She'd also noticed how the girl watched Colt as if her world revolved around him. "She's a real cutie."

"Well, she's even nicer than she looks. So yeah, I like her. A lot."

Violet put a hand to her heart. "Oh my God, could you be more wonderful? That lucky girl."

Colt snorted. "I'm not all that."

"All that and then some, honey. I bet Charish knows it, too. How many boys your age would pay as much attention to a girl's character as he does to her looks?"

Colt rubbed the back of his neck. "Maybe I should admit it wasn't her character I first noticed."

No, but it was apparently her character that swayed him into sticking closer to home. "I'm happy for you. You need to play a little more."

"I also need to work more hours. I don't mean to put you on the spot. I know the holidays will be busy around here, especially when everyone is out of school. But what about in January? Think you'd need someone more full-time, or should I look around at other places?"

Feigning grave insult, Violet drew back with a gasp. "Don't you dare work anywhere else! You said it yourself—we're like family, and family works together."

"I think that's supposed to be 'sticks' together."

"Whatever. I want you here." Where she could be a part of his life, and where she could ensure he didn't work *too* hard, or too many hours. "And yes, I'll put you full time if you want, but I'll also need to give you a raise."

"A raise?"

The wheels turned as she spoke, scrambling to find ways to make life just a little easier for Colt, while also showing him how proud she was of him. "Yes. But I have a stipulation."

Wary, he said, "All right."

"You have to work day shift the second Saturday of every month, and take off every third Saturday." That'd give him two Saturdays every month for dating.

Colt looked at her like she was nuts. "I need the money—"

"You'll have the raise, right? No reason to work every single weekend. That's my deal. I hope it's agreeable, because we need you here."

Colt laughed at her. "That's your whole motivation, huh? You're not trying to free up my time so I can go out more?"

Pretending it didn't matter to her, Violet checked a nail. "If dating is what you want to do, that's fine. Or you could see a movie with your friends, head to the creek… It's not my business."

Colt watched her with open affection. "That'd all be terrific. Thanks."

"My pleasure." She should have let it go at that, but the words burned in her throat. "You know I…well, I care a lot about you, okay?" Her voice thickened with emotion. "It's like you're my…little brother or something."

His expression went tender. "I've never been a little brother."

Did he realize that she loved him like a son? Because damn it, she did. She didn't want to make him uncomfortable by saying so. He'd lost his mother. He couldn't want her trying to fill in.

And why did she suddenly feel so whiny? She wasn't a crier, so why get choked up now? She knew why, of course.

She wanted a role in Colt's life, a role that might never be hers.

Colt squeezed her hands, then stood. "Thanks, Violet."

She nodded and, without looking at him, trying to hide her glassy eyes, shooed him away.

"I'll finish up in back." After hearing him go, she rose from the booth, turned and found Hogan standing against the wall, his arms crossed, his gaze discerning.

Violet knew he'd heard everything.

As he approached, she drummed up some false composure. "Hey, all done?"

Expression unchanged, he touched her cheek. "Do you know that the harder you work, the sexier you look?"

She hadn't seen that coming. "Yeah, right."

"It's true. I never realized how hot it is to see a woman put everything into her work."

"Well," she whispered, "not everything."

One brow went up and he half smiled. "True. You save a little energy for when I get you alone, don't you?"

She quickly turned away to finish cleaning the booth and tabletops.

Hogan took one of the cloths and helped. "So Colt and Charish, huh?"

Thrilled for the change of subject, Violet flashed him a grin. "Did you see her? I'm surprised he resisted for so long."

"He resisted," Hogan said, "because he's been working nonstop saving for college."

Violet's hand tightened on the cloth. "I know. He told me about his plan to graduate early. But there has to be a way…" She straightened and stared at Hogan.

After the day outside he looked amazing, especially wearing his Barbecue Master shirt. His windblown hair and five o'clock shadow only added to his physical appeal. She watched the muscles in his arms flex as he bent over a table, swiping the cloth across the surface.

In every way, Hogan personified the description of a gorgeous hunk. Physically, she found him almost too gorgeous for words. She only had to see him to start a slow meltdown.

He pitched in without thinking about it, didn't differentiate between guy work and women's work, or the importance of any particular job. He'd grill, help customers or, as he did now, wipe tables.

And best of all, he adored his son.

How could she *not* be crazy-nuts in love with him?

Caught in a maelstrom of thoughts and emotions, Violet opened her mouth and, without meaning to, blurted, "We could share rent."

The second the words left her mouth, her stomach sank. She jerked around and blindly cleaned an already-clean booth. Her heart drummed madly.

She'd just suggested they live together.

The silence behind her settled like lead weights onto her shoulders. Even the air felt still.

Unable to resist, she bit her lip and glanced over at Hogan. He stood there, his arms limp at his sides, his gaze fixed on her.

What did that reaction mean?

Knowing she had to say something, Violet inched toward him. "Hogan…"

Nathan and Brooklin stepped in. "Colt locked up out back. Everyone else is gone, but before we take off, I thought maybe Hogan could show me the remodel upstairs."

With the tension broken, Violet sucked in needed air, then rolled her eyes. "I take it that's your not-so-subtle way of saying you want to talk to Hogan alone?"

Brooklin said, "Yes, it is." She went to Hogan and took the cloth. "Go on, then. I'll help Violet finish up."

After a long searching look, Hogan said, "We'll only be a minute." Since Colt had already locked up in back, they went out the front door and around to the stairs by the back lot.

As soon as the men were gone, the ladies laughed.

"What are they talking about? Do you know?"

Brooklin shook her head. "We called Russell's old cell phone number, but it's not his anymore. I tried to look on his Facebook page, but it's either private now or he closed it down."

"So we don't know for sure if it was him or not."

She shook her head. "But I'd rather it be him. Russell was an ass, but he wasn't dangerous."

From behind them, a man's voice said, "That's not exactly true."

Violet jerked around. Yes, that had to be the guy. Narrow shoulders, baggy cargo pants, probably in his midthirties. He wasn't a homely man, but comparisons to Nathan weren't kind. He looked pathetic.

Except for the gun in his hands.

"Lock the door behind me," he ordered.

Neither woman moved. Brooklin said, "What are you doing, Russell?"

"You act like you don't know." He took a hard step toward her. "You ruined my life!"

Taken aback, but not looking afraid—not yet, anyway—Brooklin shook her head. "You're the one who ended our engagement."

"After what you did, did you think I'd stay with you? Do you realize how humiliating it was for me? Everyone talking, whispering behind their hands. You want to know what they said?"

"I know what they said." Now Brooklin appeared

angry, too. "I lived through it. None of it was true and you know it."

His eyes narrowed. "Lock the door. Now."

Reluctantly, Violet walked a wide path around him. Hogan and Nathan were upstairs, but if she locked the door, how would they get back in? Maybe that was a good thing, she thought, as she turned the dead bolt. They'd surely see this madman through the front window. Then they could call in reinforcements...

"Now get over here."

Violet moved back to where she'd been, wondering where Colt was. *Please don't let him walk into this mess.* Colt had hero tendencies and it scared her to death.

"What now?" she asked.

Russell flagged the gun toward the kitchens. "In there. I don't want anyone walking by, seeing us."

Brooklin's mouth pinched in anger; her face paled.

Violet took her arm, gave her a squeeze and headed where Russell pointed.

There would be big knives in the kitchen, sharp carving forks, a meat cleaver or two...

But Russell forced them to the storage area.

No windows, no weapons, only giant-sized canned vegetables and boxes of dry goods.

"Get inside."

Brooklin said, "I don't understand this, Russell. What are you thinking? What are you planning to do?"

"Planning? I'm planning to tell you what a bitch you are. Then you're going to sweetly apologize to me." He looked at Violet. "I have nothing against you except that this is the first time I've found her alone, away from the sheriff, and you just happen to be here."

"Collateral damage?" Violet asked, remembering what Hogan had called her involvement.

"Maybe you should have been more discriminating in your choice of friends." He stared at Brooklin. "Everyone whispered that I wasn't man enough and that's why you went to a kid," he sneered. "One of our own students."

She shook her head, then tried to reason with him. "You know that wasn't true, Russell."

"I know what they said." He drew a breath, but his eyes remained wild. "I got dragged into the filth with you. We were engaged, and to most people, that made me equally guilty."

"There was no guilt." With a lot of bitterness, she added, "Although you certainly believed the worst, didn't you? You jumped on the bandwagon so fast, I knew you'd never really cared about me. You couldn't have."

Incredulity carried him forward a step. "Of course I cared. I wanted to marry you. But there was a lot of evidence against you."

"No, just some ugly rumors started by a vile man."

"You're right—it was ugly and vile. I'm not stupid enough to be a part of that."

Brooklin rubbed her forehead. "So that's it? Despite everything, despite the truth, you've made up your mind?"

What mind he had, Violet thought, because Brooklin's ex looked seriously off his rocker.

"Forget what you thought back then. Forget that you never trusted me." She held out her hands. "You know the truth now."

As if Brooklin hadn't spoken, Russell said, "I couldn't stay at the school, of course. Not after all that, not with the taint you left behind."

"She didn't taint anything, you ass. She saved a girl."

Russell sent her a dismissive glance. "I didn't know

where to go. What other school would hire a teacher who'd been engaged to you?"

Violet couldn't take it. Her temper nearly imploded. "Are you that damned obtuse? *She didn't do anything.*"

He curled his lip. "You don't know anything about it. She chose them, those damn kids, over me."

Brooklin blinked at him. "That's what you think? Russell, I tried to save that girl! Her father was abusing her. He was a monster. I—"

"Shut up." He aimed the gun at her, drew in two deep breaths. "I'll hear your apology now."

Brooklin said, "If that's what you want, I—"

Violet grabbed her arm to stop her. She had the awful feeling that as soon as Russell got what he wanted, he'd kill them both. "You don't owe him anything, Brooklin. He should be apologizing to you." That made his face florid, and she rushed on, trying to think of anything to keep him talking. "You spent all this effort tracking her down. How did you find her, anyway?"

Smug, he bragged over the ease of the hunt. "With eyes like hers, she stands out."

"True. She has beautiful eyes."

Russell nodded, staring as if transfixed at Brooklin. "She does."

Disliking that obsessed stare, Violet reclaimed his attention. "But you can't track a woman by her eyes, right?"

He blinked, and his expression settled into a frown. "I spent what little money I had left on a private eye. He narrowed down Brooklin's whereabouts, and then I cut him loose. I didn't want him still around, wondering what happened to her after she's…gone."

That slight hesitation gave Violet hope. So, the man had gone mad? He hadn't always been that way or surely

Brooklin wouldn't have been engaged to him. Violet wanted to keep him talking, both to buy herself time to think and to hopefully give him time to rethink this insanity.

She assumed his current goal was to kill Brooklin, so Violet eased in front of her. She wasn't the target, and if she could deter him from hurting Brooklin, she would. "You almost ran me down, too. Why kill me? I haven't done anything to you."

He shrugged without regard. "That time on the street, you just happened to be there. Can't thread the needle with a car. I didn't particularly want to kill you, but then again, I didn't care if I did." He rubbed a hand over a smarmy smile. "You know, I thought that would scare you off. I figured Brooklin would be alone after that. But no, you started hanging out with her more, always in crowds where I couldn't get to her."

Brooklin tried to come out from behind. "So you didn't care if you got an apology then, did you?" Anger blinded her, and she tried to step in front of Violet.

Violet didn't allow it. "You know what I think? We should sit down and talk."

"I don't want to talk," Russell said. "I do want your apology now, Brooklin. You've put me to too much trouble. After all this, your apology is the first thing I'll have, and then—"

Violet raised her voice. "It takes no time to make coffee and I have some pie left. Cherry pie. Maybe pecan pie, too, but I'm not sure."

Brooklin stilled behind her. Violet could hear her breathing hard and fast.

Russell stared at her like she was the crazy one.

But so what? She'd be just as batty as she needed to

be to find a way out of this debacle. "What do you think, Russell? What's your favorite kind of pie?"

Russell slowly lowered the gun. "I like cream pies."

COLT COULDN'T BELIEVE THIS. He'd never been so divided in his entire life.

Go after the man himself?

Or go for his father and Nathan?

Even as he slipped away into the shadows, moving silently to the back door that he'd locked, it felt wrong to leave the women alone. What if the lunatic snapped and shot one of them before he could get back?

If he got his dad, he knew exactly what would happen. His father would go after the man and damn the consequences. He would not let Violet get hurt.

Colt's throat tightened, and he knew he couldn't think about that. He'd lost too much. Life was finally the way he wanted it. It couldn't change again. Not now.

He could not lose his dad.

Doing the right thing had never felt so damned difficult.

It seemed to Colt that the locks made a terrible racket as he opened them, yet no one came bursting in on him. Thank God he hadn't set the alarms; he didn't know how to shut them off and the sudden noise could spook the guy and make him react.

Once outside, Colt took just enough time to prop the door wide-open with a brick. If by some chance Violet or Brooklin got away, they needed a clear way to run.

Getting up the metal stairs without making any noise was a lesson in strained patience. He wanted to run, but even though they'd been repaired and secured, they still clanged with every footstep. Soon as he eased the door open, his dad looked up.

And knew.

Hogan came charging over. "What is it?"

In a hush, Colt said, "A man came in with a gun."

Hogan started to go, but Colt grabbed him. "Violet just offered him coffee and pie."

"What?"

"She's keeping him talking. The front door is locked."

"Where exactly are they?" Nathan asked.

"The storage area."

"Stay with Nathan," Hogan said, already moving past him in a rush.

"Damn it, I'm the sheriff!" Nathan growled low, grabbing for Hogan, but he was already out the door. Four steps down, Hogan went cleanly over the side to land in a crouch on the pavement below.

Cursing low, Nathan said, "Go around front and call 911. Explain everything to dispatch. Stay out of range, okay? Hogan would kill me if you got hurt." Then he, too, hopped off the side of the stairs.

Colt put in the call, gave the information he could and followed the men.

His blood pumping with fear and rage, Hogan edged inside the building. He couldn't lose her. *He couldn't.*

From the prep area, he heard the low voices nearby. It sounded like Russell was arguing with Violet about pie. He didn't want cherry, and she insisted he'd like it.

Crazy Violet. *Don't push him too hard, honey.*

Nathan touched his arm, and when Hogan glanced at him, he showed his own weapon.

Nathan wanted to shoot the bastard?

Worked for him.

Nathan gestured for Hogan to get the man's attention while he circled around to the other side.

At least they agreed on protecting the women first and foremost.

With a nod, Hogan continued his silent movements closer to the storage area. Nathan could stay back, and as soon as Hogan lured the man into sight, Nathan could take aim.

He inched closer.

"I don't want your pie. I don't want your coffee." Russell's voice hardened. "What I want, *right now*, is her very sincere apology for ruining me."

"Did you keep that gun in the pocket of your cargo pants? That's why you're wearing them, right? I only ask because you don't look like a cargo pants type of guy. Khakis maybe. Fitted. With a nice sharp crease."

"That's him," Brooklin said. "Casual slacks, loafers, a button-up shirt."

"So the pants were to carry the weapon?"

"Yes," Russell said. "Don't think you're so smart, though. It'd be obvious to anyone."

"Maybe." Violet paused. "Where'd you get the gun? Is it registered?"

"Don't be stupid."

"I'm not usually. But then, I've never been held at gunpoint, either. It's unnerving."

"Imminent death would unnerve anyone."

She jumped on that, saying, "So you do plan to kill us? That doesn't make any sense, Russell. Why in the world would Brooklin want to apologize to you, just so you can murder her?"

Hogan finally got in range behind the man. He'd love to rush him, beat him into the ground, but with that gun aimed at Violet and Brooklin, he couldn't take that chance.

Instead, he crept closer.

Unfortunately, Brooklin noticed him—and her eyes widened.

Russell panicked, but as he swung around, Violet screamed, "No," and grabbed for his arm.

Russell snatched her close, bringing her with him, using her like a shield. He crushed her against his chest with an arm locked around her breasts, her feet off the floor, the barrel of that gun pressed to her temple.

Everything in Hogan's world narrowed to Violet—and Russell's finger on that trigger.

"You shouldn't be here," Russell wailed, his breath coming hard and fast.

Violet's wide eyes stayed locked on Hogan.

"Let her go," Hogan said, his tone level and calm, "before I rip your fucking head off."

"No, no." Russell backed farther into the storage area. "I watched you leave."

"We didn't go anywhere." Nathan stepped out, his own gun aimed. "Lower your weapon now. It's over."

Russell's gaze darted back and forth between the two men.

"You won't make it," Nathan said. "Even think about it, and I'll shoot a hole clean through your forehead."

"No," Russell shouted. "She's not even the one who has to pay! It's Brooklin I came for."

Nathan shook his head. "You can't have her."

Brooklin said, "Yes, he can." She stepped around him, her hands behind her. "Let her go, Russell, and you and I will leave together. You'll have me."

She stood far too close to the lunatic, Hogan thought. Close enough to be grabbed. Or shot.

Close enough to push him over the edge.

"Come over here, Brooklin," Nathan ordered.

But she didn't budge except to move closer to Russell.

"Let her go," she said softly. "I'm right here. I'm the one you want, the one who ruined you. You want to hear me apologize, Russell. You want to make me pay, not her."

With a vicious snarl, Russell turned the gun to Brooklin while slinging Violet toward Nathan.

Everything happened at once.

Brooklin swung her arm out from behind her back, a large can of green beans in her hand. The blow landed on Russell's chest. His gun discharged.

At the same time, Hogan dived on him. They went down hard, tripping over a case of canned goods, hitting the floor with bone-shattering impact.

Russell wheezed, then cried out as Hogan twisted his wrist until the gun fell from his limp hand. He pounded the miserable bastard, his fist landing heavily again and again. Truthfully, he might have killed him if it hadn't been for Colt's voice intruding.

"Dad, *stop.* Violet needs you."

Nathan's restraining hands finally registered. Hogan turned Russell loose, signifying that he understood. The bloodied man dropped to the floor with an almost inaudible groan.

"Dad."

The agony in his son's voice hit like a sledgehammer. Hogan jerked around.

Colt sat on the floor, Violet leaning against him, blood everywhere, on her arm, on his hands…

A massive surge of terror slammed into him.

"She's okay," Nathan said fast. "The damn bullet ricocheted and grazed her arm. Do you hear me, Hogan? Colt's not bleeding. He's just trying to help." With that explained, Nathan went to work checking on Russell.

Hogan's thundering heart slowed to a more normal

beat and the facility to think clicked back in. He was already on his knees beside Violet. "Let me see, Colt."

Breathing fast, Colt lifted his shaking hands. Blood oozed from a raw three-inch wound gouged through Violet's upper arm. "You're doing good, Colt. Really good," Hogan told him. "I'll go grab the first-aid kit. Deep breaths, Violet, okay?"

She nodded. Her voice was thin with pain when she said, "Will you hit that jerk for me one more time?"

"I would love to, but he's out and won't feel it."

"He'll feel it when he comes around."

"True." God, he loved her attitude, finding a little comfort in it. He ran for the first-aid kit and was back in less than half a minute. He found Colt holding her close, her back supported against his shoulder.

"Colt?" Hogan infused his voice with reassurance. "She's all right now, son, okay? Why don't you go get washed up? I hear sirens. More people are going to be in here any minute now."

Shaking his head, Colt shifted, moving Violet enough that Hogan could more easily reach her while still keeping her in his arms. "I'll wait."

He didn't want to let her go, Hogan realized, and damn, that almost got him. His son had lost too many people.

He wouldn't lose Violet.

Hogan drew a shuddering breath.

"Guys," Violet said, that sassy drawl more evident than ever. "I'm seriously okay. I mean, it hurts like hell—I won't lie about that. But I'm fine." Then she leaned her head back on Colt. "I love you, Colt. Just so you know."

"Damn," Colt choked out and put his face in her hair.

Hogan didn't move. He struggled with his own emotions.

She said, "Hogan?"

"Yeah, honey?"

"Remember what I said?"

As gently as he could, he swabbed away the blood, then pressed a sterile pad to the wound. "You've said a lot, Violet."

"I asked if we could share a house."

Colt's head jerked up. "You did?"

"Blurted it right out there," she said. "I left your poor dad speechless."

Hogan concentrated on wrapping her arm without hurting her.

Colt cradled her protectively. "Well, if I get a vote—"

And together, Violet and Hogan said, "You always have a vote," then smiled at each other for that duplicate response.

"Then I say hell yes."

"Do you, now?" Hogan finished wrapping her arm, sat back on his heels and looked at the two of them. His heart wanted to burst.

Odd that being here now, with his son shaken and Violet wounded, could somehow seem so right— because they were together.

Seconds later the diner swarmed with paramedics and officers. Hogan had a hell of a time prying his son off Violet, but he understood the need to stick close. Hell, it was all he could do to let her go so her arm could be properly checked and attended.

While that happened, he kept Colt right next to him.

"You did good, Colt. I'm proud of you."

He swallowed hard. "I've never been so damned scared in my life."

"Same here."

Colt scrubbed a hand over his face. "I couldn't decide what to do. Violet means a lot to both of us, and I was afraid that by the time I came to get you, she'd be hurt."

Hogan turned his son to face him. "You did the right thing. Please don't ever put me in the position of losing you." Hogan drew him in for a tight bear hug. "I can take a lot, son. I can't take that."

Colt squeezed him, then quickly stepped back, drawing deep breaths.

Knowing they were both on the ragged edge, Hogan gave him a minute to compose himself while watching the confusion around him. Nathan controlled it all, with Brooklin held at his side.

Once Colt was breathing more normally again, he said, "So you love Violet, too, huh?"

"Too?" Colt said, and then with a slow grin, "Really? I mean, I knew it, but it's nice to hear you say it."

Making his son happy had never felt so good. "If I can talk her into our house instead of hers, I'm thinking it might be a terrific idea."

"She really asked you about it?"

"Like she said, she blindsided me with it. But it's a great idea." Hoping to leverage a little lightheartedness into deadly disturbance, he said, "It's a good way to save money since we wouldn't be paying for two houses."

Colt shoved him. "Screw that! It's not about money."

Hogan laughed, which surprised him. Just minutes ago, laughter had seemed out of reach. "That was the argument she gave me. But I wouldn't make a move like that unless I loved her. And I do. Took me a little while to work around everything, you know?"

"I do." Colt looked down at his bloody hands, curled

them into fists and closed his eyes. "Some things are tough to shake off."

This time when Hogan put his arm around Colt's shoulders, they were both in better control. "I'll talk to her soon. But tonight, I think we have other priorities."

"Hogan?"

He and Colt turned to see her struggling to her feet.

They rushed forward together, Hogan taking her hand on her uninjured arm, Colt putting a hand behind her back.

"Careful," Hogan said.

"I don't stand with my arm, guys, and my legs are just fine." She huffed. "But you're not going to believe this."

The aggrieved paramedic said, "I'm sorry, Violet, I really am."

She knew the paramedic, too? Did anyone in or near Clearbrook not know Violet?

The young EMT turned to Hogan. "You did a great job wrapping it, but it needs to be properly cleaned and she's going to need a few stitches."

Hogan said, "Another trip to the hospital isn't so bad."

She dropped her forehead to his sternum. "I'm cursed."

"You've got us," Colt said. "I hope that doesn't seem cursed."

She lifted her head and gave him a beautiful, tender smile. "No, that makes me feel like the luckiest gal alive." Cradling her wrapped arm, she asked, "Would you two very special guys mind giving me a ride? No way am I going by ambulance, but this time I'm not sure I'm up to driving."

Now that Violet was on her feet and joking, Colt further recovered. "Let me wash up real fast. I'll be right back."

Incredibly proud, Hogan kissed Violet's forehead and said, "He adores you."

"It's mutual."

Brooklin came over to them, Nathan at her side. She kept her head bowed, her hands clenched together in front of her. "Are you okay, Violet?"

"Sure. I just got my arm in the way of that stupid bouncing bullet. Though I guess, since it ricocheted, better my arm than my head, huh?"

Hogan groaned. "Don't even joke."

She frowned at Hogan. "I still think this is your fault. Until you came into my life, I was never sick, never hurt, never ever wimpy."

Brooklin stiffened even more. "No, it's my fault. If I hadn't—"

"What?" Violet challenged. "Saved a girl from her abusive father? If you weren't the type of person to do that, I wouldn't want you as a friend."

Nathan smiled. "Exactly."

"But to bring so much trouble here…"

"That butthead brought the trouble," Violet said, glaring at Russell as the paramedics worked on his bludgeoned face. Then she looked at Hogan's knuckles. "Ouch."

"Worth it," he said, carefully hugging her close to his side and feeling the fury all over again.

Nathan gave one short shake of his head. "It's going to be tough to explain how he got annihilated, but either way, he's history."

Brooklin said, "In all the time I knew him, Russell never showed any violent tendencies. He was studious, understated, very much a stereotypical teacher."

"He lost his grip," Nathan said. "It happens. But it's *not* your fault. Not any of it."

"He made terrible choices," Violet added, "and that cost him everything. The weak always find a way to deflect to others. You don't owe anyone an apology for that. Definitely not me."

"Agreed," Hogan said.

Brooklin swiped at the tears in her eyes. "Thank you. All of you." With a broken, tearful laugh, she said, "Coming to Clearbrook is the smartest thing I've ever done."

"True." Nathan pressed a kiss to her forehead, then spoke to Violet and Hogan. "I wish we could go to the hospital with you, but I've got to clean up this mess, and I don't want Brooklin out of my sight."

"Understandable." Hogan waited until Colt had rejoined them. "We'll take good care of her. Tomorrow, though, I want an update on what's happening."

"First thing," Nathan agreed, "and I'll want an update on Violet anyway."

In the car, Hogan drove and Colt sat in the back seat with Violet, doing what he could to pamper her.

They had to get through tonight, but suddenly the future looked rich with promise.

CHAPTER NINETEEN

THE NEED TO assure himself that everyone was okay drew Hogan again and again to the hallway. He peered into his bedroom to see Violet asleep in his bed. She was on her back, her bandaged arm resting over her stomach.

What if that bullet had caused more damage? Just as he'd been doing all morning, he forced aside the god-awful fear with deep breaths... And the sight of her— her hair fanned out everywhere, and from the bottom of the sheet, one small foot showed.

She would never want Colt to know, but once they'd been tucked into the bed, she'd cried. Restrained, nearly silent tears of pure emotion. She, too, understood just how badly things could have gone.

Never again would Hogan waste time on regretting his past. Now he was only looking forward to a beautiful future.

Next he looked in Colt's room. His son sprawled on his stomach, long limbs everywhere. Hogan knew he had to be exhausted, but he'd set his alarm to wake him early so he could spend some time with Charish.

Hogan wanted to get to know the girl better. He had a feeling she'd factored into Colt's decision on a local college, or at the very least, she'd made that decision easier.

He also wanted to tell Colt that he truly had choices now. Not only would he have the bonus cash flow from his accounting work, he and Violet would be splitting expenses.

By admitting his love for her, life had gotten easier.

When Diesel lifted his head, Hogan patted his thigh, calling the dog to him.

As if aware that Colt needed his sleep, Diesel picked his way carefully from the bed, joining Hogan with a wagging tail.

Life was good. This, Hogan thought, this was what he wanted.

The people he loved all together.

He and Diesel walked out to the front yard. Carrying a steaming cup of coffee and wearing only jeans, Hogan sat on the top step of his porch and allowed Diesel to take his time finding just the right grassy spot.

Morning sunshine bathed his face. A squirrel chattered. Birds sat atop the tree branches.

Life was good.

He couldn't help but think of Violet and what she meant to him. Because he wasn't a man to do things lightly, he wanted it all. Yes, her in his house, in his bed. But he also wanted his ring on her finger. He wanted the vows.

The commitment.

He knew now that he'd been seeing women differently, that he'd looked for the possible deceit—something he'd never thought about until Meg had upended his world.

Then he'd moved to Clearbrook, and there was his sister-in-law, Honor, one of the sweetest women he'd ever known, perfect for his brother.

And Lexie, who drove Sullivan nuts with her shenanigans—yet she was as caring and honorable as anyone he knew.

There was Kristy, flighty, sometimes silly, but overall a nice girl just making her way in the world.

And Joni, a definite user—as some people were, male and female.

He didn't like admitting that he'd been a shallow ass, but he had to admit that despite all the evidence, he'd continued to view women through the same lens.

Until Violet shook him out of that absurd mind-set. She was all the things he admired in other women, plus things the others never could be, because her qualities complemented his own and vice versa.

He was more with her, better, happier. Literally, just *more*.

"Any coffee left inside?"

He glanced to where his brother cut across the yard. Diesel ran to greet Jason, so Hogan stood. "I'll get a cup."

"Sullivan's on his way over, too. Might as well grab him one."

Hogan shielded his eyes from the sun and found Sullivan crossing the street.

"Got it. Be right back." As quietly as possible, he poured coffee into two cups, then made a fresh pot in case Violet woke up and wanted any.

When he turned, he almost ran into Colt. His son wore shorts and nothing else, and he made a beeline for the fridge and the orange juice.

"You sure you don't want to catch a little more sleep?"

"I'm good," Colt said around a wide yawn. He nodded at the tray Hogan held. "We have company?"

"Jason and Sullivan."

Colt nodded and, carrying a tall glass of juice, led the way back out.

When they stepped to the porch, they found Nathan just pulling into the driveway.

Diesel abandoned Jason and loped over to Colt, practically crawling into his lap, forcing Colt to hold the juice high as he laughed.

"Coffee?" Hogan asked Nathan while handing a cup to Jason and Sullivan.

"No, thanks. I finished a pot before I left." He rubbed his tired eyes. "How's Violet?"

"She's still sleeping." Hogan sat on the top step again. "If you ask her, she'll tell you she's fine. And she is. She had some pain last night, but mostly it was the aftermath of everything that made it hard for her to sleep."

"Having an asshole point a gun at you would do that," Jason said.

Hogan had called his brother from the hospital last night to fill him in, since he was bound to notice that neither Colt nor Hogan had made it home. "Brooklin?" he asked.

"Still feeling guilty, but she'll realize soon that she has no reason."

Sullivan sat below Colt and became the recipient of Diesel's affection. He stroked him idly while he sipped his coffee. "You have the guy locked up?" he asked Nathan.

"He's not going anywhere."

Jason gave a grim smile. "I heard Hogan worked him over."

"And then some," Nathan admitted. "Broke his nose and loosened a tooth, but he'll survive."

With a touch of awe, Colt said, "I've never seen Dad go at anyone like that."

"Your dad was a hard-ass in his youth." Jason lifted

his coffee cup in a salute. "Sounds like it paid off last night."

Hogan shook his head. Before moving to Clearbrook, it might have seemed odd to sit outside an hour past dawn holding council with three other men, his son and his dog. Now it just felt comfortable.

These crazy people had become the best of family and friends. For a while there, trust had seemed elusive. But Hogan trusted each of them, so he admitted, "Violet coped by focusing on the diner—if she'll have to stay closed, the damage done. She fell asleep fretting about it." Hogan pictured the mess in his mind. The over-turned boxes and scattered cans, the bullet hole in the wall, the blood—*her* blood.

"Far as the sheriff's department is concerned, she can open today as usual," Nathan said. "We already got everything we needed."

"I'll head over there first thing," Jason said, "so you can stay with her. I'll patch and paint the wall, no problem."

Sullivan said, "I have a few hours yet, so I'll help clean up."

Nathan nodded. "Count me in if you need anything."

"Well, as to that…" Hogan hoped they'd get on board. "We'd planned to open the new space next week. I have an idea on how to really get things swinging again." With all the guys waiting, he cleared his throat. "You know how that goofy column in the *Trickle* kept focus-ing on us?"

"Mainly you two," Sullivan said, referencing him and Nathan. "They're after the single guys."

Hogan shook his head. "I've been considering a big event to open the upstairs, sort of the requested 'ladies' night' that was mentioned."

"Love it," Nathan said, jumping ahead before Hogan could finish explaining. "You want the band there? We could easily set up outside."

"I do," Hogan said. "But more than that, I want us to perform."

Blank faces stared back at him.

Finally, Jason repeated, "Perform?"

"Cowboy hats, some line dancing. We'll give the ladies a real show, since that's what they've been asking for—"

"Hell no."

"Forget it."

He stared at Jason and Sullivan. Colt, he noticed, was still grinning, and Nathan just seemed to be giving it some thought. "You know it'd be a big hit."

"Nope."

Lexie, who showed up without anyone realizing it, hugged up to Sullivan's arm. Her short, pale blond hair was flattened on one side, proving she'd come straight from bed and hadn't taken the time to primp first. "You can count on Sullivan. He'll do it."

Horrified, Sullivan said, "No, I won't."

Her smile never slipped. "He's in."

"I'm not!"

"You have to. Violet needs you." She batted her eyelashes at him, stroked his chest and said, "And I really want to see it."

Sullivan stared at her a second more, then gave in. "Shit."

Hogan laughed. One down. He turned to his brother. "Jason?"

"You know I don't dance."

"It's line dancing," Honor said from behind him.

Jason jumped. "When did you get up?"

Barefoot, dressed in one of Jason's T-shirts and her shorts, her honey-colored hair mussed, she said, "When Lexie called me and said you guys were all congregated out here."

Jason slanted a look at Lexie.

"It's convenient," Lexie said, "living across the street from each other."

Honor covered her mouth as she yawned, then leaned against Jason. "Line dancing isn't really dancing. You guys could keep it simple—but sexy."

Jason groaned. "I don't do 'sexy,' damn it."

"Is that a joke?" She stared up at him and whispered, "You do sexy better than anyone."

"Hell."

Knowing she'd gotten her way, Honor hugged him.

Having the women show up had made it much easier to convince the guys, Hogan thought. Too bad Brooklin wasn't around. "Nathan?"

"Hell, I love the idea. I'm not shy. And the band will totally be on board. I even know the song we should use."

Colt, who hadn't said much, asked, "Am I invited to this dance-off?"

Hogan further messed his son's sleep-rumpled hair. "You're going to be our lead, kiddo. You'll get the younger crowd there." Then he turned to everyone. "It has to be a surprise. I don't want Violet to know about it. And it has to be a simple presentation, because we're opening the upstairs next week. We'll have to advertise by word of mouth. Think we can manage that?"

The women, Nathan and Colt gave a resounding yes.

The men grumbled, with a lot of attitude, that they'd do their best.

By now, Violet knew he wasn't concerned with keeping their relationship private. After the show, she, as well as everyone in Clearbrook, would know that she meant the world to him.

All in all, Hogan could hardly wait.

VIOLET WOKE SLOWLY, her head aching, her body heavy. When she started to stretch, pain lanced into her arm and everything came crashing back. She'd been shot.

She gasped as she opened her eyes. At first disoriented, she looked around and remembered that she wasn't in her own bed.

She wasn't home alone.

Hogan had not only insisted on her staying over, he'd insisted on her sharing his bed. Colt had been in complete agreement.

She looked down at her arm. It ached from wrist to shoulder, and around the stark white wrapping she saw bruising spreading out. She hadn't actually been shot, not directly. But the bullet, which had ricocheted off cans, cut through her arm, then embedded itself into the wall, still caused enough damage.

Moving her arm more cautiously now, she placed her hand on Hogan's side of the bed and found it cool to the touch. Sitting up, she looked around at his sparse but tidy furnishings.

Where was he?

She used the bathroom, brushed her teeth, frowned at her bedraggled appearance and then went looking for Hogan. She found him at his desk, but the second he noticed her, he closed his laptop and stood.

"How do you feel?"

"Hungover, even though I didn't have a drop to drink."

He drew her in for a warm kiss and a gentle hug. "You look beautiful."

She snorted. "Your bathroom has a mirror, you know."

He only smiled. "Coffee?"

"Please." As she looked, she asked, "Where's Colt and Diesel?"

"Colt took the dog with him when he left to meet Charish before work."

"Before work," she repeated, sinking down into a kitchen chair. "We'll be able to open today?"

"Nathan stopped by. He said it won't be a problem. Jason and Sullivan are headed over there now to fix the wall where the bullet hit and…clean up."

Violet shuddered. They were cleaning up blood. "I should do that, not them."

"Well, here's the thing." He set the coffee in front of her and pulled out a chair, turning it to face her. "We all agreed that you needed a couple of days off."

The coffee tasted delicious and cut through some of the cobwebs. "We who?"

"Everyone. Nathan and Brooklin, Jason and Honor, Sullivan and Lexie, and Colt and me." He gently cradled her hand in both of his. "I know you're tough as nails, Violet. So does everyone else. You don't need to prove anything to anyone."

"I wasn't trying to." Was she? Sure, it had taken years to prove herself, but no one had stood in her way. Mostly she'd been proving her worth to herself.

She pulled free of his unsettling hold and sipped her coffee again. "Mmm. That's good."

"Why do you refuse to rest?"

"It's my diner." Violet didn't want or need to be handled like fine china. "It's my job to be there."

"You have to take a vacation every now and then, right?"

"Well, actually…"

He sat back. "When was the last time you took off a week?"

An entire week? "Er…never?" She gulped more coffee, burned her tongue and cursed. "Look, the diner is my responsibility, okay? I can take the occasional day here and there, but not a whole week."

Hogan studied her. "I want you to move in with me."

Wow, what a switch! Quickly, she set down the cup before she dropped it. She opened her mouth, but with no idea what to say, she closed it again.

Did he mean permanently, as in she should sell her house? Or for a day or two? Maybe the week he wanted her to vacation?

When she remained silent, he said, "I like sleeping with you, waking up with you and sharing everything."

She resisted the urge to leap on him and said with placid agreement, "I like it, too."

"I never thought I'd want that with another woman. But here you are, and you mean so much to me."

He didn't say he loved her, but it was close. "Do you think maybe you're just reacting to the danger from last night?" Not giving him a chance to answer, she said, "Because I know I am. I cried last night when I hate crying."

"You cried with me," he said softly. "Just me."

He was the one she least wanted to burden. "And I'm still shaking." She held out a hand to show him. "It's all reaction."

"Yeah."

What did he mean, *yeah*? "I don't want you to say or do anything that you might regret later."

"I'll regret it a lot if I don't convince you to stay with me. We can get enough of your stuff today for you to get by, then get the rest later."

She stared at him. "Get the rest?"

He shrugged. "I'm not trying to rush you, Violet. But yes, I want you here, with me."

Her heart tried to thump out of her chest. "So we'd live at your house?"

"If you're okay with that. Colt's had enough changes, and Diesel is settled here. It's nice having my brother right next door, too."

That all sounded wonderful to her.

"Will you move in, honey?"

Reaction or not, she wanted to grab his offer with both hands and hold on tight. Nodding, she managed to squeak out, "Yes."

Relief put a happy smile on his face. "Will you also take off a week?"

"Don't push your luck, Guthrie."

He laughed. "Going forward, let's compromise on things, okay?"

"I suppose this compromise starts with me taking time off?"

"It'd be a big step toward trust, right?"

"Trust?"

"I trust you. Don't you think you could trust me back?"

Violet almost slid off her chair. *Hogan trusted her.* She let that settle in, fill her up, and finally she smiled. After everything he'd been through, he'd still let her in.

"I've always trusted you," she said. "Even when you were an ass, you were a hard worker and good brother and great dad. I figured that meant you were a great guy, deep down at least."

Hogan laughed.

"Then when I screwed up with Joni, and you let me off the hook, I knew you were the best of men."

"As the best of men, I swear I'll take good care of the diner." He scooped her up and into his lap, his mouth touching her nose, her temple, her chin. "I know what the diner means to you, Violet. I know it's *yours*, that you've built it into a successful business with your own blood, sweat and tears. It's a familiar, comfortable place loved by everyone in Clearbrook and beyond. I promise you, I'm not trying to take over and I won't let anything slip through the cracks. I'll—"

Violet leaned up and kissed him. "Compromise," she whispered. "I'll take off through Thursday, but I need to be there for the weekend."

He appeared ready to argue, then changed his mind. "Guess I better take what I can get."

Violet squirmed on his lap. "Well, as to what you can get…"

"You're wounded, woman." Holding her close, he came to his feet.

"Just my arm." Bobbing her eyebrows, she said, "Every other body part is working just fine."

"But Colt might come home anytime now. Not likely, but I wouldn't want to chance it."

Her face went blank. "I hadn't even considered that."

"You're not used to living with a teenage son. But I am." Hogan nuzzled her throat. "Monday through Friday he'll be gone to school until the afternoon."

"That gives us every morning." With Monday feeling a long way off, she sighed. "Show me where I can store my stuff, and after you go to work, I'll get Brooklin to drive so I can move over what I need right now. Toothbrush and change of clothes, things like that."

"Don't overdo it," he told her, "but feel free to bring anything you want."

In the two hours before he left for the diner, Hogan helped her get familiar with his house, showed her where to find anything she might need, and cleared out two dresser drawers and half the closet for her to use.

Then he helped her with her bath so she wouldn't get her arm wet.

OVER THE NEXT few days, Brooklin proved herself a true friend by helping her move in. With Colt's added muscle, they even managed to rearrange the bedroom furniture to make room for her big dresser.

Thanks to a special version of the Advice Anonymous column in the *Trickle*, everyone knew what had happened and that she was staying with Hogan. The author of the column made her out as a hero, describing her as coolheaded, fierce and a great defender.

That's when Violet figured out who wrote it.

For a fact, she knew Hogan, Colt and Nathan hadn't authored the advice pieces urging women to chase them down, and no one else had been on the scene—except Brooklin.

Violet didn't say anything to her. She enjoyed the column too much to chance making Brooklin uncomfortable about it.

Visitors stopped by to check on her, often with flowers, and soon the house was overflowing.

Neither Colt nor Hogan complained; they just doted on her, showing her in a dozen different ways how happy they were to have her with them.

She and Hogan slept together each night, and each morning after Colt left for school, they indulged each other.

Diesel kept her from being lonely when both the guys worked. He rarely left her side, except for when he slept with Colt. Each evening when her guys got home they told her how the day had gone.

It was a surreal time, wonderful but very different from what she was used to—since she usually worked sunup to sundown. She *liked* being busy, so by the time Friday arrived, her arm felt much better and she was anxious to get back to her normal routine.

She and Hogan rode to the diner together. A lot of progress had been made in the upstairs area and they were all set for their grand opening.

Of course, when she went out back to talk to Hogan, she noticed the outdoor stage right away. Prepping for the bigger crowd expected, Hogan loaded his grills.

Violet nudged him. "What's up with the stage?"

He kept his gaze on the grill, saying, "Nathan and the band are going to play for our grand opening. Nice, huh?"

The band had performed at Screwy Louie's many times, so that still didn't explain things. "They've never used a stage before." Usually they set up their equipment around trees and tables and made do.

"Maybe he's trying to impress Brooklin."

"Hmm. Maybe." She put that aside as she oversaw their new signature burger, the Colt. Because of his part in handling Russell's intrusion, Violet had insisted.

Colt laughed every time they mentioned it.

It was a big juicy burger with all of Colt's favorite toppings. She expected it to be a hit, and the perfect way to introduce the feature.

The upstairs looked amazing and a new spotlight at the outside stairs helped showcase the additional entrance. Charish would help tonight, directing the young people to the special area.

Violet had expected a crowd, but the number of people filling the diner, the upstairs and the yard exceeded her expectations. By seven o'clock, she was ready to happily collapse. When the music started, she and most of the other guests moved to the outdoor area.

People were everywhere. She beamed with the pleasure of it. If this kept up, she thought, expanding the space might be a good idea.

"Always thinking ahead," Hogan whispered near her ear, as if reading her mind. "I like how you do that."

"It's amazing, isn't it?" She opened her arms and turned a circle, taking it all in. "First you with your sinfully delicious ribs, and now that awesome area upstairs." She threw her open arms around him. "You've been great for business, Hogan."

He kept her close. "Have I been good for you, too?"

She filled her lungs with the joy of it. "You've been amazing for me."

"Amazing enough to make it permanent?"

Good grief, would he always throw her for a loop?

Crowds literally swarmed around them. Nathan and the Drunken Monkeys wrapped up their song with a loud crescendo. People applauded.

"Way to keep me in suspense," Hogan said with a grin. Then he kissed her.

Not a quick peck, either, but a toe-curling, tongue-sliding, damp-heat kiss that turned her knees to noodles.

Soon as he let up, Violet gasped, "I moved in. Did you think it was temporary?" Good thing she hadn't put her house up for sale yet.

As if he'd read her mind, he said, "But we still have two houses. And we're not married."

Her knees gave out and she clutched at him to keep from falling. "Marriage?" she croaked.

"I love you."

Oh my God. He said that like he wasn't confessing something monumental. Violet nodded fast. "I love you, too."

"Tell me you'll marry me. Quick. I only have about fifteen seconds left."

Was the marriage proposal going to expire? She had no idea, but blinded by the sudden tears, she whispered, "Yes, I would love to marry you."

Hogan kissed her hard and fast. "Stay put, okay? This is for you."

"What—"

Just then, Nathan announced, "Come on, Hogan. Let's get the show going."

Violet stared as Hogan stripped off his Barbecue Master shirt and laid it over the chair. The crowd went nuts, especially when he pulled a cowboy hat out from under his table and slapped it on his head.

Completely off balance, Violet grabbed the chair to steady herself.

Until Hogan started for the stage, she hadn't realized he wore cowboy boots.

Putting her hand over her mouth, she laughed. What in the world!

Bounding onto the low stage and smiling toward Violet, he said into the mic, "She said yes."

The cheers erupted into a deafening roar.

Colt came to stand beside her. He wore a cowboy hat and boots, too. Putting his arm around her, he said, "I'm glad you'll be official, Violet."

She nodded and whispered, "Me, too."

The music started, and other than moving away from the mic, Hogan stayed put.

Nathan and the Drunken Monkeys started playing.

Her eyes widened. "I recognize that song!"

"Good." Colt kissed her cheek, stripped off his shirt and headed for the stage. Charish, along with a whole group of friends, egged him on.

While singing "Save a Horse, Ride a Cowboy," Nathan unbuttoned his shirt, shrugged it off and donned his own hat. Brooklin sat near the stage and she whooped—along with all the other women.

As if on cue, Sullivan and Jason emerged from the crowd, both already shirtless, jeans slung low, their hats tipped forward to hide their faces.

Lexie and Honor bounced and cheered.

Violet couldn't stop laughing. Far as surprises went, this was the best. She couldn't remember the last time she'd been so tickled.

And that proposal? She hugged herself to contain the utter joy.

When all the guys were onstage, they lined up and started to dance.

She laughed until she doubled over, loving the show, loving life.

Loving Hogan Guthrie.

The audience began to clap in time to their movements so that everyone seemed involved.

The tears overflowed, happy tears.

When at last they finished and the raucous applause began to fade, Hogan again took the mic. "One Friday night each month will be ladies' night. I can't guarantee a show every time—"

He had to wait for the protests to end before he could continue.

Wearing a huge smile, Hogan said, "—but Violet has some great ideas on how to keep you all happy."

That brought out renewed celebration and a chant of her name.

"Come on up here, Violet."

She tried to shake her head, but suddenly Kristy was there, urging her forward. And once she was close enough, Hogan took her hand and brought her up.

Grinning, Hogan said again, "She's going to be my wife."

The place went nuts.

He calmed them down, saying, "One more dance, and this time, any guy who wants should join in."

The band immediately stripped off their shirts, even though two of them looked much better with them on. Their hats, a mix of straw and felt and, for Stan, decorated with a big feather, had everyone chuckling.

Nathan set a big box off the edge of the stage. "Help yourself to some hats, boys."

She looked at Hogan, and he whispered, "Costume hats. Cheap, I promise."

Aww, even now he had her bottom line in mind. "It's an amazing idea," she said, impressed and madly in love.

There was a general rowdy removal of shirts as men flaunted their not-so-impressive chests and wore the comically small cowboy hats in a variety of black, brown and white.

Nathan said, "Don't forget your hardworking servers, okay? Show them some appreciation."

Kristy, busy refilling drinks, gave him a thumbs-up.

When Nathan fired up another fast-paced country song, Hogan led Violet in a dance on the stage.

Sullivan went after Lexie, Jason after Honor. Colt

abandoned them for Charish, and Nathan brought Brooklin up to join them.

It was, by far, the best night of Violet's entire life.

With his hands holding her hips, Hogan gently swayed them, saying close to her ear, "I know it doesn't make up for missing dances in school. But I promise you, going forward we'll fit in lots of fun." He brought her closer, slow dancing even though the music raced. "Not that I ever want to neglect your diner."

"*Our* diner," Violet said, leaning back to smile up at him. "We'll share everything, okay?"

Hogan studied her face, half smiled and nodded. "I'm a lucky man."

It amazed her that he could think so after all he'd been through. She stopped dancing. "I'm sorry that the past was so hard on you, but I'm glad life eventually brought you to me."

Hogan glanced out at Colt dancing with Charish, surrounded by his friends, then to his brother, who laughed with Honor. When he smiled down at Violet again, he said, "Being here, now that I have you, I wouldn't change a single thing."

And that, more than anything, told Violet that the past was where it needed to be, no longer a part of their lives.

* * * * *

*Read on for an exclusive sneak peek at the next
sizzling book from* New York Times *bestselling author
Lori Foster,* Cooper's Charm...

CHAPTER ONE

THE SUN SHONE brightly on that early mid-May morning. The crisp, cool air smelled of damp leaves—an appealing, earthy scent. A mist from the nearby lake blanketed the ground, swirling around her sneaker-covered feet.

Phoenix Rose stood at the high entrance to the resort and looked down at the neat, winding rows of RVs and fifth wheels in various sizes, as well as the numerous log cabins and the rustic tent grounds. All was quiet, as if no one had yet awakened.

She could have parked in the lower lot, closer to her destination, but she wanted the time to take it in.

Besides, after driving for a few hours, she'd enjoy stretching her legs.

Breathing deeply, she filled her lungs with fresh air, also filling her heart with hope.

It was such a beautiful morning that her clip-on sunglasses, worn over her regular glasses, only cut back the worst of the glare; she had to shade her eyes with a hand as she took in the many unique aspects of Cooper's Charm RV Park and Resort.

Before submitting her résumé to the online wanted ad, she'd scoured over all the info she could find. She'd also studied the map to familiarize herself with the design.

The website hadn't done it justice.

It was more beautiful than she'd expected.

Dense woods bordered the property on one side and at the entrance, giving it a private, isolated feel. To the other side, a line of evergreens separated the park from an old-fashioned drive-in that offered nightly movies not only to the resort guests, but also to the residents in the surrounding small town of Woodbine, Ohio.

At the very back of the resort, a large lake—created from a quarry—wound in and around the land before fading into the sun-kissed mist, making it impossible to see the full size. Currently, large inflated slides and trampolines floated in and out of the mist, randomly catching the sunshine as they bobbed in the mostly placid water. Phoenix couldn't imagine anyone getting into the frigid water today—or even this month—but the online brochure claimed the lake was already open, as was the heated in-ground pool.

She was to meet the owner near the lake, but she'd deliberately arrived fifteen minutes early, which gave her a chance to look around.

After six months in hotel rooms, and a month familiarizing herself with the park, Cooper's Charm already felt like home. She could be at peace here and that meant a lot, because for too long now, peace of mind had remained an elusive thing.

Knowing her sister was waiting, Phoenix pulled out her phone and took a pic of the beautiful scenery, then texted it to Ridley, typing, Arrived.

Despite the early hour, Ridley immediately texted back, Are you sure about this?

Positive, Phoenix replied. She hadn't been this certain in ages. Hope the interview goes well.

Loyal to the end, her sister sent back, He'll take one look at you and fall in love.

Phoenix grinned even as she rolled her eyes. Ridley had the misguided notion that everyone else shared her skewed but adoring perception. I'll settle for a job, thank you very much.

Keep me posted. Love you.

Her heart swelled. Through thick and thin, Ridley was her backup, her support system, and the person she trusted most in the whole world. Her parents were great too, very attentive and protective, but it was her sister who best understood her. It didn't matter that Ridley lived a very different lifestyle, or that their goals in life were so different.

Phoenix loved working with her hands, staying busy, and took satisfaction from a job well done.

Ridley enjoyed seeing the world, traveling nearly non-stop to posh destinations, had an exquisite flair for the latest fashions, and detested being messy in any way.

Different, but still best friends through and through.

Phoenix signed off in her usual way. Love you, too. Byeeeee...

She knew Ridley was still worried, and that bothered her. Much as she appreciated her sister's dedication, she wanted to portray an air of confidence and independence...just as she once had.

She didn't like being weak, and she didn't like allowing others to impact her life, yet both had happened. This was her chance to get back to being a strong, capable woman.

If all went well, today would be a start toward reaching that goal.

Taking her time, Phoenix strode through the grounds, familiarizing herself on her way to the lake. She really wanted to explore the woods, and the small, quaint cabins where she would live.

More than that, though, she wanted to be at the lake when Cooper Cochran arrived. She wouldn't be late, wouldn't be nervous, and wouldn't screw up her fresh start.

Unfortunately, just as she rounded a play area filled with swings and slides, she saw the lone figure standing along the sandy shore, a fishing rod in hand.

Was that Cochran?

Good Lord, he was big, and impressively built, too, with wide, hard shoulders and muscular thighs. She hated to admit it, but that could be a problem for her.

After all, she'd learned the hard way, on a very basic level, that big men were also powerful men.

Pausing to stare, she pressed a hand to her stomach to quell the nervous butterflies taking flight at the sight of him.

The sunrise gilded his messy, sandy brown hair. As he reeled in his line, then cast it out again, muscles flexed beneath a dark pullover with the sleeves pushed up to his elbows, showing taut forearms and thick wrists dusted with hair. Worn denim hugged his long legs.

He seemed to stand nearly a half foot taller than her five feet four inches. God, how she'd prayed he'd be a smaller, less…imposing man.

Finding information on the resort had been easy. Finding information on Cooper Cochran…not so much.

She stood frozen on the spot, trying to convince her feet to move, doing her best to conquer her irrational reservations, but she was suddenly, painfully aware that they were all alone on the shore. Logically, she knew it wasn't a problem. Plenty of people were around, though in their RVs or cabins, so there was no reason to be afraid.

Not here, not now.

Lately though, fear had been a fickle thing, often re-emerging out of nowhere. She'd always been able to hide that fear from her parents, but Ridley was a different matter. Her sister would take one look at her and understand.

But Ridley wasn't here now, and this job was important...

As if he'd known she was there all along, he glanced over his shoulder at her. Reflective sunglasses hid his eyes, and yet she felt his scrutiny and a touch of surprise. She knew his gaze was burning over her and it caused her to shift with nervous awareness.

She guessed him to be in his midthirties, maybe nine or ten years older than her. No one would call him a classically handsome man. His features were as bold as his body, including a strong jaw, masculine nose and harshly carved cheekbones.

Not typical good looks, but he certainly wouldn't be ignored.

She could see that he hadn't yet shaved this morning, and she wasn't sure if he'd combed his hair. The breeze and fog off the lake might have played with it, leaving it a little wavier than usual.

She couldn't look away, couldn't even blink.

His scrutiny kept her pinned in place with a strange stirring of her senses, unpleasant only in its unfamiliarity.

Releasing her by turning back to the lake, he said, "Ms. Rose?"

The words seemed to carry on the quiet, cool air.

Phoenix swallowed. "Yes." She watched as he cast

out yet again. It almost seemed that he gave her time to get herself together. Of course, he couldn't know why she was so reserved. Still, his patience, his apparent lack of interest, finally helped her to move forward.

She watched the way his large hands deftly, slowly, reeled in the line.

Her feet sank in the soft, damp sand. "Mr. Cochran?"

"You can call me Coop."

He had a deep, mellow voice that should have put her at ease but instead sharpened her awareness of him as a large man.

"I like to fish in the morning before everyone crowds the lake. Are you an early bird, Ms. Rose?"

"Actually, yes." A white gull swooped down, skimmed the water and took flight again. Ripples fanned out across the surface. By the minute, the mist evaporated, giving way to the warmth of the sun. "You know I had my own landscaping business." She'd told him that much in their email correspondence concerning her application. "In the summer especially, it was more comfortable to start as early as possible. I've gotten in the habit of being up and about by six."

"You won't need to be that early here."

"Okay." She wasn't sure what else to say. "The lake is beautiful."

"And peaceful." This time when he reeled in the line, he had a small bass attached. "Do you fish?"

He hadn't faced her again and that made it easier to converse. "When I was younger, my sister and I would visit our grandparents for the weekend and we'd fish in their pond. That was years ago, though." This was the strangest interview she'd ever had. It was also less stressful than she'd anticipated.

Had Cooper Cochran planned it that way—or did he just love to fish?

"You don't fish with them anymore?"

"They passed away just before I turned twenty. Granddad first, and my grandma not long after."

"I'm sorry to hear that. Sounds like you made good memories with them, though."

"Yes." Fascinated, she watched as he worked the hook easily from the fish's mouth, then he bent and placed it gently back in the water before rinsing his hands. "Too small to keep?"

"I rarely keep what I catch." He gestured toward a picnic table. "Let's talk."

Until then, she hadn't noticed the tackle box and towel on the summer-bleached wooden table.

She followed Cochran, then out of habit waited until he'd chosen a spot so she could take the side opposite him—a habit she'd gotten into with men. These days she preferred as much distance as she could manage.

He stepped over the bench, dropped the towel, pushed up his sunglasses and seated himself.

Golden-brown eyes took her by surprise. They were a stark contrast to his heavy brows and the blunt angles of his face.

She realized she was staring, that he merely stared back with one brow lifted, and she quickly looked away. Thankfully, she still wore the clip-on sunglasses, giving her a hint of concealment.

She retreated behind idle chitchat. "I studied the map online and feel like I know my way around. The lake is more impressive than I'd realized. The photos don't do it justice."

"I've been meaning to update the website," he said.

"It's been busy though. We lost our groundskeeper and housekeeper at the same time."

"Someone had both positions?"

He smiled with some private amusement. "No. Either position is a full-time job. But without any of us noticing, the two of them fell in love, married and then headed to Florida to retire."

"Oh." She expected to find many things at the resort, but love wasn't on the list. Love wasn't even in her universe.

Not anymore.

"You said you checked out the map online?"

"Actually, I researched everything I could about the place, including the surrounding grounds, and I'm sure I'd be a good fit for the job."

When he looked past her, she quickly turned her head to find a woman approaching with a metal coffeepot in one hand, the handles of two mugs hooked through the fingers of the other.

Cooper stood. "Perfect timing, Maris."

The woman's smile was easy and friendly. "I was watching." Long dark blond hair, caught in a high ponytail, swung behind her with every step. Soft brown eyes glanced at Phoenix. "Good morning."

"Morning."

"Coffee?" She set one mug in front of Cooper and filled it.

Phoenix nodded. "Yes, please."

Maris filled the second mug, then dug creamer cups and sugar packets from a sturdy apron pocket, along with a spoon wrapped in a napkin. "Coop drinks his black, but I wasn't sure about you."

Anyone who presented her with coffee on a cool morning instantly earned her admiration. "I'll take it any way I can get it, but I prefer a little cream and sugar, so thank you."

Cooper reseated himself. "Maris Kennedy, meet Phoenix Rose. Maris runs the camp store. Phoenix is here about the position for groundskeeper."

Slim brows went up. "Really? I was assuming house-keeper."

Cooper's smile did amazing things to his rugged face, and disastrous things to her concentration.

He explained to Phoenix, "We've never had a woman tend the grounds." Then to Maris, he said, "Ms. Rose used to run her own landscaping company. She's more than qualified and we'd be lucky to get her."

Phoenix perked up. Did that mean he'd already made up his mind to hire her?

"Especially now." Maris leaned a hip against the end of the table. "I don't know if Coop told you, but we're starting this season short-handed. We were all taking turns with the grounds and the housekeeping, so every-one will be thrilled to take one thing off their list."

Still unsure if she had the job or not, Phoenix said, "It'd be my pleasure to make things easier. If I'm hired, I can start right away." She glanced at Cooper and added, "Today even."

Maris straightened. "Seriously?"

Already feeling a sense of purpose that had been missing for too long from her life, Phoenix nodded. "I'm anxious to get to work."

Cooper put his elbows on the table and leaned for-ward. "Then consider yourself hired."

Behind the glasses, her eyes widened. "Just like that?"

"You expected a different outcome?"

"Well, no, but—" She could barely contain her excitement. If she didn't have an audience, she would have danced across the sandy shoreline.

"I bet you already packed, didn't you?"

Heat rushed into her cheeks for being so presumptuous, but she admitted the truth with a grin. "My car is full."

"Glad to hear it." He took a drink of his coffee, then said, "You had a great résumé, so meeting was just a formality."

More than a little dazed, Phoenix said, "Thank you."

"So you accept?" Maris asked.

"Of course!"

"Fantastic. So where are we putting her?"

With his gaze on his coffee, Cooper said, "I was thinking cabin eighteen."

Maris paused, subdued a smile, and nodded. "Okay then. Give me thirty minutes and I'll get it set up."

"I can do it," Phoenix quickly offered. "I don't want to put you out."

"It's not a problem. I'm just glad you're hired. Now hopefully Coop will find a housekeeper, too—hint, hint." She looked up at the sky and pretended to pray.

Cooper shook his head. "You're the queen of subtlety, Maris. As it happens, I'll be interviewing a woman next week."

In an aside to Phoenix, she said, "He interviews someone every week. Trust me, most don't get hired so easily." Then to Cooper, she added, "If she's not a serial killer, hire her."

He snorted. "You're going to make Ms. Rose think I'm a harsh boss. She'll run off before she ever gets started."

Maris rushed to say, "Coop is the *best* of bosses. Working for him is a dream."

Phoenix laughed. "You don't need to sell me. I'm excited for the opportunity."

"Just because you're a positive person, meaning you'll be fun to have around, I'll make sure you get some extra towels and one of our better coffeemakers." With a wink, she headed off.

As Maris disappeared into her store, her words hung with Phoenix. If most people weren't so easily hired, why was she? She knew she had good credentials, and she knew she could do the work. Was he so desperate to fill the position that a formal interview wasn't necessary?

She wasn't used to things going smoothly these days, but she wanted the job enough not to question it.

Silence dragged on. She was aware of Cooper intently watching her while he drank his coffee. It made her twitchy.

Determined, she turned to him. "I'm really looking forward to the job." Damn it, she'd already said that—or something like it. She didn't want to babble.

"Maris hasn't given you second thoughts?"

Phoenix shook her head. "Actually, she seems really nice."

"She is. I'm fortunate that everyone who works here gets along really well."

Perfect. The last thing she wanted was drama in her life. She'd had enough of that. The plan now was to work hard enough to keep the demons at bay, and otherwise live peacefully. "They all live on-site?"

"Yep." He stood. "Come on. I'll show you around while Maris opens your cabin and gets fresh linen inside." He paused. "You're aware that the cabin is small, right?"

"Yes. It's just me so I don't need a lot of room." In

fact, it'd be nice to have less to take care of. Recent events had proven to her that material things were far less important than she'd thought.

"We have some premium cabins, and a few available rental campers, but I try to leave those open to guests." He carried his tackle box, towel and rod as they walked. "Over there is the cabin you'll be using. There aren't any units around it, but it's close to the lodge, so there'll be a lot of foot traffic going by. We have quiet time from 11:00 p.m. to 8:00 a.m., so no one should disturb you during that span."

She gazed at the small wood cabin that would be her home for the foreseeable future. Screens enclosed a front porch just big enough for a rocker. A lattice skirt circled the base of the cabin. She envisioned some colorful pots filled with flowers to brighten the all-wood exterior, maybe a wind chime or two and a floral wreath for the door.

Decorating it, making it her own, would be fun.

"You're welcome to get your breakfast from the camp store, but you do have a full refrigerator and a small stove. Each cabin can sleep four, but since you're alone, I assume you'll use the loft bed without unfolding the couch. There's only a small TV, but you have WiFi."

She already knew all that from the brochures, so she only nodded.

Cooper paused, his light brown eyes staring down at her. "I know it's not much—"

"I love it. It's perfect."

His gaze lingered. "I think you mean that."

Every word. With a confidence she didn't always feel, she said, "I intend to be very happy here."

"Glad to hear it."

She cleared her throat. "There is one thing…"

"What's that?"

"I'm not very tech-savvy." At her age, it was a terrible thing to admit. "Is there anyone to help me set up the WiFi?"

Looking somehow relieved, he smiled. "We'll make sure you get set up. No problem." He continued on, his pace easy. "My house is up there."

Phoenix glanced in the direction he indicated, shading her eyes as he continued to speak.

"I have two high school boys who come on Mondays to cut the grass. If it's raining, they bump it back to the next day. It's your job to keep track of their hours and to supervise them when necessary. Overall they do a good job, but sometimes need to be prompted to stay off their phones and to clean up afterward."

"I'll take care of it." She looked back at his house again. Situated diagonally from her cabin, it sat atop a rise and overlooked the rest of the park.

"You can see that we've had some recent storms. A lot of cleanup needs to be done. Also, this is the time of year we check trees for dead branches. We don't want any falling on a camper's awning and doing damage."

"I'll go through the park and assess them all." Though she walked alongside him, her attention kept returning to his home. Like the little chapel they passed, it was made mostly of stone with arched entryways and it had a wooden addition on the left side. A path led down to the deepest section of the lake, with posted signs indicating that part was private to him.

"I cut my own grass," he said, as if he thought she was wondering.

"Really? It'd be a simple thing to add that area to the rest." With a riding mower, it wouldn't take much longer to keep the manicured lawn looking great.

"Not necessary." He gestured ahead. "The supply building is this way, and the maintenance building is at the end of the lane."

When Cooper took her arm, she automatically jerked back and would have fallen if he'd let go. Startled, she stared up at him and tried not to look so rattled.

Expression enigmatic, he slowly released her and indicated the limb in her path. "You would have tripped over it."

Because she hadn't been paying attention. *Way to make a good impression.* She forced a smile. "I'm sorry. I was admiring your house."

He looked back at the house as if he'd forgotten it was there—and didn't like remembering. When he returned his scrutiny to her, he looked different, more distant. "Did you catch anything I said?"

"I think so." Not really, but she dutifully pointed, "Supply building, lodge, showers—"

Consideration brought his brows together. "Ms. Rose, you told me you researched the park to get familiar with it, right?"

"Yes." Even without the tour, she probably could have told him where everything was located.

"I did the same."

Not understanding, she asked, "You researched the park?"

"No." He looked away as a woman opened her camper door and carried a bag of garbage to the curb for pickup. "I research all my employees prior to meeting them."

He'd researched...*her*?

Well, of course he had. That was the responsible thing to do. But how detailed had he gotten?

He watched her as if he could hear her breathing, which had the effect of making her hold her breath.

With too much gentleness, he explained, "Social media being what it is, it's not difficult to do."

"No," she said on a sharp exhalation. "I guess it's not."

"With you, I also found multiple news articles after a simple search of your name."

Horrified, she took a step back.

"I do background checks and research on everyone I hire," he repeated.

She wanted to leave…but knew she couldn't. Where would she go anyway?

To her sister? No, Ridley was already too concerned. When next she saw her, Phoenix hoped to be back to her usual self, a woman her sister could admire rather than one she fretted over.

Her parents? God no. She loved them dearly, but the last thing they needed was to start worrying about her again. They'd done enough of that already.

Back to a hotel? Though necessary at the time, it had turned into a miserable existence, like a self-imposed exile. Now that she was out, she never wanted to do that again.

She preferred to feel the sun on her skin and the earth on her hands.

This was her chance to make it happen, an opportunity to start over, to reclaim her life. She wouldn't give it up just because her privacy had been breached once more.

Far too serious, Cooper said, "I haven't mentioned your personal history to anyone else, and I won't. Nothing I found factored into my decision to hire you."

Well, that was something at least. "Thank you." She

drew a deep breath and, putting it in the simplest terms, said, "I was hoping for a fresh start."

He stared out toward the lake. "I'm sorry for what you went through."

With more accusation than she intended, she asked, "Why do you even bring it up?" She didn't want to think about it, much less talk about it with a stranger. She definitely didn't want his pity.

As if he couldn't help himself, his gaze met hers again; neither of them looked away. "I mentioned it in case you need anything."

Phoenix couldn't blink. The sun behind him set a glow around his brown hair, emphasizing the breadth of his shoulders, his height. It was the oddest thing, but his size didn't really intimidate her. Not anymore.

And it had nothing to do with what he'd just said, but rather it was something about him, some vague sincerity...or sadness?

She shook her head. What exactly did he think he could give her?

And why were they both standing there staring at each other?

Shifting her stance to break the spell, she said with conviction, "I'm fine." Then thought to add, "Thank you."

He didn't look convinced. "If you change your mind—"

"I won't."

Maris called her name, catching up to them. "I have your cabin all ready. Would you like to see it?"

Cooper stepped away. "Thanks, Maris. You'll help her get settled?"

"Sure. Should I finish giving her the tour, too?"

"If you wouldn't mind." Smiling, he said, "Get her

set up for our WiFi, too." He glanced at Phoenix. "You can start tomorrow, Ms. Rose. I'll email you the names and phone numbers of your helpers, along with our usual schedule."

Phoenix realized she must have offended him to have him walking off without finishing his instructions, but she wasn't sure how to fix it. "I'll be ready."

He flashed her a subdued smile. "Welcome to Cooper's Charm. As the sign says, it's a good place to get away."

Don't miss
Cooper's Charm
by New York Times *bestselling author Lori Foster!*

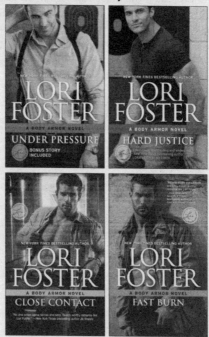